MÉ 9

# EVERYDAY KINDNESS

– A COLLECTION OF UPLIFTING TALES
TO BRIGHTEN YOUR DAY

# EVERYDAY KINDNESS

– A COLLECTION OF UPLIFTING TALES
TO BRIGHTEN YOUR DAY

EDITED BY
LJ ROSS

ISBN: 978-1-912310-00-5

First published in November 2021 by Dark Skies Publishing



Typeset by Riverside Publishing Solutions Limited

Printed and bound by CPI Goup (UK) Limited

# CONTENTS

# FOREWORD

Dear Reader,

Thank you for buying this copy of Everyday Kindness. Your purchase has made a donation to Shelter*, the housing and homelessness charity.

The Covid-19 outbreak has been devastating and unpredictable, causing the loss of freedom, friends and family. At the same time, we have seen communities come together to support each other with kindness, love and generosity. This collection of short stories hopes to continue this and brighten your day.

Shelter exists to defend the right to a safe home and fight the devastating impact the housing emergency has on people and society. We do this with campaigns, advice and support—and we never give up. We believe that home is everything.

Over the decades, governments have failed to build enough social homes. Without access to safe and secure housing, thousands of families are living in temporary accommodation. Many others are forced to sleep on the streets and some of them die there.

The shortage of social homes has fuelled the growth of the private rental sector. A lack of regulation means that renters must navigate a minefield of sky-high rents, poor conditions, and the threat of unfair eviction. Too many people are living in poor quality homes that they can barely afford. They're often too afraid to complain and feel like they have to put up with bad conditions. And life is made even more difficult by a welfare system that simply doesn't provide enough support to people when they're struggling.

This is the housing emergency and this is what we're up against.

Your donation will go towards Shelter's services. Our free emergency helpline is open 365 days a year to answer calls from anyone struggling with a housing issue or homelessness. On our website, find expert information about everything from reclaiming your deposit to applying as homeless, or speak to an adviser over webchat. Our solicitors provide free legal advice and attend court to help people who've lost their homes or are facing eviction. In towns and cities across the UK, our advice and support services offer one-to-one, personalised help with housing issues and homelessness.

Once again, thank you for your support. You have joined the fight for home.

Max Newton
Head of Community Fundraising, Shelter

To find out more about our work, please visit **www.shelter.org.uk** or search for Shelter on social media channels.

*When referring to Shelter, this encompasses both Shelter and Shelter Scotland.

# A NOTE FROM THE EDITOR

The Covid-19 crisis had a devastating impact on so many communities and individuals around the world, but none more so than those who were already amongst the most vulnerable in our society. This 'Everyday Kindness' anthology came about from a desire to pool our collective skills and resources to raise awareness and funds to support our chosen charity partner, Shelter, whose vital work focuses on preventing homelessness and bad housing. Our anthology brings together literary talent from over fifty new, established, award-winning and internationally best-selling authors from across the spectrum of publishing, each of whom have contributed a story designed to promote kindness or hope. Each story is very different, but all are moving and uplifting, reflecting our shared desire to publish something uniquely positive and give back to our wider community. We hope you, the reader, enjoy this fine collection, and express our gratitude to all those who contributed to this endeavour—not least, the authors, who have given of their time and talent. Particular thanks must also go to: Andrew Davidson, who donated the beautifully painted artwork which graces the cover of our book; Stuart and Natasha Bache of 'Books Covered', who donated the layout and remaining cover design work; James Ross, who donated considerable editorial and 'back office' time bringing the project together; Duncan and Paul at Riverside Publishing Solutions, who donated their typesetting and layout work; Samantha Missingham, Kate Baguley and Danielle Price, for all their valuable help and insights during the making of this anthology; Dani, Liz and Zekra of Colour PR; and, Katherine and Martin, for all their assistance bringing our charitable endeavour to the attention of bookshops around the UK.

LJ ROSS
September 2021

# JACKALS

*By Adam Hamdy*

If it wasn't for bad luck, I wouldn't have no luck at all.

I've never been good with words, but I've heard enough to recognise the good ones. If you put a hurt on me for the elevator pitch of my life, those are the words I'd choose. Don't feel sorry for me though. God never gave a body a heavier load than their shoulders could carry. At least that was my grandma's wisdom, but as time passes, the words my child ears took as true start to buckle under the strain of experience, and as my load gets heavier and heavier, I find myself wondering if she was right.

It was another fine day. Least it was for those with electro-compressed cold air. For us smog-breathers, it was brutal. The heat could crackle a pig's skin, and every breath was like a lungful straight from an oven.

I stood at the intersection of Topanga Canyon Road and the Pacific Coast Highway, holding my tray. A few loose smokes and some sticks of gum, melting in their wrappers. I bought my stock at Ralph's on the corner of Sunset Boulevard, where I loitered in the air-conditioned aisles until one of the bosses gave me the side eye. When I'd restocked, I'd split my packs of cigarettes and gum into singles and set them on my tray. Everything was a dollar, but I wasn't trying to cheat anyone. When drivers dropped their windows to give me notes, I'd offer them something from my tray. A trade made everyone feel better, even though I knew whatever they took would most likely be trashed. I mean, what Californian millionaire would eat a half-melted gum from a homeless guy?

But it was my way, and habits, good and bad, had brought me to this furnace on the edge of paradise. Malibu lay north, with its multimillion-dollar white sand, rock star mansions, and to the east were the secluded mountain homes of Hollywood story folk, who conjured dreams for us all. South was the road to Los Angeles, city of a million broken promises, and to the west was the Pacific and the edge of the world. At the heart of it all was me, standing on my regular spot, a traffic island in the median of the valley road. When the lights shone red, I'd walk the line of cars backed up Topanga Canyon Road, and smile at each and every driver.

Some made like I was invisible, others gave me a brush off, but a few wound their windows down, and shared a little kindness. I had a dozen regulars, glad-hearted souls who always had a nice word and a couple of extra bucks for me. I always gave them a brighter smile and gospel thanks.

Their kindness was magic, at least to my mind. The bills they gave were meaningless to them. What was a dollar to a man driving a quarter-million Lamborghini? But the moment that paper hit my hand, it was transformed into life. Food in an empty belly, drink for a parched throat. On a good day, I could buy medicine to keep my pain at bay, or spend a few cents on a book to read in the moonlight to remind me there are other lives better than this one.

Did the people who gave me money feel the magic? Did they know what their money meant to me? I doubt it. When I was like them, with a car and a house and a job, I never gave a second thought to a buck here or a five there, handed out to broken men and women whose faces I don't remember.

*Goldie is coming.*

I recognise the Mercedes GL from a distance, shining bright as an angel's wings. I have no idea what her real name is, I just gave her the moniker Goldie on account of her blonde hair, which is always perfect, just like her tan, makeup, clothes and figure. She used to be one of my regulars, but then she took up with the Mobster, a cruel jackal, my grandma's word for a scavenger who fed off the lives of others. He always scowled and brushed me away from the car. I don't know if he really was a crook, but he certainly was a villain in my book, and he dressed like one too; dark suits, pressed shirts and woven ties. Probably a lawyer or banker, so if not a criminal, at least a cousin to them. He had a nasty face, but in a certain light, and with enough desperation, a body might call him handsome.

The lights changed and the Benz glided to a stop three cars up from the intersection. I walked the line and got two brush offs from an Escalade and a Camry. I pinned a broad smile to my face in the hope I could finally win the Mobster over, but he wasn't looking at me. He was too busy yelling at Goldie, who flinched at his words as though each was a blow.

I've been brave in my life, and I've won and lost wars, but that was long ago before age took me, and ill health broke me. I wasn't brave, or certainly didn't feel that way when I knocked on the driver's window.

Goldie looked at me with desperation, and the mobster turned his curled wicked scowl on me and shooed me away like a bug. And I'm ashamed to say I floated on like the pest he thought me, and walked to the next car. When I looked back, I saw the Mobster leaning between the headrests, raising his fist and shouting. His words were lost to the rumble of north-south traffic on the PCH, but he wore a red mask of anger, the kind my daddy used to slip on after a few drinks.

Maybe it was the thought of my pa wailing on my mom? Or maybe I'd grown so tired of life I could afford bravery? Whatever the reason, I shuffled back to the Benz, rehearsing my intervention, but when I reached for the driver's door handle, the car sped away.

The lights had turned green.

* * *

I thought about Goldie the rest of the day, and wondered whether her afternoon had been as difficult as mine. Five hours in the sun for twenty-seven bucks.

Take your smiles where you can find 'em, grandma used to say. So I took my twenty-seven to Ralph's, lingered in air-cooled comfort, easing off the scorch of the day, and restocked my tray. I spent twelve sixteen on smokes and gum, and six sixty-five on some ice-cold water and a meatball sub. The rest would go in my belt, and one day, if the angels smiled on me, I might have enough for a roof.

I ate my sub on a bench by a bus stop, sitting with my back against the face of Maggie Li, a Malibu Realtor. It spoke to my mischief that I, a man without a roof, could block the message of someone who traded multimillion-dollar dream homes. I sat there for a while, nodding at the bus drivers who didn't bother stopping. They knew I never went anywhere.

When it was dark, I walked along the PCH, dazzled by the never-ending stream of lights, and shuffled my way onto Topanga Beach. The long stretch of sand was off-limits after dark, so I moved as quickly as I could to avoid being seen. I hurried across the golden powder and went to the disused pipe that jutted out from a cluster of rocks at the north-eastern edge of the beach.

I didn't know where the six-feet diameter outlet came from, or what it had once been used for. All I knew was that it had become my home.

I'd found the pipe a few months ago when I'd left Venice Beach. I'd trawled the PCH looking for a new base and had discovered the lock on the grille that covered the outlet was rusted. It had taken me less than an hour to break it off, and I'd bought a new one from Ralph's, which only I had the key to.

I unlocked it now, opened the grille and climbed inside. I shut the grille behind me and secured the padlock. There was another grille about thirty feet into the darkness, but that one was fixed in place and couldn't be broken, so I had never been able to explore what lay beyond, but I didn't much mind. Thirty feet was more than enough for me. All my stuff lay neatly stacked along its length, and I had a habit of checking everything each night before I went to sleep to make sure nothing had been taken. My clothes, little trophies and interesting driftwood I've scavenged from the beach, and my roll, a towel that doubled as a place for keepsakes and which I used as a pillow. When I was sure everything was where I'd left it, I took the eight dollars and nineteen cents from my pocket and put it inside the waterproof money belt I kept hidden under my T-shirt. Topher, my friend and mentor, who'd taken me under his wing when I'd arrived in Los Angles, told me, "Get yourself a belt for your greenbacks. Keep it close and make sure it's waterproof because you can't control when rain will hit your shoulders."

I think about Topher most nights when I lie with my head on my roll and my hands tucked in either end. But this night I thought of Goldie and how frightened she looked, and I wondered what I would have done if I'd managed to get that door open. Bravery came easier for people with a roof. Especially white people. A black man pulling open the door of a Benz was likely to get himself shot.

I'd keep an eye out for her tomorrow and check she was OK. Maybe if she was on her own, I'd strike up a little chatter like we used to, and put a smile on her face with one of my jokes.

* * *

I woke, as always, in the grey light that told a body dawn was coming. Everything was black and white movie monotone and the PCH was quiet. I had a drink of water and climbed out of the pipe. I checked the beach was clear and took off my T-shirt. The cool air felt good, and when I got down to the water's edge, I slipped off my sneakers and stripped down to my underwear. I had a habit of taking a bath in the grand old Pacific each morning before most folks were awake, and I waded in until the water reached my chest. Another habit, a ritual maybe, a baptism each morning, a fresh chance at life and maybe today would be the day that I'd catch some of the ocean magic that had flowed thousands of miles from China or Japan or Hawaii.

I ducked underwater and ran my hands through my hair. It was getting long and tangled. I'd need to pay a visit to Hector, the street barber in Venice, who'd shave a skull for three bucks.

When I surfaced, I felt eyes on me and saw a man in a hoodie at the shoreline, near my clothes. I felt him making a calculation.

"Shit," I said out loud, as he grabbed my shoes and clothes and ran.

I waded out of the water, cursing myself for not being more careful.

Old wolves don't die of age. Youngsters learn how to put them down.

My running days were long behind me, but I limped and shuffled my way across the sand to the edge of the PCH as fast as I could. The young thief sprinted across the six lane highway and shot up a mountain trail that led into the bluffs.

He was gone.

My stuff was gone.

But the worst was to come.

My heart, already pounding with exertion, skipped a hard beat when the sound of a siren cut the air, and a Malibu sheriff's black and white pulled up a few feet away.

The deputy, a square-jawed white man in his twenties could have made good money as a TV extra. He looked at a loss, and I suddenly saw myself through his eyes, a scrawny, soaking wet old black man with tufty salt and pepper hair, teeth crying out for a dentist, naked save for a pair of six-year-old jockeys and a waterproof money belt.

We both knew what would happen next.

***

They held me for 24-hours, while they checked my identity and made sure I had no outstanding warrants. I got some torn sweats to replace my stolen clothes, and three square meals, so it wasn't all bad. But I worried about my money belt, which had been taken from me on booking, and my stuff in the pipe which had been unguarded and unchecked for a whole day.

I'd told the deputy a version of the truth; that I'd been strolling by the beach and decided to have a swim. That some punk had stolen my clothes and my wallet and phone. He seemed content to pretend to believe the lie.

Finally, the morning after I'd been arrested, they cut me loose and I shuffled along the cell block to the booking desk to sign my release and collect my belt. There were three deputies on duty and they all ragged on me, cracking wise at my expense. They wore light brown uniforms, the colour of jackals.

"Is your butler coming to collect you, Mr Millionaire?"

"Hope you make it back to your mansion."

"Blow your Bitcoin on new briefs."

And so on. They called out my teeth, my hair, just about anything that could make a man feel smaller than small, but I knew better than to respond.

"Yes, sir."

"No, sir."

"Yeah, very funny, sir."

*Please don't get mad, sir. No brutality, sir. No knee in my neck, sir.*

The unspoken contract. Play nice and they wouldn't end me.

I knew the nature of these beasts, so I just signed for my belt and kept smiling, but the moment I picked it up, I knew something was wrong. I unzipped the main compartment and my guts flipped when I saw it was empty.

"Excuse me, sir," I said to the jackal on the desk. "My money. What happened to my money?"

"What money?" he scoffed.

"I had six-hundred and thirteen dollars in here, sir, and some ninety-six cents." I tried to sound composed, but inside I was already crying.

That money was my roof. At least part of it. There was a place in the City of Industry that would give a man a roof for eight hundred, and with a roof I could get a job, and with a job insurance for my health, maybe not for the pre-existing, but certainly for any new ailments, and all that, everything, it was all gone. It was gone, and the laughing, smirking jackals had taken it.

But jackals are dangerous. Especially in packs.

"That's how it was booked," the desk jackal replied.

"Maybe you left it in your safety deposit box?" one of the others jeered.

"Or in your safe at your mansion?" the third said.

The trio howled at their miserable jokes.

"There's been some mistake, sirs. I had my money in here," I said.

That killed the laughter, and the jackals turned up their lips in ugly snarls.

"What are you saying?" the desk jackal asked.

"Where's the deputy who brought me in? Maybe he put it somewhere safe for me."

"Boy!" the desk jackal barked. "You think we're thieves? We're the law."

*You look like thieves*, I thought, but the words never passed my lips.

Maybe he saw them in my eyes, because he got mad.

"Get him out of here," he said to the others, and they grabbed me and marched me into the street.

"Get lost," one of the them said, and he went inside.

The other jackal lingered, and when his pack-mate was gone, he leaned forward and whispered, "Consider it a tax."

He left me with an evil smile that made my toes curl, and as I watched him turn and go inside, I realised I'd never wanted to hurt a man so much. I felt sick with anger. He'd taken my life. He'd stolen my dreams for a few hundred bucks.

The jackal looked back, almost goading me to strike him, but I didn't. I watched him go inside and I turned away and shuffled along the sidewalk to the PCH. I could feel them watching me from the stationhouse window, but I didn't turn around. I wouldn't give them the satisfaction of seeing me cry.

* * *

I was back in the oven, standing on the median in my spot on Topanga Canyon Road, starting from scratch. All I had was what was in my tray, and I need to make enough to buy food and water before sundown.

I couldn't shake the injustice and kept picturing myself beating hell out of those three jackals. Theirs was the latest in a long line of cruelties the world had inflicted on me, and as I stood there sweating, I spiralled back through all of them, freewheeling through the disasters and failures that were my life.

My pinned smile wavered and when there were no cars around, I yelled at myself.

"Why are you so weak?" I shouted. "Why are you so stupid?"

But no one wants to see an angry, crying old man. Smiles win dollars, but my act wasn't good enough to hide my rage, and by late afternoon I'd only made three bucks.

It was going to be a thirsty, hungry night, and the thought of my empty belly gnawing on itself brought back memories of the early days, when I'd first lost my roof and hadn't learned how to survive. My eyes filled with tears. I was right back there at the beginning, with nothing. How could those jackals be so cruel?

*A jackal doesn't know any other way*, I thought. *It is what it is.*

Born evil, live evil, die evil.

I wouldn't let their evil beat my good, so I wiped my eyes, and refreshed my smile as a convoy of automobiles came rolling down the valley. I saw the stunning white angel, Goldie's Benz, stop fifth in line. She'd help me.

I ignored the other cars and shuffled straight to hers, but she wasn't in any position to help. Goldie, beautiful, perfect Goldie was crying. She had a black eye and a puffball purple cheek and the Mobster was yelling at her.

Something inside me broke. I didn't care. I walked into the road, and he was so engaged in abusing Goldie with vicious words he never noticed me go to his side and open the door. I'm not a strong man, least not anymore, but in that moment he became every jackal who'd ever been cruel to me and I punched and kicked him like the evil creature he was. I shouted things I can't remember and I cried and roared and the younger, fitter, stronger man stood no chance against my storm. Goldie was crying and the Mobster was crying, and I think I was crying, and somehow in the chaos, I dragged him out of the car and put him on the ground, and I kicked and I kicked and I kicked him until her voice cut through my anger.

"Stop!" she said. "Stop!"

The Mobster was a quivering bloody mess. People were out of their cars, some filming, some on their phones, a few trying to muster the courage to approach me.

Goldie said, "Get in."

Street life had given me the sense to know when danger was on the wind, and I didn't waste a moment. I climbed in beside her, slammed the door shut, she pulled a U-turn and the Benz shot into the mountains.

"Thank you," she said.

We turned off Canyon Road onto Grand View Drive, and she took us to a quiet spot where we parked in the shade of a big old tree. I could see why people paid top dollar for roofs up here. The Pacific looked magical. It shimmered at the foot of the green mountains like a mirror that had been scattered with diamonds.

"You were very brave," Goldie said.

"I couldn't let him get away with that, ma'am," I replied. "No one deserves, well…"

I left the words unspoken, but we both knew I was talking about her face.

We sat in the car for hours and talked about how life had made victims of us. She told me her name was Julie and that the Mobster was called Rick. She hadn't been with a man for years, since her first marriage went bust, and had met Rick through an online dating app. He'd started out perfect, but once he'd moved in he'd turned mean and nasty and controlling, and Julie, a successful attorney, had grown smaller and smaller.

Prey to a jackal.

I told her my story. A child with big football dreams knocked down to size when I broke my back in junior year. My reserve dream of becoming a rock star died over the years because I didn't quite have what it took. Or maybe I did, but I was never in the right place at the right time. I told her about my drift into becoming a roadie for other bands, getting sucked into the rock and roll lifestyle without rock and roll money. My failed marriage, my estranged son, who I abandoned with his mother when the going got tough. My second career-ending injury when I dropped an amp case on my foot. My move to construction just so I could get healthcare. Ten hard years working sites until my third and final injury on a badly-run yard. Unfit for work. Unemployable. Homeless in Michigan. Unable to face the cold winters on the street. The journey to California. To Los Angeles, where the sun always shines and anything can happen.

I told her about Topher, my friend and mentor. I met him on Venice Beach and he took me under his wing and schooled me on the importance of good habits. I told her how Topher had died a month after I met him. Set alight by a wannabe gangster who had been given the grim task to earn full colours. I told Julie about my good friend's ugly passing, but I spared her the screams I can still hear today, or the smell, or how I'd been held at bay by a gangster at gunpoint. I wasn't brave that night. And I never went back. I travelled the PCH and found my home in the pipe on Topanga Beach.

We traded misery and sadness and I think we made each other feel better, and after the pink sun had disappeared beneath the edge of the world, Julie drove me back down the mountain and set me in my spot. There was no sign anything had ever happened.

"Here," Julie said, reaching into her purse.

She gave me a handful of bills and I wasn't too proud to take them.

"Thank you," I said.

"No. Thank you."

I counted the money as she drove away. Two-hundred and eighty bucks in tens and twenties. I did the last of my crying, but these were happy tears. I could get my meatball sub and bottle of water, and was well on my way to my roof.

* * *

I stayed clear of my spot for a few weeks in case the Mobster had tipped the police to my description. I guessed he wouldn't want them digging into his violence against Julie, but life had taught me to be careful. I worked the intersection by Ralph's, but it wasn't as good as my Topanga median. The lights changed too quickly and people were always in a hurry.

My first morning back on Topanga Canyon was spent smiling and joking with whoever was kind enough to wind down their window. It was like nothing had ever happened. In the afternoon, I saw the white Benz come down the valley, but instead of joining the line of cars at the lights, it pulled into a layby. Julie lowered her window and waved me over. She was smiling and I was real glad to see her face had healed.

"Get in," she said, as I shuffled across the street. "I want to show you something."

I felt a little awkward climbing in her clean, fresh car. Last time I'd been drunk on violence, but now I was sober and I felt the vast distance between her world and mine. But she made me welcome.

"I've been looking for you," she said. "What happened? Where did you go?"

"I thought I'd better lay low," I replied as she swung a U and took us up the valley road into the mountains.

They shone perfect and green in the afternoon sun and as we drove, Julie told me she'd finally plucked up the courage to move the Mobster's stuff out. He'd been hospitalised for a few days, and when they finally discharged him, he was homeless. His meal ticket had kicked him to the kerb and no matter how much he begged and pleaded, Julie wouldn't let him back in. After a few days he gave up trying to win her with sugar and turned sour. He threatened her and tried to intimidate her, but when she held strong, he finally gave up and crawled back to whatever jackal world he'd come from.

We drove through the town of Topanga with its hippy cafes and street stalls and turned onto Entrada Road towards the state park. When we were near the park entrance, Julie slowed and turned into a driveway. She used a remote to open a solid metal gate, and when it had swung wide, she drove me into paradise.

Julie's two-storey home stood on a three-acre piece of mountain she'd filled with fruit trees, water features and tropical plants. The house itself was a designer's dream made real, all glass and brushed black steel with jaw-to-the-floor views of the ocean.

Julie followed the driveway down past the house, through the bountiful garden to a scrap of scrubland behind a row of trees at the bottom of the lot. There was a ride-on mower and a small digger, and beside them, raised on some slabs, was an old Airstream trailer.

"I bought this the day after you helped me," Julie said. "Arrived last week, but I couldn't find you."

She parked in front of the trailer and got out.

"Come on," she said, but the lump in my throat was so heavy I could hardly move.

Finally, I got out, and the warm breeze blew tears from my eyes.

"I decided to do something real for once. Actually help someone. Someone who helped me."

"I…" I began, but I couldn't go on.

"I won't tolerate any nonsense. Not after Rick. If you're trouble, I will call the police," she said. "I'm done with villains."

"I'm no villain," I assured her.

"Good. It's not much," she said.

But she was wrong. To my eyes, the little silver trailer looked better than her palace up the hill.

"I don't know what happened to me. I kind of lost myself with Rick. You reminded me how to be strong and stand up to him."

"I didn't…" I tried to say, but she cut me off.

"It's yours for as long as you need it. You can use my address for mail and to apply for jobs or social security or whatever."

"Thank you," I said, clasping her hands fondly. I didn't know what else to say. "Thank you."

* * *

We drove to the beach and I picked up my roll and other stuff from the outlet pipe and moved them to my new home.

I wish I could say that was the happy ever after, but my road has never been smooth and like I said at the start, if it wasn't for bad luck, I wouldn't have no luck at all. Seems I couldn't get a mouthful of sweetness without a bitter aftertaste, and three weeks later, I woke in my little bed to see a figure sat in the armchair Julie had bought me from the used furniture yard beside the PCH.

"Nobody lays a finger on me." I didn't have to be a genius to figure out who the deep voice belonged to. "Not without paying for it."

He pushed his right arm forward and I saw the silhouette of a pistol in the gloom.

"She thinks she can throw me out? And move in some cripple old lapdog?" I had no doubt he'd rehearsed this speech and worked up his anger many times. "Not in my world. That's not how this story ends. I'll tell you what happens. I'm going to put this gun against your skull and blow your brains out. And then I'm going to the house to shoot her, and when the cops find your bodies they'll think an eccentric rich woman made the mistake of bringing some homeless wild animal into her life and the dog turned around and bit her."

"Don't do this, Rick," I said, but my words only agitated him.

"Don't use my name," he yelled, getting to his feet. He moved towards my bed. "You should have stayed in your miserable little lane."

He raised the pistol and started moving it towards my head, and that's when I knew he wasn't bluffing.

Topher taught me many things about life on the street, but the hardest and most lasting lesson had been the one he'd taught me in death. Never assume you're safe.

Habits. Bad ones kill you. The good ones keep you alive.

No matter how many pillows Julie bought me, I still liked to sleep with my roll tucked under my head, with my hands in both ends, fingers touching the 22 revolver I bought from a pawn shop on Crenshaw the day after Topher had been murdered.

I slid my right hand out of the roll, curled my left index finger around the trigger and pulled. There was a crack of thunder and my ears started ringing.

Rick cried out as the bullet hit him in the thigh. He dropped his gun, grabbed at the wound, and fell to the floor.

I rolled out of bed, picked up his pistol and held it on him until Julie came. She called the police and they took Rick away in an ambulance.

* * *

Rick got fifteen years for attempted murder and a heap of other charges, including his violence against Julie.

Me? I'm still living in the trailer and every morning Julie drops me off at an air-cooled paradise, the Ralph's on the corner of Sunset, where I've got a job packing bags.

I may not be the fastest packer, and my injuries mean I have to take regular breaks, but my boss says I make the customers feel good with my jokes and smiles, and I'm happy to spread the joy, because life is being good to me.

---

Adam Hamdy is a Sunday Times, Kindle and international bestselling author and screenwriter. Prior to embarking on his writing career, Adam was a strategy consultant and advised global businesses in the medical, robotics, technology and financial services sectors. Adam has a law degree from Oxford University and a philosophy degree from the University of London. He is a seasoned rock climber, skier and CPSA marksman. Adam is a co-founder of Capital Crime and is on the board of the International Thriller Writers Organization. He lives in Shropshire with his wife, Amy, and their three children.

# SNAP

*By Alex Smith*

"And that isn't where it goes, Alice, not even close."

Billie pushed through the door like a mule navigating a narrow mountain pass, rucksacks clattering, her handbag strap catching on something outside and halting her like a tugged rein. Two-year-old Moira pushed between her legs, oblivious, marching after her oldest sister and trampling the coat that Alice had left in the hall. Outside, Evie was still moaning about the fact she hadn't been able to walk home with her best friend, even though she *had* walked home with her best friend, right up until the corner of their street. She'd had to struggle along by herself for all of forty-eight seconds. The rising pitch of her voice was like a kettle coming to boil, and something squirmed in Billie's empty stomach.

"Alice," she called into the dark interior. "Coat, now."

Kitchen cupboards clattered in reply, drawers opening, then the fridge. Billie tried to move past the door but her bag was still caught, and Evie was too involved in her own drama outside to do anything about it. She wrestled the strap over her head, the weight of Alice's schoolbag popping her free then falling at her feet, tripping her.

"*Fudging* hell!" she said as she stumbled into the hall, a flare of anger lighting up the shadows. She braced a hand on the wall to stop herself falling, Evie's bag sliding off her shoulder onto the floor. The four-year-old followed her in, wailing as she stomped over Alice's coat.

"Really?" Billie called after her.

"I just want Fiona!" Evie said as she vanished into the kitchen. "I just want Fiona. Hey, that's my scone!"

Moira squealed, then so did Alice, the kitchen suddenly full of stray cats. Billie closed her eyes for a moment, breathing stale air, the smell of it still so unfamiliar even after all the months of living here. The house seemed to pulse around her, the silence of it somehow even louder than the screams of her three girls. She reclaimed her handbag from the mat and shut the door, the darkness wrapping her in its arms, making her feel for a moment like she was suffocating.

"Right," she whispered to herself. "Tea."

She hung the bags by the door then scooped up Alice's coat, well aware that she shouldn't. When she kicked the assortment of little shoes beneath the telephone table, two of them rebounded, skittering down the hall like mice. By the time she'd reached the kitchen all hell had broken loose, Alice doing her best to hold on to the last remaining cheese scone as Evie and Moira wrestled her for it. Evie was holding back but Moira was deadly serious, raking her nails down her oldest sister's arm.

"Go away!" Alice shrieked, her face and fists clenched. "Stop hurting me!"

"Girls," Billie said, the anger painful, poisonous. "That's enough!"

"Want it," Moira said, slapping Alice's stomach.

"Have it!" Alice roared, throwing the scone across the room. It hit the cabinets then the floor, in pieces.

"I said *enough*! Alice, pick that up."

But Alice had retreated inside herself, her wrists pressed to her ears, the fingers of both hands clicking. She lurched back and forth like a rocking horse, an unexploded bomb of anxiety.

"That wasn't kind," Billie said to her. "You're an unkind girl."

She took two steps towards her before she noticed Moira picking pieces of scone off the dirty lino.

"Wait," she said, feeling something about to detonate inside her own chest, the fizz of panic like a burning fuse. "Moira, wait, I'll get you something else."

"No!" the youngest girl said, running from the kitchen with her hands full of crumbs. Billie turned to ask Evie to stop her but Evie had already gone. There was just Alice, rocking hard, her eyes like moons in the half light of the small room, her clicking fingers an engine.

*Snap snap snap snap.*

"Enough," said Billie, resting a hand on her oldest daughter's shoulder, feeling her resist for a second before giving up. She pulled her into a hug that was tight enough to stop the rocking, but those staccato pops were relentless, loud enough to make Billie's ears hurt. "Alice, that's enough. Stop."

"I'm hungry," Alice said after a moment. "I just want my scone."

"I'll make you something else," Billie said. "Just stop clicking, please."

Alice twisted her body free, grunting quietly as she walked out of the room. One hand was rooted in her own hair, the other beat out the same rhythm of percussive clicks.

*Snap snap snap snap.*

She'd been doing it all her life, the stimming, but the snapping fingers were new. She'd only just learned how to do it.

*Snap snap snap snap.*

All the way down the corridor into the living room.

"Just stay away from your sisters for a little while, okay?" Billie called after her. "Watch your iPad."

Dead words, falling on deaf ears, but for now it was quiet. Billie inhaled through her nose to loosen the knot of resentment that noosed her insides. Then she grabbed the kettle and turned on the tap, fingers of pain drumming against her temples. She returned it to its stand, her finger hesitating over the button.

*It's okay. There's time.*

And even though she reassured herself this was true, it still took a moment for her to find the strength to switch the kettle on.

*So stupid.*

So stupid, yes, and yet here she was, her fingers steepled on the old wood of the counter to stop them from trembling. She watched the kettle and it seemed to watch her, something animal-like in those first few seconds of silence, as if it was trying to figure out whether to trust her. Then a hiss, snake-like and unwelcome. The kettle was old, it had been here when they'd moved in, its insides clogged with a nest of limescale thanks to the hard Norfolk water. It had a burnished copper finish and she could see her outline there, her features erased, ghostlike.

From the living room, Evie squealed.

"Wait a minute, I'm bringing some food," she called to her.

*Just wait, please just be kind to each other.*

Billie opened the cupboard above the kettle, finding a lonely bag of pink crisps that seemed startled by the light. The fridge was right behind her but even that seemed too far away. She turned and pushed herself from the counter like she was in a small boat on rough seas, opening the fridge to find a couple of squeezy yoghurts. She grabbed them in one hand, taking the milk in the other, making it halfway back before one of the yoghurts slid free and slapped to the ground.

She swore, dumping the milk on the counter, listening to the sound of the kettle. The hiss had become a low growl, like a distant plane. There was time. She picked up the yoghurt and took the crisps from the cupboard, all the while the storm in the living room grew in volume.

"Alice," she called. "Food."

Her oldest was screaming again, full of rage. Billie stepped to the kitchen door.

"Hey, there's food here."

The kettle hissed, the first tendrils of steam reaching for the ceiling. There was time, but not much.

*Hear the kettle snap*, said a voice inside her head.

"Don't," she said to it. Then, louder: "Evie, Moira, food!"

They wouldn't hear her past the screams, past Alice's guttural, awful, accusatory voice. Evie was crying again, and Billie stepped into the hall—but only one step, before cowardice turned her back. She flicked the switch on the kettle, listening to it ebb into dissatisfied silence.

*So stupid*, she thought again, only to hear her thoughts answer her: *Hear the kettle snap, break your daughter's back*.

"No," she said, making sure the switch was off before gathering the yoghurts and the crisps and walking into the living room. Evie and Moira were on the sofa, sharing what little scraps of scone hadn't fallen into the cushions. Alice stood in front of them snapping her fingers, her arms like steel wires.

"Hey," Billie said. "Calm down, all of you."

"Mine," Moira said, spotting the yoghurt. Alice turned around, her hair wild, her face wilder.

"Come here," Billie said to Evie, who was smudging tears from her crimson cheeks. The four-year-old slid from the sofa and ran over, wrapping her short arms around her as best she could. She was hotter than the sun, sticky with sweat and tears.

"It's okay. You're tired. Thursdays are always hard. I'll put the telly on, you can eat the crisps."

Evie nodded, sniffing her way back to her seat. Billie opened the crisps for her—her fingers still shaking—then unscrewed the yogurt and handed it to Moira.

"I want one," said Alice, snapping her fingers.

"Sit down then," Billie said. "And ask nicely."

"Please," grunted Alice, collapsing to the floor like her strings had been cut.

Billie knew not to push it, dropping the yoghurt into her lap. She switched the TV on at the wall and handed the remote to Evie, whose eyes glistened with gratitude. Her mouth was sandpaper-dry by the time she'd made it back to the kitchen, and she clicked the kettle on again. It answered with an immediate growl and the tension in her gut ratcheted up another couple of notches.

*Empty it, start again*, said her head, and she shook it like the words were bluebottles.

"So stupid."

*Hear the kettle snap, break your daughter's back.*

She hated it, *hated* it, but unlike the kettle she couldn't switch it off. She drummed her fingers on the counter, waiting as the kettle's hiss morphed into a dull rumble once again, as the steam began to explore the bottom of the cabinets, as it caught in the sickly light from the window.

Out in the hall, her phone began to ring. She ignored it, grabbing a cup from the drainer and dropping a teabag into it. She caught the reflection of her movement in the kettle, her ghost-self trapped in the copper sheen. A prisoner, she thought, and the irony wasn't lost on her. But what was the alternative? Walk away, let the kettle snap, *chance* it?

*Nothing will happen. Nothing.*

But what if it did?

*Hear the kettle snap…*

Her phone cut out and she tuned in to the sound of her girls again. Still arguing, as if they ever did anything else. It hadn't always been this way, had it? They'd been feisty, and that was no bad thing, but it had never been this bad. The scratches, the occasional bites, the constant, endless screams.

Those bloody clicking fingers.

*Snap snap snap snap.*

She didn't know what to do. She didn't know how to make it better, because they didn't seem to be able to listen to her anymore. It was the same thing every day, the same arguments, the same mess, and each day she felt the weight of it grow, pushing on her shoulders, buckling her back, compressing her, making her eggcup small. She couldn't go on like this forever because something inside her was close to breaking, and she didn't know whether it was something that could be fixed.

Maybe it was already too late. Because why else would she be standing here, her hand hovering by the kettle switch as it started to rattle on its perch? Why else would she believe—and she *did* believe it, with her whole heart, with some undeniable, misplaced instinct—that the entirety of her health and happiness, the lives of her children, the safety of the entire world would depend upon her switching the kettle off before it tripped itself.

*So stupid. So utterly, pathetically stupid.*

And yet…

"Mum!"

Evie's voice, and full enough of genuine fear to punch Billie out of the kitchen. She ran into the hall, seeing her middle daughter first, seeing the open front door behind her, the flash of blonde hair as Moira made a run for it. Billie managed two steps before her mind screamed.

*The kettle! The kettle!*

And she couldn't stop the machinery of her body from turning back to the kitchen, from running to the kettle which rumbled on the counter.

"No!" she said, snapping it off. "Moira, wait!"

She pushed herself away, back through the door, Evie blocking the corridor.

"Moira!"

That little blonde head running for the street.

"Jesus, no!"

Through the door, into the bitter cold, Moira's laughter the loudest thing in the world—that and the growl of an engine.

"Moira, stop! Stop!"

And she did. Thank god, she did. The girl reached the line of cars parked along the kerb and planted a hand on one, still laughing, her foot hovering over the street as a delivery van choked its way past—the driver oblivious. Billie ran to her youngest daughter and scooped her up, held her so tight that she squealed in protest. The girl's damp hands pushed against her face, smudging her lips into her teeth, but she didn't let go, she didn't relax.

"No, Mumma, run! Run!"

Didn't let go all the way back to the house.

"Run!"

Billie closed the door, putting Moira down so that she could lock it. She slid the safety chain into place too, just to be sure. Her youngest had collapsed to her backside, her fingers squeaking on the bare boards as she protested her imprisonment. Billie felt dizzy, felt like the house was on ropes, spinning fast. Evie stood in the hall, her eyes wider than ever. She pointed up the stairs, answering a question Billie hadn't even asked.

"Alice," Billie said, just a whisper. She cleared her throat, tried again. "Alice, get down here."

"She opened the door," Evie said. "She told her to go away."

The anger was there, sharp, dangerous. The strength of it scared her. She checked the locks again, stepping over Moira then past Evie, entering the kitchen. Had she turned the kettle off, or had it snapped by itself? For an awful second she couldn't remember, but the seconds that followed were even worse because she saw herself turning away from the open door, from her escaping child. She saw herself running back to the kitchen.

*She could have died. Oh god, she could have died.*

"Alice!" she shouted. "Now."

And her oldest daughter must have known how serious she was, because Billie heard the rising sound of clicking fingers, as neat as tap shoes.

*Snap snap snap snap.*

The girl rounded the newel post and walked down the hallway, drowning in darkness. Moira watched her from where she sat by the door, Evie crouching beside her with a little arm looped over her sister's shoulders.

"I didn't do it," Alice said.

A hundred things boiled their way up Billie's throat at once and she swallowed them all down.

"I didn't do it."

*Snap snap snap snap.*

Alice's fingers were a clockwork mechanism, the tick of an organ-grinder's music box, the snap of a toy monkey's cymbals. Billie almost laughed at the image, at the *horror* of it, feeling the reality of the dark room start to peel away, unpicked one click at a time until she could bear it no longer. She moved in and took Alice's hands, holding them hard, feeling those slim fingers twitch and struggle like they were things with lives of their own, suffocating in her grip.

"Ow!" Alice said, trying to pull away. Billie didn't let her, she held on to those hands with a force that scared her, her own fists locked tight. "Mum, you're hurting me."

Billie opened her mouth but still the words wouldn't fit up her throat. She was a broken thing, unable to speak, unable to move.

"Please," said Alice.

Billie remembered herself, her fingers releasing like steel traps. Alice pulled away, her hands to her chest like they'd been burned.

"I'm sorry," Billie said.

Alice blinked at her, confused.

"Don't ever do that again," she said. "Promise me."

The girl nodded, her long hair falling in front of her face. She made no attempt to move it away, her hands in front of her now, the pads of her thumb and middle fingers pressed together, cocked. She clicked one experimentally, quietly. Out in the hallway Moira and Evie were laughing, the little one chasing her big sister into the living room as if she hadn't almost met her end on the street outside.

*How easily they forget*, Billie thought, *how easily they let things go.*

Alice snapped the fingers of her other hand.

"I won't," she said.

"Won't do it, or won't promise?"

"Won't do it. I won't. I didn't think the door would even open, it wasn't my fault."

*It was my fault*, Billie thought, seeing herself turn away from her child, seeing herself run back to the kitchen. She looked at the kettle now, at that hateful thing.

*Hear the kettle snap, break your daughter's back.*

She couldn't bring herself to switch it on. She didn't know how she'd ever be able to do it again.

"What is it?" Alice asked.

"Nothing," said Billie, resting her trembling hands back on the counter, feeling crumbs beneath her fingertips. Alice snapped away, like castanets. "Why do you do it?"

"I didn't—"

"The snapping," Billie said. "Why do you snap your fingers so much?"

She looked back to see her daughter shrug her bony shoulders. She listened to Alice's heavy breaths, to the giggles that came from the living room, to those endlessly snapping fingers and the silence of the house that sat behind it all. Once again she was struck by the unreality of it all, the sheer impossibility of it. She was paper-thin and the tears were right there, the pressure of them enough to rupture her.

"I like it," Alice said eventually. "I like the way it feels."

Billie perched against the counter.

"Feels?" she said.

"I like the ending of it," Alice said, shrugging again, struggling.

"How do you mean?"

"The ending of it, the feel of it. Like a full stop."

A smile found its way to Billie's face, fragile and unexpected.

"It feels like a full stop?" she asked.

"Sometimes things go on too long," Alice said, staring at the middle of Billie's chest the way she always did when she was thinking. "Sometimes things go on and on and it's too much to see all in one go. Like in a book when it won't stop talking. It makes my head feel too full, like it's going to burst."

She snapped her fingers again, her left hand then her right.

"So I make a full stop. And it makes my head less fizzy and full, and I can start thinking again."

"That's clever," Billie said. "Really clever."

Alice smiled, genuinely happy, genuinely relieved.

*Snap.*

"You can do it too," she said. "Try it. I can show you."

"I will," said Billie.

"Can we have food?"

"I'll see what I can do."

Alice wheeled around on her heels, running down the hallway. She stopped outside the living room door, and Billie watched her as she watched her little sisters, so curious, so unsure, as fragile as old glass.

*Snap snap snap snap.*

And something in Billie's heart seemed to both marvel and break when she turned and made for the stairs instead.

"Alice," she called after her. A head appeared over the bannister. "I'm sorry I said you were unkind. You're not unkind. You're the kindest girl I know. I love you."

"Thanks," Alice shot back, clattering away like a train.

Billie turned and leaned on the counter, looking at the kettle.

"You, though," she told it. "You are just a bastard."

It had almost been the end of her youngest girl, her little Moira.

*What's wrong with you?* she asked, answering herself. *Alice is right, the world is too much. It makes my head feel too full as well.*

She reached out, and hesitated.

*Hear the kettle snap, break your daughter's back.*

"No," she said.

She pushed down the switch, a fist of adrenaline hitting her right in her stomach. The kettle was primed, the water already hot, and the rumble was immediate. Curls of steam reached for the ceiling, ghostly hands held up in worship, in reverence. It seemed as if something was coming to boil in Billie's head as well, something awful, something that couldn't be undone. A stream of thoughts sluiced through her, a current of bad things. She reached for the switch, hesitated again.

*Too much, too fast.*

The kettle was shaking, the rumble of a plane crashing, a continent shaking, a world ending.

*Her* world ending.

But she ignored it, thinking of her Alice, her infuriating, wonderful, kind Alice.

*I make a full stop. And it makes my head less fizzy and full, and I can start thinking again.*

She closed her eyes, gripped the counter, everything contracting to that one singular, inevitable sound.

Snap.

Just a full stop. Not an end, but a pause. A chance to think. A chance to breathe and start again.

Billie opened her eyes to see the kettle. Just a kettle, quietening slowly, its job done. The rumble faded and the world was still here, *she* was still here.

Just a full stop.

And the kitchen might have been ten times bigger, the sun right outside the window. She took a breath and waved the steam from the air, exhausted.

*Hear the kettle snap*, said her head.

"And all will be fine," she said. "All will be well."

And the strange thing was, she believed it. She believed it, and she knew nothing would be the same now.

She emptied the kettle into the sink, refilling it and easing it onto its cradle.

"Just a full stop," she said, pressing the switch.

From the living room, Evie laughed, and Billie moved towards the sound like a mote of dust lifted by a shaft of sunlight. She paused by the door, a lifetime of uncertainty holding her back.

But only for a moment.

"Just a full stop," she said. "The story goes on."

She left the kettle to do its job, and went to check on her girls.

---

Alexander Gordon Smith is the author of thirteen novels for children and young adults, including the Escape From Furnace series, which is loved by millions of readers around the world. As 'Alex Smith' he writes the internationally bestselling DCI Robert Kett books, about a detective who juggles solving crimes and looking after his three young daughters—the three girls who appear in *Snap*. Gordon, as he is known to friends and family, lives in Norwich with his wife and his own three daughters.

# AN UNEXPECTED VISITOR

*By Alison Stockham*

Her shadow flickered across the front door, as the first light of the morning rose from behind clouds that would clear soon enough to reveal a beautiful spring morning. Everything was covered with a delicate misting of dew from the still-cool nights, washing the world new by daybreak. Looking around her, she knew she would have to work fast if she wanted to stay unseen. There were the faint sounds of households waking around her and she still had more houses to see to. A toddler's cry of 'Mama' came sharply through the window she was crouched under and she froze.

Still holding her breath, she raised her head just above the window line to see through the glass. At the back of the house, through the bright open-plan space, she could see the outline of a woman, holding the child on her hip as she went about her morning routine, making coffee and getting a family breakfast ready. The silhouette of a man joined her, kissing her cheek and ruffling the hair of the small child who held out their arms to him. A restful morning scene, a family blissfully unaware of the person crouched outside the front of their house, uninvited. Finishing up her task, she checked that the coast was clear before moving on to the next house, taking deep breaths of relief that she had not been seen.

She knew from before that this next house did not have young children living in it. It was a family with teenagers and so she knew it was likely that she would not be disturbed, the family taking the opportunity to sleep in on this spring Sunday, after many years of early morning starts, unwelcomed by all but the then enthusiastic youngsters, who now would take multiple attempts to be prised out of bed before lunchtime. The house would later be filled with boisterous behaviour and bursting at the seams with life, but as the day slowly woke up around her, she was able to do what she was there to do uninterrupted and make her way to the next house.

Each house conveniently had a low brick wall at the front. It was a row of whitewashed Victorian terraced villas, a line of respectability stretching over a hundred years back and all the way down the street. Several properties could be completed at one time. She could hide below the wall and then peep up to check the coast was clear, before she put one be-suited leg over the small adjoining wall, as it turned perpendicular to the outside wall of the house, then climbing over to next door. Had anyone seen her do this, they would not have considered it elegant nor graceful and her dismount to the neighbouring side was anything but balletic. Had she been a gymnast, no score cards registering ten would even have been considered.

Once she had completed her work at the quiet house with the teenagers, she had then to only hop across the joined front doorsteps to the next house, crouching again behind the wall that screened her from the street. The birds singing in the trees could see her at her work, but there was no one out walking, no one cycling past, even the dog walkers were not out yet. As the street woke up, faint smells of coffee and bacon wafted into the air to join the delicate yellow fragrance that the daffodils gave off as they swayed in the breeze. She lost a few moments' focus as she enjoyed the tranquillity that was draping itself along the road, before the rough bark of a nearby dog made her jump and remind her to concentrate on the job in hand.

This next house was an even quieter property, one rarely visited or filled with people. It was inhabited by a solitary, elderly lady. She knew this. She had observed her on various occasions, standing at the window, watching the world go by, waiting for someone to see her and wave so that she could wave back. The same routine day after day after day with only the dark hours of night to differentiate one from the other. She knew that this lady would be awake, would have been since before the first light of the day had dawned, stretching its luminance across the front room that looked onto the street. The lady would be in the garden by now, watching the birds as they hopped about on the multiple feeders that she had asked her son to set up for her in the occasional visits he managed. The birds were her reliable company, so long as the food stations were full. She knew from her previous visits that this lady had regular deliveries of bird food to her door, often seeing the milkman delivering it with his single bottle of milk. More food for the birds than for her. So much solitude, all the more reason for this house to be included in her morning's work. A good result from this house, no doubt.

She was overheating now, a combination of nerves and exertion and it was making her task harder, her hands warm and slippery. She tsked at herself, she should have worn gloves. Too late now. She had to get this done, get home and get out of her disguise. There were more people around now, the sun fully up. If she were to be able to enjoy the fruits of her labour from a safe distance, she needed to get it done. Speeding up, and taking more risks as she did so, she snaked her way along the street, making sure no house was left out. The whole street was part of the plan; her masterplan that had taken weeks to develop. She only had this chance to get it right and her nerves were starting to crack. A mistake now could ruin everything

A few early risers were making their presence known. A jogger here, a dog walker there, and they gave her odd glances as she nodded at them nervously, hoping that her disguise was enough not to blow her cover, enough that should they be asked, they would not be able to identify her. She had barely had time to finish at the last house in the row when there came a shout.

'Oi! You there! Oi! What do you think you're doing?!'

A man from the other side of the street had seen her, as she peered into the living room window at the final house, having caught sight of the shadow of someone coming down the stairs through the stained-glass window of the slate-grey front door. She snapped her head up, turning to look at him as he marched towards her. He was slowed by his dog, straining at its leash as it tried to mark its territory on the street sign, and by the car that was slowly making its way down the road, pausing to allow a bored pigeon to strut backwards and forwards in the way. There was enough time to bound over the wall and hightail it away to the back of the houses, where a narrow alleyway snaked its way along the houses' back gardens, a way for householders to bring their bins out and their bikes in. In her panic, her head span as she whipped round to see if he was following. She saw his dog first as the leash let it turn the corner before him. She grabbed the cool metal handle of the wooden back gate, slamming it shut behind her, her breathing fast and her heart hammering in her chest. This was not part of the plan.

She was grateful that she had made it into this back garden. She knew that this house was empty. There would be no one watching from the kitchen at the sight she revealed whilst stood on the lawn. Having locked the gate behind her, she listened to hear if the man had followed her. He had not. He must have glanced down the alleyway and seen it was empty and, not wanting to investigate further, gone on his way. There was no noise but the birds and the gentle songs drifting from the Sunday morning radio show that the next-door house was listening to. She breathed in and out again feeling herself calm. She had gone along the whole street. She had done it.

She walked to the back door, grateful that it had been left unlocked when she tried the handle and walked inside. The house was silent. Empty.

Just as she had left it. She missed being in a house full of people, full of life. She wanted this to be a fresh start, a new beginning. Her old home had been such a sad one, a place of loneliness and sorrow, that she wanted this one to be full of magic and joy. Which is how she came to find herself, at seven in the morning on Easter Sunday, dressed in a giant bunny costume. She laughed at herself and took off the giant head, the ears flopping into her face as she did so. She turned the head of the costume in her hands and looked at it. *What must that man have thought?!* she chuckled to herself as she imagined him noticing a giant white rabbit hiding behind the potted cherry tree, its first blossoms spreading their delicate scent in the air. And how she had hopped away, her woven wicker basket emptied of all its treats, ready for her neighbours to find.

Heading upstairs, she quickly changed into more everyday clothes and, grabbing the thermos of coffee she had made beforehand, she slipped out of her front door to officially welcome the day by sitting on the wall of her own house and watching the magic unfold.

She leant over and knocked on her neighbour's door, before sitting back down. A truncated version of knock down ginger.

The door was opened by her neighbour.

'Oh, morning Lauren, how are you?' she said, looking a little surprised at such an early visitor.

'I'm good. Happy Easter!' Lauren replied smiling before silently pointing at the small collection of brightly coloured, foil-covered eggs sitting snuggly on the doorstep, next to a chalk outline of a pawprint. 'I see the Easter bunny has been!'

Lauren gave her neighbour Sally a look. One that said that it was okay to accept this treat, a knowing look that said that it wasn't something dodgy, it wasn't left by some madwoman (or had it been?!) and that it was a little parcel of joy to share with her house. But a look that also said *Don't ask me about it, don't spoil the magic.*

'Eh?' Sally said, initially confused. She then looked at Lauren's doorstep where she had remembered to leave some for herself and at the house on the other side and seeing that the offerings had been left for all, Sally turned back into the house and shouted excitedly, with an element of the childish thrill of an unexpected surprise that Lauren had been hoping to create, 'Children! Come and see who's been!'

The thundering noise that Lauren usually experienced through the walls, echoed out of the door as the children of the house came running to see what their mother was talking about and, on seeing the pile of eggs glinting in the sun, smiled and said 'Mummmm!'

'It wasn't me!' she protested. 'I've already given you your eggs.'

Lauren smiled. 'Must be magic.'

'Do you have any?' the boy asked, offering one up to her.

Lauren nodded. 'I do, thank you! In fact, I'll have one now,' she said and she bent to pick one up, slowly feeling around its curved shape, her fingers, warmed by her coffee cup, melting the chocolate beneath the wrapper. She opened an egg and popped it into her mouth whole. The sweetness melted onto her tongue and the creaminess coated her mouth. It was delicious.

The boy followed suit and then leant over to the other side of their dividing wall.

'Look! Max has some too!' he said, and he leapt over to knock on their door.

Lauren watched in delight as house by house, neighbour by neighbour, each house opened their doors to find their unexpected gifts. And, once they were out, each house stayed for a while, chatting and passing the time of day with each other, with the people they lived their lives with, side by side. The house with the boisterous teenagers, with the house with the fragile elderly lady, all standing next to each other, enjoying this moment in the spring sunshine.

'This is nice,' Lauren said absent-mindedly to her neighbour. 'We should have a street party or something in the summer.'

'That's a great idea! I've often thought that but never knew where to start. You should come over for coffee and we can talk it over.'

'I'd love that,' Lauren said truthfully. She wanted so much to be part of a community and she glimpsed the possibility of that unfolding in front of her. She hugged her cup to her chest and smiled, warmth spreading inside her chest.

'In fact, would you like to come to lunch today? We've not had you round yet and we've an Easter spread planned.'

Lauren hesitated, checking that the invitation was genuine, or one made purely out of politeness, but on sensing that it was, replied with a beaming smile.

'That would be wonderful! If you're sure? Though, I was going to see if Patricia further down wanted any company today. Her family are so far away now, she seems a bit lonely. But I don't know her too well.'

'We've spoken a few times. Maybe she could come too. More the merrier. I'm sure the *Easter Bunny* would approve!'

Sally said knowingly, smiling at Lauren. 'Why don't we go and ask her now?'

Sally nodded her head towards the elderly lady's house but stopped, briefly, to whisper at Lauren.

'By the way, I think the suit suited you!' she said with a kind grin on her face.

'Huh?' Lauren said confused.

'I saw the Easter bunny out of the window this morning as I got up. What a lovely idea.'

Lauren paused, initially unsure, but then, a wide smile grew across her face as she took Sally's arm in hers. 'I'm sure I don't know what you mean!'

'I'm sure you don't, must have been someone else then' Sally nodded.

'It was. It was the Easter bunny.' Lauren laughed.

---

Alison Stockham has always written, training with the Script Factory as a script editor, working in film drama before moving into TV documentary production, predominantly for the BBC and Channel 4. Whilst working in television, Alison continued to write, drafting short stories and novellas. Her first full-length novel, *The Magpie Sister*, was long listed for the Lucy Cavendish Fiction Prize 2020 and she began work on a subsequent novel, *Under A Different Sky*, on a Faber Academy course. Both novels are currently works in progress.

# PLANTING OUT

*By Anne O'Leary*

Mam was scared because the forecast was for ice. I told her she'd be grand as long as she took it handy. The car did slide a bit as she backed out the driveway, but I said that in the event of an emergency I would help by grabbing hold of the steering wheel. She told me I was not to do that under any circumstances. She's a martyr to her nerves.

It was still dark and there were only a few early morning lights on around our estate. In our house, all the lights are kept on when we're at home and not asleep. We are a family that doesn't like the dark. Well, Mam and I don't, anyway. Dad loves complaining about the electric bill and who's expected to shell out for it. It always gets paid, so I don't know what his problem is. *Because I'm the eejit expected to magic up the money, Paulie Boy,* he told me when I said it out loud once. I usually hum something in my head when he calls me that instead of just Paulie, which is my name.

Where the road widens at the entrance to the estate was a bit of a skating rink, in fairness. It was powdery white, like icing sugar under the streetlamps. We obviously weren't the first adventurers, because it was covered in big, swirly loops of tyre marks. They made a pleasing pattern, evenly done. I pointed them out to Mam, but she couldn't look because she was watching out for danger. She called the Holy Name under her breath as she made her way across, even though she never normally swore. Her knuckles were white on the steering wheel, and though she was doing that crawly old lady driving I have no patience with, the back of the car swung left. Still, she made it out onto the main road, which the council are great for gritting when there's a severe weather alert.

I had the map ready in my hand. The night before, I'd highlighted the route in green, and in my notebook I'd written a list of particular landmarks to watch out for. I'd also brought my gardening book in case there was time for a bit of last-minute studying. I felt nervous, but it was a good kind of nervous.

Mam had packed a flask and sandwiches in case we got stranded, and the number for the AA. Dad said it was a set of rosary beads and some holy water she'd need, but she paid him no heed. He had refused to drive, and advised us not to risk it, so his opinion wasn't welcomed.

Mallow town centre was still asleep, shutters down and shop awnings up, eerily empty. We drove by the flat where I'd lived for a while during my twenties, the one over the chip shop. Everything I owned stank of cooking oil for ages after I moved back home, and I hated the smell because it reminded me of that frightening place, of trying to sleep at night with drunk people fighting out on the street just below me. Fellas would be throwing punches at one another without letting go of their cheeseburgers, and there I'd be, shaking in my bed in case they tried to break through my front door. Dad said the rough crowd was the reason for the cheap rent, but by all means to come home if that was what I wanted. Mam was delighted and said she hadn't slept with an easy mind the whole time I was out of the house. So my moving back worked out fine, though I'd still get a fierce knot in my stomach any time I had to pass by the chip shop, and would hold my breath not to let the chip fat fumes seep into me.

As she drove, Mam kept rubbing one eye and then the other behind her glasses. I was worried she might not be able to watch the road properly, but she insisted she was fine. The rubbing made a sickening squelchy sound, so I asked her to stop.

Plus, after rubbing them, her eyes looked more lined than usual and I had to look the other way because I don't like to think about getting old as it makes me think of death, in particular hers, and that is upsetting.

I tried reading my gardening book to pass the time, but the streetlights made the pages flash yellow, then black, then yellow. I wanted to put on the radio, but Mam said, *Oh, not at this hour, please, Paulie. It would wreck my head*. But it was boring with nothing to look out at and I was starting to feel stressed, so she said I could listen as long as I kept it nice and low. The radio wasn't great at that hour and the songs tended to be slow, sad ones, so I had to keep searching. But then I remembered there was a Proclaimers CD in the glove compartment that always made me feel happy, and I turned it up high so I could belt out my favourite songs. Mam didn't sing along, she just went back to rubbing her eyes. At least the music covered the squelching.

I'm not sure where we went wrong, but by the time we realised it, we were very lost. I had my notebook open, waiting to tick off the landmarks as we passed them, but we didn't come across any. We were off the main road by then, Mam having taken a left where the road sign told us to. We'd almost forgotten about the ice while we were on the gritted motorway, and she started *OhJesusMaryandJosephing* as soon as we got onto the back road and felt the slide. Because she was concentrating on keeping the car pointed forwards, she must have missed some turn or other.

There were no lights this far into the countryside, and no sign of a church at a T-junction where there should have been.

My anxiety levels were getting bad by now. Mam said it could have happened to anyone, and that I was shouting at her again, though I wasn't.

We drove past dark bungalows and lonely farmhouses and a closed Co-op, but no signs of life. Between the old lady driving and the getting lost, I was scared I was going to be late. And being late would be disastrous because I wouldn't get the placement.

Finding a job is hard. You can go to a dozen interviews and not be offered a single one. Or you can get the job and then find out it's not what you expected so you've no choice but to leave. Or you can keep applying for jobs, but not have a clue what kind of work to say you're suited to when they quiz you at the employment place. This was the first thing I'd ever seen that I felt was something I might like to do. It was also the first time I wasn't asked about the long gaps in my CV. I knew if I could get there I'd convince them I was the right man for their trainee programme.

I had done my homework. I liked browsing gardening books at the best of times, and I've always been fascinated with nature, the shapes of leaves and the smell of lavender and the colour of long grasses when the sun shines through. Plus I enjoyed watching gardening programmes when I was younger—Monty Don, Alan Titchmarsh, all those fellas. Something about nurturing plants appealed to me. I knew egg boxes were ideal for sowing seeds in, and that marigolds grown alongside tomato plants would trick aphids. I knew how to take cuttings to create independent new plants, and how to carefully plant out fragile seedlings for some hope of survival. Dad said I should help him in the garden for a bit of hands-on practice, but that didn't work out. It was the wrong time of year, for one thing, so the ground was too hard for digging and there wasn't much to do other than pull cabbages. He got mad when I advised him to grow rocket in the spring instead of butterhead lettuce—seeing as Mam and I both hate it—and threw a fit when I refused to rake leaves. But they're dead things and I don't like dead things.

Anyway, I was thinking on a bigger scale, and working on the grounds of a stately home was a far cry from deadheading dahlias in a council house back yard.

I was beginning to feel a terrible darkness pressing against the car, squeezing the breath out of me inside. The headlights showed only tiny slices of road. Mam cursed every time she felt the spin of the tyres on an icy patch. She wasn't even bothering to do it under her breath anymore, and I had to call her up on her language more than once. It wasn't helping my stress levels one bit and made me wish I had gotten around to learning how to drive.

After what felt like hours, I noticed a change in the sky, a faint purple strip on the horizon. We'd been travelling uphill for some time, so we pulled in at a gateway to a high field and got our bearings. In the valley below was a dotting of houses and, in the distance, a church. If we could get to that, Mam reckoned, we'd be right. She asked if I fancied a quick sandwich and tea from the flask as we hadn't yet had breakfast, but I said, *Are you mad, when we're in the middle of bloody nowhere and the interview's in twenty minutes?* To be honest, Mam is something of a noisy eater and at that precise moment I couldn't bear the slurp of tea and the grinding of dentures.

It was a straight run down to the church, which turned out to be the one on my list, so I ticked it and we took a right at the T-junction. It was a relief to see a brown signpost for the stately home and, soon after that, huge black gates with golden scrollwork. My stomach flipped from worried-scared to excited-scared, and I leaned forward to get a good look as we drove through the park. It went on for miles, first woodland, then fields, then formal gardens. There was no ice on the gravel driveway so Mam was able to get the Mini up to a good speed, arriving at the entrance in a spray of stones like a cop car on a callout. There were two minutes to go to my interview so I tore in through a door twice my height. It was marked *Private* to stop just anyone from marching through uninvited.

They told me on the spot I had the placement. They were impressed I'd made the journey on such a shocking day, and in fact there were only two interviewers present as the other two from the panel hadn't made it in.

*Your determination is admirable, Paul,* they told me, shaking my hand and smiling. I did my best to smile back and look them in the eye, the way Mam had instructed me to do.

*No bother,* I said. *I enjoy a challenge,* I said.

Mam was waiting in the car, eating a sandwich with shaky hands. She cried when I told her.

*You'll have to drive me, though,* I said, when she calmed herself. *I've no hope of getting here otherwise.*

*Anything,* she said, her eyes wet and those lines worse than ever. *Anything at all for my boy.* She stroked my face and I let her because I really was very pleased. She said she knew things were going to work out perfectly this time.

I celebrated with The Proclaimers on full blast all the way home.

---

Anne O'Leary lives in Cork, Ireland. She won the Molly Keane Award 2018 and 'From the Well' Short Story Competition 2017, was a runner-up in the Irish Novel Fair 2016 and 2021, shortlisted for the Colm Tóibín International Short Story Award 2016 and Highly Commended in 2017, and longlisted for the Cambridge Short Story Prize 2020 and RTE Guide/Penguin Ireland Short Story Competition 2015. Her work has been published in literary journals and anthologies in Ireland and the UK.

# A WAVE OF LOVE

*By Barbara Copperthwaite*

'...Happy birthday dear Brian, happy birthday to you!'

The song rang out, bouncing off the high ceiling with a slight echo, as Brian Meeks carried his usual noon cuppa from the kitchen to the lounge. As it was a special occasion, he'd treated himself to a custard slice from the corner shop, too, although he hadn't bothered putting 80 candles on it. He was so looking forward to it that he didn't notice the runner in the hallway was rucked up until his toe caught and the slice almost flew off the plate—he managed to save it, but slopped tea everywhere instead.

'Sorry, Hattie,' he sighed. 'I'll clean it up.'

If she'd been there, his wife would have insisted on clearing up herself. She was one of those people who took charge—not bossy, just loved being busy. But Hattie had been gone for three years now, and Brian was celebrating his birthday alone. Still, he spoke to her as if she was there. It made him feel less lonely.

With a grunt of effort, he bent over and flicked a tea towel around the skirting board, but didn't get all the splashes.

'That'll have to do, girl,' he said, standing with an even louder groan. 'No one's going to be looking at it, anyway—and if I managed to get down there to wipe it, it'd take a crane to get me up again.'

He chuckled, and imagined Hattie laughing back. She always laughed with a whoop to start, her belly shaking, eyes closing as she wiped at them. He missed her. Missed company and connection with the outside world. That was why he sat in his armchair all day every day, looking out of the bay window, waiting for passers-by to wave to. A wave was a universal sign of hello and goodbye, of friendliness that requires no speech and has no language or age barriers. Through it, Brian tried to connect with a world that he increasingly felt isolated from.

Not long after Brian had settled down in his usual place and taken his first bite of custard slice, a man in jeans and smart arran jumper, his shirt collar showing over the neckline, appeared at the bottom of the street. His head down, he hurried along as he talked on his phone, pushed by the urgency of the words Brian couldn't hear through his window. Brian waved. The man didn't notice. Perhaps he was getting bad news; Brian hoped not and sent a silent prayer after the man's disappearing back.

Ten minutes later, a long-haired fella with holes in his jeans at the knees meandered by. He looked embarrassed when he saw Brian's greeting, and didn't break stride or pull his hands from his pockets.

That was the usual reaction from people. They didn't seem to realise the elderly man lived for that brief connection through a gesture.

Brian settled his head back on the antimacassar that Hattie had crocheted, and waited. He'd been born in this house. As a child, he'd walked to the school around the corner, and always gave a wide grin to Mrs Panton, the widow who had been known locally as Mrs Wavey because of her habit of sitting in the front window. Everyone had known her. It had been different back then, though. Nowadays people barely recognised their neighbours, and children were driven to the school around the corner rather than walking past his house.

By 2pm, the lunchtime rush of three passers-by was over. Brian pushed his finger around his plate just in case he'd missed a crumb of custard slice, then decided it was time for his own lunch. He picked up the unfinished and now cold mug of tea, just as a woman in her twenties turned into the street and walked slowly along, young shoulders hunched, wearing those tiny white headphones that everyone these days seemed to wear to cut themselves off from the world. She carried a brightly-coloured handbag by the strap so that it almost trailed on the ground.

He waved. She slumped on, staring at the pavement as if it contained all the woes of the world and none of the answers. Brian's hand dropped…then he decided to give it one last go because today was his birthday and he was, if he was totally honest, feeling a bit sorry for himself, which wouldn't do at all. The movement must have caught the corner of her eye, because she looked up, but her gaze slid away as if he was invisible.

Silly, really, but the rejection from a stranger hurt.

'You're being a daft old man,' he scolded himself. 'Young people are busy, too—'

He stopped. She'd walked back, hesitant, and given a smile. The sort of smile that makes someone look worried, but then she raised a hand, paused for a second, looking at him, then walked on.

A little act of kindness that made his day.

Her eyes reminded Brian of Hattie's. Her mouth smiled, but her eyes had a sadness that could be spotted by those who truly looked.

Brian had been only 18 when he and the love of his life had met. They married five years later. He'd had to propose three times before Hattie accepted, because she was ten years older than him and she'd worried about him making a mistake or changing his mind. No chance of that. They had shared one of those rare and wonderful loves that lasts a lifetime and never fades. When he thought of their life together he thought of laughter because they were always happy. Even when they'd realised their dream of a family of their own wouldn't happen, she'd tried to smile through the heartbreak, though sometimes her eyes had given away the secret.

He wondered what secret the passer-by kept.

The rest of the day passed as usual. No one waved at him. At 5.30pm he ate, as always, and then put the telly on for a bit of company. He liked to argue with the newsreaders.

The next day he got up bright and early, the sun streaming in all morning, creating patches of warmth through the house as he waited and waited and waited for someone to catch his eye, to make him feel he wasn't invisible. He saw a boy of about 12 on a red bike, who really should have been at school; a young mum pushing a pram and looking content but lost in a world of her own; and a group of six pensioners, though younger than him, all talking together so intently that only one of them at the back of the group gave a shy wave.

Just as Brian was about to stand up for his lunch, the young woman appeared—and this time she seemed to be looking for him as she passed the houses approaching his. His heart gave a little skip that someone might actually be eager to see him. When she spotted him, one side of her mouth pulled up into a smile, the other side still indecisive. She gave a wave at the exact same time he did. Paused for several heartbeats, then walked away.

Brown eyes, like Hattie's. Kind. Chestnut hair.

Brian spent the rest of the day whistling to himself, and didn't even get annoyed when he watched the news.

The following day Brian decided to have his lunch a bit later, so he wouldn't risk missing her. At just past 2pm, she came and waved as she strode by. She seemed to be standing a little straighter, and her bright handbag sat on her shoulder, where it should be. Brian's belly growled as he raised his hand, so the next day he had lunch on a tray on his lap, like a heathen; it was worth it so that he could see his new friend.

When the weekend arrived, Brian realised the Lunchtime Girl's routine would probably be different, which made loneliness gnaw at him the way his dog Susie used to gnash at a bone, until she'd got too old and lost half her teeth. Susie's squishy bed still sat in the corner, beside the fire. It had been empty now for five long years, apart from a well-worn leather collar that sat in the middle of it, the tag highly polished.

Sometimes, he still talked to Susie, like he did Hattie. So as he ate lunch he chattered aloud, trying to make conversation. He'd just swallowed his last mouthful when a movement made him look up—it was her, the Lunchtime Girl, walking by with sa big, enthusiastic wave.

Brian couldn't help wondering if she'd made the effort to wander by just to see him.

Every day without fail, she'd step past at around 2pm. Some days she waved even before he did. Her eyes seemed to light up and her smile was always bright. Every time he saw her turn into the top of his street his heart lifted and he felt tethered to the outside world.

He looked forward to seeing this friend—and they did feel like friends, even though they'd never spoken.

One night, about a month later, Brian spent another evening watching television and talking to it as though Hattie were still there. Then he had a cup of Horlicks, as usual, put the fire guard around the fire, which he'd lit because it had been a nippy night despite the earlier warmth of the spring day, and headed into the hall to go up to bed when...his toe caught on the rucked up hallway runner.

A sense of weightlessness; Brian was flying, twisting through the air. The floor rushed towards him. With a thump, he hit it hard and his breath huffed out and refused to come back in. Panic for a second…then he was able to breathe again.

Then he tried to pull himself up. Pain flared in his hip.

'I'm just going to lie here a minute and gather my strength,' he gasped out loud.

Brawn refused to appear, though. He didn't have the strength to stand. He called for help but his voice quickly grew small and croaky. As time passed, he curled up. At least it was warm, and he was sure he'd be able to stand soon.

'Look at the state of the skirting board,' he said. 'Sorry, Hattie. I've not been dusting as often as I should.'

The drips of tea that hadn't been wiped up from the other day were suddenly so obvious. Hattie would give Brian hell if she saw.

She would have done, if she could see.

Only she wouldn't have done, of course, because although she was house proud her first concern had always been for people not things.

'Is this one of your daft jokes? Up you get,' Hattie would have told him had she been there.

*Up you get.* He'd said that to her when she'd fainted. He'd said it to jolly her along, to show her he wasn't worried so then she wouldn't worry, even though his mouth had been as dry as the bottom of a budgie's birdcage, and his heart had beaten as fast as it had back in the day, when they'd first met at the local dance hall. Ballroom dancing it was. Kids today would probably laugh at the formality of it, but back then it was the only chance to hold a girl close and chat, one on one, no interruptions for as long as the music was playing.

He'd only gone along that night—the night that had changed his life—because his pal, Ray, had wanted to learn to dance to impress someone he was giving the glad eye to. As Brian had walked across the dance floor to sit down, he'd been intent on the empty seats in front of him, choosing where to sit. Until a girl walked behind them. Chestnut hair, kind eyes. *Boom.* It was like being physically hit by something right in his chest.

From somewhere, he'd found the courage to ask her to dance. Was it courage? He'd felt like he was drawn towards her and wouldn't have been able to stop if he'd wanted to, like two magnets pulling together. She'd told him her name was Hattie and given a laugh that made him go weak at the knees. He'd been utterly captured by the way her wavy hair shone in the light and curled against her neck; the glow in her eyes; the radiance of her skin across plump cheeks; that smile that was wide enough for the world but felt like it was only for him. When Hattie slid into his arms it felt as if they were made for each other, and when the music stopped he hadn't wanted to let go.

Lying on the floor now, Brian hugged his arms around his chest at the memory, as if holding Hattie close. A warm glow spread through him. He had had a small life in many ways, but he'd had a big love.

He shifted and gasped at the pain shooting through his hip. That was the only sound. It was so quiet in the house that he heard the cinders from the fire shift and fall as it died.

'I've got myself in a pickle, Hattie,' he whispered. 'Still, I'll be able to see you soon, girl; you and Susie and, God willing, our little Mable.'

A tear quivered then spilled at the thought of seeing the precious daughter they'd almost had. She'd been born too soon; so early that she didn't even have a grave. They'd never had the chance to hold her. To the world, Mable hadn't existed, but to Hattie and Brian she'd meant everything and always would. They'd been parents, even if only for seven months while she'd sheltered in Hattie's womb.

There was a birth certificate, though. A little fake one. The midwife had made it for them, just so they had something real to remind them that their daughter hadn't been imagined. Such a thoughtful thing to do. There'd been some tears shed when it was handed over, of sadness but also gratitude.

'You don't know what this means to us,' Hattie had said, hugging her.

'It's nothing. I wish I could do more.'

Funny, how often kindness is brushed off as 'nothing'. Hattie had been inspired by what the midwife had done, though.

'Little acts of kindness are like stars that light up the night sky. They seem too tiny to matter but they have the power to transform darkness, and by them we can navigate our way,' she'd said.

It was a bit deep for Brian, but his Hattie had always had a beautiful way with words, and he could still remember the day she'd come out with that. Could see again the tears in her eyes, and feel once more the painful pride he'd felt at watching her find something positive out of something so devastating.

Hattie had transformed the darkness of losing Mabel by helping others. She'd become a hospital volunteer, visiting people who didn't have anyone; and if it was young mums, she'd always knit a little outfit for their new-born. She'd been particularly good with those mums who went in to have a baby but came out with their arms empty. She always knew what to say, what to do. Kindness was her gift. That was the thing about Hattie, she made the world a better place without realising it.

'It's nothing,' she'd say.

But she'd get cards and letters of thanks passed on by the hospital from people telling her the difference her visits had made to them, or how cherished the knitted clothes had been, especially to those with little money.

Brian had tried to do his bit, too, knowing that each gesture was just a drop in the ocean, but that oceans are made up of drops. On his days off he'd offer his services out to drive people to and from the hospital; people who couldn't afford the transport costs of having to get to the hospital to visit a loved one or even to get treatment. It wasn't much, but it made their lives a bit easier just when they were often going through the hardest of times. Brian would get cards of thanks too, but he didn't see why; what he was doing wasn't a big deal.

He'd stopped volunteering altogether after Hattie's death. It was too painful to visit the place where she'd passed away from pancreatic cancer, just two months after she'd taken that giddy turn right there in the hallway.

For a long time afterwards, Brian had felt shell-shocked. Life had changed irrevocably, and it kept on changing as friends moved to live closer to their children and grandchildren. That or they were dead. At one point he'd gone to a funeral every month for a year. When that stopped he was shocked to realise funerals had been his social life. Without them, he saw no one. Getting out and about became harder, too, because he'd had to give up driving not long after Hattie passed away—he just couldn't see well enough any more, and his reactions weren't what they used to be. At first he had travelled by train to see friends in their new homes, but being away from home for periods of time had started to feel epic. He liked his bed, grew anxious away from his routine.

Getting old was no fun. Without a family of his own to rally around him, Brian became increasingly isolated and lonely. But sitting around feeling sorry for himself wasn't going to change anything, he'd decided—which was when he'd remembered Mrs Wavey and, about a year ago, turned his armchair to face outside instead of staring at his TV endlessly. He'd hoped to stay connected with the world that way…

Bright sunshine on his face woke Brian. He felt stiff and sore. Once again, he tried and failed to stand. He tried to call out but all that came was a papery whisper.

No one was going to come to his rescue. There wasn't a single person in the world who would notice his absence.

Time passed. The shadows had shifted, Brian must have fallen asleep and not realised. He was cold now the patch of sun that streamed in first thing had disappeared, and the residual heat from the long-gone-out fire in the lounge had dissipated. His throat was so dry it burned.

'I'm on my way out, old girl,' he told Hattie.

There was no fear, he realised. Instead he pondered life and its meaning, now that he was so close to leaving it. He thought of the little acts of kindness and how easy it was to make a difference to someone's life. No big gestures required. Like the waving—every person who had returned his silent greeting had reminded Brian that he was still part of the world.

He thought of the Lunchtime Girl. Of how she reminded him of Hattie. She made him think of Mable. Of the grandchildren he might now have if life had panned out differently.

He drifted through his thoughts and floated away.

A sound stirred him. Knocking. Then footsteps. Fading. He'd woken too late. Tried to call out but could only manage a croak.

Perhaps he could pull something over and attract attention with the crashing? When he attempted to move, his head span with weakness.

Not much longer now until he saw Mable and Hattie.

In fact, could he hear Hattie? It sounded like she was shouting at him through the letterbox. Telling him to wake up. That she was going to call for help.

Was it Hattie? She sounded different…

Suddenly there was a commotion. A loud bang that made him flinch and squeeze his eyes shut. The door flew open, then people surrounded him. People with soft voices and gentle touches, and Hattie's voice insisting she was going in the ambulance with him.

No, it wasn't his wife, it was the Lunchtime Girl. But how could she be here, in his house? Nothing made sense.

Someone else was talking now. 'You're very dehydrated, Brian. We're going to put a drip in to get some fluids into you, okay?'

Something scratched the back of his hand. Moments later came the sensation of being lifted.

Things were coming into focus more. Brian was in the back of an ambulance now, covered in a foil blanket.

'I look like a chicken ready to be roasted,' he chuckled weakly. He expected Hattie's little whoop, followed by her belly laugh. But what sounded was deeper, softer. The person holding his hand, it wasn't Hattie. As their eyes met, the young woman smiled at him and gave a little wave.

'Hello. How are you feeling?'

'You're the Lunchtime Girl,' he replied.

'That's right. Though you can call me Tracy. But let's talk later, you need to rest for now—and don't worry, I won't leave you.'

'Why are you here, though? How did you find me?'

Tracy explained how she'd grown worried about Brian when she walked past his house and he hadn't been at the window. 'I knocked on your door, and when there was no answer I peered through the letterbox and could see your legs, so I dialled 999.'

'You know, you waving at me brightens my days but I never imagined it'd end up saving my life. I can't thank you enough.'

Tracy became suddenly serious as she took his hand. 'No, Brian. You saved my life.'

'I think you're getting in a muddle,' he laughed. 'Either that, or I am.'

'That first day I saw you, I was feeling so low. I had been for weeks—months, even. The last year or so has been hard on everyone, but living alone has really taken its toll on me. Then I lost my job after furlough ended and have had no luck finding a new one.' Tracy's eyes revealed their secret sadness as she spoke. 'It just reached a point where I couldn't see anything to carry on for; like the world wouldn't notice if I wasn't part of it because I didn't *feel* part of it any more. I went for a walk and all I could think about was that if I died no one would care.

'Then you waved at me. Suddenly, I was seen. You smiled and it was like a light switching on at the end of a long tunnel. I went home that night and cried for the first time, actually letting out some of the bottled up emotions.'

Brian could hardly believe what he was hearing. Someone else felt the way he did? But Tracy was just a young slip of a girl who had her whole life ahead of her. He didn't dare interrupt, though, seeing that she had more to say.

'The next day I walked the same route, hoping to see you again—and there you were, waving again. It seemed as if you looked forward to it as much as me.' A tear made its lonely way down her cheek, even as her mouth lifted into a smile. 'That little bit of positivity every day made me feel so much better, and started to spill into other areas of my life. You saved me that day you decided to wave to me.'

For a moment all Brian could do was stare at Tracy in shock. Then he looked into her eyes, so like Hattie's, and realised his own cheeks were wet with tears.

'If you ever feel lonely, you come round and talk to me. I'm always home,' he offered.

'Are—are you sure? I'd hate to—'

'Impose on a lonely old man? Don't be daft—I'd love it! I could cook you dinner. I miss cooking for two sometimes.'

'It's a deal—as long as I'm allowed to bring dessert. It's been a while since I baked a cake, but I used to really enjoy it.'

Brian patted Tracy's hand and shook his head and nodded and didn't know what to say, he felt so overcome. He'd always felt that the people waving to him were doing him a kindness; he'd never for a moment suspected he might be helping someone, too. It seemed so silly, too tiny a thing to count for anything.

Then he remembered Hattie's words.

*'Little acts of kindness are like stars that light up the night sky. They seem too tiny to matter but they have the power to transform darkness, and by them we can navigate our way.'*

---

Barbara Copperthwaite is an Amazon, Kobo and USA Today bestselling author of psychological thrillers. Her career started in journalism, writing for national newspapers and magazines, and interviewing the real victims of crime—and also those who have carried those crimes out. She is fascinated by creating realistic, complex characters, and taking them apart before the readers' eyes in order to discover just how much it takes to push a person over a line. When not writing feverishly at her home in Birmingham, Barbara is often found walking her two dogs, Scamp and Buddy, or hiding behind a camera to take wildlife photographs.

# THE PERFECT MATCH

*By Caroline Mitchell*

I stiffen as our police carrier jolts from the force of the crowd. There are only so many chants of 'f—the police' I can hear before questioning my life choices. Protestors are currently engaged in the futile exercise of rocking our van from side to side. Given Gazza 'brick shithouse' Newman is sitting across from me, I'm surprised they've managed to move it at all. So, I sit here, rocking and sweating buckets in my body armour as I await further orders. The steady motion might even be soothing, if it wasn't for the petrol bombs. I hope I get home in one piece tonight. Being a Met police officer isn't always this exciting. Sometimes, entire days are spent on scene guard. The boredom spurred my decision to become Level 2 tactical trained in riot control. Call it a mid-life crisis if you wish. I'll give you that. At my age, many female officers investigate crime from the safety of their offices, away from the madding crowd. But oh no, old Gwen here (if you call 42 old) fancied a bit of rough and tumble. It helps that there's nobody at home, wringing their hands as they wonder how I am, and texting to see what time my shift ends. Not that I'm totally on my own. To my right is Rochelle. It's her first proper riot. She's twenty three and literally shaking in her tactical boots.

The rest of my colleagues are men. This is a male-dominated environment. I'm not tutting as I say that. No eye-rolling here. The guys I work with are accepting and considerate. They have my back and I have theirs. As for Rochelle…she'll be alright.

Gazza belches with his usual flair, and I join in with the chorus of groans as the stench of cheese and onion crisps fill the air. My adrenalin is pumping as any second now, the back doors will open, and I'll be thrust into a violent crowd. It's the horses I feel for. We're here by choice, but why hurt the police horses? It makes my blood boil. I glance around at the band of officers packed into this rocking tin can. Believe it or not, we're here because we want to help. The protesters' chants have grown louder. I take comfort in being part of a bigger family.

Rochelle wasn't all right. She got crushed in the crowd and suffered a broken arm and a black eye from where someone managed to pull off her helmet and stamp on her head. My legs feel like lead as I walk home from the Slug & Lettuce, warmed by several whiskey and cokes. The lads are still there, decompressing after a stressful day. Rochelle's injuries have affected everyone. Tomorrow her hospital room will be filled with flowers of every shape and size.

As I amble down the street, I see a familiar figure in a fluorescent orange tabard. My head shakes as it always does when I see Millie out at this hour on her own. Millicent Mumford is seventy-five years old and a proud street angel. She lives with Thomas, and by the way she talks about him, I presume he is her son. One of these days, I'll be having some stern words with him. As dashing and handsome as he sounds, he should be taking better care of his mum. I watch Millie as she hands an intoxicated young lady in stilettos a wet wipe to clean the vomit off her face. 'Have some water dear,' she says, digging a bottle from her backpack. 'It'll help with the hangover.' Millie thinks of everything. Something tells me she's been there, many moons ago. I imagine her as a hippie, all flower power and free love. I've never been able to prise her backstory out of her. She gives me a wink as she ushers the drunken girl into a taxi, interrogating the driver at the same time. 'I've got a photo of your vehicle,' she warns the middle-aged man who looks more like Santa Claus than the serial killer Millie obviously sees him as. 'So, you make sure and bring her straight home. No funny business.'

'Will do, officer Millie!' The driver laughs. The corners of my mouth turn upwards in a rueful smile. It seems he knows her too. I watch as she slips him the fare and my heart is warmed by her generosity. Sometimes, a little bit of Millie is all you need after a long day.

'It's late.' I state the obvious as I gain her full attention. 'Want me to walk you home?' It's an offer I've made many times before. I already know her response. I'll be going home alone. It breaks my heart to think of anything happening to this frail little woman, but despite her stature, her wits are sharp.

'No thank you.' As she turns her blue eyes upon me, I swear she can see into my soul. 'You look tired. I hope you're taking care of yourself.' A siren blares as a police car speeds up the city streets, and the traffic parts to make way. The air smells of diesel fumes and takeaway food. Music blares from a nearby club. It's been manic since lockdown was lifted and the police have never been so overworked.

'I'm fine,' I sigh, but she stares at me with the gaze of someone who knows better.

'Alright,' I concede, raising my hands in surrender. 'I've had a bit of a rough day. One of my colleagues ended up in hospital but she'll be alright.' I've no doubt Rochelle will recover, but I don't think I'll see her in the carrier again. I dread to think what would have happened if we hadn't scooped her up from the road. Millie's eyes are twinkling as she smiles.

'You need to spend time with Thomas. It's not right, you going back to an empty flat.'

I don't have the heart to tell Millie that I'd be more receptive to a Thomasina, if such a name exists. 'I'm sure he's lovely but I prefer my own company,' I say, unconvincingly. But Millie won't let me off the hook that easily. 'Oh, but you don't know my Thomas,' she says, pulling her tabard together as it flaps in the wind. 'You two would make a perfect match.' I watch as she cases the street, looking out for young women, alone and vulnerable as they wobble home. I wonder what happened in Millie's life to make her like this. 'What do you say?' She pins me with a gaze. 'About Thomas? Would you like to meet him? It will be love at first sight, I know it.'

Her enthusiasm makes me laugh aloud. 'Do you try to marry off Thomas to everyone you meet or just me?'

'Just you dear. You need someone to curl up in bed with…' She breaks off from her sentence which is a relief as our conversation is taking a bizarre turn. I follow as she trots after a woman in a leopard-print dress. 'Get lost, Grandma!' the woman shouts, as Millie offers her a taxi home. I join Millie, placing my hand on her arm. Leopard-print woman joins a man coming out from the alleyway, as he pulls up his flies. Delightful. What is it about drunken men and peeing in alleyways? My jaw tightens as I steer Millie away. One of these days, she's going to get hurt.

'I'm worried about you,' I say. 'Thomas should be here, keeping an eye out.'

'He's where he should be—in front of the fire watching television,' Millie smiles. 'It's far too dangerous for him here.'

These streets *are* dangerous for men at this hour of the night, as drunken revellers look for excuses to pick a fight, but Millie isn't immune to trouble either. After five minutes of trying to persuade her to volunteer her time during the day, I give up.

'At least use an app that pays for the taxis. That way, you won't have to carry cash.'

'If it makes you happy.' She casts her glance over the litter-strewn pavements. 'I know I can't help everyone, and you're right, there are bad people out there. It's why I stay on this street, in public, right under the eye of that camera…' She raises a finger and points. 'There. She gives it a tinkly wave. 'Dinesh operates that one. It's for a private security firm. We go way back.' She nods happily as she agrees with herself. I concede. Millie is more streetwise than I give her credit for.

'All right, I know when I'm beat,' I say, raising my hands in the air. But Millie's attention is already on a young girl who can't seem to get a signal on her phone. 'Use mine, dear,' she says to the teenager on the verge of tears. 'I can get you a taxi home if you like…' She pulls a shawl from her bottomless backpack and places it over the girl's bare shoulders. It's the last time I see Millie alive.

It's twelve weeks later and I'm sitting in the waiting room of an office that my mother would have described as 'swanky'. My presence has been requested as I've been mentioned in Millie's will. Don't feel too bad about Millie's death. She had terminal cancer and lived way beyond the time specialists gave her. She died peacefully, in her sleep. I'm sure Thomas never left her side.

The last few weeks I've thrown myself into work, feeling the pang of loneliness even stronger than before. I love my job. I just hate going home. I know you won't tell anyone as this is deeply embarrassing but if I could sleep in the nick, I would. Last year I came out of a bad relationship. I said, 'never again'. But sometimes life has a way of taking you by the ankles and shaking you upside down. Call it copper's instinct, but I have a feeling that when I come out of this office, things won't be the same again. I pick at my nails as I wait to be called.

At last, Mr Geoffrey Fairholme calls me in. He'd had a job finding me apparently, given Millie didn't know my exact address. He ended up writing to the Met, who took some time to track me down. Thankfully there weren't any other Gwen Dunne's in the Metropolitan police (my grandad was Irish, in case you're wondering). So now I'm sitting in his London office, which is huge. It's a glorious day, too warm to be sitting in freezing cold air-con. It's another reason why I never progressed past the ranks of uniformed police. I love the outdoors.

Millie's solicitor is a large man with a red, bulbous nose. I sense he likes a drink or three judging by the broken veins in his skin. He has a kind face and I like him already. If he's good enough for Millie… He begins by telling me that she has left me something very specific in her will. I don't *have to* accept her gift, but it meant a great deal to her. I'm sad but intrigued. He pushes an envelope across the mahogany desk. 'I've been instructed to wait while you read her letter,' he says, watching me with a curious eye. This is all very cloak and dagger. I imagine Millie watching from afar with her mischievous, twinkling eyes.

I open the envelope with care, my pulse picking up pace. I can face a crowd of angry thugs without blinking an eye, but this is throwing me for six.

*Dear Gwen,*

*I hope this letter finds you well. Thank you for always looking out for me. This will come as a surprise to you, but I was proud to serve in the Metropolitan Police for twenty years of my life. I retired due to illness. I was a police superintendent. I've been exactly where you are now. That should answer the question as to why this batty old lady was using up the remaining years of her life helping young women get home. Because like you, I care. I even care about the people who spit in the street and call me names. But there is one thing I have that you don't. Company. Please don't roll your eyes at this sentiment. Don't think I haven't seen it when I've brought up Thomas before. But Gwen, this is as much for him as it is for me. I need you to care for him. He can't do this on his own.*

*He's a funny sort. He doesn't need to be fussed over night and day. Just a couple of hours company in the evening will suffice. Your lifestyle is as close as I could get to my own. I know you will be happy together and I have provided well for him. He has no shortage of takers, but I want him to live with you. I'm smiling as I write this as I'd love to see your face. Believe me when I say, this is a match made in heaven. Please open your heart to him.*

*Much love,*
*Millie*

My mouth dropping open, I stare at Mr Fairholme in disbelief. 'She can't be serious. Do you know what she's asking?'

'It's all in the will,' Mr Fairholme says. But his eyes crinkle and his expression betrays that he is in on the joke of the year. He leans over his desk, speaking in a conspiratorial whisper. 'Thomas is her cat.'

It takes about three seconds before the news kicks in. A burst of laughter leaves my lips. 'You're kidding,' I say, my shoulders shaking as I try to hold back. I laugh like a four-year-old child. My colleagues constantly wind me up about my childish laugh. I struggle to control it and today I am in full flow. The thing is, it's highly infectious. Mr Fairholme is laughing now, wiping away a tear from the corner of his eye. I laugh until my stomach aches. If Millie had set out to play a trick from beyond the grave, then she had well and truly succeeded. Millie and I may not be related but we are from the same police family. Like me, she didn't have children. She cared for other people's daughters, sisters and mothers instead.

So that takes me to Thomas. Oh yes, he's here now, curled up on my lap. How could I say no to such a request? It still makes me smile, how Millie never corrected my presumption that Thomas was her son. Perhaps he was the closest thing she had to family. Thomas is actually quite young, at only three years of age. He's one of a long line of Millie's cats, and young enough to settle with me. She was right. He's not a morning person but is partial to an open fire and the TV being left on. He enjoys my lap of an evening and is happy to see me when I come home. My life feels balanced now. I have the best of both worlds. We are a perfect match.

---

A native of Ferbane in Southern Ireland, Caroline Mitchell moved to the coast in Essex with her family in 2003. In she joined Essex Police on 12th February 2007 and worked in various roles whilst in uniform in Walton on the Naze, Clacton on Sea, and Colchester. She then passed her ICIDP exam and worked in CID as a detective constable dealing with serious crimes. She also worked as an on-call SOTO (sexual offences trained officer) and was trained to a high level in interviewing vulnerable victims and victims of serious crimes. She later became a DASO (domestic abuse safeguarding officer), safeguarding high risk victims of domestic abuse, victims of stalking and honour-based abuse. In 2016, she left her police career to write full time.

# KINDNESS IS MAGIC

*By Chris McDonald*

It had been exactly one week since the strange event that had started this whole episode.

The usual Friday afternoon carnage had been raging; the teacher had been barking orders and holding up odd bits of clothing in the hope of reuniting them with an owner, while the children largely ignored her. In fairness, Tommy *had* been flitting around the classroom, delivering invitations to his birthday party, which was much more exciting than forgotten joggers.

Robin watched from the back row as his nemesis made a song and dance about handing out the envelopes to everyone else in the class but him, and tried not to care. Sure, Tommy and his gang of friends made Robin's break and lunchtimes a living nightmare, but still. The emotions that came with being excluded were hard for an eight-year-old's brain to compute.

It was with almighty surprise then, that Tommy sidled up to Robin with his final envelope. He set it on the desk and looked Robin in the eye.

'My mum made me,' he sneered, just loud enough for the children nearby to hear, before moving back to his own desk.

During the week that followed, Robin's mood had ebbed and flowed. One day, he was excited about the prospect of attending the birthday party, and the next, he felt physically sick at the thought of walking up the path to the local Methodist church, clutching a present.

He hadn't slept much the night before, and now that he was here in the church hall, Robin wondered why he had bothered to turn up. He watched the other children play, though had no inclination to join in. He was afraid that whatever game they were playing would suddenly involve hurting him in some way, and so waved away any adult that tried to get him out of his seat. Instead, he remained sat in the corner of the room with his head down, keen not to invite any attention to himself.

'Alright, everyone,' Tommy's mum shouted suddenly, 'we've got a very special guest in the next room who wants to say hello.'

Robin watched the other children push and shove their way through the wooden door into the smaller room. When he was sure that he was the last, he followed the group in and chose a chair at the back.

The guest, it turned out, was a well-dressed man who was standing at the front of the room. He was wearing a black suit with a red bow-tie, a top hat and a cape. A bushy moustache sat above his wide smile, and twinkling eyes surveyed the unruly crowd. At his feet sat a rickety treasure chest.

The door closing behind Robin seemed to be his cue, for he silenced the crowd with a booming voice.

'My name is Marvin the Magnificent. Today, you are going to witness magic before your very eyes.'

From nowhere, he produced a bunch of flowers, which he sniffed and threw into the crowd to much astonishment.

For the next forty minutes, he worked through his repertoire of tricks. The children started off entranced, though quickly grew bored. The fidgeting preceded the hushed (and then the not-so-hushed) plans for the games they would play just as soon as the show had finished. The adults tried to keep some sense of order, but divvying up the teams for football was serious business.

The end of the show was greeted with enthusiasm, but not in relation to the magician's talents, more for the fact that it was finally over. The children left the room in the manner of a jailbreak that might be stopped at any moment.

Only Robin remained.

He had sat in quiet awe for the duration of the show. He was amazed by Marvin's showmanship; in the stories he wove during the set-up and in the perfect delivery that accompanied the climax of each and every trick.

It was only when Marvin addressed him that he realised the show was over.

'Did you enjoy that?' he asked.

Robin nodded. He'd always been shy around adults and couldn't find the words, nor the courage, to show Marvin just how much he had loved the show.

Marvin seemed to know this, because he smiled and thanked the young man sitting in the back row.

'You're not like the other kids, are you?'

Robin lowered his head and looked at the stone floor.

'I mean that in a good way,' Marvin went on, while packing away his things. 'I saw you during the show. You believe in magic, don't you?'

Again, Robin didn't know what to say. He'd never heard of magic before today. His life so far had been as unmagical as it was possible to be. He'd never met his father, who had left his mum before Robin had been born. He lived in a bedsit with one bedroom and slept on the sofa. His mother had frequent companionship, though the same man rarely visited twice.

She was an emotional woman, and Robin was unsure how to help her, except to tuck her into bed when she'd had too many glasses of wine.

He'd seen and experienced things an eight-year-old shouldn't. But, today was different. Though he didn't know it, what he'd seen today would change his life.

He lifted his gaze from the floor and summoned all his bravery. He opened his mouth and spoke to the man.

'How can I be magic?'

'You already are,' Marvin replied. 'I can tell. You just haven't found it yet. But you will.'

Marvin threw the rest of his things into the treasure chest and said goodbye to Robin.

The young boy waited a few minutes before sneaking out of a side door and walking home, with a little spring in his step and a feeling in his stomach that he had not experienced before. Perhaps, the magic was stirring, he thought to himself.

* * *

The next day, Martha walked up the main street of the town, wishing her son would shut up about wands and bow ties.

Her hangover was raging; her head thumping and her body pushing back waves of nausea. The alcohol from last night was obviously the cause—two bottles of wine will do that to you—but there was also the guilt that was eating away at her.

Poor Robin had bounded into her room early this morning, snuggling under the duvet with her, keen to find out what she'd bought him for his birthday. He'd laughed when she'd said that she hadn't got him anything yet, though his face had fallen when he'd seen she wasn't joking. He shuffled to the edge of the bed and jumped down, and she'd heard him start to whimper as he'd pulled the door closed behind him.

Now, here they were, braving the rain and wind with what little money she had scrabbled together, heading for the toy shop.

A bell tinkled above their heads as they pushed their way inside. The shop was empty, aside from Mr Fletcher, who was sat behind the counter, hunched over a thick weekend newspaper. He looked up as they entered, and flashed a wide smile at the mother and son.

'You need any help, folks, just let me know,' he said, before turning his attention back to the crossword he was half-way through.

Martha trailed after her son, listening to him gabble excitedly about what he was going to choose. She worried that his expectations were too lofty for the amount of cash she currently had available, but he was a clever boy who knew that things were tight.

Robin rushed past the Hot Wheels and Ghostbusters toys, and came to an abrupt stop when he reached the magic sets, his eyeballs travelling at triple speed, so keen was he to take in every detail of the bounty available to him.

They finally settled on a box with bright bubble writing and a boy smiling manically at a range of magical items that were floating in mid-air. Robin recognised the paraphernalia needed for the trick that Marvin the Magnificent had finished his show with; the one that had really blown Robin's mind.

He picked the box up and showed it to his mum.

She smiled, and then checked the price tag, before shaking her head.

'Please, mum,' Robin whispered.

'I can't,' she said, shaking her head. 'We don't have enough money.'

She picked up a similar looking box that was within their price range.

'How about this one?' she asked.

'I want that one,' he cried, pointing at the original box. 'That one has…'

'Listen,' she said, interrupting his pleas while getting down on her knees to look him in the eyes, 'I don't know how to explain this in a way that will get it through your thick skull, but we do not have enough money for the one you want.'

She regretted the harshness of the words as soon as they had left her mouth, but her head was sore and her patience was waning.

Robin felt like he'd been slapped and tried hard to keep the tears at bay, but couldn't. They began rolling down his face just as Mr Fletcher rounded the corner and started to make his way down the aisle.

In his hand was a pricing gun.

'Ah, sorry,' he said, seemingly ignoring the scene in front of him. 'I'm a bit behind on my tasks today.'

He slipped past mother and son and stood looking at the shelves. Glancing at the floor, he noticed the set that the boy was clinging to, and reached for the same box on the shelf.

'The set you're holding, son, isn't selling for toffee, so I'm putting it in the sale. Fifty percent off.'

Robin tried to work out what that meant, but wasn't very good at maths. His mother wasn't much better, but she knew what Mr Fletcher was doing. She was about to tell him that they weren't a charity, but he glanced her way and gave a knowing nod and smile.

'Kindness is magic,' he said, and led them back to the counter where he took the note from Martha, handed the magic set to Robin and bade them goodbye with a wide smile.

He watched Robin through the window, and could see the excitement dancing in the boy's eyes. When he was sure they'd gone, he walked back down the aisle to the magic sets and peeled the discounted sticker off their best-selling toy, before heading back to finish his crossword.

***

*Ten years later*

Mr Fletcher sat on his sofa with a huge smile plastered on his face. It was the first smile that had touched his face in over a year. Or, at least, that's how it felt. There hadn't been much to feel happy about recently.

Thoughts of his poor wife, lying in the hospital hooked up to all of those machines that beeped and whirred, were hard to push out of his mind. The images seemed to be imprinted on the inside of his eyelids, reminding him constantly of what he stood to lose.

It was hard to think of anything else.

Except, on the television right now was a show he'd seen advertised and had finally found the time to watch.

On screen was a face he recognised.

The King of Magic, dressed in a top hat, black cloak and red bow tie, was currently performing an intricate trick involving several silver rings and a lot of showmanship.

Little Robin had come a long way.

Mr Fletcher watched in awe as the suspense built; Robin had the audience in the palm of his hand. With a final flourish, the trick reached its climax. Robin smiled at the camera and the screen faded to black.

As the credits rolled, memories of Robin in ill-fitting clothes, trailing behind his drunk mother burst into the old man's mind. The little boy had escaped the clutches of the small town and had really made something of himself.

With the show finished, Mr Fletcher pushed himself up from the sofa and hobbled over to the sideboard, picking up the leaflets the hospital had given him about experimental surgery. The corners were worn and tattered because of the hours he'd spent poring over every word, even though he'd known from first glance that the treatment was unattainable.

The cost was just far too high.

A quiet knock on the door tore him away from the information on the glossy pages, and he crossed the room with a confused expression etched on his face.

He opened the door and peered out into the darkness, though only a gust of wind greeted him. He looked up and down the street, but aside from a young couple walking their dog further down the cul-de-sac, there was nothing to see.

Thinking that maybe it was some of the children trying their luck early for some trick or treat goodies, but had given up in the time it had taken him to cross the room, he began to close the door when he noticed something on the doorstep.

A black, rectangular block sat on its side. With creaking knees, Mr Fletcher bent down and picked up the object.

It was a suitcase.

He closed the door behind him and walked back to the sofa, where he sat down. He turned the suitcase over in his hands, though it had no distinguishing features—black plastic handle, black leather covering. Something a businessman would use daily, but an object Mr Fletcher had certainly no need for.

Had someone got the wrong house?

He set it flat on the coffee table and fumbled with the clasp. It popped with a quiet click and Mr Fletcher cautiously opened the suitcase. His jaw dropped with surprise.

Inside, wrapped in bundles, was more money than he had ever seen in his life. It looked like some unattainable prize on an over-the-top gameshow, though Mr Fletcher's first thought was gangsters!

His second thought was that the money was more than enough to cover his wife's surgery. Tears sprung to his eyes.

After staring at the money for a long, long time, and thinking about the love of his life receiving the treatment she so desperately required, his eyes were drawn to a handwritten note taped to the inside lid of the suitcase. He freed it and unfolded the page, before reading it aloud.

'Mr Fletcher, it's because of you that I am where I am. I never forgot what you did that day in your toy shop and I remain forever grateful. I hope your wife gets better. Kindness is magic.'

---

Chris McDonald is the author of the DI Erika Piper series and Stonebridge Mysteries, a cosy crime series. He is also a regular voice on the 'Blood Brothers' Podcast. Chris is a primary school teacher and lives near Manchester with his wife and two children. He is a fan of heavy metal and dogs.

# IMAGINATION AVENUE

*By C.L. Taylor*

No one could quite remember how it started, the infection that transformed the residents of Inverness Avenue; a short, steep but otherwise unremarkable street on the outskirts of Brighton. But start it did and some claim it was never completely wiped out.

Lisa Matthews was watering the potted basil plant in her kitchen when she first noticed something was wrong. Her pot-bellied neighbour was conducting his daily post-work tour of his stamp-sized garden. Lisa watched through narrowed eyes as he reached into the overgrown lavender that populated his border. She knew what would come next; he would remove a snail from the purple buds, hold it gingerly between his fingers and thumb and launch it over the dividing fence into her own garden. Her hand hovered on the window catch. Today she would say something.

But Gary didn't toss the snail over the fence and into her prize patch of lilies. Instead he reached back into the lavender and plucked out another snail. Lisa frowned as he turned, a snail in each hand and looked directly at her.

"Snails," he shouted. "Look, snails."

It wasn't what he shouted that made Lisa gasp, it was the child-like expression on his middle-aged face and the way he waved the molluscs at her as though they were fighter planes, dive-bombing through the air.

He's obviously drunk, Lisa decided as she returned to her living room with her microwaved lasagne for one. She paused, her finger over the remote, and listened. Were the Italian couple on the other side of the wall arguing again? It was something they did loudly and regularly several times a week. And if they weren't arguing they were drowning out the television with the three-minute rat-a-tat-tat of their frantic making up. It was the sound of life, of love, of being part of a couple. It was more than Lisa could bear. She forked a frazzled piece of pasta into her mouth and, almost on cue, voices filtered through the dividing wall.

"You can hide and I'll seek," a female voice said in broken English.

"Make sure you count all the way to a hundred," said a male voice. "And don't cheat or I'll tell."

Lisa signed. She had never played hide and seek with a lover, although she had played "Doctors and Nurses" with Joe once, a long, long time ago. She reached for the remote and turned the television up, loud enough to block out her thoughts.

It was Thursday evening when she finally accepted all was not right with her street. She trudged up the hill, her laptop bag over one shoulder, two heavy supermarket bags bulging with meals for one in the other. The street, normally full of cars trawling for a space in the post-work rush, appeared to be hosting a game of five-a-side football. Lisa stopped at the foot of the hill and stared. Adults and children of both sexes were charging down the street, an errant football rolling with increasing speed towards her. Those who weren't running were clutching their sides and squealing with laughter.

"Excuse me," said the father of three from number eleven as he drew near. "Excuse me please lady but could we please have our ball back?"

Lisa looked from the grubby-kneed man in front of her to the ball that nestled against her shoes.

"Has everyone completely lost the plo…" she began, then changed her mind. "Is this some kind of street party?"

"We're just playing," said the man. "Wanna join in?"

"Um," said Lisa reaching for the ball. "No thank you. I have some cleaning to do."

"Boring," shouted the man as he booted the ball up the hill. "Why would you want to do that when you could have fun instead?"

*Has everyone gone mad?* Lisa wondered as she retrieved her shopping bags and made her way to her front door. *What was next?*

What was next, she discovered when she opened her front door and plucked a copy of the local paper from the carpet, was a possible explanation. "Imagination Infection" blared the headline. "Residents of Inverness Avenue struck down by mysterious illness." Instead of switching on the kettle, emptying her bags of their contents and stroking the cat, Lisa sat down and started to read. Apparently she wasn't alone in noticing her street's unusual behaviour. Several postmen and a team of refuse collectors had complained to the council about the "strange goings on" in Inverness Avenue that had included: three old ladies playing hopscotch, a gang of university students playing "Cowboys and Indians" (with lampposts as totem poles) and all of the street's single residents playing a mixture of knock-down-ginger meets kiss-chase. The Argus reporter who had been sent to investigate the story said he had failed to find a single plausible explanation for the change in behaviour and the joyous grins on the residents' faces. There was nothing wrong with the drinking water, the symptoms were not synonymous with any known disease, sales of alcohol at the local pub had dwindled away to nothing and, he jokingly concluded, no one had reported any alien landings in the vicinity. When asked for his view on the situation, Mr John Peterson from number 23 Inverness Street had simply replied, "We get to play games again, like when we were children and we don't have to think about rubbish adult stuff. We're having fun and we're happy. Why would we want this to stop?"

Lisa closed the paper and moved to the window. The game of football had morphed into a new game, a mixture of British Bulldog and rugby. Joe would know what to do, she thought. He'd help her make sense of the world. But Joe wasn't around to give advice. He was sleeping quietly in a grave two hundred miles away. It had felt right to bury her husband where he was surrounded by memories of their life together, but Lisa couldn't stay. She couldn't cope with the pitying looks and the word "widow" rushed out on sympathetic breath. Too young, they said, two young to be a widow at just twenty-eight, but the way they said it made her feel eighty years old.

That's why she had to move away. She wanted to be surrounded by people who didn't peer at her curiously, who looked at her as though she was just another young woman with the rest of her life ahead of her, rather than the best part of her life spent. And if the people of Brighton looked at her like that, Lisa had reasoned, maybe she'd be able to look at her reflection in the mirror and see herself the same way.

Only she'd taken it too far hadn't she? She was too shy, too nervous to introduce herself when she first arrived and even at work people only knew her by name. Now her street was squealing and laughing, hopping, skipping and charging around and she was alone, at her window, her cat mewing plaintively as it wound itself around her legs.

The sun was setting outside when Lisa opened her front door and stepped onto the pavement. She glanced in the direction of the single mum from two doors down who was jumping, two feet together, over a twirling skipping rope.

"Who will I marry?" the woman chanted as the rope whirred and her trainers thudded on the pavement. "Darren, Eddie, Gordon, Matthew, Alex..."

When the singing stopped Lisa looked down at her feet. It had been a stupid idea to go outside.

"Excuse me," said a female voice.

Lisa looked up. A red-haired woman was panting at her side.

"Excuse me," the woman said again. "What's your name?"

Lisa released her bottom lip from its grip between her teeth. "Lisa. Lisa Matthews."

"Hi Lisa. I'm Sandra. Jessie had to go back inside and we need someone to twirl the rope. Do you want to play?"

Before Lisa had a chance to object, Sandra had taken hold of her hand and skipped her across the street. Sandra's palm felt sweaty against her own but it also felt warm, and real. Lisa smiled.

"I'd love to play," she said.

"There's your end," said Sandra, pointing to the discarded skipping rope. "Make sure you turn it in time with Anna over there."

*This is ridiculous*, Lisa thought as she picked up the wooden handle and started to twirl the rope. *I'm a grown woman. I don't do playing. I don't know how to.*

"Faster," screamed the red-faced woman as she jumped up and down. "Faster!"

Together the women turned their handles, faster and faster until the rope, the chant, the street and the world blurred into one. Lisa smiled, grinned and then screamed with joy.

The next day the police arrived, as did five ambulances and a crowd of men in what looked like, to the street's residents anyway, white astronaut suits. The street was cordoned off at both ends with yellow tape stamped in black with the word "HAZARD". A crowd of paparazzi, television cameras and reporters buzzed like flies beyond it, turning in circles as they tried to get closer to the action. The adults playing on the street glanced at the commotion, but continued with their games.

A wiry policeman removed his facemask, approached the cordon tape and raised a loudhailer to his lips. "Could everyone please listen?"

The street's residents stopped playing and stared. Some of them giggled.

"What do you want?" Lisa shouted. She was surrounded by her new friends and felt particularly brave.

"To take you all to a safe place," said the policeman. "We've got a medical team who need to take a look at you."

"Why?" shouted a man with greying hair and a football under his arm.

"Because we need to find out what's wrong with you. You're putting yourselves, your children and the general public at risk."

The man with the football seemed to shake at the mention of his children and strode towards the yellow tape. Lisa watched, confused, as his expression grew hard and cold as he ducked under the cordon and confronted the policeman. He didn't look like a child anymore. Lisa drifted closer, pulling Sandra behind her.

"Do you think he'll tell them to go away?" Sandra asked.

"I don't know," Lisa said. "They seem quite angry with us."

They turned to look at the grey-haired man who was now red in the face and shouting at the policeman. When he raised his arms and pounded the air with his open hands the football slipped from under his arm and rolled under the cordon, gathering speed as it tumbled down the street. No one ran to collect it.

"This isn't a disease and we're not imbeciles," he shouted. "We still go to work and we're still responsible adults when we need to be. We can control our impulses to play when our children need us."

"Calm down sir," said the policeman, taking a step back. "We'd just like to take you all somewhere safe while we carry out our investigations. We need to understand what's happened to you."

As the grey-haired man opened his mouth to reply, the policeman raised a hand in the air and a dozen policemen surged forward, their batons raised, their shields covering their faces. The grey-haired man paled and stepped backwards, one hand on the yellow and black tape.

"Grab him," shouted the policeman. "Get him before he goes back onto the street."

Lisa and Sandra screamed as the man disappeared beneath a blanket of fluorescent yellow jackets.

"Run," the man shouted at them as he was bundled into the back of a police van. "Run or they'll take you too."

Lisa turned to see her neighbour Gary storming up the street, his generous belly wobbling as he ran. As he neared the cordon he paused and crouched down, scooping something up from the gutter.

"No," he shouted as he hurled the bouncy ball towards the policemen, hitting the one with the loudspeaker on the cheek. "You can't take us away. You can't do that to us."

There was a shout, a roar and the sound of two dozen boots on concrete as the police breached the cordon en masse and flooded the street. The street's residents screamed and fought as they were grabbed, some of them pinned to the ground, and herded over the flattened tape and towards the waiting vans.

"Run Lisa," Sandra screamed as each of her arms was grabbed by female officers. "Find somewhere to hide."

Lisa took off with a start, weaving her way between the outstretched arms of the police until she reached the front door of her flat. She poked her key into the lock and sprinted through the rooms, gathering milk, blankets and food as she sped out of the back door and into her shed. She slammed the door behind her and curled up on the floor, the blanket thrown over her head.

"Please don't take me," she whispered. "Please don't take me. I've only just come back."

The next afternoon, when the sound of sirens, heavy boots and raised voices had subsided, Lisa crept out from her hiding space and peeled back the living room curtain and peered outside. The street was empty, even the makeshift goalposts at either end had disappeared. She bit down on her bottom lip to stop herself from crying and turned on the TV, keeping the sound on low so she could hear her Italian neighbours if they came back.

Two days later, the street's inhabitants returned. They stepped out of taxis, pale-faced and drawn, and unlocked their front doors without acknowledging the neighbours that shuffled up the pathways on either side.

*Why is no one talking to each other?* thought Lisa as she skipped up the street and knocked on Sandra's door. *Is this the start of a new game?*

"Hello," said Sandra, opening the door as far as the safety chain would allow. "Can I help you?"

Her wild red hair had been scraped into severe bun and she was wearing tartan slippers and a white towelling dressing gown instead of trainers and pink shorts.

"It's me," Lisa said. "Do you want to come and play?"

Sandra laughed and closed the door half an inch.

"Play?" she said. "I'm thirty-two."

"But," Lisa said, her smile slipping. "What about the skipping?"

Sandra shook her head and moved to close the door.

"Wait," Lisa said, cramming her hand between the door and the frame, her fingers brushing Sandra's. "Don't go."

Sandra froze. She looked from her hand to Lisa's and felt a familiar warmth flow through her body. Her tight, polite smile dissolved into a wide, open grin.

"Skipping?" she said, as she slid back the chain and opened the door wide. "Brilliant! I'll just get my rope."

---

C.L. Taylor is an award winning, Sunday Times bestselling author of eight gripping psychological thrillers including *Sleep*, a Richard and Judy Book Club pick for autumn 2019 and *Her Last Holiday*. Her books have sold two million copies worldwide, hit the number one spots on Amazon Kindle, Audible, Kobo, iBooks and Google Play and have been translated into 25 languages and optioned for TV. She has also written two Young Adult thrillers: *The Treatment* and *The Island*. She lives in Bristol with her partner and son.

# WHEN ANGELS ARE NEAR

*By Casey Kelleher*

Franky's eyes fix on the photograph of his nan as he tries so desperately to hold on to her gentle, soft face. Those piercing green eyes that always seemed to be smiling.

And then, just like that, she's gone forever.

The sombre sound of the organ fills the room. The heavy, morbid notes only adding to the sense of finality as the coffin disappears behind the slowly closing curtains.

Franky gets up. His legs weightless, like they are floating. Like they are no longer attached to the rest of his body. Yet somehow, he moves in time behind his mother, following her out of the chapel.

But none of this feels real.

His mind still can't process that he's just said his final goodbye to his nan.

And he knows that his mother is suffering. Even more than he is. Yet she hides it so well. Or at least she tries.

He watches her closely now. As she wanders outside, her expression dazed and woeful. Nodding and smiling in all the right places as the gathering well-wishers and distant relatives all offer their condolences.

Franky fights back his tears then, because he knows that she's trying her best to stay strong for him.

For as long as he can remember it was always the three of them. His nan, his mum and him. And now that she's gone, there'll be no more family dinners, all sitting laughing around the dining room table. There'll be no more movie nights, snuggled up together on the sofa. No more trips to the skate park, where Franky could show off his skills to his mum and his nan, whilst making them both watch on from a distance, so that they wouldn't damage his street-cred.

All he feels now is the empty gaping hole that has been left behind.

And his mother feels it too. Of course, she does.

Her grief has left her immobilised. Moving and speaking so robotically as she tries to hold herself together.

Franky reaches for her hand.

The two of them walking side by side, taking in the sight of colourful wreaths and flower arrangements. His mother stopping frequently to read the heartfelt words written on each card.

She pauses at the end of the pathway. Her eyes lingering on the last display. The display from her.

'MUM'.

Spelt out with his nan's favourite flowers, purple chrysanthemums. Or something like that? He hadn't been paying proper attention.

But he is now.

He's taking it all in.

Holding his breath and his tears as his mum crumbles in front of him. Sinking down to her knees in front of the wreath.

Only it's not the flowers that his mother is looking at, he realises.

As she reaches out her hand and touches the small white feather that has landed on the bright floral display.

'She's here,' Eve whispers, her voice so small that for a moment Franky isn't sure if she's talking to him or just out loud.

Turning then, she offers him a small smile of reassurance.

Her face lighting up, as a glimmer of hope shines out through her own tears.

'There's a saying. "Feathers appear when angels are near." Your nan said it all the time. She is here. I can feel it. This is her sign.'

Wrapping her fingers around the feather, she picks it up and leans towards Franky.

Placing the feather inside his top pocket.

'She's telling us that she's okay, Franky. That we're both going to be okay. She hasn't really left us.'

Franky sees his mum stand taller then as she walks towards the waiting car and wonders if she really believes that.

Because Franky doesn't.

Pulling the feather from his pocket he stares at it.

And for a few seconds he wishes more than anything that it was true.

That his mother's belief in angels and feathers were real.

That his nan really is here.

But he knows that she isn't.

'It's just a stupid feather…' he says, throwing it back down on the floor before wiping his hot, angry tears away and making his own way toward the car.

She was gone. She'd left them both.

* * *

'Franky! You've got ten minutes.' Placing a saucepan down on the hob before pouring a scoop of porridge oats inside, Eve opened the fridge and scanned the meagre contents in search of the milk.

They'd run out, she realised as she eyed the few aged-softened vegetables that were well past their best and a couple of almost empty condiment jars.

Reaching inside for the sandwich she'd made for Franky's lunch, having used up the last of the ham and bread, she placed it down on the kitchen side, before going back to the saucepan and tipping a cup of water into the powdery mixture.

Her eyes deliberately avoiding the pile of post she'd left unopened on the kitchen side, that she didn't have the energy to deal with right now.

What was the point?

It would only be more bills that she couldn't afford to pay. More final notices. More rejection letters from the hundreds of jobs she'd applied for.

And she was so tired from it all.

This wasn't the life she hoped for. This wasn't the life she planned.

Living here in this decrepit flat on an estate in Hackney. Jobless. In constant debt while forever borrowing off of Peter to pay back Paul.

'I haven't got time for breakfast Mum, Tommy will be here in a sec,' Franky said, strolling into the kitchen, having dressed in his school uniform in record time for a change.

'Make time! You're a growing lad and you need to eat. And here, stick this in your bag,' Eve said, passing Franky his lunch. 'You've got a few minutes…' Slopping the gloopy mixture into a bowl, Eve sprinkled it with an extra generous spoon of sugar in an attempt to hide the watery blandness from her son before placing it down in front of him. 'And I expect you'll need all your energy let loose in the Science Museum with Tommy. Speaking of energy…'

Eve switched the kettle on. Resigned to drinking her coffee black, as long as it meant she'd get the hit of much-needed caffeine she craved. Anything to take the edge off her chronic tiredness.

The feeling of exhaustion consumed her these days.

She spent so much of her day napping that by the time she went to bed, she just lay there. Restless and battling with the grief of losing her mum. Her head consumed with worry of not being able to cope.

"Shit. Not again!' Eve sighed, as the flat plunged into sudden darkness and the noisy bubbling of the kettle ceased as abruptly as it had started. Remembering that they'd used the emergency electricity on the key just a few days ago and that she hadn't topped it back up. Eve picked up the kettle and poured out the tepid water into her cup, hoping that it would do.

'Another power cut?' Franky asked, raising his brown eyes and playing along as his mother nodded her head as he knew she would.

Spooning the thick, gooey mixture into his mouth, Franky kept his own counsel and forced it down. Wondering quietly to himself when his mother was going to realise that he saw things.

He knew things.

Like how the electric meter worked.

And how his mother had stuffed away a huge pile of bills inside the kitchen drawer. Scary sounding letters from people threatening to come to their flat and take their stuff away.

Still, he knew not to bring it up.

For the same reason that he never asked about the big dark circles around her eyes each morning or mentioned that he'd heard her lying awake each night crying.

Some things just couldn't be fixed.

'Tommy's here!' Franky said, grateful that the loud shrill of the doorbell just seconds later allowed him to push his bowl away and that he didn't have to finish the thick gloopy paste that his mother had tried to pass off as porridge.

'I can't remember the last time I went to the Science Museum!' Eve said, watching as Franky stuffed his sandwiches down inside his rucksack before shoving his feet into his tatty-looking trainers.

A flutter of shame ran through her then, as she spotted the sole hanging loosely from the back of one.

Thinking of the latest pile of rejection letters that sat on the side, she wished more than anything that she could give him more.

And she really was trying.

She'd only given up her job so that she could care full-time for her dying mother and now she was reapplying her best just didn't seem good enough.

Because for every role as a cleaner, dinner lady or shop assistant that she went for, so did a dozen or so others. And the problem was, they were all more qualified and experienced applicants than her.

'You were a toddler.' Eve smiled as she finally recalled the memory. Her beautiful, inquisitive little boy running around and taking all the sights and sounds in.

Things had seemed easier back then.

Though Franky was really no different now at the age of ten, she thought as she watched him hurrying to leave the house, full of excitement at the day ahead.

She couldn't remember the last time she'd felt that either.

Excitement.

'Here. It's not much but get yourself some sweets,' Eve said, reaching into her purse and scooping up the last four pound coins that lay at the bottom.

'Nah, you're alright, Mum,' Franky said, wavering. Knowing that his mum could use this money to top up the electricity key for a couple of days.

'Please, Franky. Take it,' Eve insisted, as if reading her son's mind. 'I want you to have fun.'

Because he deserved it.

To have some normality. Some enjoyment.

There had been too much sadness lately. And what was a few pounds?

'Thanks Mum!' Franky said, taking the money and flashing her a grin.

Part of him thinking how his mother's words sounded more like an order. Like an instruction.

To have fun. Because one of them needed to. Because Franky knew that the second he was gone, the second that he closed the front door behind him, his mother would do what she did most days and crawl back into her bed.

Leaving him with that sinking feeling that something was very wrong, and it made him feel scared that he didn't know how to help her.

So, they both just pretended now that this was normal. That everything was okay.

'See you later, Mum!' Franky said, yanking open the door and hoping that if they both pretended enough, then eventually it would be.

* * *

'Astronaut food? What! Ahh, I'm getting some of this. Look, Franks! Can you even imagine? Sitting in space, looking down at the world and eating Neapolitan ice-cream sandwiches. Man, they have the best job! I'm going to be an astronaut when I'm older.' Tommy screeched excitedly as they made their way around the Science Museum's gift shop at the end of the trip, and he picked up the strange package of food from the shelf.

'And this, look! A mini drone. This is the coolest shop! I want everything! What are you getting, Franky?' Tommy asked, eyeing the shining crystals that his friend stood admiring.

Both their gazes scanning the huge clumps of brightly-coloured gems and rocks.

Franky shrugged before pointing towards the black ones.

'I dunno. These ones look pretty cool.' Not wanting to admit to his friend that he only had four pounds to spend, and the rocks were probably all he could afford.

'A rock?' Tommy scoffed, narrowing his eyes. Clearly not impressed.

'It's not just a rock. Look. "Hematite crystal." They're special or something...' Franky said, leaning in and reading the information card at the front of the display. 'It says that it's one of the most powerful stones and it's connected to the root chakra. For healing and protection.'

'What's a chakra?' Tommy said, still unconvinced.

'I don't know? It's something to do with your body and the crystals have healing powers. Or something...'

'Magic rocks?' Tommy laughed. 'Mate, you really believe that?

'My nan used to have some...I dunno. They just look cool I guess!'

'Yeah, I suppose they do look kinda cool.' Tommy shrugged. Knowing that talking about his nan was still hard for his friend and not wanting to upset him.

'You know what, you should get one! I can always let you try some of my spaceman ice-cream so you don't miss out!' Tommy said with a grin. 'I'll go and pay for mine. I'll see you back on the coach, yeah?'

Alone again, Franky watched his friend making his way towards the tills before eyeing the length of the aisle. Boxes and boxes piled high to the ceiling, full of every gadget and toy you could think of.

Tommy was right. This was one of the coolest shops that he and Franky had ever been in. And it dawned on him then that he didn't feel sad because he didn't have enough money for all the amazing things that Tommy could afford to buy. He felt sad because, the truth was, he didn't really want any of this stuff anyway. Even if he could afford it.

Because that's all it was, just stuff.

And none of it would make him happy. Not really.

The only thing he really wanted was for things to be better again at home, for him and his mum.

Like she had been when his nan was alive.

God, he missed her.

Turning back to the crystals, his eye was drawn to an unusual shaped one at the back.

Reaching inside the shelf he picked it up, taking in the sight of the small black carved figurine of angel wings.

He smiled then. Running his fingers over the outline of jagged feathers, recalling his mother's words about feathers appearing when angels are near.

She'd say that this was another sign.

Seeing these angel wings right at the time he'd been thinking of his nan.

And who knows, maybe it really was?

Flipping it over, Franky winced at the price. Eight pounds. The sign wasn't for him.

It was just a coincidence.

About to put the crystal back, he jumped then when a woman behind him interrupted his thoughts.

'Oh, now that's one of my favourites. It's small, but that hematite crystal packs a real punch. They say that it's a stone for the mind. That it helps build courage and can take away sadness. Pretty cool stone to have, I'd say.'

'It's too much,' Franky said, disappointed then, jangling his coins in his hand, about to put it back.

'How much have you got?'

'Four pounds.'

The woman took the crystal from him and turned it over. Swiping a pricing gun over the top of the old tag.

It was only then that Franky realised the woman was dressed in the museum shop's uniform.

"Well would you look at that!' the woman said, handing the angel wing figurine back to Franky and flashing him a warm smile. 'It's only four pounds now, in the sale. Looks like it's meant to be yours after all!'

* * *

'The power came back on then?' Franky said as he sat down at the dinner table.

Surprised to have come home from his school trip to see his mother dressed and her hair done how she used to do it.

The lights were all back on now and the sound of the TV spilled through the flat.

'We ran out on the meter," Eve admitted. 'I know you're not stupid. And sometimes I forget just how grown up you are.'

Placing the dish down in the centre of the table, and sitting opposite her son, she added playfully, 'I've done meatballs for dinner. They're still your favourite right? You're not too grown up for them though are you?'

'They're still my favourite.' Franky grinned. And they really were. They hadn't had proper homemade meatballs in such a long time.

'Good. Now sit down and tell me all about today. How did it go?'

'It was wicked, Mum! Me and Tommy did an interactive treasure hunt, and we went on a space rocket simulator. It was so cool...' Franky said, recalling the fun he'd had. 'The gift shop was almost as big as the museum. Tommy got some real astronaut food! Did you know that they eat ice-cream in space?!' Franky laughed. His excitement infectious as Eve laughed too.

"I didn't know that, no.'

'I got you something...' Franky said, feeling coy then as he reached into his school bag and took out the wrinkled paper bag he'd stuffed at the bottom, before sliding it over the table towards his mum.

'You spent your money on me?' Eve said, confused.

Opening the bag, she pulled out the beautiful hematite angel wings and held them tightly in her hand.

'Franky!' she cried, fighting back the thick emotion in her voice as her eyes filled with tears as she read the small card explaining the stone's meaning.

Happy tears this time.

'It's beautiful. But you shouldn't have. That money was for you.'

'But I wanted you to have them, Mum. I want you to be happy again...'

Eve looked at Franky then.

The beautiful grown-up young man that he was becoming, and she smiled.

'You make me happy, Franky. Every single day. I know things have been really tough lately and I know that I've not been myself, but I promise you Franky. Things are going to change from now on.' She wiped her tears. 'We'll always miss Nan, of course we will, but she wouldn't want us to be sad. And I'm sorry that you've been so worried about me.'

Eve got up and kissed Franky on the forehead.

'Thank you for my angel wings. I think they may have brought me some good luck today, already!' Eve smiled. 'That's why I wanted to make you a special dinner tonight. To celebrate...I've got a new job, Franky. I start on Monday. And your nan's solicitor called me. She left us some money in her will.'

Placing the angel wings down on the table, Eve nodded over to the photo of her mother displayed on the windowsill.

'She's still here, Franky. Still watching over us. She always will be.'

---

Casey Kelleher was born in Cuckfield, West Sussex, and grew up as an avid reader. Whilst working as a beauty therapist and bringing up her children together with her husband, Casey penned her debut novel *Rotten to the Core*. Its success meant that she could give up her day job and concentrate on writing full time. Casey has since written fourteen books. Her newest book, a psychological thriller *I'll Never Tell* will be published on 3rd December 2021.

# DO THE RESEARCH

*By C.K. McDonnell*

Razor looked at his screen and shook his head. Balander69 was such a newb. The idiot probably believed that man had really been to the moon. Mind you, some of the young guns you meet on these boards, nothing would surprise him. Razor had been in a chat last week that had descended into a flame war, an increasingly common occurrence since the schism. He'd dismissed the other guy as a tourist who didn't even know who JFK was. The guy had hit back that he'd been into him since his early demos. Kids.

He was about to get into it when the doorbell rang. Lucky escape for Balander69. Razor would rip him a new one about how international banking really worked some other time. Right now, dinner was here, and he was starving. He'd spent the entire day researching whether the foot-and-mouth supposed animal 'cull' was actually an operation to stockpile meat stocks for the chosen few after the great reboot. It was all coming together. Everything was there if you dug deep enough.

He pulled the cord to draw the curtain he'd installed to cover his charts. Security was paramount. He couldn't have civilians stumbling upon what he was working on. The deep state had eyes and ears everywhere. Razor needed to stay off the grid. It was the only way. As far as anyone else was concerned, he was just an ordinary dude living in a terraced house in Salford and that was how he wanted it to stay. Be the unseen enemy.

The doorbell rang again.

'All right. I'm coming,' said Razor, tightening the belt on his dressing gown.

'Do it faster,' responded a female voice at the other side of the front door, 'I haven't got all night and your pizza is getting cold.'

That was odd. The normal guy was, well, a guy to start. Razor looked through the spyhole in the door. A girl was standing there, long blonde hair but totally shaved on one side. A ring through her eyebrow and a streak of red through her hair added to her distinctly punk look. She was chewing gum with a ferocious intensity while glowering at the door. As if on cue, she held up a pizza box and pointed at it with a sarcastic smile. How the hell did she know he was looking? There was no way she could see that.

'Thanks,' said Razor, 'just leave it on the step.'

'I can't do that,' she responded.

'The normal guy does.'

'The normal guy did a lot of things, that's why he got fired. Although some of them, to be honest, were not that normal. I'm not allowed say but, you might want to check you aren't pregnant.'

'What?' asked Razor.

'Nothing. I'm joking. I have a very dry sense of humour. Not everybody gets me. I also have a pizza. Nobody gets that unless they open the door.'

'I don't normally open the door.'

'Cool,' said the girl. 'On behalf of myself and the other drones trying to make a living in the zero-hour-contract minimum-wage service industry, may I thank you for your big tipping ways. Still, in the twenty-five-minute-long unpaid training session I had before starting this gig tonight, they made it really clear we can't just dump the pizza. You've got five seconds to take it from me like a human being or I'm going to eat it while you watch.'

'You've got a real attitude problem,' said Razor.

'And yet my finishing school voted me most likely to succeed. Five…'

'Hang on.'

'I have been. Four…'

Part of Razor's brain was tempted to tell her exactly where she could go. However, a much larger part of his brain really wanted pizza. He began unlocking the four locks he had installed. He decided he'd give her a piece of his mind right after he got the food.

'Two…' said the girl.

'What happened to three?'

'It got bored and left. Can't say I blame it.'

Razor finished unlocking the door and went to open it. 'OK, give me the—'

He was interrupted by his own front door smacking him straight in the face, propelled by a well-placed Doc Martin boot. He stepped backwards, stumbled and fell over the coffee table. When he looked up, the girl was in his house, closing the front door behind her.

'What the hell?' shouted Razor.

'Yeah,' said the girl sounding infuriatingly calm, 'you shouldn't have opened the door. That was a good instinct you ignored there.'

Razor held his hand up to his face. 'You broke my nose.'

'No I didn't, you big baby. It's just bleeding a little.'

'I'm going to ring the shop and complain about you.'

'Seriously?' she said with a smirk, 'You're part of an outlaw group, fighting to open the eyes of the sheeple about the true nature of the global elite. Somebody kicks in your door and you still think they're from the local pizza place?'

Before she could stop him, Razor turned and threw himself under his desk. He reached a hand out in each direction, simultaneously hitting the two large red buttons that sat under either end of it.

He looked up at the girl and smiled. 'I've just wiped clean every last one of my hard drives.'

She shrugged. 'Cool.' She turned her head to take in the rest of the front room and looked into the open-plan kitchen behind. Her face formed into a mask of disgust. 'Fingers crossed this is the start of the full-on cleaning blitz this whole place needs.' She nodded pointedly at the pile of pizza boxes in the corner. 'You're going to other shops too? Wait until the guys at home base hear about this, they'll be so upset.'

'I'm calling the police,' said Razor.

'Interesting,' replied the girl, 'I thought you'd be all 'the cops are the pawns of the global fascist elite, working for Bill Gates, blah, blah, blah, blah.'

'Who the hell are you?'

'See,' said the girl, 'now you're actually asking semi-sensible questions. That smack in the face did you a world of good. Besides, I'd imagine that raggedy beard you've got going there took most of the damage. You look like Tom Hanks in that *Castaway* film only, y'know, sadder. Anyway, I'm Tina. What should I call you?'

'People call me Razor.'

She barked a laugh. 'Well, I'm not going to be able to do that with a straight face. Let's go with Brian, seeing as it is the name your mum gave you. She says hello by the way.'

Brian/Razor narrowed his eyes. 'My mother is dead.'

'Well,' said Tina, 'that would certainly explain the smell.'

'I think you should leave,' said Brian as he started to stand.

'I feel you,' replied Tina. 'I didn't even want to come here in the first place but, well—I got myself into some trouble and let's just say this is like my community service.' She flipped open the pizza box, to reveal it was empty except for some crusts. 'Thanks for the pizza by the way although, seriously—cheese-stuffed crust on a Quattro Formaggi? C'mon dude, that's less of an order and more of a cry for help.'

'I don't want to hurt you,' said Brian, pointing at the door, 'but I will if I have to.'

Tina nodded. 'Thank you for the information, Brian. I'll be honest, I don't think it is going to become an issue but nevertheless, good to know. Take a seat.'

'I don't want to…'

It was hard to say what confused him more. The fact that even as he was objecting to the very idea of sitting down, he did it, or that the chair from his workstation was suddenly behind him. It hadn't been there before. Then again, he had just been hit in the head so perhaps he wasn't thinking straight. Yes, that must be it.

'So, as I was saying, your mother—may she rest in peace—is not, in fact, resting in peace. Her spirit is highly agitated because she is worried about you.'

'Oh please,' said Brian, 'you've not seriously come here to peddle some ghost mumbo-jumbo, have you?'

Tina sighed. 'First off, you fuzzy-faced incel, I'm not here peddling anything. I'm here because I did the teeny-tiniest bit of messing about with a traffic warden who was being rude and it was "do this thing for Big John or end up in front of one of his meetings again", and second'—she moved across and pulled the cord that revealed the wall full of charts—'you believe that there is a link between the Clintons, a mining company in Peru, UFOs and is that Phillip Schofield from off the telly?'

'I wouldn't expect someone like you to understand.'

'Good,' said Tina, 'because I don't and have no interest at all in trying although, with…' She pointed at the board again. 'Is that the comedian David Baddiel?'

'That is need to know information,' said Brian.

She leaned in. 'It's written below the picture, so now I know. So yeah, with David Baddiel as my witness, if at any point you speak the words 'do the research,' I will not be responsible for my actions.'

Brian said nothing, instead staring back at her in a way he hoped could be described as defiant.

'I'm here because your mother's spirit is bugging Mrs Shanyaski from three doors down night and day and she has had enough of it. Her downstairs is giving her terrible trouble and she doesn't need any more stress right now. I appreciate you didn't want or need to know about Mrs S's downstairs issues but neither did I. I just came from there. Honestly, I'm not sure if she meant downstairs in an architectural or biological sense but some questions you just don't ask. I'm here, we're going to sort this out and then we can both get on with our lives.' She looked around again. 'Or at least, whatever you're doing in lieu of having one.'

'Right,' said Brian. 'Well let's just say for one second I believe you, which I don't, how come Mum is bothering Mrs Shanyaski and not me?'

Tina didn't take her eyes off the board, seemingly transfixed by the lines of thread interconnecting the various pictures. 'Not to go all Bruce Willis on you but Mrs S has a strong sixth sense. It's like any other sense—sight, smell—some people are a lot more sensitive than others.' Tina turned to Brian. 'Speaking of which, can you really not smell that?'

'What?'

She waved a finger around. 'All of this. This place reeks of old socks, stale food, body odour and sadness. You're really not getting that?'

'No.'

'Do your eyes work?' asked Tina, looking around. 'I mean, seriously. If I photoshopped in a picture of a seal living in this squalor, you'd have Madonna protesting on your doorstep by morning.' She pointed towards the desk. 'Has that jar got wee in it?'

'Of course not,' said Brian. 'It's Snapple.'

'Drink it.'

'I'm not thirsty right now.'

'Look,' said Tina, softening her tone considerably, 'how long has it been since your mother passed away?'

'Two years.'

'And it was always just you and her?'

Brian nodded.

Tina looked around for somewhere to sit, and then thought better of it. 'Do you think that maybe you're not dealing with it great?'

'I'm doing fine.'

'Brian, quick realty check—if I set fire to your house, I'd be done for burning rubbish in a suburban area. When was the last time you went outside?'

'I've been very busy.'

Tina shook her head. 'Oh come on, Brian. You're a young man. You have your whole life ahead of you. You're only what thirty-seven? Thirty-eight?'

'I'm twenty-four!'

'Wow. You really need to get some sunlight.'

Brian jabbed an angry finger at the pinboard. 'Look, this is important stuff. I don't expect you to understand.'

'Is it though? What are you, QAnon?'

'No,' said Brian, scoffing. 'How dare you. Nothing like that. QAnon was just a false flag disinformation operation carried out by the deep state to hide what is really going on. It's all there if you…'

Brian stopped himself.

'Say it,' said Tina, her eyes narrowing, 'I dare you.'

'…look into it,' finished Brian.

Tina puffed her cheeks out. 'Look, dude. I get it. We all go through some stuff and it is easy to get side-tracked, but you need to get yourself back in the game. Do it for your mother if not for yourself.'

'Right,' snapped Brian, 'can we just skip to the bit where you give me the pamphlet about joining your church or whatever this is?'

'You are one stubborn so-and-so, do you know that?'

Brian jabbed a finger at the pinboard again. 'This is vital. All right? You have no idea how the world really works, what kind of stuff is secretly going on behind the…'

Brian stopped talking. A jar of your own urine floating across the room in front of you will do that. He sat open-mouthed as it stopped and hovered a couple of feet in front of him.

'Oh, I'm sorry,' said Tina, 'did I break your concentration? You were explaining how the world works?'

'But…'

'And by the by, it's not my area of expertise but that's looking a little cloudy. You might want to get that checked out.'

'How are you doing that?' asked Brian in a near whisper.

'What?' asked Tina. 'Oh that? The floating jar of cloudy pee-pee? That's nothing. This on the other hand…'

Brian watched dumbfounded as the pile of pizza boxes in the corner rose into the air and proceeded to dance around each other, like low-rent UFOs. Brian had to duck as the jar of pee returned to its place on his desk. 'This is the kind of stuff you learn when you have way too much time on your hands.'

'It's incredible,' said Brian, unable to keep the awe from his voice.

'Here's the reality of how the world works, Brian,' she said, as the eight pizza boxes continued their display. 'Most politicians are just power-hungry narcissists who weren't hugged enough as children. Rich people just want to get richer because it's how they keep score. The vast majority of the bad crap that happens is not part of some big evil plan but just people not thinking about anything other than making a tonne of easy dirty cash. Life is terrifyingly random and if you're wondering how the planet is still here, well you're not the only one.' The eight pizza boxes had now formed themselves into a big smiley face hanging in the air in front of him. 'Any questions?'

'How?' asked Brian.

'Oh,' said Tina, clicking her fingers theatrically causing the pizza boxes to pile themselves back up in the corner again. 'All of this? Well, Bri, there really is magic in the world. Wonders more than you can possibly imagine and there actually is a battle going on between good and evil,' she pointed at the pinboard behind her, 'but none of it involves the Clintons, Beyonce, 5G, the Rothschilds, David Baddiel or Phillip Schofield. What is more, I guarantee, you'll find none of it on your websites, chat forums, or wherever else you are 'doing the research.' She pointed at the front door. 'The only place you'll find out about it is out there.'

'Are you a…'

'What?' asked Tina.

'A witch?'

'We don't use that word. It has a lot of negative connotations. Wizard on the other hand—see the difference? There's your basic sexism. So no, we prefer practitioner. Also, people don't tend to burn practitioners at the stake.'

'And there's lots of these practitioners? What can you do exactly? So ghosts are really real? What does that make UFOs? Which—'

Tina raised her hand. 'I can see you've got a lot of questions and I'll answer all of them I can…'

'Cool.'

'…in exactly two months' time. When I'll meet you in the Canky's Rest pub at 8pm.'

'What?'

'By which time,' continued Tina, 'you'll have restarted your university course in…' she looked at him pointedly.

'Electronic engineering.'

'Yep, that. You'll be dressing in clean clothes every day, leaving the house, having showered. You'll have dropped a good ten pounds. This place will look fit for human habitation and, in the name of all that is good and holy, you pee in another jar in your life, and I will stop you doing that permanently in a way you definitely won't like. Are we clear?'

'I have to do all that before you'll tell me anything?'

'No, you've to do all that to allow your poor mother to move on, safe in the knowledge she didn't raise the next Unabomber. Then, I'll tell you a little of what I know.'

Brian ran his fingers through his hair. 'What am I supposed to do in the meantime?'

'Do you mean other than cleaning?'

'Yes.'

Tina looked around again. 'I mean, I think that will take up most of the time.'

'Please?'

Tina puffed her cheeks out and tapped her foot. 'Hmmm.' She clapped her hands together. 'I got it.' She pulled a rolled-up newspaper from her pocket and handed it to Brian. 'Here you go.'

He unfurled it. '*The Stranger Times*? This is that weird paper full of all the lunatic stories.'

'People who live in bad *X-Files* re-runs shouldn't throw stones but yes, that's the one.'

He held it up and pointed at the headline, 'A Dragon Ate My Pasty. You're telling me this is real?'

'Oh no, most of it is nonsense. Most of it. Still, if you know what to look for…'

'And how will I…'

'You'll figure it out. You're a smart boy when you're not being an idiot. Besides, it has a cartoon strip that I always enjoy.' Tina rubbed her hands together. 'Right, my work here is done.' She turned towards the door.

'Wait!'

'Nope. I'm making a dramatic exit.'

'Please?'

The note of pleading in Brian's voice made Tina stop with her hand on the door handle.

'My mum,' said Brian. 'Can you give her a message? Tell her I love her and I'm sorry.'

Tina looked at Brian for a long moment and then, 'She knows. And for what it's worth, the reason she can't move on is she clearly loves you too.'

Brian looked at the carpet and nodded, tears pushing at his eyes.

Tina opened the door and waved. 'Later gator. Two months to be exact. Next time I see you, you better be wearing trousers.'

And with that, she slammed the door shut.

Alone again, Brian looked around the room. He coughed to clear his throat. 'OK Mum, I guess I should get cleaning.' He scratched at his beard. "Where do we keep the sponges?'

---

Born in Limerick and raised in Dublin, CK (Caimh) McDonnell is a former stand-up comedian and TV writer. He performed around the world, had several well-received Edinburgh shows and supported acts such as Sarah Millican and Gary Delaney on tour before hanging up his clowning shoes to concentrate on writing. He has also written for numerous TV shows and been nominated for a Children's TV BAFTA. His debut novel, *A Man With One of Those Faces*—a comic crime novel—was published in 2016 and spawned The Dublin Trilogy books and the spin-off McGarry Stateside series. They have been Amazon bestsellers on both sides of the Atlantic. C. K. McDonnell lives in Manchester. To find out more, visit: whitehairedirishman.com.

# THE BIRTH OF GOODY MERRYMAN

*By Claire Sheehy*

The slap of fists against cheekbone, the grunt of pain as ribs absorbed brutal kicks, jarred Detective Lizzie March out of her thoughts. She'd taken a short-cut to town, striding down the steep steps behind the church, towards the side street leading to a bustling Market Street. Even as her instincts kicked in and she rounded the corner at a run, she cursed her decision to go the quieter way, causing her to stumble across a mugging—or worse—on her rare afternoon off.

Her boots ringing off the tarmac spooked the gang of youths viciously stamping on a moaning pile of clothes. Her appearance and shout of anger had them scurrying away, yelling obscenities and high fiving each other.

Lizzie contemplated chasing after the scum-bag kids. Petty crime had been rising in recent years, gangs of boys and girls roaming the streets like feral cats. She, more than most, knew how teenagers could get sucked into the darker side of crime, not only ruining the lives of their victims, but sending them down a path to an even scarier future. More than anything, she wanted to catch them and dish out her own form of justice. To put real fear into them, but she knew the living bundle of clothes needed her more.

Bending down, gently pulling a tartan scarf away from the figure's head, she found herself staring into a pair of pained, grey eyes. The anger in them fighting to overcome the fear. Blood oozed from a cut on the bald head, just above the left eye. Lizzie immediately pulled out a packet of tissues, pressing one to the cut. She did a quick assessment of the other bruises and marks already beginning to show up, checking for any serious damage.

"Where else are you hurt?" she asked gently, not wishing to alarm the middle-aged man attempting to rise.

"I'm okay." The gruff answer came out strong, before he winced and fell back as his injured ribs protested the lie.

"Sure you are, and I'm the Tooth Fairy," she scoffed, offering him a hand and getting her first proper look as she hauled him to his feet.

He wasn't particularly tall, about 5'8, but still much taller than her 5'2. What really struck her was how he was dressed. He really did look like a bundle of clothes all mixed up in the wash. His mismatched outfit hung on his skinny frame, unusual layers peeking out from under each other. His grey baggy trousers were paired with an oversized plum coloured sweater, a white pussy-cat-bow blouse rising from the neckline and cuffs. A terracotta leather-look mini skirt over the trousers added to the colourful picture. The image was completed with the tartan scarf now wrapped around his head in a type of turban. Only his shoes could be classed as conventional. Brown, leather brogues, scuffed and in need of a polish, but none-the-less strikingly 'normal' compared to the rest of his outfit.

"I think we need to get you checked out, and report the incident," Lizzie declared, seeing him favour his right leg and press a hand to his ribs.

"No! No doctors, and definitely no police."

Lizzie frowned. She wanted to argue but the mulish look on his face and his move to step away made her realise he meant it. If she pushed the issue he might just disappear, and she didn't relish spending her afternoon off hunting him down to check he was okay.

"Okay. No doctors," she agreed, hoping he wouldn't notice her omission, "on one condition".

Suspicion flared in the man's eyes and he took another unsteady step back from her.

"Don't worry," she soothed, "I'm not going to rob you or make you an improper offer. I just think you need to have a sit down and maybe a cup of tea before you head off. You're still shaken up and I need to know you aren't hiding any more serious injuries before my conscience would let you leave. Do we have a deal?"

Before she'd finished speaking, the man was shaking his head. "I can't, they took my wallet. I have no money on me."

"My treat," promised Lizzie, her voice letting him know it wasn't up for negotiation.

At his reluctant nod Lizzie smiled and indicted a sign in old fashioned script, 'Vintage Tea Room and Thrift Store.' It was hanging above a red-brick building, almost hidden by a screen of over-grown bushes and rampant ivy.

"This is my favourite place," she confessed, pleased to see he'd relaxed a little and was keeping pace with her slow walk. He didn't reply but nor did he bolt. Lizzie chalked it up as a win. The tinkle of the bell above the door startled the man, to the point she could see his heart rate speed up at the pulse in his neck. Lizzie was impressed when he forced himself to take a deep, fortifying breath and walk through the door ahead of her.

"Ooh!" The squeal of excitement shifted Lizzie's attention away from her companion. Looking up, she was almost bowled over by a tiny dynamo barrelling towards her. In one smooth motion Lizzie scooped up the little girl and gave her a huge hug. The child was about three years old, and absolutely adorable. Her bright blue eyes shone with excitement, her wide mouth curved into an infectious grin. Turning, the beautiful child still in her arms, Lizzie made the introductions.

"This is Angela," she told the man, "Carole, who owns this place, is her aunt. Angela helps her out when she's not in nursery, don't you sweetheart?"

The child's enthusiastic nod drew a small but genuine smile from the man.

"What's your name?" Angela demanded.

Seeing how uncomfortable this made the man, Lizzie shushed the child.

"You can't ask strangers personal questions," she explained.

"But he's not a stranger," argued Angela, "he's with you. You're a good guy, so he must be too."

Lizzie wished it was so simple. Her instincts were rarely wrong, and at this moment they were telling her to believe the bruised and battered man next to her was a good guy.

"Are you a goody or a baddy?" Angela asked, cutting into Lizzie's thoughts.

"Umm..." The man seemed unsure how to answer the question, glancing at Lizzie for help.

Deciding to listen to her gut, she answered, "A goody. He's a goody." Satisfied with the answer, Angela wriggled out of Lizzie's arms and, waving a hand at the man chirped, "Nice to meet you Goody!"

Before either of them could speak, Angela turned and waved over a well-dressed woman emerging from the kitchen, "Auntie Carole, look it's Lizzie and she's brought a friend with her," Angela announced as though Lizzie had just brought a unicorn into the tea shop. Smiling, Carole greeted both Lizzie and her guest.

"Hi Carole," Lizzie returned, "do you have a table in the back for us?"

"Of course. It's very quiet today so the back room is empty. Are you planning on browsing the rails? There's a gorgeous leather trench coat just arrived, I think it would be perfect for you."

"Sounds lovely, but first, tea and cakes. Can you also bring your first-aid kit?" Lizzie asked as Carole's eyes slid to the cut on the man's head.

Curious, but too polite to ask, Carole agreed and ushered them through the main part of the tea shop into the back room. Lizzie loved it here. It was so peaceful and calm. The large arched window overlooked a cobbled courtyard and flooded the room with light.

"You've changed things around. I love it," Lizzie declared, as Carole nodded and beamed with pride.

There were a couple of armchairs next to a coffee table situated in the arched window, a squishy sofa against the adjoining wall with another coffee table, and three circular tables with mis-matched chairs finishing the seating. Lizzie's eyes drifted around the room and landed on the five rails of clothes near the far wall.

"Is the leather trench over there?" she asked, scanning the rails.

Carole shook her head. "No, I put it to one side. I know you're going to love it and didn't want someone else to choose it before I could show you."

"You're a good friend Carole," Lizzie smiled, "but someone else might have paid more for it than I could afford. The hospice could have benefitted more."

"Nonsense. A few pounds difference on the coat is easily made up in different ways. You're always buying things here, and I know for a fact most of them end up at the homeless shelter or the young mother's centre," Carole replied.

Lizzie backed down. Carole had her pegged as a saint, and nothing would change her mind. She was far from it, but it gave her a warm feeling so she didn't argue. Smiling her thanks, and ordering two afternoon teas, she led her new acquaintance to the comfy chairs in the window, helping him into the soft cushion. Seeing him wince, Lizzie frowned.

"Are you ok? Is it your ribs?" she asked, concern colouring her voice.

"No, I'm fine," the man replied, an embarrassed flush tinging his cheeks, before another grimace flashed across his face.

"You're certainly not ok!" Lizzie declared in exasperation.

"It's the skirt, it's too tight for sitting in," the man mumbled, his face now beetroot with embarrassment.

"Pardon?" Lizzie asked, not understanding his mumbled words.

"Goody said his skirt is too tight. He can't sit down in it," Angela chimed in helpfully. Watching the man close his eyes, obviously wanting the floor to swallow him up after Angela's loud comment, Lizzie's heart swelled with pity.

"Angela, be a good girl and go get the first aid kit from your aunt?" Lizzie asked, ushering the little girl out of the room. As soon as the pitter-patter of Angela's shoes had faded Lizzie helped the man to his feet and slipped the skirt zip down his hip, giving him breathing room around his waist.

"There you go. Now you can sit and eat, Goody," she announced.

"Goody?"

Lizzie grinned. "It's as good as any other until you feel confident to share your real name with me."

The newly-christened Goody just shrugged his acceptance, saying nothing else as Angela returned with her aunt. Her little hands carried the old first-aid tin, as carefully as Carole carried a tray heavy with teacups and overflowing cake stands. The little girl ceremonially offered the tin to Lizzie while her aunt placed the contents of the tray onto the table before them.

Lizzie inwardly winced as she saw the extra item Carole had put on the table. It was a glass jar with a large sticker on, boldly stating 'Lizzie's Swear Jar'. Beneath the title was a list of rude words and profanities with an increasing price next to each.

"We'll leave you to it now," Carole said, smiling at Lizzie, mischief dancing in her eyes. "Come on Angela, I need help decorating the gingerbread men."

Eagerly grasping her aunt's hand, Angela waved goodbye, leaving Lizzie and Goody alone in the stream of afternoon sunlight shining through the huge window. Goody picked up the jar and peered at it closely. Lizzie watched his eyes light up with amusement when he realised what it was. Snatching it from his hand, Lizzie put it back on the table.

"It's nothing, Carole's just winding me up," she explained.

"It looks pretty legitimate to me," Goody grinned.

Rolling her eyes, Lizzie explained how at the beginning of the year she'd vowed to cut back on her swearing and if she ever slipped up, she'd put money in a jar for the local hospice. Along with this one at the café, she had jar at work and another at home.

Goody picked it up again and gave it a shake, "I see there are a few fivers and lots of pound coins in here," he teased. Lizzie took his teasing with good humour, pleased he'd relaxed enough to find some lightness in his day.

"May I?" asked Lizzie, indicating the first aid box and the cut above his eye. At his nod she rose and came round to his side of the table. Gently, she used an antiseptic wipe to clean the cut.

"It doesn't look to be too deep. It's pretty superficial. You won't need stitches," she informed him, sticking a small dinosaur plaster across the wound. He muttered a "thank you" and Lizzie sank back into her chair.

"Let's eat, I'm starving!" she declared, pouring tea into his cup before helping herself. They ate in companiable silence for a while, until her curiosity started to build. Lizzie watched the man across from her. He darted his eyes around nervously every so often, but she was happy to see he had dropped his guard a little. She couldn't help him if he didn't allow her in, and for some reason she really wanted to help this man. She had no idea why she felt so drawn to him, but he'd piqued her interest and she was determined to find out more. Hell, his name would be a start!

"I'm Lizzie. Lizzie Marsh," she offered once he seemed relaxed enough to hold a basic conversation. He nodded politely but didn't offer his own name. Lizzie lifted her shoulder in a small shrug. She was used to people refusing to give their name when she asked. She tried a different tack.

"Do you live or work around here?"

The man nodded, obviously not concerned about sharing that information. "Both. I got off the streets about a year ago and have a bedsit behind the bus station now. I work from home, with computers. During the day I help various organisations protect their data and online presence."

"And at night?"

Lizzie felt his narrowed eyes assessing her and waited patiently. He was either going to tell her or not. It was that simple. She really hoped he would. Something about him, his vulnerability and cloak of loneliness, tugged at her heart. She knew he wouldn't want her pity, so she kept a polite smile on her face—a skill she had honed over many years.

"Can I trust you?"

Lizzie felt her smile fade.

"I'd like to think so. But if you're going to confess to staying up late breaking the law, doing dodgy things online, it might be best not to. *Are* you breaking the law?"

"No," Goody returned. Then clarified, "Not exactly."

"Not exactly? Then what, exactly?"

Goody looked down at his hands, picking the sultanas from the fluffy scones and squeezing them hard until they mushed between his fingers. Lizzie waited patiently. She knew the golden rule better than most. Whoever spoke first broke the stand-off.

"I told you, I'm good at computers," he said.

Lizzie nodded.

"I'm really good." It wasn't a boast, it was said in a matter-of-fact way. The same way someone might say they were good with languages, or numbers. Lizzie relaxed her tension a little and picked up her scone, slathering it with butter and jam.

"Go on", she encouraged. All she really wanted to do was lean across the table and demand more details. Unfortunately, it wasn't an interrogation, so all she did was raise her eyebrows, showing polite interest.

"The day job pays my bills, barely, but it doesn't use my skills and I didn't want to get rusty. So, I sort of dabble in other things at night. I don't sleep well, so if I'm awake I get active online."

"Okaay," Lizzie replied, drawing out the word, turning it almost into a question.

"Are you familiar with the dark web?" he asked.

"I've heard of it but can't say I'm personally familiar with it. What I do know is there are some pretty sick things on there, and layers upon layers of criminal stuff. Are you telling me you work on the dark web at night?"

Lizzie watched Goody flush, whether with guilt, embarrassment or something else, she couldn't tell.

"Well?"

"I don't do anything to hurt anyone, or against the law, if I can help it. I kind of police the darker corners of the web. I look for scammers who target lonely men and women, stringing them along for money, bleeding them dry. You know the sort. They meet them online in a chat room or dating site and reel them in, telling them they love them. Then once the victim is in so deep, they start asking for money for their sick mother, or to pay immigration fees. I even found one person pretending to be a woman in her twenties with a sick child. She was"—he put his fingers up to make quotation marks—" 'engaged' to four different men, all of whom were bankrupting themselves to finance life-saving surgery abroad for her non-existent child."

Lizzie felt Goody's gaze on her. "How do you stop them?" she asked, "I mean, these are sophisticated criminal gangs, and you're just one person."

Goody's posture became more upright and he lifted his chin, meeting Lizzie's eyes.

"I told you, I'm good. Really good. I find the threads of these scammers and the people they are targeting and follow the path to change the code. The scammers think the people they are targeting have lost interest, and the targets are suddenly ghosted by the scammers."

Lizzie blinked in astonishment. "Wow, I had no idea. Where did you learn how to do that? I can just about figure out how to turn my phone on." She watched the light in Goody's eyes dim and kicked herself for causing it to happen.

"I used to work at a computer firm. A big, global one. I specialised in code breaking, building and protecting firewalls, general cyber security. That sort of thing. I worked my way up the ranks and was in line for a huge promotion but then everything went wrong. I had to leave."

"What do you mean? Why?"

"A month before the promotion was to be announced, I was called into the CEO's office and asked to resign."

Lizzie just stared at the gentle man sat across from her. His tartan scarf-turban had started to slip slightly, and she watched as he absentmindedly adjusted it.

"I had a secret." He shrugged. "I thought I'd managed to keep it from everyone, but apparently I didn't do a good enough job. My wife found out and went straight to my boss. It was a choice of either being fired, and everyone finding out why, or resigning and keeping my dignity."

"Ok, you've hooked me now," Lizzie admitted, really hoping he was willing to tell her, curiosity burning a hole in her brain.

"It's not a secret anymore. One look at me and everyone knows."

Lizzie stared at him puzzled.

Goody waved a hand down his body, indicating himself. "My clothes."

Lizzie raised her eyebrows. "Umm, you had to resign because you wear an eclectic choice of clashing colours and over the top layering?"

He smiled ruefully. "No."

"Then what? Did you rob a bank dressed like a clown?"

"No, of course not. It's because..." He hesitated. "As you can see, I like to wear women's clothes." The devastation in his voice was painful to hear.

"They didn't want a pervert working at the company, dragging their good name through the mud," he muttered, pain lacing his words.

"What?" Lizzie burst out. "The clothes you wear don't make you a pervert. Unless you turn up naked or just in a tiny thong, then I guess it might be a bit inappropriate. Did you actually go into work dressed in women's clothes?"

"No. Never. I always wore my Saville Row suits and silk ties. Perfectly turned out, as my wife would say."

Lizzie was genuinely puzzled. "So why did it matter?"

Goody shrugged. "My wife went crazy, screaming at me. Saying I wasn't normal, I wasn't a real man. You know. To make matters worse, my wife is also the CEO's niece. He took her side in it and I was finished."

Lizzie was outraged. "I can imagine it must have been a shock for her but it's hardly the crime of the century! There was nothing else, no other secret?"

Goody hung his head, gazing at a spot on the floor as he spoke. "I used to go to a private club for cross dressers, no questions asked. I could be myself there. She thought I was having an affair and followed me one night. I supposed she was half right. I was cheating on her, but with myself. Dressed as a woman."

Lizzie shook her head, trying to understand. "*Were* you cheating on her?"

"Of course not! I wouldn't."

Lizzie dug deep into her memory, trying to pull out information from a long-ago course on equality and diversity she'd been forced to attend. It had covered a whole range of areas, focusing mainly on gender, ethnicity and disabilities but it did touch upon LGBTQ+ issues, albeit briefly.

"Can I ask you a personal question?" she asked.

"I thought you already were," Goody muttered, biting into a sandwich.

Ignoring his comment, Lizzie leaned across the table to fill his teacup again before settling back in her chair. "Are you trans, or maybe gay? I'm not judging, I'm trying to understand."

Goody shook his head, paused and shrugged. "I'm not transgender. That much I do know. I'm a man in a man's body. It must be so hard for people who are living in the wrong body.

I don't know if I'm gay or not. It's complicated. None of the labels seem to fit me. I'm attracted to women and men. It depends on who they are, and I guess more who I am at the time too."

"Who *you* are at the time?" Lizzie queried, pleased he was opening up but feeling like she was walking through a verbal minefield risking being blown up by one wrong comment at any moment.

Goody indicated his strange attire. "I don't normally dress like this. Today I was feeling very unsettled and didn't know if I wanted to be in boy mode or girl mode. So, I opted for both. As you saw, it didn't go down too well with the locals," he added wryly.

Lizzie smiled sympathetically, putting another sandwich on his plate. "Kids like those little hooligans will always find something to use as an excuse to bully and harass people. Don't let them put you off being yourself."

Seeing the look of sorrow flit across his face, Lizzie bit her lip. "Did I say something wrong?"

"No, not at all. You're being very kind."

"Then what is it?"

"You said I should just be myself," he answered

"I did," agreed Lizzie

"What if I can't be the person I was?"

"I'm sorry, I don't understand," Lizzie admitted

Goody's sad eyes clouded again, and Lizzie wanted to scoop him up in a huge hug. Her last set of foster parents had been the best. They had showered her with affection and were constantly hugging her when she was sad or angry. As a teen she had been sad *and* angry most of the time, but the hugs from Eileen and Charlie had been the best and she had caught the hug bug from them. She also had learnt all about taking in waifs and strays from them too. She knew the man across from her wasn't an injured fox cub, or a stray kitten. She couldn't take him home to look after, but her instincts were screaming to do something for him. As the silence stretched and she thought he wouldn't continue, Goody finally answered.

"My wife, well ex-wife now, demanded I never use my name again as part of the divorce settlement. I just wanted to get away from everything and so I agreed."

"Seriously?"

"Seriously. Her father is high up in the government and threatened me with all sorts of retribution if I sullied his daughter's reputation by dressing as woman and keeping my own identity. It was just easier to agree."

"So, did you change your name by deed poll?"

"No."

"No? Then you still use your name?"

"No, I have no name now."

Lizzie was stunned. The man before her seemed gentle and kind. Yes, he had an unusual way of dressing, but so did a lot of other people. In her book it didn't make an ounce of difference. It was the person under the clothes who mattered.

"Let me get this straight," Lizzie stated, her voice incredulous, "your wife decided, because you occasionally like wearing female clothes, that you were not worthy of using your own name? The name your parents gave you, the name your ancestors had?"

Goody nodded.

Lizzie's eyebrows pulled into a scowl and without filtering her thoughts she proceeded to tell him exactly what she thought of his ex-wife. The swear jar was overflowing with coins and a £20 note by the time she'd finished. Finally running to a stop, Lizzie noticed Goody staring in fascination. Sheepishly, she smiled at him.

"Sorry, I got carried away."

Chuckling, he shook his head. "Don't apologise, everything you said was pretty much on the mark. She definitely cared more about her image and what her friends would say, than saving our marriage and working out..."

Lizzie grinned. "Working out who wears the trousers?"

His snort of laughter surprised them both. Lizzie smiled, pleased to see her new acquaintance so amused.

"Right," she declared, when most of her sandwiches and scones had disappeared, "Time to browse. Come on Goody, you can drink more tea later!" Goody slowly rose from his chair and followed her to the rails of clothes, shoes, bags, and even a jumble of wigs.

After a little persuasion by Lizzie and the returned Angela and Carole, Goody agreed to try on a few outfits, just for fun. Most were complete disasters, making him look more like a pantomime dame or lap dancer than anything else, but a simple shift dress in navy blue hung beautifully off his bony shoulders, while a fuchsia pink trouser suit fit like it had been bespoke for him, making his legs look a mile long.

Lizzie pulled out two wigs, one a peroxide pixie cut, the other a tumble of red curls, and insisted Goody try them on. The hair pieces transformed him. The brown brogues were swapped for a pair of black sling backs. Gone was the slightly awkward and apologetic man, in his place was a fierce and confident woman.

All too soon, Lizzie realised the café would be closing and reluctantly assisted Goody back into his own clothes. Still laughing and giggling over the impromptu fashion show, they were again joined by Angela who'd been popping in and out of the room most of the afternoon.

"You're happy now!" she announced, delight shining from her.

"I am, and it's all thanks to you and your friend Lizzie here," agreed a much more relaxed man. "I'm a lot merrier than I was earlier."

A smile split the little girl's face and lit up the room as she did a happy jig on the spot. "You're a merry man now!" she giggled.

Carole came into the room, looking for Angela, and Lizzie beckoned to her. As Goody and Angela chatted, rating the vintage ragdolls and tatty teddy bears scattered around the room, Lizzie paid the bill, before asking her friend for a favour. Carole nodded and with a practised hand scooped up all the clothes they had been playing dress-up with.

"Come with me and I'll find the leather coat I saved for you," Carole said. Hearing her aunt about to leave the room, Angela patted her new friend's arm before telling him to 'wait right there.' At Goody's nod she skipped from the room, following Lizzie and Carole.

When Lizzie came back to the table, she was wearing a soft leather trench coat. It reached her ankles and fit her curves like a glove. The pale buttery colour complemented her perfectly, the lightness of the leather a perfect foil for her green eyes and almost black hair. In her hands was a brown paper parcel.

Goody looked much better than he had when she'd first met him, only a couple of hours ago. He smiled up at her when she neared and reached for his teacup. He took a final swallow and gave a sigh, slumping into the soft cushion at his back, as though it was the first time he had truly relaxed in a very long time.

"Thank you. I've had a wonderful afternoon," he said, the frown lines of stress and pain smoothed by the laughter lines.

"You're more than welcome," Lizzie smiled.

"I'll tell you my name if you like," he hesitantly offered.

Lizzie shook her head. "No, I already know your name."

At his puzzled look, Lizzie continued, "You're Goody Merryman and today is your official birthday. Here's a birthday present."

Lizzie grinned and handed over the parcel. Goody stared at the brown paper and string in his hands, not moving or speaking.

"Well, go on, open it," Lizzie urged.

Goody pulled on the string and the parcel fell open to reveal a treasure trove of clothes and the black heels. He stared, running his fingers over the soft fabric of the navy shift dress, and playing with the buttons on the pink trouser suit. The two wigs he'd looked amazing in were lying on top. With a sheen of tears in his eyes, he looked up at Lizzie.

Leaning towards him, Lizzie patted his knee. "Welcome to the world, Goody Merryman. Be as fabulous as you can be and never let anyone take away who you are again."

---

Claire Sheehy was born in Manchester but moved around the North West as a child, finally landing in Chorley a year before starting high school. Claire attended Liverpool University and then did a Post Grad in Watford, before entering the crazy and creative world of London advertising agencies in the early 1990's. Claire has always loved writing, scribbling little stories for her younger sisters for fun, and writing articles for a whole host of magazines, whilst toying with writing a novel or a screen play on numerous occasions. She finally took the plunge in 2019 and published a short story, *ShopLift*, introducing her character Detective Lizzie Marsh. She is currently working on her first full length crime novel. Her stories are based in the North West, but she draws inspiration from her time living and working in London, Leeds and the Yorkshire Dales.

# A FINE PAIR OF SHOES

*By Clare Flynn*

*1851*

She'd only worn the shoes once. Twenty-five years earlier, on her wedding day. After John Somerton carried her over the threshold of his terraced house, she'd slipped them off her feet, stuffed them with tissue paper, wrapped them in a piece of cotton and put them in a box on top of the bedroom cupboard. Since that day—a lifetime ago—there'd been no opportunity to wear the shoes again. Now, Maria fetched a stool from the kitchen, clambered up and brought the wooden box down. Once she'd wiped the dust off the lid, she opened it and took out the precious shoes. Cream satin with silk bows on the front. So dainty. So delicate. A wedding gift from her mother, who had put a penny aside whenever she could as Maria was growing up, determined her only daughter would have something special that wasn't homemade like the rest of her trousseau.

Maria cradled the shoes in her hands, remembering that day and the mixture of happiness and fear she'd experienced. John Somerton had been a virtual stranger to her then. They'd exchanged only a few words, their courtship consisting of quick stolen glances, with Maria dropping her gaze whenever she thought there was a risk he might notice her watching him, as he made his way up the hill past her family's house on the way to the cotton mill, where he was responsible for maintaining the spinning machines. Maria worked in a different mill, carding and spooling the cotton, so there had been no opportunity for a casual workplace encounter and the exchange of a few words.

The girls at the mill gossiped and shared stories about the young men who caught their eyes, but Maria said nothing about the engineer who had captured her heart simply by walking past her up the street. It had taken her months to discover his name and even longer before she ventured a smile when at last their eyes met. But after that smile everything changed, and John began to wish her a good morning and eventually asked her name. One Sunday after church, there was a knock at the door and there he was bearing a posy of flowers for her mother and a big smile for her.

'I was wondering if you might care to take a walk with me. Just a stroll. The bluebells are flowering and they make a wonderful sight. Have you seen them yet?'

She told him she hadn't. It was a lie of course. She walked past the bluebell woods every day on the way to the mill, but seeing the swathes of flowers with John beside her would be seeing them anew.

They said very little on that walk and those that took place on the following Sundays, both of them being painfully shy. Yet Maria had felt increasingly comfortable in his company, her heart beating faster every time she saw him coming up the street. A month later, John asked her father for her hand in marriage. She was just seventeen and he was twenty-five.

Maria had no idea what she might expect from marriage—but John proved to be the best and kindest husband she could have wished for. Within a year she gave birth to her first baby. The boy had died as an infant, as did three others, another boy and two girls, but she and John had been blessed with seven surviving children and while times were often hard, he had always provided for his growing family.

With the shoes in her hands, Maria thought back to her wedding day. How young, innocent and in love she had been. How handsome and strong John had looked, towering over her as they stood together at the altar, his eyes full of love.

A quarter of a century later, she thought him as handsome as ever. Yes, there was a hint of grey at his temples, but he was still the type of man to whom people looked up and showed natural respect. John was firm of jaw, his thick hair still lustrous and his eyes bright and full of intelligence. Despite the familiarity bred by all those years of marriage, she often found herself glancing at him and thanking God that he had chosen her—as well as doubting how he could possibly still love her now that she was no longer the pretty young girl he had fallen for.

She stared at her own reflection in the mirror. The years had taken a harder toll on her than on her husband. Not just the years—it was the long hours working on the cotton machines and having all those babies. At only forty-two, her hair had lost its youthful gloss, scraped back always into a scrawny bun. Her shapely figure and trim ankles were distant memories. The woman staring back at her already showed a spider's web of lines with chubby rolls under her chin and around her thickened waist.

Maria turned away, pulling her shoulders back and holding her head up. No time for vanity and no point in dwelling on the past. Today she had a reason for great excitement. After all the years that her wedding shoes had lain in state on the top of the cupboard, now at last she had an occasion to wear them again.

Lady Gerard up at Garswood Hall had invited the women of the parish to tea at the Hall and regaled them with tales of her visit to the Great Exhibition in London. She told them the magnificent Crystal Palace was filled with every kind of wonder of man's creation from locomotive engines to all the treasures of the Empire. Her ladyship said they should all do everything they possibly could to travel to London and witness the wonders for themselves. Easier said than done. A trip to London was a regular occurrence for Lady Gerard but beyond the dreams of working-class women like Maria.

Maria had rushed home afterwards, filled with awe about what she had heard but knowing there was no possibility she would ever have the chance to visit this magical place.

'Oh, John, you can't imagine what wonderful things her ladyship saw at the Great Exhibition. There's everything you can possibly think of in your wildest dreams and it's all there under one roof. She told us to do what we can to try to get there. Oh, dearest, wouldn't it be a fine thing to be able to visit it? There's even a stuffed elephant! I would be thrilled to see such a thing.'

John reached across the table and took her hands in his.

'Well then, my darling wife, we shall have to go and witness all these wonders for ourselves. I've quite a fancy myself to see a stuffed elephant.'

Maria bounced up and down in excitement.

'You mean it? All the way to London?'

'If it's good enough for Lady Gerard then it's good enough for Maria Somerton. As it happens, I was going to suggest it anyway but I didn't know whether you'd be prepared to travel all that distance. The Mechanics Institute is arranging transport for as many as want to travel from Ashton. I'll sign us up tomorrow. A big group will be going from the mill. It'll be quite an adventure.'

'But can we afford it?'

John winked at her. 'Where there's a will. This is a chance of a lifetime, my dearest. It would be criminal not to seize the opportunity. We'll manage somehow.'

'Oh, John! Thank you.' Maria flung her arms around her husband.

Maria had never set foot outside Ashton-in-Makerfield before. John had occasionally travelled to Liverpool to visit his brother and had once been to Manchester to look at a new type of spinning wheel but had never gone further than the borders of Lancashire. The prospect of a journey to the capital city was almost too much to conceive.

Maria discovered they were far from being the only ones in Ashton-in Makerfield to join the trip to London. The Mechanics Institute had arranged a special train for hundreds of millworkers, then they were to stay in a lodging house with a full day to visit the Exhibition, before returning home to Ashton the following morning. With heavily subsidised prices, her anxiety about the cost receded.

Three whole days away from Ashton. They would have to leave the children behind. Thinking about that, she almost changed her mind, but Margaret, the eldest was sixteen and there was also Maria's mother to help with the little ones. They'd manage. There would never be another opportunity like this in her life. It was something she would one day tell her grandchildren.

On the morning of their departure, the Somertons dressed in their Sunday best clothes. Maria had trimmed her bonnet with a piece of ribbon she'd been saving for years and she slipped the satin shoes on her feet. They were about to leave the house, when John, frowning, put a hand on her arm.

'You're not planning to go all the way to London wearing those shoes are you?'

'I most certainly am. They're my best shoes from our wedding. I've waited twenty-five years for another excuse to wear them.'

'I can see that, my darling, and very fine shoes they are too, but don't you think you might be more comfortable wearing your everyday ones? The Crystal Palace is said to cover eighteen acres of land so there will be a lot of walking to do. It will be a long day and could be very tiring.'

'Nonsense. I am not going all the way to London to mix and mingle with the high and mighty, wearing an old pair of clodhoppers. What do you take me for?'

John shook his head. 'Those are indeed a dainty pair of shoes, but no one will see them underneath your skirts, my love. Are you sure you wouldn't prefer to be comfortable in these old shoes?'

Maria was outraged. 'Certainly not! I am wearing these and that's the end of the matter. They're as comfortable as a pair of soft leather gloves.'

They stood outside the lodging house. John read the sign on the front of the large brick building.

'This is it. *One and thruppence a night. Bedstead, woollen mattress, sheets, blankets, coverlets, soap and towels all included. Facilities for ablutions. Gas lighting in all dormitories*. That'll do us proud, missus.'

There was a meal of cold roast beef and boiled mutton, with pickles, bread and fruit pies, but Maria was far too excited to eat more than a couple of mouthfuls. That night it felt strange sleeping in the big, crowded dormitory, full of working people like them, here in London for the first time, whispering in the dark about how thrilled they were about what lay ahead.

The next morning, the Somertons dressed and readied themselves bright and early and set off for Hyde Park. All the omnibuses heading in that direction were overcrowded so, rather than queue, they decided to proceed on foot. It was no more than a mile but, as they approached the park, Maria could feel the binding around her satin shoes cutting into her feet and the back of the shoes chafing against her heels.

The roads were thronged with people. Street traders were everywhere: hawkers carrying trays containing miniature models of the Crystal Place, boys pulling barrows laden with nuts and baskets of oranges, or pushing carts selling ginger beer for a penny. Huge Union flags hung from the windows of public houses in a festive display of pride and patriotism. Everywhere around them the crowds of people were smiling and bubbling with anticipation.

As they entered the park, there it was—the great glass building. Lady Gerard had not exaggerated. Maria and John had never seen anything like it. It rose up ahead of them, a towering colossus, sunlight shimmering through it, so that despite its enormous proportions it seemed a light and airy creation, made of ice rather than iron and glass. A huge sign proudly proclaimed *The Great Exhibition of the Works of Industry and Art of All Nations*.

Once they had paid their shilling entrance fee, the world inside the glass pavilion bedazzled them. So vast was the edifice that it had swallowed up several of the tall elm trees of the park, now growing inside the building and dwarfed by its mammoth proportions.

'Oh, John, can you believe it? You could fit Garswood Hall in here several times over! How clever the men must be to make a building as grand as this one.'

'There's never an end to the invention of mankind, dearest. I can honestly say I have never before felt so proud to be a part of the British Empire.'

They walked the length of the building, fascinated by everything they saw from the carpets and tapestries to the dental equipment and printing presses, from the giant Egyptian pharaohs to the steam turbines, Jacquard lace machines and the Koh-i-Noor diamond. But no matter how overwhelmed she was by the wonders around her, Maria could think of nothing but the pain in her feet. By now she was limping badly, the bunions of forty-two Lancastrian winters pressing against the cotton lining of the flimsy, satin shoes, the soles of her feet separated from the hard ground by only a wafer-thin, leather sole. The tiny feet that had slipped so easily into those shoes on her wedding day were swollen and hardened after years of married life. She limped on, cursing her vanity and stupidity and wishing she had listened to John's advice to wear her work shoes. But she was too proud to admit it and, besides, what good would it do now?

At last, they stopped for a pot of tea in the refreshment court beside the great Coalbrookdale iron gates. Maria sipped the tea, happy to be seated at last, surreptitiously slipping off her shoes under the table and wiggling her toes. The relief was exquisite. A tingling release as the blood rushed to her burning soles.

A fountain tinkled and the sounds of violin music played beyond the palm trees that surrounded the refreshment area. Maria would have happily remained there for the rest of the day but John was already itching to see the latest advances in cotton-spinning machinery. She forced her swollen feet back into the shoes, wincing with pain as the blisters were squeezed. Biting her lip to hold back the tears, she stood up. The brief respite had made her feet swell even more and now the shoes were tighter than ever. Excruciating torture. Like walking on shards of glass. She couldn't go on. Even the delights of the exhibition couldn't lure her to put one foot in front of the other. It was no good. She would have to confess and ask John to take her back to the lodgings. Knowing she had ruined their day, she choked back the tears. Would he ever forgive her? Would she ever forgive herself?

'Oh John, I'm so sorry. I hate to admit it, but you were right about the shoes. I can't walk another step. What am I to do? I've spoiled our day.'

John took her hand and led her back to the seat. From the depths of the pockets of his voluminous caped greatcoat he pulled out first one and then the other of her battered work shoes. Without a word, he knelt down on the ground in front of her, removed the satin wedding slippers, gave her aching feet a gentle rub and slipped her old clodhoppers onto them.

---

Clare Flynn is the author of thirteen historical novels. A former International Marketing Director and strategic management consultant, she is now a full-time writer. Born in Liverpool and having lived and worked in Newcastle, London, Paris, Brussels, Milan and Sydney, home is now on the south coast, in Sussex, England, where she can watch the sea from her windows. An avid traveller, her books are often set in exotic locations. Clare is a Fellow of the Royal Society of Arts, a member of The Society of Authors, The Alliance of Independent Authors, the Historical Novel Society and the Romantic Novelists Association.

# THE BIG BURN BOOK

*By Darren O'Sullivan*

You get to a stage in your life when you spend more time looking back than looking forward. I watched my grandmother do so when I was in my teens, her life reduced to only thinking and talking of the world before the two great wars. I saw the same thing happen to my mother when she grew old; she seldom spoke of new things, instead, she reminisced about Vera Lynn, ration books, the hardships she faced during it all. She would regale us with a sort of sad nostalgia. And this past year, since my husband died, I've discovered it is now my turn. I don't look forward anymore, instead I dig as far back as I can remember. I can just about recall my childhood with my mother, father and big brother, Alan. I can still smell the endless summers in the field behind our home where I chased crickets. I remember Alan leaving to join the war effort. He was too young to go to France, so he joined the Home Guard. I explicitly recall the day he didn't make it home. His life ending in central London at the hand of a German bomb. But really, when I think about the past, I think of the large part that was with my Stan. I think about the day we met, our wedding day, the holidays we took, the children we had. I think about how we grew old together. I think about the way he smiled out of one side of his mouth when he was being mischievous, and how he liked to be mischievous often. I think about the sad day that cancer took him away. At night, when I cannot sleep, I drift back to a memory of him reading one of his favourite Sherlock Holmes mysteries to me. He read to me for 42 wonderful years. I can feel his hand gently stroking my hair as he reads.

I don't look forward to the nothing that is to come—just like those before me, I think back to when my life was good.

Now, life is just life—not much living, more waiting for it to run its course. It sounds bleak, and I'm sorry for that, but the truth is the truth. I miss who I once was, I miss who I was once with. There are no more adventures, no more new experiences, because I'm old and that's just how it is. I live, from day to day, in a pleasant and yet somehow morose old people's home called Sunnyview. Sunnyview has been my home for the past year, since Stan died and it was deemed I couldn't live alone, and every day I do the same thing, I have the same experiences. I wait for the end, just like everyone who lives here. We never speak of it, but it's there regardless, hanging in the silence between breaths in speech.

And that was okay for me, at my age. I had made peace with how I would see my life out. At least, I used to.

Then, I met Maggie Constance.

Maggie moved in on a wet Tuesday morning, and at first glance, she didn't look any different to the other elderly ladies who lived here. If anything, she looked more fragile than most as her tiny frame shuffled across the dayroom to a chair near to the patio door. As Ricky, the kindest employee at Sunnyview, introduced her to us all, I smiled politely, and she smiled back, one that was wide and toothy. I usually wasn't curious about new faces. As I have said, most come to this place to die. But there was something about her, something different to the others. She must have felt me staring as she spun in her seat and flashed me another toothy smile. I wanted to say something to her, offer my name at least. But I didn't. Then, she turned in her chair to face the window again and looked out into the garden, drawn to it by the sound of rain hitting the window as the heavens had opened. I thought that that would be it for my interaction with Maggie Constance. I knew her name, exchanged a glance, and now we would both go back to thinking about our lives before here, never to speak again, and then, one of us would die, eventually, we both would, and two more ladies would move in, to wait their turn.

I didn't speak to Maggie for that first week of her living at Sunnyview. But I felt myself wanting to. She had odd ways. On her second day, I watched her bite into an orange like it was an apple and then proclaim to Ricky that it tasted totally different. On day four, she missed breakfast, and when she eventually joined the lounge at lunchtime, she said she had a hangover that could kill a horse. I asked Ricky—apparently, she snuck out and went to a pub. There was a rumour she was brought home by a man who was much younger than she, and from the way they kissed goodbye, it definitely wasn't her son. Day five, she escaped through the front door and from my bedroom window, I watched her play in the children's park across the road. And all the time, in her possession, a little black book that she wrote in, and scribbled things out of. We all had to wonder whether Maggie Constance was unwell, perhaps a degenerative brain disease. I asked Ricky if she was in need more support. His response confused me.

'She's not unwell, Joy, she's trouble.'

On day seven, a day that was miserable and bone-achingly damp, Maggie waddled in, dressed in her finery, an expensive-looking handbag over her shoulder, and smiled at me before she sat in a chair facing the back window. Her tiny, diminutive features just showing around the wingback. She reached into her handbag and removed her small, black notebook with a pen attached. Removing the pen, she opened the notebook, and scribbled in it quite excitedly. Then she did the most remarkable thing. She put the book face down, on the arm of the chair, open on the page she had written in, stood, opened the back door, and before the staff had time to react, Maggie Constance was outside, stamping in puddles, her face up to the heavens, dancing in the April rain. Ricky dashed out to grab her, concerned that she would 'catch a death.' She tried to evade him by hiding behind a pear tree, and we could all hear her teasing him as she did. Eventually, she gave up and let him bring her back inside, whisking her off to her room so she could get dry. And as she passed, her clothes soaked to the bone, she smiled at me again, confirming my suspicion that she was in fact very unwell. I watched until she and Ricky rounded a corridor toward her room, and then I looked back at the chair—her little book was still there, she'd forgotten it. From across the dayroom, at their table where they were playing cards, Tim, Janice and Frances—my only friends at Sunnyview—saw the book too. Standing up, I approached and picked it up. The book was unremarkable, something you would find in any supermarket, and as I turned it over, I saw her writings. I closed the book before I could be tempted to read any.

'Well? What does it say?' Tim asked in hushed tones.

'I'm not reading it.'

'Give it here, I will,' he said.

'No, Tim.'

I looked to Janice for support, but she smiled mischievously, even Frances, who was normally a stickler for doing things properly seemed interested. Truth be told, I wanted to look, but only to then speak with Ricky about her perhaps needing to be upstairs in the ward for those who needed more support. Everything she was doing looked like a degenerative mind disease, but who I was I to say?

'Quick, before she comes back.'

Giving in to peer pressure, I opened the front page, its entire contents consisted of four words.

*The Big Burn Book.*

'Joy, look out!' Frances said, and panicking, I put the book back on the arm of the chair just as Maggie Constance came back in, her clothes changed, but her hair was still wet. I must have looked guilty, as when Maggie drew closer, she looked from me to the book.

'Did you take a look?' she asked.

'No, no of course not, I was going to pick it up and return it to you.'

'Shame, I would have looked if it was yours,' she said, picking up the book and tucking it under her arm. I suspected Maggie was then going to leave, maybe sit down, but she just stood there, looking at me.

'Joy, isn't it?'

'Yes, hello.'

'Hello.'

The silence hung over us, and I looked over to Tim, Frances and Janice who pretended to be busy with their game. Maggie unsettled me, and needing their support, I offered to introduce her to my friends.

'Oh, yes, that would be lovely.'

Taking Maggie Constance into the dining area, I formally introduced her to the others. Janice said hello and couldn't stop staring, like Maggie was other-worldly. Frances said she was charmed, putting on her best posh voice, but watching suspiciously. And Tim, well, Tim nodded, gruffed and offered nothing else. Taking a seat with the group an awkward silence fell over us, and I realised, I didn't know what to say. In the past week, we had spoken a little unkindly of Maggie, mainly Tim, who called her batty at everything she did. I opted for 'quirky' but was now aware, that was just as unkind. I felt uncomfortable, as did the others, but Maggie didn't. She settled into the chair and we watched as she looked up towards the ceiling as her mind drifted to lord knows where. Then, she opened her little black book and scribbled something down furiously. From where I was sat, I could just about make out the page she scrawled on, but her handwriting was illegible. I really wanted to know what the book contained, and what 'the big burn' meant. Flashing a glance to the others, I could see they all wanted to know as well, but none of us wanted to ask. Of course, Tim had no such issue with etiquette.

'Mrs Constance, what is in that little book of yours?'

'I wondered when someone would ask. Do you really want to know?' she said.

'Of course, I bloody do, or I'd not raise the question.'

'Tim!' exclaimed Frances. 'Manners!'

'I'm sorry about him.'

'Don't be, he's fun, and you, do you all want to know too?'

We all nodded.

'This, well this is my Big Burn Book.'

'The big what now?' Tim asked.

'The Big Burn Book,' Maggie said.

'I see,' Tim said, but clearly, like the rest of us having no idea what she meant.

'Could you elaborate?' I asked.

'Of course, but to answer, I need to ask a question first. Tim, how old are you?'

'I'm not sure what's that got to do with anything.'

'Humour me'

'I don't wish to.'

'He's 81,' Janice butted in.

'And you?'

'I'm 83,' she said.

'Frances, Joy?'

'85 next week,' Frances said, rather proudly, and I told her I was 84. She nodded, as if our answers cleared up the mystery of the book.

'Well, I've just turned 86,' she said. 'We are no spring chickens anymore.'

'No,' I said quietly, we were far from a spring chicken, we were the fat old used-up battery hens.

'Tim,' she continued, breaking my macabre thoughts, 'do you know the average life expectancy for a man in England?'

'Well, as you know my age now,' he said, flashing Janice a scowl, 'shall I guess 81?'

'79,' she stated matter-of-factly, then paused, to let the number sink in.

'And ladies—what's our average life expectancy?'

I looked at the others—it was clear, we didn't know.

'82. Every one of us has passed that number now. We are living beyond what is expected of us.'

'That's a grim thought.'

'Perhaps, or perhaps knowing this liberates us from what is expected, as we are doing the unexpected by simply breathing. To quote Dylan Thomas, *Do not go gentle into that good night, but rage, rage against the dying of the light.*'

I was stunned, as were the others, Maggie had just touched on something none of us had thought of before. Perhaps she wasn't that mad after all?

'Charlie, my husband, suffered before he went,' she continued. 'He suffered for a long, long time. Bed-ridden, losing his dignity by the day, and being his wife, I stood by his side, spoke kindly in his ear and listened as he told me all of the good things of his life. I loved him fiercely until the day he drew his last breath.'

'I'm so sorry,' I said.

'What for?'

'Your loss.'

'You're seeing it all wrong. I've not lost Charlie; I'll be with him again one day. No, I've gained something in the absence of Charlie.'

'Your book?'

'Yes Joy, my book.'

'I don't understand, Maggie.'

'Charlie lost himself to his illness. Day by day, he forgot who he was, who I was.'

'That must have been so difficult.'

'It was, but, on his good days, on those moments when he remembered everything, he started to write in this book, something I didn't know about until after he was gone.'

'He wrote in that book. May I ask, what does it say?'

'Look for yourself.'

Maggie Constance handed me the book and carefully, like I was holding some ancient text, I turned over the first page to see a letter. It started, 'My dearest Maggie…' I turned over, knowing that whatever it said wasn't for me to read. On the next page was two items of a list. The second had been scribbled out:

1—Swim naked in the sea
~~2—Have a hangover that could kill a horse.~~

The rest of the page was filled with doodles of sunsets and other sentences, the words illegible. 'Swim naked in the sea?' I said, trying not to blush.

'Yes, when I was young, I was too body-conscious to do it. Charlie knew it was something I always wished to do.'

'As in fully naked?' Janice asked.

'Like the day I was born.'

'I couldn't...'

'Why Janice? Who cares what we look like anymore? Do you?'

'No.'

'Then what would stop you?'

'Getting into trouble.'

'At our age, we can but hope.'

'And your husband wrote for you to do this?' I asked.

'He did.'

'Why?'

'To make sure I tried to rage against it, in his absence. My husband wanted me to do all those things I wished I had, but never did.'

I let her words sink in for a moment.

'He is no doubt enjoying my antics elsewhere. When I'm with him again, we will laugh until we cry at what he made me do after he died.'

I liked the idea of that and wondered what my Stan thought of me as he looked down, and a sadness washed over me. I was doing nothing of worth.

Turning my attention back to the book, which was captivating me, I saw 'ride a motorbike' and 'scuba dive'.

'This list is bonkers, Maggie.'

'Joy, my dear, sometime in the near future, I'm going to face the Big Burn.'

'What is the Big Burn?'

'It was what Charlie called being cremated. He often said, it would soon be his time for the Big Burn. We all get there in the end.'

Her words slapped the smile from my face.

'I have lived through the Second World War. Countless elections, a pandemic. I have a son who is 55, a daughter who is 49. I have a grandson who is off to university next year. I have lived a very long time, and I've had a good life. However, there are still things I wish I had done. Do you have those things too?'

'Yes, I mean, I don't think about it much, but I guess everyone does, don't they?' I said.

'Well, what are they?' she asked, and I struggled to articulate a single thought.

'I always wanted to see the world,' Janice jumped in. 'I have lived in the fen my whole life. I wish I saw things—buildings, sights, landmarks. If I could do my time again, I would want to travel.'

'Where would you start?'

'Oh, Maggie, I've not even made it to London to see Big Ben.'

'What about you, Frances?' Maggie asked.

'I don't know, I had a good life really, I guess, I wish I got into more trouble.'

I laughed at this unexpected response from the normally-sensible Frances. 'Really?'

'Oh yes Joy, yes, I wish I was arrested,' she said, laughing with us too.

'Tim?'

'There is no point wishing for things that cannot be done,' he said, not wanting to participate, but he listened none the less.

'I always wanted to get high,' I said, surprised at myself for saying it. 'I guess, I would have done that.'

'These are all great,' Maggie said, writing them in her little black book. 'Now, I have to ask, what is stopping any of you doing these things?'

With that, Maggie stood, smiled at us, thanked us for the company, and wandered back to her room, leaving us to ponder her question, the answer to which was…nothing. Nothing was stopping us.

For the rest of the day, we didn't speak, we didn't play games, we just thought of our lives, not thinking back to what we did, but what we could have done differently. Dinner approached, and Maggie didn't come out of her room. Worrying I had offended her by lying about looking in her book, I went to her room, and tapped three times gently on the door.

'Who is it?' her voice sounded from within.

'It's me, Joy. I'm not interrupting, am I?'

'No, dear, no, come in.'

I opened the door, and saw Maggie Constance packing a bag on her bed.

'Maggie?'

'I'm leaving.'

'Leaving? What do you mean? Where are you going?'

'My list isn't going to tick itself off, Joy.'

'You can't.'

'Says who? I may be old, but I'm not dead yet. Join me, Joy, all of you. Let's bust out of here, tonight.'

'Tonight?'

'Yes, tonight.'

'Maggie, I—'

'Think about it, tonight at midnight, I'll be in the dayroom, if none of you come, I'll leave at five-past. You better go, before someone sees us,' she said.

Unsure what to say, or do, I nodded, said goodbye and closed Maggie's door.

Back in the dayroom, I told the others what I had learnt.

'We have to tell someone,' Frances said.

'Do we?' I replied.

'Joy, you cannot be suggesting we let her do this?' Tim said.

'Well, why not, is there any rule to say she cannot?' There wasn't, as far as I could tell. At no point had I signed away my liberty just because I was old.

The evening seemed to drag on longer than any other evening I had spent in Sunnyview, and just after 8pm Frances excused herself for bed. I followed shortly after, and as I said goodnight both Tim and Janice gave me a look as if to say, 'I hope you know what you are doing'.

In my room, I tried my best to sleep, managing only an hour or so before my alarm clock sounded, telling me it was ten to midnight. Rolling out of bed, my limbs feeling heavy, I dressed. I didn't know what I was doing—was I going to stop her, convince her it was a bad idea, or was I going to leave too?

As I tiptoed towards the dayroom, careful not to disturb anyone else, or be caught, I was shocked to see that in the darkness, Tim, Janice, Frances and Maggie were all there.

'Joy, I'm so glad you are joining us.'

'Us?' I asked.

'Well, it seems we all want to rage,' Tim said, smiling, perhaps for the first time since I met the man.

'I cannot believe we are doing this,' Frances said. 'We could get into so much trouble.'

'You don't have to,' Maggie said.

'I know, but since you showed your list, I have thought of the things I wanted to do, and I realised, if I didn't right now, in this moment, I wouldn't ever.'

'Carpe diem,' Tim said. 'I had the same thoughts. One day, I won't be mobile enough for one last adventure. Christ, I'm barely mobile now. Like Frances, it's now, or it's never.'

'I think, Maggie Constance, we are all with you,' Janice said, beaming a wide and youthful smile.

'Right, lets rage a little, shall we?' Maggie said.

As we made our way towards the front door, to the clear night and the adventure that waited for us, I realised that this step outside would be the first I had taken in almost a year that was an independent step. A step because I had chosen to take it.

But no sooner had we arrived at reception to leave; I saw that step wasn't going to happen. Blocking our escape, our impromptu adventure, stood Ricky.

'I knew you lot were up to no good. What the bloody hell do you think you are doing?' he said, and I was taken back. I hadn't heard him swear before, even something as minor as the word 'bloody'.

'We are leaving,' said Maggie Constance, defiantly.

'You are not!'

'We are not prisoners here, Ricky. If we want to leave, we will leave.'

'But…' He hesitated. 'No, you can't, it's not safe.'

'Says who? Says you? I don't mean to be rude Ricky, but I survived the blitz as a small child. I think I can handle myself.'

'But now, your…' He trailed off.

'We are what? Go on, say it,' Maggie said.

'Fine, I'll say it. You're old.'

Before Maggie could come back with a no-doubt compelling argument, I stepped forward and placed my hand on Ricky's arm.

'Yes, we are old. We are all very old. And this is why you need to let us go.'

'I can't, what if something happens?'

'We are hoping something will.'

I watched as his eyes widened, misinterpreting my words.

'I don't mean something terrible; I mean something wonderful.'

'Ricky,' Maggie Constance chipped in, 'our lives are short, and we want to enjoy what we have left.'

'We've all got things we want to do before we go,' Janice added.

'Please, Ricky,' Frances pleaded. 'We need to do this, we need to leave right now, before we lose our courage—we don't have the same time you do.'

Ricky looked from me to the others in the group, weighing up what was best. I understood why he felt compelled to stop us, I truly did. And if I was him, I would be doing the same. I just hoped our reasoning would be enough for him to ignore that side of himself. Maggie spoke, calmer, softer than before.

'How old are you dear?'

'39,' he replied.

'Still so young.'

'I don't feel it.' He smiled.

'Ricky, what would you do, if you could?'

He thought about it for a moment. 'I was once with a woman called Joanne, she was wonderful, my world.'

'What happened?'

'She wanted marriage, mortgage, all that. I wasn't ready, I felt I was too young, so she moved on. If I could do my time again, I would have been braver.'

'Do you think you might find love again?'

'Maybe,' he said, a sadness in his words. 'One day.'

'Ricky, we don't have one day, we have now, and that's it.'

'We just want to rage, Ricky,' Tim said quietly, all of his bluster and anger gone.

'Rage?'

'Yes, rage. One day, you'll understand.'

'Dear Ricky,' Maggie said, turning her attention to him. 'We just want to rage. Whilst there is time.'

He considered us one more time before sighing. 'You have until 6am, then I'm going to have to tell someone you're all missing.'

'That's all we could hope for, thank you dear Ricky.'

'Go on, get out of here,' he said, stepping to one side to let us pass. And as we did, each and every one if us, including Tim, gave him a hug. Maggie was last, and just before she joined us in the cold spring night air, she smiled at him.

'You're a goodun, Ricky.'

'Yeah, tell my landlord that when I'm sacked and cannot pay my rent. Now go on, before I change my mind, or someone else sees you.'

Maggie joined our side, we began to move through the carpark, and as I was on the far left, I could see across the line. A bunch of old age pensioners, shuffling and plodding into adventure. My dear Stan was an old rocker at heart, and I couldn't help but hear Immigrant Song in my head. The lyrics that seemed to make everyone feel angrier or more dangerous back when it was first released. I still couldn't believe we were doing it. We were going out. And it terrified me. As we waited for a taxi Maggie had booked to take us to our first destination—London, for Janice—I wondered if we were making a terrible mistake. Maggie saw it on my face, and gently took my hand.

'Joy, time waits for no-one, you either used it, or it is lost forever.'

She was right, and I had already wasted so much of it.

So, as we climbed into the taxi and drove away, I closed my eyes, and took a deep breath. We must rage, tell our stories, leave our legacies. Yes, we were old; yes, we were almost invisible. But we weren't entirely gone, we had love to share, joy and laughter to find. In just one day, I had learnt the most valuable lesson in my life—despite my age, despite what the world expected from me, I was still able to live, to learn, to do new things. It was never too late to start again, to have an adventure, it was never too late to rage against the dying of the light.

---

Darren O'Sullivan is the author of bestsellers, *Our Little Secret*, *Close Your Eyes* and *Closer Than You Think*, *Dark Corners* and *The Players*. He also writes under the pen name, 'BB Thomas'. When Darren isn't writing, he is teaching English for a crime prevention charity, directing theatre, or spending time with his six-year-old, which is his happy place. You can follow him on Twitter/Instagram @Darrensully or on Facebook via his author page, Darren O'Sullivan-author.

# A MOTHER'S GIFT

*By David Leadbeater*

In the cold, dark, desolate hour before dawn there was a sharp knock at the front door.

I heard it as I drifted in that comfortable state between napping and waking. It was an alien and unwelcome noise, a sound you don't want to hear or be forced to act upon. A sound that makes you want to hide under the covers until it goes away.

Eventually, as the knocking persisted, I swung my legs out from under the duvet, rose and slid my feet into my slippers. In this ungodly hour beyond the dead of night a creeping chill crawled over my exposed arms and legs. I wrapped a dressing gown over my pyjamas, tied the sash securely, and exited my room. The green glow of the bedside clock read *04:55* and I wondered who might be abroad at this hour, at my door, and what mischief they might be here to make.

The stairs stretched downward before me, a long, dark chute leading to the unknown. At their base, the front door and its single lock was all that stood before me and the outside world. Right now, that didn't seem enough.

Two shadows hulked beyond the door, outlined by the obscure vision panel that formed the top half. They weren't moving, just standing there. I jumped as the knocking sound came again.

Here I was, on my own. My wife left me years ago, dragged to the grave by a broken heart. At forty-six, life shouldn't be over, should it? I'd never felt so desolate and alone.

I padded down the stairs on bare feet, put my head to the front door and listened. Whoever was out there wasn't talking. I said, "Hello?" and right then, *after* I spoke, I realised I'd left my phone, and all means of protection, upstairs. I recalled those days when my mind had been as clear as cut crystal, not befuddled by bourbon, but the halcyon days of my twenties and thirties were unfortunately long gone.

A young voice penetrated the glass. "Mr Richmond? Is that you?"

I frowned, startled. Yes, it was me, but who on earth was this young woman? "What do you want? It's early."

An obvious statement, but one I felt better for pointing out.

"Mr Richmond, we need to talk to you." A deeper, older woman's voice spoke up. "Please."

I couldn't figure out a reason not to, so unhooked the chain and unlocked the door. I pulled it open a crack, letting the cold air stream in. One look at the women outside told me they were strangers and that they shouldn't know me. The older woman was dark-haired, shivering, and in her thirties. The younger was clearly nervous, had scruffy blonde hair and appeared to be of college age. Maybe eighteen or nineteen.

I addressed the older woman. "Honestly, how could I possibly help you at this time of the morning? Are you hurt? Broken down?"

The younger woman answered. "I'm Sarah," she said. "This is my mum, Jayne. Thank you."

I blinked, taken aback. My daughter had been called Sarah, but she died a long time ago. Every mention of that name pierced my heart with frozen barbs. I coughed to gain a moment before answering. "Right, well, you're welcome. I'm Jack. What is it that you want?"

Sarah moved closer, holding my eyes as she climbed the step to my porch. "I want to tell you a story," she said earnestly. "I've come a long way to let you know. To put your heart at rest. I'm here to help."

I stared at them in the stark false light of dawn, at their fresh faces framed by a haze of cold vapours, the greying skies laden with storm-clouds above their heads, and wondered what I was letting myself in for. You see, call me crazy but I'd already decided to grant their wish. I don't know why. Maybe it was the early morning shenanigans, the surprise that caught me off guard—or maybe it was the mention of the young girl's name.

I couldn't refuse that.

I pushed the door wider and beckoned them in, waved them to continue down the long hallway and into the dark kitchen at the far end. I closed the door and locked it after them, feeling a turbulent mix of confusion, numbness and anxiety.

"Are you...alone here?" Sarah asked with surprise in her voice. "All alone?"

"Yes." I moved past them, not sure what she meant by that. I flicked the lights on and waved at the kitchen table. "Sit down. I'll switch the heating on and get us some drinks. Is coffee okay?"

"Perfect." Jayne, the girl's mother, rubbed her hands and exhaled a faint trail of fog from her mouth.

"Thank you," Sarah said.

I bustled for a few minutes, overflowing with questions, holding onto them with great difficulty. I placed the steaming mugs before the women and backed away, standing with my back to the kitchen radiator so that the burgeoning heat would soon start to warm me through.

"What is this story?" I asked Sarah.

"A tale of sorrow and heartbreak," she replied, looking down. "And one of ultimate kindness. Forgive me if I need to catch my breath along the way."

I focused on her serious face, captivated by the solemn and profound directness of one so young. Clearly, her teenage eyes had witnessed tragedy beyond their years; a fact that made me recall just how alone I was in this washed-out and merciless world.

"Go on and don't worry," I said, trying to put this stranger at ease.

*"It was one of those warm summer days that dawn with an eternal kind of promise,"* she began. *"You know the kind. Your spirits lift. Worries slough away like unnecessary skins. The whole day lies ahead of you, boundless, yours to attack. And when you're young—say seven, or so—the world is one big playground. No boundaries. No evil. Our eyes and hearts are full of excitement and adventure and endless, golden, untroubled days."*

I sipped my coffee, feeling a sense of warmth spreading through my body that emanated from her words, rather than from the heater at my back.

*"My brother and I had been allowed to catch the bus to the seaside accompanied by an adult. It wasn't far, just twenty minutes. He was thirteen and I was seven. We were trusted. That day, that beautiful, terrible day, we begged our mum and dad to let us go alone. Him and me. A trip to Scott's arcade, an ice cream at the Harbour Bar, fish and chips and scraps and a freshly-made donut from Emma's. That's all we asked. We wouldn't be too long. We wouldn't overstep our bounds. I could tell…I could tell from my mum's face…that letting us go hurt like hell. It cowed her, you know, made her fold inside. She didn't want to let us go alone but my brother was thirteen, I was seven, and we'd done the trip a*

*hundred times already. My dad said okay, and we walked off down the garden path. At the end, near the gate..."* she stammered. *"...near the gate...we turned and waved. We...waved goodbye."*

I held on to her every word, wondering why the old cracks in my soul were already starting to ache.

*"I saw my mum's face one last time. My dad was at the bedroom window, grinning. I'll never forget it. I so wish we hadn't left them alone that day. I feel so sorry for what happened to them."*

I plonked myself into a chair opposite her and sent a quick, questioning glance at her mother. Jayne only smiled in return, but the corners of her eyes were already full of tears and her mouth was drooping. I didn't understand. No doubt she'd heard this story before, but it was affecting her greatly. Even as I watched she shuddered, a look of fear sweeping across her face.

*"We caught the train that day, and rode it all the way to the coast, to the beach,"* Sarah went on, tears leaking down her face. *"It was so busy we had to stand the whole way. The heat hit hard when we disembarked. We headed straight for the beach, tired but still full of promise. I remember feeling so happy that my big brother wanted to spend the day with me, so grown up and full of love and life and expectation. It didn't get any better. But I was tired. The whole day was ahead of us. I asked my brother if I could cat nap, just for twenty minutes. I'd been awake for four hours and it was only ten a.m. He laughed and agreed, threatening to leave me behind for fun. He left me napping on a bench whilst he crossed the road to grab us a couple of ice creams and some slushies. It wasn't far, just a hundred yards. Before he went, I remembered saying that we couldn't miss the train back and made him promise to make sure we were on it. Above all, we didn't want to worry mum and dad any more than they already were. He left me in sight of the train station, on the beach, and I...never saw him again."*

I was so grateful that I was sitting down. My legs were jelly. My heart hammering. Her story was chilling me to the bone.

*"When I woke it felt later, much later. My brother wasn't back. I was stiff and cold. I had no watch, no money, nothing. I looked up, still drowsy and befuddled from sleeping, and there was a train at the station. A big one. I was filled with fear. How long had I been out? Was this the last train? Had my brother done as he threatened and left me behind as a cruel joke? I couldn't let the train go and, without thinking any more, ran and jumped aboard just as the doors were closing. I sat and I searched, and I hoped my brother was on board. I roamed the carriages. I soon realised that the journey home* should *be short, only this train kept on going. It never stopped."*

Sarah fixed me with a distressed stare. "Later, I realised it took me over one thousand miles to the south. Sheer across the country. So far from my parents that I would never see them again. I had no identification. I didn't know the name of my hometown, my province. I was herded into an orphan camp and, later, adopted by two incredible parents who brought me up as best as anyone could." Sarah turned to Jayne. "My Mum."

"It's not a story I've heard before," I whispered. "But it has some close similarities to one that I know. Why the hell are you telling me this?" A little anger slipped the guard I'd erected a decade ago. "Are you trying to hurt me?"

"I'm almost finished," Sarah said. *"I was adopted and allowed to keep my given name. I was so happy because it was everything that I remembered of my old life. Almost,"* she smiled. *"Because, you see, my new mum took the time to draw me a map based on my recollections. An act of kindness that lodged in my heart. I remembered things you see. Though I was a thousand miles away I never gave up hope, even at seven years old. I drew everything I recalled. The layout of our home. The shape of the twin lakes that lay twenty homes south of ours. The old pond to the west.*

*Old man Mason's tree—the biggest in the province—sitting proud in his front yard. I remembered the alley that ran alongside our home, the water tower to the north and the parkland to the west. It sat in my journal for years and I got on with life. But I never stopped searching...*" She held my eyes like a deathbed memory, like an unforgettable, life-changing experience that moulded the remainder of all the days of your life.

I saw her only through a blur of rolling tears.

"Sarah," I cried. "But how?"

She wiped her eyes and smiled. "I never stopped searching, Dad. *Never.* I never gave up on you. On Mum. On my good-for-nothing brother. Though I *still* don't know why he left me on my own that day." She smiled openly and expectantly.

How could I tell her? I searched hopelessly for the words. "Your brother, George, was hit by a speeding car as he crossed that road," I said, gritting my teeth to hold back turbulent emotions. "Carrying ice cream and slushies, he didn't see the car and the driver didn't see him due to the way the sun glared off the road. George died instantly. He hadn't taken anything to identify him to the authorities, so it was hours before they contacted us. And by then...you were gone too. Your mum, she held on for years. We did everything that we could to find you but, here, resources aren't good. In the end"—I cleared my throat—"in the end she couldn't go on without the both of you."

Sarah closed her eyes, sobbing. I was broken. Her stepmother was broken. We sat in the kitchen and held our mugs and cried as a rising dawn started to bleed crimson streaks across the horizon.

Finally, achingly, I reached out a hand and touched my daughter for the first time in ten years. I touched a hand I'd thought long dead and felt warmth the like of which I'd never expected to experience ever again. I wiped tears from my eyes and tried to speak.

"But how?" I stuttered. "It's been ten years. How did you find me?"

Sarah gathered herself and turned to Jayne. "This one's act of kindness," she said. "She never let me forget the sketch I'd made and, incredibly, took six months of earnings and bought a computer just so that I could start scouring Google Earth. It took me eight years," she said, closing her eyes in wonder. "Eight years of looking. Every week, day after day, I searched until I found something that I barely remembered. I scanned every patch of ground. Every village. If it hadn't been for the gift of the original sketch and then the computer, I would never have found my home."

I gasped, unable to speak. I rose so fast my chair fell over, and rushed around the table. I stood next to the daughter that I thought I'd lost and failed so long ago. So close now, I remembered her smell, her cheekbones, her sparkling eyes. I remembered everything I'd been trying to forget, and I felt renewed. My life that had been so hollow was now filled with an elation beyond all bounds. There were no words to describe my feelings.

Sarah leapt up, straight into my arms, grabbing me tightly. At first, I wondered if this was all a dream but then I found myself staring, both grief-stricken and deeply overjoyed, straight into the tear-filled eyes of her stepmother.

She'd brought Sarah up. Raised her from the age of seven, for over a decade. Back then, and ever since, and especially now, she'd always know her act of kindness might one day make her lose her daughter.

I held out a hand. Jayne smiled and rose to join us.

---

David Leadbeater has published more than 40 novels and sold over a million Amazon Kindle e-books. All 27 instalments of the Matt Drake series were international bestsellers and continue to top the charts. The first part of his 'Relic Hunters' series won the inaugural Amazon Kindle Storyteller award in 2017. For a chronological reading order of the Matt Drake, Alicia Myles and Disavowed series, please visit his website, www.davidleadbeater.com.

# CHRISTMAS GINGER

*By Debbie Young*

"Christmas tree, May Sayers?" Billy wrapped his arms across his chest for warmth as he stood on my doorstep. "I've just got one littl'un left that's a steal at twenty quid."

At the far end of my front path, his handcart of festive evergreens was blocking the pavement, its load much depleted since his visit the previous week. His assistant, a scruffy teenage boy, was nowhere to be seen, but that was not surprising as it was Christmas Eve.

Billy began to stamp his feet to boost his circulation. "I can bring it in and help you set it up, if you like, May."

It had been decades since I decorated a Christmas tree. In my younger days, I left it to my parents. Since retiring from my peripatetic career as a travel writer, I've spent my Christmases with my nephew and his family in Inverness. By the time I arrive there, his wife and daughter Sophie have already set their tree up. But this year, for the first time ever, a snowstorm in Scotland had scuppered my plans and I'd be spending Christmas alone in my cottage.

"Well, why not, Billy? It would give me something to do. I think my mother's old box of baubles is still in the cupboard under the stairs. While you bring it in, I'll put the kettle on. You look like you could do with a cup of tea to warm you up."

"Shall I add some mistletoe to your order?" Billy gave me a cheeky wink. "You never know when you might get lucky."

I fixed him with an old-fashioned look. "I'll give the mistletoe a miss, thank you, Billy."

Like me, Billy had never married. As he'd lived all his life in the village, the local girls of our vintage saw him more as a brotherly type than as husband material, and a naughty little brother at that. What miles I had put between us, pursuing my career far away from Wendlebury Barrow since we were at school together.

Once Billy had heaved the tree into my parlour, he set it up in front of the window. My wastepaper basket provided a makeshift pot, and he wedged it into position with a few bits of kindling from the hearth. I rewarded him with a cup of tea and a slice of the Christmas cake I'd bought from Carol at the village shop the previous afternoon, when I'd realised I'd be spending the festive period at home.

"I thought you finished selling your Christmas trees a week ago, Billy."

He replied through a mouthful of crumbs. "Aye, but I didn't have enough mistletoe to go round last week, so I'm dropping off some orders before I packs up for the season. I had just one little tree left over needing a good home. Then when I stopped in the village shop just now for a box of matches, Carol Barker told me your trip up north was off, so I thought I'd bring it down to you. You must be put out, now you won't be seeing that little cutie of yours."

As I stirred my tea, watching the whirlpool I'd created, I pictured the River Ness, feeling the pull of its waters as they rushed out to the Moray Firth on their way to the North Sea. When Sophie was little, I'd hold her hand on our riverside walks, nervous of her stumbling into currents that could so easily bear her away from me. I confess I was afraid of a British river—I, who had stood beneath the spray of the Niagara Falls, crossed the Zambezi on a rickety rope bridge, paddled down the Amazon in a canoe, all without a thought for my own safety. On my last few trips to Scotland, Sophie had felt too old to hold my hand, looping her arm companionably through mine instead.

"What's her name again? Suki, isn't it? Or Susie?" Billy was saying. Sophie had been spending her summer holidays with me since she became old enough to stay away from her parents for any length of time, so he'd seen her about the village. "What's up? You two fallen out?"

"You mean Sophie. And no, it's the weather that's keeping us apart, Billy. Inverness Airport is snowed in and unlikely to reopen for days."

"Why don't you just drive up there? Save all that hanging around at airports."

I sighed. He meant well.

"I'm afraid I don't have the stamina for such a long drive these days. It's the best part of a day's journey by car, even in midsummer. Besides, if the airport's closed, it's likely the A9 will be impassable."

Billy looked blank.

"Why? Do they park the planes on it when they're not using them?"

As Billy seldom leaves the parish and doesn't drive, he has only the haziest idea about long-distance road travel. Even locally, he refers to roads by their traditional names rather than the official road numbers: the Fosse Way, the Bath Road, the old London Road.

"The A9 would be the final part of my journey by car, heading north from central Scotland. It runs all the way from Falkirk to Scrabster Harbour on the north coast. It's a high road, very exposed, so prone to snowdrifts. At the roadside, there are poles to indicate the depth of the snow. Once it reaches a certain height, they close the snow gates until it's safe to drive again."

When Billy held out his empty cup in the direction of the teapot, I took the hint and refilled it.

"It's not like you to be so defeatist, May Sayers. What's wrong with the train? You're not short of a bob or two. Why don't you spend some of your money on a train ticket? You can get a train almost all the way from Land's End to John O'Groats. I've seen it on the telly."

My lips twitched into my first smile of the day.

"And get stuck in a train in a snowdrift? Have you never read *Murder on the Orient Express*?"

Billy chortled. "No, but I seen the film. So Hercule Poirot's not your type?" He leaned forward to prod my knee with a grubby forefinger. "But we all know who is, don't we?"

My cheeks began to burn, and not from the fire.

"Oh, for goodness' sake, Billy, that was decades ago, when he and I were both young, free and single."

He drained his cup and set it in its saucer on the coffee table with a clatter.

"Well, now you're both old, free and single. You sure I can't interest you in a bit of mistletoe just in case? I ain't got much left to get rid of before I can get home to my fireside."

I fished my purse out of my handbag and found a twenty-pound note to pay him for the tree.

"Well, if you hadn't stopped for tea, cake and gossip with every delivery, you'd have got home a lot quicker."

As he pocketed my payment, he frowned. "What sort of a scrounger do you take me for? I haven't had tea and cake at every stop. I had a smoked salmon sandwich at the vicarage, and very nice it was too."

He patted his round tummy before buttoning his ancient tweed jacket across it and rising to his feet.

"Why aren't you wearing an overcoat, Billy? Or at least a scarf, hat and gloves. You want to wrap up warmer at your age."

He guffawed. "You mean our age."

I followed him to the hall. As he opened the front door, a gust of icy wind made us catch our breath.

Billy braced himself to step out into the cold. "We'll be having snow ourselves before too long, you mark my words."

I took down from the hallstand a colourful stripey scarf, woven by an old Turkish lady in a tiny, rough cottage where I'd once spent the night. I wasn't keen on the colours, but I'd bought it to supplement the paltry fee she was charging for my accommodation. The scarf had hung on the hallstand ever since I'd brought it home, reminding me every day of the contrast between her home and mine.

As Billy turned to say goodbye, I looped the Turkish scarf about his neck.

"Merry Christmas, Billy."

I stepped quickly back inside before he could get the wrong idea. He'd never caught me at kiss-chase in the playground, and I wasn't about to let him start now.

His face lit up in delighted surprise.

"Why, thank you very much, May Sayers, that's most kind."

Tucking its ends inside his jacket, he bustled down my front path to retrieve his cart. As he headed off to finish his mistletoe rounds, he was still smiling.

And so was I. It was the first time all day that I'd heard someone say my name.

As soon as I'd closed the front door, I dragged my mother's old box of Christmas decorations out from the cupboard under the stairs. I'd have decorated my little tree faster if I hadn't stopped to reminisce about the origin of each bauble as I took it from the box.

These days, people think nothing of buying new decorations each year. I swear Sophie's mother throws hers out come January, because I've never seen their Christmas trees look the same twice. My parents kept every single bauble from year to year, protecting the wafer-thin glass with layer upon layer of newspaper. Unwrapping them now was like playing the children's party game of pass-the-parcel. Just like Mother used to do, I flattened each piece of newspaper as I took it off. At the end of the process, just as she did, I laid the pile of sheets back in the box, ready to receive the baubles back again on Twelfth Night.

Some of the newspapers dated back to the Second World War and were frailer than the decorations. A few of them were in foreign languages. I recognised the Egyptian newspaper in which I'd wrapped a ceramic ashtray I'd brought my parents from Cairo.

When I came home that Christmas, Mother and Father had been expecting me to settle down and marry Joshua, the boy next door—now the elderly gentleman next door. As I smoothed out the last piece of newspaper, I noticed the skin on the back of my hands was papery too. Back then, Joshua had beautiful hands, supple and bronzed from his active outdoor life. These days, they'd probably be as delicate as mine. But they'd still be Joshua's hands.

I'd had to break it to all three of them that my return was only temporary. Straight after New Year, I was due to take up a part-time office job at the British Embassy in Cairo. The post came with a nice bed-sitting room in a safe compound, where I could spend my free time writing. But the biggest perk of my new job had come the following March, when, serving drinks to guests at an Embassy reception, I got chatting to the visiting features editor of a British newspaper. Taking a shine to me, he commissioned my first column, which turned into a monthly spot. After a year, my track record with the newspaper made it relatively easy for me to secure a publishing contract for my first book. Its title was simply *Cairo*. It did very well and was to become the first in a series about ancient capital cities.

Meanwhile, Joshua continued to write me long and frequent letters, full of love and hope and expectation. To my shame, I replied sporadically and only by postcard, too caught up in my new career to think far beyond the vibrant, bustling city that was flooding my senses.

While I went on to travel the world, ever thirsty for new places and fresh faces, Joshua stayed in Wendlebury in the house where he'd been born. Before long, Edith, the pretty new barmaid at The Blackbird, caught his eye—and the rest of him followed. When Mother wrote to tell me ruefully they planned to marry, I dismissed the news. A whirlwind romance on the rebound wouldn't last five minutes. I hadn't been gone that long. How could he have found a replacement for me so quickly?

Eventually, I realised time passes more slowly in Wendlebury Barrow. But by then, I had lost him forever.

After I'd hung the last bauble on the tree, I placed the Egyptian newspaper on top of the pile in the box. The Arabic characters conjured up the scents and sounds of Cairo, the adrenalin that fuelled my solo outings, and the strange new tastes and textures I encountered in the local cafés and bars. I've long since forgotten any Arabic I once knew, but the shapes of the words were familiar old friends. I had plenty of memories from my travels to treasure besides those of my lost love.

If I couldn't be in Scotland for Christmas, I could journey there in my head as easily as I could to Cairo, to Athens, to Patagonia, and everywhere else I'd ever travelled for my career. All over the house, souvenirs prompted memories of my many destinations.

A watercolour of feluccas on the Nile hung just inside my front door; blue and white Chinese plates were displayed above the stairs; and the handwoven Persian rug I'd bought from its maker nestled beneath my feet in the front parlour. In my kitchen, I could sip mint tea from jewel-bright Moroccan tea-glasses and imagine myself back in the souks of Marrakech. Snacking on tapas from my Spanish pottery platter, bright with primary colours, I'd hear classical guitar tunes playing in my head.

One day soon, I must catalogue all of these things, so that when I'm no longer here to explain their origin and value, they'll still be understood and treasured. Sophie is to have my cottage when I'm gone. Not that I'm letting on, as I want her to go out and make her own way in the world first, but when it's hers, I'd like her to know what's what.

The same goes for my garden. Not that I brought many plants back from abroad—import and export laws are too restrictive. Most of my plants have come from the nearest garden centre at Slate Green. But after I inherited my cottage from my parents, I planted something to reflect every trip I'd made, from a Japanese flowering cherry to an Australian eucalyptus. It was how I made the garden my own.

Now, before I did anything else, I needed to clear away the tea things from Billy's visit. As I set the tray on the draining board in the kitchen, I lingered by the window for a moment, admiring my imaginative planting scheme. In my parents' day, the garden had been an uncluttered rectangle divided into strips for growing vegetables, framed like a sampler by the original dry stone walls. Now very little of the walls could be seen behind my flourishing trees, shrubs and perennials. I hoped they were holding up against the weather. Cotswold stone wicks up rainwater like a sponge, and in a cold snap, ice forms inside it. As the ice expands, it shatters the stone from within.

As far as I could see now, the walls were still intact, even the weaker patch where there had once stood a gate between our garden and Joshua's. When Edith married him, she made him block it up, because that was where he and I used to meet in our teens. We'd spend the lazy hours of our summers lying on our backs in his garden or mine, in the shadow of our raspberry canes or his apple trees, cloud-gazing by day, watching for shooting stars at night. At least, that's what we told our parents.

The first time I came home after their wedding, the fresh blond stone plugging the gap had seemed unnecessary and a little spiteful. When I complained to my father, he gave a wry smile, quoting Robert Frost: "Good fences make good neighbours".

Little did I know then that for years to come, Joshua would blow a kiss to every passing plane, just in case it was the one bearing me home. It didn't matter that I was always more likely to travel by train and ferry; it was his way of reaching out for me.

Those blond stones soon weathered to match the older part of the wall, thanks to Wendlebury's exposed position high on the rolling Cotswold hills. "When it's jacket weather down in Slate Green, it's overcoat weather up in Wendlebury Barrow," my father used to say. But I can still tell where the gate once was, even if no-one else can.

Not that it matters to Edith anymore, as she'd died the previous summer from a sudden heart attack. According to Carol, she fell to the floor like a domino as she was clearing away her tea things. She was gone before the ambulance arrived.

Now Joshua would be spending his first Christmas alone. Well, not entirely alone. Although he and Edith had not been blessed with children, since his parents died, his kind nephew had always invited the two of them for Christmas. At least Joshua could still get to his nephew's. There were no snowdrifts between Wendlebury and Bristol.

Closing the wooden shutters, I returned to the parlour to give myself a firm talking-to. I had plenty of food and drink in the house, and the radio, television and books to keep me amused. There was a great stack of logs and a wicker basket overflowing with kindling on the hearth. The fire in the wood-burner was glowing cheerfully, reflected many times over in the pretty baubles on my tree.

Of course, there were no presents under the tree. Mine would be under Sophie's tree right now, awaiting my arrival. I'd packed my gifts to her family in my suitcase three days ago, and there they would stay, waiting for when my flight could be rebooked.

Fortunately, my nomadic career has equipped me with a useful knack for turning disrupted plans into opportunities. Some of my best reports sprang from serendipitous events rather than from carefully choreographed journeys. My story on the great Kefalonian earthquake of 1953 came about only because my ferry to Patras had been cancelled, leaving me wandering the streets in the wake of this terrible natural disaster. As I stayed longer, exploring the island and beyond, I wrote about a community abandoning its village, which had been damaged beyond repair. The article was syndicated around the world.

Half a century later, it had another lease of life in a follow-up piece. When I returned to light a candle in what I presumed to be the abandoned tiny Greek Orthodox Church in the ruined village, I found a lantern still burning. Someone returns each day to keep the flame alight, and I tracked them down. Their simple faith boosted mine.

Now I switched on the radio to listen to the traditional carols from King's College, Cambridge. Singing along, I decided to do something constructive to lift my spirits. Whenever my travel plans were disrupted, I used to find it helpful to restore order to my immediate surroundings, perhaps by repacking my bag with immaculate precision, or by dusting my hotel room. As a traveller rather than a holidaymaker, I've stayed in plenty of places that had never seen a duster until I got there. I never packed a duster in my luggage, instead improvising with a headscarf. But I did always carry a candle and matches. Sometimes we have to ignite our own hope.

So, this Christmas Eve, I set about dusting. Before getting stuck in, I set up a reward for my labours: I poured half a bottle of red wine into my jam kettle, dropped in some slices of orange and lemon studded with cloves, stirred it with a cinnamon stick and sprinkled on dried ginger. After I'd set it on top of the wood-burner to warm, with duster in hand, I began to work my way through the house. Every time I finished a room, I topped up my cheery hand-painted Spanish mug, chosen for its festive reds and greens. I didn't dare risk the heat of mulled wine in my favourite violet Bohemian crystal wine goblet, even though it would have looked spectacular.

No-one has a cottage quite like mine. They're all different in these parts, built to suit the whim and the budget of whoever was first to live in them. Nor does anyone have the same vast collection of souvenirs of globetrotting scattered about the house. In the days when I made my living mostly from travel journalism rather than book commissions and royalties, other hacks on the circuit were dismissive of my penchant for souvenir-hunting. They thought it made me less professional. They took home only items that could be bought from airport duty-free shops. There was a saying among them, mutilating Samuel Johnson's famous dictum on London, that if a man was tired of duty-free, he was tired of travel writing. Perhaps they were right. None of my immediate peers stayed the course in travel journalism, nor did they graduate into writing books. I was glad to separate myself from that pack as soon as I was able to pay my own way to wherever I wanted to write about.

I pitied their wives (in those days the hacks were mostly men) and their children, who might reasonably expect gifts from wherever their daddy had been on his latest facility visit—those thinly-veiled bribes to write reports on hotels and resorts. Some of the men sneaked in last-minute gifts at the airport alongside the endless bottles of Calvados or ouzo or sake. Toblerones, the equivalent of fuel-station flowers in the gift stakes, don't count as thoughtful presents unless you're travelling from Switzerland.

I prided myself on never resorting to airport presents. The gifts I brought my parents, and later my nephew, then Sophie, were always carefully chosen from local craftsmen or women. Choosing Sophie's presents was fun—a pretty Black Forest dirndl; wooden clogs in the right shoe size from Amsterdam; a traditional hand-painted wooden Swedish Dala horse, as unique as a fingerprint.

But I bought far more for myself than for anyone else.

"More to dust!" my mother would mutter at every new item I brought home. My parents' cottage was always my base, as I never had a permanent home abroad. In those days, Mother was the one who did the dusting. Now I have to do it myself, I never mind. As I run the duster over each item, I admire it afresh, remembering with perfect clarity the moment and the place of acquisition. Some items need more delicate handling than others, such as an ornamental clamshell from Hong Kong, in whose open jaws lies a miniature carved landscape as creamy as the shell, complete with a lake, a river, a house and tiny Chinese people amid foliage daubed red and green. It's far too small for my duster, so I just blow it to dislodge any debris. Then the working water wheel dips into its painted river, spinning as if in a storm surge.

I can be as heavy-handed as I like with my chunky wooden carvings from the Caribbean. As bright as tropical fish, they look out of place in the pallid English light, but I love them all the same. Polishing my cobalt wooden parrot, I feel Bahamian sunshine burnishing my face.

Other items have been thoughtfully fortified by their makers against careless cleaners, dipped in resin or drenched in varnish. It's ironic that someone felt the need to embed my piece of Berlin Wall in protective plastic. And yes, it is genuine. I was there when the Wall came down. I stayed on in the aftermath, helping enterprising souls from both sides to collect fragments of communist concrete, as in their enthusiasm they prised it apart with penknives, hammers and bare hands.

"Good fences make good neighbours?" I murmured now, slipping the piece of Berlin Wall into my pocket. "I don't think so."

When I returned to the parlour, both the fire and the mulled wine were low. The heavy scent of spices and citrus hung in the air, melding with the sharp bite of pine. My hand slipped as I topped the jam kettle up from the rest of the bottle I'd left breathing on the hearth. I didn't mean to empty it, but why not?

I raised my next glass to the angel on top of the Christmas tree. Decades before, on a pavement in Durban, I'd watched a local boy with skin as dark as the sun was bright, conjure up this concoction of red and white beads. Cleverly twisting them into shape on fine wire, he was so intent on his craft that he seemed oblivious to the seductive view of the Indian Ocean across the promenade. I wondered what had become of him.

Then my focus slid sideways from my South African angel to its backdrop. Night had fallen while I'd been dusting. I'd closed the upstairs shutters as I'd left each room, but not the ones downstairs. I've always liked the Dutch custom of leaving your front curtains or shutters open after lighting-up time to share the warmth of your home with passers-by. Now a very gentle rain was drifting slowly down behind my tree-top angel, turned into flecks of glitter by the streetlight across the road. Except the flecks were falling too slowly for rain.

Those sparkly flakes were very definitely snow.

On the radio, the carol service had long since finished, and now I caught a snatch of the weather forecast:

"In the south-west of England, all non-essential travel should be avoided." There was a note of apology in the weatherman's voice. Perhaps he felt guilty at wrecking people's holiday plans. "Treacherous conditions…warnings of ice…" I wondered whether he'd obey his own instructions.

Would Joshua have arrived safely at his nephew's? Stepping over to the window, I pulled aside just enough branches of my Christmas tree to peer beyond my front path and around to Joshua's garden. The pool of light on his frosty lawn told me he hadn't gone away after all. He was holed up in his parlour, same as me, with only his memories for company.

My close proximity to the astringent scent of the pine needles was starting to make my eyes water, so I let the branches spring back into place. Then I opened the wood-burner to fling another log inside, refilled my tea glass, and settled down in my fireside chair to think.

In our childhood days, Billy had been notorious for playing knock-down-ginger. In this silly, selfish game, youngsters think it the height of wit to rap at an innocent neighbour's door and run away. Then they hide, staying just close enough to witness their victim's puzzlement on opening the door to Mr Nobody. Did the latest generation of tearaways still play that game? I'd seen no evidence. Doubtless they're too busy playing with their electronic gadgets to find such foolishness entertaining.

So I wondered whether, when Joshua heard a knock on his front door late on Christmas Eve, his first thought would be of Billy. Except Billy never left presents on people's doorsteps. Especially presents wrapped in vintage Egyptian newspaper.

Before Joshua could answer the knock, I darted back inside my house and closed my door as quietly as I could. The sharp trill of the telephone diverted me from ascertaining Joshua's reaction. As I picked up the receiver, I was still catching my breath.

"Merry Christmas Eve, Auntie May!" Sophie's sweet smile warmed her voice as she regaled me with the fun she and her friends were having in the snow. I was glad she didn't yet consider herself too old to build a snowman. Then she outlined the family's plans for Hogmanay. The New Year celebrations are so much more exciting in Scotland than they are south of the border in England, even if the revellers do need an extra public holiday on 2 January to get over them.

"She'll be writing to you in between times, May," I heard her mother call in the background.

"I'll look forward to that, my dear," I replied, though I knew full well that as the child was growing up, her letters were getting shorter and less frequent. Soon I'd be lucky to get so much as a postcard, but that's OK. Hadn't I done exactly the same in response to Joshua's letters?

Sophie's father was next on the line. "You will come as soon as you can, won't you, May?" Beneath his gruff voice, I could detect the plaintive plea of the little boy he'd once been. "And you can stay as long as you like now that you're retired."

"Yes, yes, of course, dear. Your delicious Highland air is just the tonic I need."

And to see their dear faces, of course.

"I'm saving a drop of my best Highland whisky to share with you, May. But hang on, is that your doorbell?" He sounded miffed to have a rival for my attention. Frankly, I was as surprised as he was.

"Indeed it is. I had better attend to it. I'll call you tomorrow, dear. Merry Christmas."

I set the receiver back in its cradle. As I made my way through to the hall, I steadied myself on the doorhandle. Through the small stained-glass window set into the front door, I could just make out a tall figure, slightly stooped.

My hands were shaking as I opened the door. To Joshua.

As he raised his cap and gave me a slight bow, a shy smile played beneath his still-handsome moustache.

"Miss Sayers, may I wish you a merry Christmas?"

He didn't need to ask my permission. As I stepped back and motioned to him to come in, I saw that in his other hand, he was clutching the Egyptian newspaper in which I'd wrapped my symbolic gift to him: my piece of the fallen Berlin Wall. The package was no longer a flat slab, but chunky and round. At least he wasn't returning my gift unopened. But what had he wrapped in the paper for me?

He stamped the snow off his stout shoes and hung his cap on my hallstand before following me into the parlour, where he offered me the package. My hand dropped slightly as I took it. It was much heavier than it looked.

"I hear recycled wrapping paper is all the rage these days, May." The familiar twinkle hadn't left his eyes. "You may open it now. I won't make you wait until after church on Christmas morning." Trying hard to sound casual, he seemed as nervous as I felt.

I sat down heavily in my fireside chair and set the package on my lap. Joshua remained standing in front of me.

I tried to contain my emotions as I peeled back the newspaper to reveal a lump of honey-coloured Cotswold stone, cold and rimy. When I gazed up at him for an explanation, he just smiled.

"The first of many stones I plan to remove to restore the dear old gate between our gardens." His eyes locked onto mine. "We can never go back to where we left off, May, but I believe it's not yet too late for us to harvest a little more precious time together. I do hope you agree."

I clapped my hand to my mouth, covering a smile broad enough to hurt my cheeks. I don't know why I, the unshockable seasoned traveller, said what I said next: "Well yes, of course, but whatever will the neighbours think?"

Joshua threw back his head and laughed, slapping his tweed-covered thighs.

"Oh, my dear May, does it really matter what anyone else thinks? Just allow me to assure you that your closest neighbour"—he tapped his chest—"deems your consent cause for celebration." He pulled a small glass flask of sloe gin from the sagging pocket of his trousers. "And tomorrow, let's spend Christmas Day together. The first of many special days that we might share."

As I nodded, loneliness slid from my shoulders like the snow from an Alpine chalet roof. I set his stone gently on the hearth, where it still lies today.

When he reached out his hands to pull me up from my armchair to face him, I wished I'd bought some of Billy's mistletoe after all.

---

Debbie Young writes warm, witty, feel-good fiction set in the rural Cotswolds, inspired by the village in which she has lived for thirty years. Her novels and novelettes combine original, surprising mystery plots in delightful settings with gentle romance, and each story is underpinned by subtle messages about tolerance and understanding. Books in both her series have been shortlisted for 'The Selfies', awarded by publishing industry news service Bookbrunch for the best self-published fiction in the UK—*Secrets at St Bride's* (first in the Staffroom at St Bride's series) in 2020 and *Springtime for Murder* (fifth in the Sophie Sayers Village Mystery series) in 2021. Debbie is a frequent speaker at events for readers and writers, a judge for various writing competitions, and UK Ambassador for the Alliance of Independent Authors.

# THE BEST LAID PLANS

*By Deborah Carr*

'This isn't the first time you've done it, though, is it?' Emma groaned, slapping the newspaper she was holding in front of her disinterested father's face. 'How could you humiliate us like that?'

He swiped the paper away with the back of his gnarled hand and glared at her, reminding her of one of the gargoyles that glowered down at them from the old municipal building in town. 'If people are ignorant enough to sell their belongings for less than they're worth, then why shouldn't I benefit?'

Emma took a deep breath and tried unsuccessfully to steady her rage. 'Because any decent human being would never be tempted to do such a thing.'

'That's rubbish and you know it. Now get lost and leave me in peace.' He took a swig out of his half-empty can and shook his head. 'You should be grateful I make enough money to keep this family going.'

She couldn't be bothered arguing that it was her and her mother who supplemented his meagre and very occasional income. She was sick of him and had had enough. It was bad enough that all their neighbours knew that Steve Page was a scheming trickster, but now some poor elderly woman, who she now knew lived only three streets away, had sold her story to the local paper telling them about her shameful father. Emma cringed as it dawned on her that a lot of her colleagues at work would read the story and know the depths her father stooped to. It was just too embarrassing.

Hearing her mother working in the kitchen, Emma went to join her. 'Why do you put up with him?' she asked, stopping to watch the tired, once-glamorous woman who was, as usual, standing in front of the sink peeling potatoes for his supper. 'He's not even nice to you anymore. He's not nice to anyone.'

Her mother gave her a sympathetic smile. 'He can't help it, love,' she said, making the usual excuses that Emma no longer believed. 'He's changed since his accident.'

Emma picked up a knife to help her mother prepare the supper. 'Come on, Mum. We both know that him being bumped on the head by a sandbag three years ago made no difference at all to his personality. He's lazy and corrupt and there's no excuse for screwing old ladies out of money. I don't care how many times you try and defend him, you'll never manage to persuade me that he's a nice person.'

Her mother stopped what she was doing and gave Emma an apologetic smile. 'I'm sorry.'

Emma shrugged. She knew it was pointless even having the conversation because nothing would ever change, but the thought that people would know how selfish he could be was mortifying. 'What about my colleagues at the office? I know some of them will have read the article. How am I going to show my face at work tomorrow?'

She watched her mother give her question some thought. 'Maybe they won't connect the two of you?'

If only that were true, Emma mused miserably. 'I think we both know that's unlikely. Most of them know you're my mother and at least half of them know you're married to him. Anyway, never mind me, what about you?'

Her mother finished peeling the potato in her hand and dropped it into the bowl of water in the sink. 'What about me?'

Emma couldn't believe her mother was being so calm. Was it because she had spent her entire adult life trying to ignore the trouble her husband regularly got himself involved in? Probably, Emma reasoned.

'I meant what about when you're serving locals at the café tomorrow. How will you cope if someone says something?' Emma pictured a couple of the less friendly women she knew visited the café most days. It worried her that they might pick on someone as gentle as her mum. The thought infuriated her.

Her mother shrugged her narrow shoulders. Guilt coursed through Emma. What was she doing adding to her mother's pain by ranting at her in this way? It wasn't her mother's fault that she had married someone who had turned out not to be the perfect man she had imagined him when they first met. According to her mother, he hadn't always been sly and devious.

Emma wasn't sure if that was the case though, especially as she had spent her entire life being let down by him. She thought back to when she was younger and had been given a lift home by the police because her father had forgotten to collect her from a netball match. She had insisted to her teacher that she was fine to walk home but had ended up waiting two hours until eventually two policemen patrolling the area offered to give her a lift home when it became dark and they stopped to check if she was alright. Instead of her father being apologetic to her for forgetting her while drinking with friends, he had given her a hiding for letting the police bring her to their house. Her mother had pacified the policemen by pretending she had been the one to forget Emma and typically her father hadn't taken responsibility for anything. Why should he do so now?

This last escapade of his was too much though. A frail pensioner, living alone and surviving on her pittance of a pension had been taken advantage of by a man not even in his fifties. He was disgusting, and Emma was determined he would pay the old lady back somehow. But how?

She knew her father well enough to be sure there was little point trying to reason with him. The only friends he mixed with were found in the same dingy pub as him each day at the end of their road, so they wouldn't be any use to her either. Her mother had learnt years before not to waste her limited energy bothering to stand up to him, so it was going to be up to Emma to do something about the situation.

She decided to wait until the following morning to try and find out what he had done with the porcelain ornament he had all but stolen from the lady. She set her alarm earlier than usual. Knowing that it was market day and the one time her father got out of bed early, she set to work making him his favourite slap-up breakfast. As he stepped through the kitchen doorway, Emma smiled in his direction and motioned for him to sit down at his place at the head of the table. She placed a full mug of the strong tea he loved in front of him. It was heavily laced with four heaped teaspoons of sugar, just the way he liked it.

'Blimey, to what do I owe this honour?' he asked, folding over a piece of buttered bread from the side plate and taking a large mouthful. 'I thought you hated me.'

'I was annoyed with you,' she admitted. 'But Mum explained to me that it wasn't your fault. I thought I could say sorry for having a go at you yesterday by treating you to your favourite meal. I don't have to cook it though, not if you'd rather I didn't bother.' She went to turn the cooker off, but he yelled angrily.

'Hey, steady on there, my girl. I was only making a remark. You carry on with that fry-up. I'm starving. I've got a lot going on today and I could do with this grub.'

She cracked three eggs on the side of the pan and as the whites of the eggs spluttered, she flicked them with the hot oil. Soon they were just how he liked them with the yolk soft and runny. Emma then transferred the eggs to a plate where she had already placed rashers of bacon, sausages, beans and a tomato.

'There you go,' she said, placing the gargantuan meal down in front of him. 'Enjoy your breakfast.'

Too greedy to be interested in asking any further questions, as she knew he would be once his attention had been taken by the food, Emma sat down opposite him with her bowl of cereal. 'So,' she said, 'market today, isn't it?'

He pushed another mouthful of egg and sausage into his mouth and, after a couple of chews, slurped tea from his mug before nodding.

'Do you still have that ornament you bought from the lady then?' she asked, giving him her most innocent smile as he stopped chewing for a second and gazed across the table at her. He didn't answer her question, but she knew he had been reassured by her innocent smile when he turned his attention back to his food and continued eating.

After a few moments, he dropped his cutlery noisily onto the bare plate, leant back and belched. 'You've done me proud with that lot. You cook almost as well as your mum.'

His table manners made Emma feel sick and reminded her why she had made excuses not to eat with him for so many years. She pushed her spoon around her now soggy cereal, having lost her appetite, and decided to try once more to find out about the old lady's property.

'I hope you managed to get its full worth when you sold it?' she asked feigning little interest.

He glowered at her. 'Are you still on about that bloody ornament?'

Emma shrugged. 'I'm just interested, that's all.'

He gulped down the remainder of his tea. 'I thought you said I was disgusting to get it in the first place. Why would you want to know what I've got paid for it?'

'Because I thought about what you said yesterday and realised I was wrong,' she fibbed. 'Anyway, you're always moaning to mum and me that we never take any interest in anything you do. Now that I am, you're moaning at me. I can't win with you, can I?' She hoped her indignant reaction might tempt him to want to appease her slightly and give her more information.

'All right, calm down,' he sighed. 'If you must know, I haven't sold the little treasure yet. It's with a mate of mine. You know, Sammy, with the auction house.'

'You mean the second-hand dealer?' she asked, wishing she could stop from baiting him quite so readily.

He mimicked her words. 'Snotty cow. Yes, him.'

'When's the, um, auction being held then?' She hoped she had time to come up with some sort of plan.

'In three days. Now, if you don't mind, I'm off. I don't want to be late today.' He stood up and, without pushing in his chair or bothering to carry his plate the couple of feet to the sink, he left the house, slamming the front door loudly behind him.

Emma kept her head down at work to avoid being caught in the small kitchen by any of the other staff. The last thing she needed was to have to answer any questions about her father's actions. Despite keeping to herself for the morning, she couldn't help overhearing pointed comments shot her way by some of her colleagues. Miserable and desperate to do something positive, she left the office as soon as the clock struck one and ran most of the way to Sammy's yard. She was determined to persuade him that the lady had been conned out of her ornament and that it should be returned to her.

'Don't be soft,' Sammy said, laughing in her face. 'Your dad would have a fit if I didn't sell it for him.'

'Well, at least let me pay you what he paid her for it,' she reasoned. 'Then you can tell him someone made you an offer.' When he didn't look convinced, she added, 'Or maybe you could say it was cracked or something, and you were forced to sell it to someone who made you an offer for it.' She sensed she was wasting her time but had to at least try to persuade the man to do the right thing.

Sammy raised his thick black eyebrows thoughtfully. 'Do you know your old man at all? He would have my guts if I screwed him like that. Nope, sorry girl, not a chance. I'm going to sell this like I agreed to do.'

'Thanks for nothing,' Emma grumbled, aware she had no choice but to pay the old woman a visit and see what damage control she could come up with once she got to her house.

She glanced at a large clock on Sammy's office wall and realised she didn't have time to do anything apart from returning to her job. The rest of the afternoon dragged and as soon as five o'clock came, Emma left to go to the woman's home. She found the right house easily and knocked on the dusty, green front door. Emma's heart raced as she waited for the door to be opened. Recognizing Mrs Slattery by her photo, she took a deep breath and explained who she was.

'I'm so sorry,' Emma said once she had introduced herself. 'I did try to get your precious ornament back for you, but I didn't manage to, I'm afraid.'

She watched the old lady's lined faced and couldn't believe it when her mouth drew back into a wide smile for a few seconds before the woman threw back her head and laughed.

'I don't understand,' Emma said, confused by the reaction.

'Dear girl, don't fret so,' the lady said, wiping her eyes with her palms. 'I only realised after I'd sold that story that the ornament your father bought off me wasn't the original.'

Emma frowned. 'I'm sorry? What do you mean?'

The lady placed a hand on Emma's forearm. 'My son, Peter, came to see me last night, as he does most days. He had read the article in the paper and told me that I'd made a mistake.'

'Mistake?'

'Yes. You see the jug I sold to your father wasn't the original piece.'

'Pardon?' Emma couldn't believe what she was hearing. Did this mean that her father hadn't fooled the woman after all?

Mrs Slattery leant closer and lowered her voice. 'You see, I bought one years ago. Dead proud I was of my purchase. Only my son told me it was a fake. I was so upset by my mistake that for my next birthday he treated me to the real thing. Bless him. He's always been a good boy. Anyway, I kept them both. It always amused me to see them standing near to each other. They're very similar, you see, and my son says that to the untrained eye the fake one could be mistaken for an original.'

Emma sighed with relief. 'That's brilliant! I'm so happy that he didn't manage to fleece you.'

The woman sighed. 'To tell you the truth, I did feel a little bad for your father at first. Especially when it occurred to me that he had paid me over the odds for the fake. But then Peter explained that your father has spent years conning others like me and he reckoned he deserved to be caught out for once.'

Emma giggled. Then she saw the twinkle in the old lady's eyes and the thought of her father's face when he discovered that instead of tricking someone, the trick had been played on him, tickled her enormously. She began laughing at the poetic justice of what had happened to him. 'I couldn't agree with you more,' she said, when she managed to stop laughing.

Emma left Mrs Slattery's home happy to know that although this outcome would not help lessen her embarrassment with her friends and work colleagues, at least they would forget about it long before her father was able to do so.

She only wished she could be a fly on the wall when Sammy broke the news to her father.

---

Deborah Carr writes historical fiction for Harper Collins, One More Chapter. She is the USA Today bestselling author of *The Poppy Field* and the 'Mrs Boots' series, inspired by the life of the woman behind the Boots empire. She lives with her husband and three rescue dogs on the island of Jersey and also writes contemporary romance series set on the island as 'Georgina Troy'.

# DETENTION

*By Emma Robinson*

It was only stubbornness that had kept Laura here this last week; a refusal to accept that everyone had been right.

Despite the cold February weather, the classroom was hot and unpleasant. Partly because of the archaic heating system which was centrally controlled and partly because of the twenty-eight bodies which had just piled out of it in a cacophonous mass. Laura took a deep breath and started to clear the detritus left behind: pencil shavings, balled-up paper and forgotten pens and rulers. On top of the bookshelf beside the whiteboard, she found a paper aeroplane with a blunted nose, poorly fashioned from the worksheet that had taken two hours to create on Sunday while her friends were out at the pub. She snatched it up and shoved it in the waste bin she was carrying around. What was the point of any of it?

The classroom door pushed open followed by a red head and grubby shirt collar. 'Can I go now?'

In her eagerness to release the rest of them, she'd forgotten the student she'd sent out into the hallway. Now there was the problem of what to do with him. 'Just sit down, Mitchell. I'll speak to you when I'm ready.'

Mitchell threw his too-long legs under a desk in the back corner. As far away from her as it was possible to get. Scowling downwards at the desk, he started to pick at a hole in its corner which may have been there for years or might have been started in her lesson just this afternoon. The relentless click of his fingernail on the exposed wood was torture, but she didn't have the energy to tell him to stop. Tactical ignoring. That's what the lecturer in the behaviour management seminar had called it last week. 'You can't take on every small piece of bad behaviour or you'll never get through the lesson.'

Obviously, there was no way she could have tactically ignored Mitchell's outburst this afternoon. Ten minutes before the end of the lesson. So near to the finish line. On the home stretch, rounding up their learning about conjunctions. For the last three months, she'd tried so hard to make their lessons interesting and enjoyable. Had even sat up late last night making individual bingo cards with connectives on, thinking it would be fun. And look how they had repaid her. Was it any wonder she was so upset?

It wasn't as if she had even seen it coming. Writing Liane Patterson's ideas onto the thought shower on the whiteboard, Laura had had her back to the class for a matter of seconds, before Mitchell's roar made her spin around in time to see him lurch forwards towards Katie Lewis, desk scraped forwards by his thighs, the chair clattering backwards onto the floor.

Even now, she said a prayer of thanks to whoever the god of trainee teachers was that Mitchell's flailing fist hadn't made contact with Katie. Laura wasn't even supposed to be on her own with a class yet, but there were so many staff off at the moment that there were no qualified teachers spare to sit at the back of her room. The volume of her voice had surprised even her. 'Mitchell Jennings! Get out! Now!'

As he'd left the room, he hadn't even bothered to lower his voice when he called her a 'stupid cow, anyway.' Twenty-seven pre-teen faces had whipped round to look at Laura to see what she was going to do.

From the moment she'd applied for the teacher training course, Laura had been determined not to be one of those who shouted at the kids. Having experienced first-hand the unpleasantness of booming male and screeching female teachers at her own comprehensive school—never at her, she'd always been one of the good kids—she'd been determined to be firm but fair. It was almost funny how many preconceived ideas she'd had before actually standing in front of a class of disengaged, disinterested 11-year-olds, intent on testing her mettle and seeing how long it would take to make her shout or cry.

It was that advert's fault. *Those who can, teach.* They'd been in the cinema to watch some god-awful action film—she couldn't even remember what it was called—but she'd spent most of it thinking how bored she was. Not just with the film: with Tom, with her job, with the flat. Before the film trailers, there had been an advertisement for people to train to become a teacher. On the screen, four metres high, a woman about her age was pointing out the metaphors in Sonnet 116, *Love is not love where it alteration finds.* The children seated in front of her, in neat rows of clean modern desks with their smart uniforms, tidy hair and perfect teeth, were rapt. *I could do that,* she'd thought. *I* want *to do that.*

Almost everyone she cared about had told her she was crazy. Even her mum and dad, who had always supported everything she'd wanted to do from being the first in her family to go to university, to travels in South America, to taking a low paid admin job in marketing when she returned. Even they had seemed hesitant when—after six years and several promotions—she'd given in her notice as UK Marketing Manager and taken out a student loan to retrain as an English teacher. Still, they'd smiled and told her that they were proud of her whatever she chose to do.

Her friends had been less tactful. 'Are you actually off your actual head?' Heidi had looked at her as if she'd told them she planned to bungee jump off the Grand Canyon. Charlotte had been gentler, but no less surprised. 'You know that you'll have to take a massive pay cut, right?' Tom had merely laughed at her. 'No way have you got the patience for that.' It had been the beginning of the end for their relationship, the death knell on which had been rung when she could no longer hop on a plane for a last-minute break because she couldn't afford it and could only go away in the more-costly school holidays now, anyway.

This was what she wanted to tell Mitchell as he sat there with a thunderous face, the beginnings of acne around his hairline. She had given up so much to do this job. In her old life, she used to speak to a conference table full of director-level suits. Take clients out to lunch at beautiful restaurants. Drive a car which had cost more than she would make in two years of teaching once she was qualified. If she ever got that far.

Mitchell stopped picking at the table for a moment. 'Can I go now? You're only allowed to keep us for 30 minutes, otherwise you have to call my mum and ask for permission.'

She still had no clue what she was going to say to him. 'I am well aware of the rules, Mitchell. And you've been here for the sum total of'—she looked up at the clock on the wall, the arch enemy who always seemed to go too fast or too slow for the lesson she had planned—'seven minutes.'

Mitchell tutted loudly and kicked the legs of the chair in front with the Nike trainers she had only just realised he was wearing in contravention of the school uniform rules. *Tactically ignore.*

Under one of the desks in the front row, she found two empty crisp packets and a balled-up party bag of M&Ms. Who had been sitting there? She checked the required seating plan on the wall which had been changed at least five times that term as she'd worked out which kids talked, hated or disrupted each other. What a surprise: Bradley Smallman. Now there was a misnomer for the lump of a lad who had a pretty good side-hustle selling chocolate bars on the Year 7 playground. How had he managed to eat all of that in a one-hour lesson without her noticing?

It wasn't just him. Every hour with this class had been a slog. Since taking over their English lessons back in November, she'd spent more time trying to keep them in their seats than explaining about sentence structure. There was no way of getting through to them: if she was strict, they would laugh at her behind their hands; if she made a joke, they looked at her like she was the most pathetic excuse for a human being they'd ever encountered.

And this was only a Year 7 class. It was only going to get more difficult. What happened when they gave her a Year 11 class? Sixteen-year-olds in their last year of school before they were let out into the world. Boys who towered over her with their gruff voices, wisps of facial hair and a pungent mixture of perspiration and body spray. Girls with their fake nails, skirts rolled over at the waistband, and heavy earrings that spent more time in the school office confiscation box than they did in their ears. If she couldn't manage a class of eleven-year-olds, that lot would eat her alive and throw the bones into the Biology Department's hazardous waste bin.

There was a thud as Mitchell slammed his elbows onto the desk and dropped his forehead into his palms. The theatrics were for her benefit. Under his breath he muttered, 'This is stupid.'

Mitchell had been particularly difficult. According to the list she'd been given by the Special Needs Coordinator, he had no diagnosed learning difficulties; but he'd barely managed to write more than a couple of untidy misspelled sentences in the three lessons a week he'd spent with her. Half the time, he looked like he was about to fall asleep, cheek down on the desk, looking sideways at his exercise book as he doodled on the page. She'd called home to speak with his mum. All she'd got for her trouble was a dismissive, 'Well, he's a boy, isn't he?'

Today's lesson had been her last with this class; her last day in the school. As part of the training programme, she was due to start at a second placement school after the February holiday. Maybe this was a good point at which to call it quits. She'd tried—she'd really *really* tried—but it was just too hard. Whatever it was that good teachers had, she didn't have it. Enthusiasm and good intentions weren't enough. This weekend, she'd make a final decision, then call her course supervisor on Monday. Maybe her old boss would consider taking her back?

First, though, she needed to deal with Mitchell. Still holding the waste paper bin, she pulled out a chair from the desk next to his and sat down. This was the moment she should give him a lecture about his behaviour, his choices, where he wanted to go in life. All of that, though, required more energy than she had left in the tank.

Instead, she told him what was really bugging her. 'The thing is, Mitchell, I think I have always been kind to you and showed you respect. That's why I'm sad that you…'

She hadn't even finished her sentence when he leapt up, arms in the air like a football player arguing with a referee. 'It wasn't my fault! It was her! It was Katie! She wouldn't let me sign the card! It's not fair. Why am I the one in detention? It's her fault!'

Laura rubbed at her forehead. She had the beginning of a headache and absolutely no clue what he was talking about. 'Slow down, Mitchell. What card? What do you mean?'

He flicked a hand in the direction of the teacher's desk at the back of the classroom. At her leaving drinks, Laura's former colleagues had joked about her 'sitting at the teacher's desk' with her 'teacher's coffee'. Little did they, or she, know that she would never actually get to sit at that desk during lessons when she had to circulate the classroom constantly, playing whack-a-mole with kids turning around to chat to their mates.

'It's there. On your desk. Katie made it.'

Sure enough, there was something on her desk. Laura recognised the yellow card which she'd bought out of her own funds to display their work. It had been inexpertly folded in half and there was bubble writing on the outside, every letter written in a different colour sparkly gel pen: THANK YOU MISS ROBERTS.

Laura swallowed and opened the card. Inside, she recognised Katie's writing across the middle. THANKS FOR TEACHING US. The rest of the card was filled with the signatures of the rest of the class. Some were just a name: Ben's was smudged, Oliver's so tiny you needed a magnifying glass, Janie's had a heart as the dot of the *i*. Others had left little messages: Sorry we were a pain! Thanks for the stickers! Come back and see us!

The words blurred and she couldn't look up at Mitchell when he spoke to her, though she could hear the squeak of him kicking one trainer into the other. 'That's why I got mad. She said I couldn't sign it. She said you didn't like me anyway. Everyone else signed it. I wanted to sign it.'

She could hear him whipping himself up to another angry outburst. Someone needed to help him with that. Teach him how to manage disappointment in a way that didn't involve his fists. She turned to him and held out the card. 'Would you like to sign it now? I'd love it if you would.'

He stopped kicking at his own foot and looked up, she could almost see in his face the stubbornness and the eagerness wrestling for control. His shoulders let go of their anger and he nodded, held out his hand to take it.

'Yes, please, Miss.'

---

Emma Robinson is the bestselling author of *My Husband's Daughter* and other women's fiction novels. She also blogs about the funny side of parenting and has contributed to podcasts such as 'Funny Women'. Whilst her early novels are humorous, her recent work focuses on emotional themes and these novels are both heart-breaking and life affirming. Emma enjoys writing stories which explore the power of family and friendship in the most challenging circumstances. Emma currently lives in Essex with a husband, two children and a small black dog.

# NEXT DOOR

*By Graham Brack*

The removal lorry pulled away and Sylvie and Martin were left to begin a new phase of their lives.

Leaving the old house and their friends had been difficult for the children but they had understood that Daddy's job had changed and he needed to be nearer to his new work. Moreover, the new house was bigger, and had a larger garden to play in, circumstances that filled Sylvie with the hope that her increasingly fevered attempts to obtain a puppy would finally bear fruit.

Sylvie pulled herself away from the gate and wandered inside, so Martin followed suit. He was often described as "Sylvie's shadow", wanting to be independent but feeling happier when he tagged along behind his big sister who was, as she proudly declared, nearly ten. She had been "nearly ten" since the third day after her ninth birthday, but now it was literally true.

Her parents were both busy. Daddy had decided that the time to paint the lounge ceiling was before they got used to it, so all their furniture was covered in dust sheets and she was immediately ordered out, while her mother flitted from room to room fitting sheets and blankets on the beds.

'Don't get under my feet, Sylvie!' she ordered. 'Why don't you go out and play?'

Playing is never as much fun when you have been ordered to do it, but there seemed no other option, so Sylvie picked up a ball and invited Martin to join her for a game of catch. Since Martin was only six, this was a contest that favoured her, except that he could not throw reliably either, so she found herself sprinting in all directions to retrieve the ball. They had instituted a rule that it did not count as a drop if the ball did not land within two steps of where the receiver was standing, but while that made the scoring more equal it did not improve Martin's throwing.

It was only a matter of time before the ball disappeared over the fence to bring their game to a halt, and that time turned out to be around four minutes.

'Oh, Martin, you always do that!' Sylvie screeched in frustration.

'Sorry,' Martin replied. 'It slipped.'

In their previous home they had been lucky to get the ball back at all. The old lady there regularly lectured them about her entitlement to take a knife to the ball on her property before reluctantly returning it after a day or two, so Sylvie looked around for something else to play with. She had a bicycle but the garden was not that large and Martin could not join in. Similarly, she had roller skates and there was a long driveway to the garage, but Martin had none. He optimistically produced a cricket bat, only to be reminded by his sister that they no longer had a ball, unless he could find the old, bare tennis ball they normally used. Martin rummaged in a crate for a while before conceding that he could not, and flopped on the back step with a profound sigh.

Sylvie felt a responsibility to keep her younger brother entertained, but she had no idea how. She was still thinking about it when she heard a voice.

'Hello, young lady!'

Glancing up she saw a man's upper body at the fence, and an arm was swiftly raised so that she could see their ball.

'Is this yours?' said the man.

Sylvie nodded.

'And what's your name?' he asked, so Sylvie told him, introducing Martin for good measure.

The man smiled, though only the lifting of his cheeks proved the point, since the lower half of his face was wrapped in a thick white beard. He gently lobbed the ball back over the fence.

'There you are!' he said. 'See you later!'

Over the next few days, the ball crossed the fence more than once, and each time it was thrown gently back after a little while. Mindful of her mother's instructions about speaking to strange men, Sylvie had shared her encounter with their neighbour, to be told that she mustn't bother Mr Robinson, though she could speak to him if he spoke first.

From the bedroom window, Sylvie could sometimes see Mr Robinson as he busied himself in the back garden. He had a favourite chair there where he sat to read a book or the newspaper; always the right hand one as she looked at them, never the one on the left. The garden was tidy but not immaculate; he did not spend enough time gardening to make it prettier, she decided, not failing to notice his resemblance to one of the gnomes that guarded the short curving path to the shed. Maybe that was what he was—a professional gnome or gnome model.

There came a day that was to change a great many things. Sylvie had seen Mr Robinson in his garden while they were playing but now he had vanished from sight. Martin had found the tennis ball and they were playing cricket when Martin unexpectedly managed to hit the ball and sent it over the fence in a steepling arc. The problem was that she did not hear the gentle plop of ball hitting earth, but rather the dull clunk of ball on old man. She instinctively ran towards the back door as if to demonstrate that she was no part of the cricket match when she was interrupted by Mr Robinson's voice.

'That was some hit, young Martin!' he chuckled.

To her surprise, he was not angry. If his cheeks were red, that was because they often were.

He held the ball out towards them.

'I'm sorry,' said Sylvie.

'Sorry? What for? You didn't mean to hit the ball over the fence, did you?' he grinned.

'No. And it wasn't me anyway. It was Martin,' she added, pointing at the guilty party to reinforce her innocence.

Their mother must have been watching from the kitchen and came out, if only to provide assurance of punishment to a potentially irate neighbour.

'I'm sorry if they're a nuisance…' she began.

'Not at all, not at all!' Mr Robinson replied. 'Children have to play somewhere, and the streets aren't safe these days. If their ball goes over the fence again, I'm very happy for them to come round and collect it themselves. I'm sure they won't damage anything deliberately.'

'Isn't that nice of Mr Robinson? Say thank you nicely, children,' said Mother.

'Thank you,' said Sylvie obediently.

'Thank you nicely,' added Martin.

The test, of course, came on the next occasion that the ball crossed the fence. After some deliberation, Sylvie decided to put the invitation to the test and carefully opened the side gate to Mr Robinson's garden, found the ball, and managed to escape without being eaten or turned into a toad.

It could not last, and the day came when Sylvie entered the garden to find that the ball was not immediately visible, though, after a brief inspection, she suspected that the decapitated gnome lying on its side might indicate where the ball had gone. With much trepidation she picked the gnome up and tried to fix it by pushing the head back in place, but the break was not a clean one and she had to admit defeat. Being an honest and well brought-up girl, she felt the need to confess what had happened to Mr Robinson. Picking up the gnome she carried it to the back door and knocked.

'Hello, Sylvie,' said Mr Robinson, squatting to bring his eyes down to her level. 'What can I do for you?'

Wordlessly, Sylvie put the gnome's head in his hand and bit her lower lip to stop it trembling.

'Did your ball hit it?' he asked.

Sylvie merely nodded.

'Well, there's no harm done. I'm sure you didn't do it deliberately. Accidents happen.'

Sylvie could not doubt the last two propositions but was not sure that she could assent to the first.

'We're sorry,' she whispered.

Mr Robinson put his hand on her shoulder. 'Don't be. There's no need.' He lowered his voice confidentially. 'I never much liked the wee fellow anyway.'

Sylvie could not resist a smile at this.

'But you did the right thing owning up. Honesty is the best policy, even if it isn't always the comfortable one.'

Sylvie was so surprised at this display of reasonable behaviour from an adult that she mentioned it over the dinner table. When she was brushing her teeth, she caught a little of the discussion her parents were having downstairs.

'Is he safe with the kids? You read such things…'

'Of course he is, Brian. He's just a nice, lonely old man. And you know what he's going through.'

At Sylvie's insistence, Mr Robinson was invited to her birthday party. He came, bringing a small present, and had a cup of tea with her mother in the kitchen. If the other children were surprised to see him, they said nothing. Perhaps they thought he was her grandad, she supposed, although she already had two of them, and neither was as nice as Mr Robinson. He did not stay long, but ruffled her hair as he left and called her "Princess" which she quite liked.

A few months later, she stood on tiptoe to see over the fence, and saw Mr Robinson in his usual seat. He wasn't reading, just staring into space. As she called and he turned to her, she could see he was wearing a tie, which was unusual, and a dark suit.

'Are you all right?' she asked solicitously.

'Oh, I'm fine in myself,' he answered. 'Just having a wee moment.'

She had no idea what he meant but he forced a smile.

'All the better for seeing you, Princess. Tell me what you've been doing.'

She launched into a description of her school day, together with her appraisal of the various teachers with whom she interacted, their faults and foibles.

'What's your favourite subject?' Mr Robinson demanded.

'English,' she replied at once. 'I love stories.'

'Don't we all? Being able to tell a good story is a great gift.'

'I'll write you one,' she responded impulsively, convinced that he would be a good audience for her efforts.

'I'd like that,' he smiled. 'Will it have bears in it?'

'I don't think so,' she replied gravely. 'I'm not fond of bears.'

He laughed. It was good to see, she thought.

'Well, whatever the story is, I'm sure it'll be wonderful.'

She ran indoors to start work, but her mother grabbed her as she ran through the kitchen.

'I hope you haven't been bothering Mr Robinson, especially now.'

'I'm no bother,' she protested. 'He said he'd like me to write him a story.'

Her mother relaxed her grip. 'He's had a nasty shock,' she explained. 'He's probably quite sad.'

'Why?'

'Because Mrs Robinson died last week and she was being buried today.'

'Mrs Robinson? Who's Mrs Robinson?'

'His wife, of course.'

'I've never seen her. I didn't know he had a wife.'

As she delivered the story a day or two later, she felt she had to say something.

'I'm sorry Mrs Robinson died,' she said.

'Thank you, Sylvie. That's kind of you.'

'I never saw her.'

'No, she'd been unwell for a long time. But she saw you.'

'She did?'

'Oh, yes. You see that window up there?'

'With the cream curtains?'

'That's the one. That's our bedroom. She used to sit by the window and sometimes she told me she'd seen you or Martin in our garden. It cheered her up to see children.'

'Do you have children, Mr Robinson?'

'No, I'm afraid we don't, Sylvie. I wish we had, but it wasn't to be.'

'What was Mrs Robinson like?' she asked.

If he was surprised by the question, he quickly recovered. 'She was beautiful. When I met her, I couldn't take my eyes off her hair. It was golden and wavy. And she was a wonderful dancer. When we went out, I just knew all the other boys were looking at her and thinking how lucky I was.'

'Was she a Princess too?'

'Oh no, Sylvie. You're my Princess. She was my Queen.'

Sylvie was very content with that explanation.

As time passed, Sylvie became less interested in play, but still visited Mr Robinson. Almost every Saturday when Martin was playing football, she went next door and told Mr Robinson about her week. It was, she thought, strangely like a conversation of equals. Somehow he understood her in a way that one's parents never can. When she only got a B in English, he dissected her essay with her and pointed to areas she could do better next time; he taught her a couple of mnemonics that he had learned at school; he allowed her to draw him for an art project.

He was so easy to talk to, thought Sylvie. She found herself discussing things that had previously seemed very private.

'Why are people mean?'

'Has someone been unpleasant to you, Sylvie?'

Sylvie nodded. 'There are a couple of the girls in my class who keep telling me I'm plain and I ought to make more of myself or I'll never get a boyfriend.'

Mr Robinson chuckled. 'Believe me, Sylvie, you'll get a boyfriend. Someday you'll have more than you want. But aren't you a bit young for a steady boyfriend now?'

'I don't want to be engaged or anything. But it's good to have someone to go out with.'

'Yes, it is,' agreed Mr Robinson, 'but it doesn't always have to be the same person. And remember that while we're sitting here talking like this, somewhere there's a lad saying the same thing. All you have to do is meet up and you'll both be happy. You see, Sylvie, if you don't really want a boyfriend why should it upset you that you don't have one? I'd say those girls are trying to grow up a bit too fast. Being an adult isn't all it's cracked up to be, you know.'

'Mum won't let me use make-up.'

'Good for her. You don't need it.' Mr Robinson pointed at the chair she was occupying. 'Why do you think that chair is painted?'

Sylvie shrugged. 'Was it ugly?'

'Well, a bit scratched and battered. They were sound chairs, but over the years they'd lost their looks, so I painted them. The same thing can happen to people, but until it does, don't worry about make-up. You don't need any decoration.'

A couple of years later, they were having a similar conversation, but this time about boys. Sylvie had gone out with a boy who, according to his friends, had made unflattering remarks about her afterwards.

'Why did he need to do that?' she wailed.

'Well, first, young lady, you don't know that he did. It may be just talk. Ask him outright. If he said it, then he isn't fit to be your friend, but you'll decide that for yourself. If he didn't say it, then he may need to think about his own friends.'

'Why are boys so immature?' she snapped.

Mr Robinson considered for a moment. 'Being adult brings lots of responsibilities,' he decided. 'Who can blame anyone wanting to put that off as long as they can? Girls can't avoid it as easily. They're expected to look after their wee brothers and sisters and learn how to run a house of their own. Things are changing, and that's good. Why shouldn't girls become engineers or pilots if they want? If I had a daughter, I wouldn't want her to face any more barriers than a son.'

'I'd much rather be a boy. I can't think of one good thing about being a girl.'

'Oh, I can!' said Mr Robinson. 'Handbags. There's only so much you can get in your pockets.'

He smiled, and Sylvie laughed.

'What were you like as a boy?' she asked.

'Me? Oh, I was as immature as the rest of them, I suppose.'

'Have you got any pictures?'

Mr Robinson scratched his head, and then levered himself out of the chair and walked through to the lounge, rubbing his hip as he did so, returning after a few moments with a wedding photograph.

'That's the youngest one I have, I think.'

Sylvie inspected it closely. 'Goodness, you're very different.'

'It was over fifty years ago, Sylvie. Of course I was different. It'd be rather sad if I'd looked like this then.'

'Mrs Robinson is really pretty.'

'Oh, she was quite a looker. Especially in a mini-dress.'

Sylvie was quite shocked. 'In a mini-dress?'

'Ah, now, I see where you're coming from. You can only think of her as an old woman. But whenever you see an old person, Sylvie, remember that they were like you once. Some youngsters like to make fun of old timers. They may have trouble getting out of a chair now, but they may have been a fabulous dancer at your age. I was quite a footballer in my youth, you know. If I tried it now, everyone would laugh.'

'I'd never make fun of you, Mr Robinson.'

'I know. But I also know I'd be more hurt if you did it than anyone else I know, because you're a very understanding young woman. It would be thoughtless, and I don't think you'd ever do anything without thinking.'

The day came when Sylvie was leaving for university. The excitement of her future was so great that she failed to realise how difficult her departure was for her parents and, in particular, for her younger brother, who would be deprived of the person with whom he most enjoyed arguing.

There was, however, one person that Sylvie was prepared to admit that she would miss, and she was sufficiently self-assured by this age to believe that Mr Robinson might feel the same way about her.

She tapped on the back door, and Mr Robinson presently answered. He was growing older, and perhaps he was a little less cared-for than had been the case before. Sylvie's mother had taken to delivering a Sunday lunch to him each week because she was worried that he was living on microwaved dinners or tinned food.

'So this is it?' he said, and produced a resigned smile.

'Yes, I'm off. But I'll be back for a reading week before you know it.'

'That's good. Well, enjoy yourself and learn everything you can, because you'll never get another opportunity like this. And don't let what other people get up to steer you off your course. Live your life, not theirs.'

Sylvie nodded, then, realising that she was about to cry, impulsively jumped forward and hugged Mr Robinson tight so that his head was over her shoulder and he could not see her tears until she had flicked them away with a finger.

'I'll make you proud of me,' she promised.

'You already do,' he replied. 'But it's not me you need to impress. Do it for your Mum and Dad.'

She nodded, and turned to walk away, circling to wave one last time.

'I'll keep an eye on Martin,' Mr Robinson said.

She had been at university for a little over four weeks when her mother rang to tell her that she had found Mr Robinson dead in his chair. Looking out of the bedroom window one morning she had noticed his kitchen light on. He was a man of habit, so she had gone to investigate. The front curtains were closed, but she could see Mr Robinson's feet. The back door was unlocked, so she had gone inside and found him. He must have died the evening before, thought the paramedics when they came.

Sylvie was unprepared for this. How could he have died without seeing her one last time? They had unfinished business. There was so much she had wanted to tell him about university life, a boy she had met, her dreams…

She came home for the funeral, cried throughout, and remembered nothing of it afterwards; except that a very smart man approached her at the end, offered his condolences, and explained that he was Mr Robinson's solicitor, handing her an envelope and his business card.

'I'll leave you to read this in your own time,' he said, 'then we can have a chat.'

Sylvie sat at the dining table and opened the manila envelope to disclose some papers and a pale blue envelope. Opening that, she found that it was a handwritten note from Mr Robinson.

*Sylvie,*

*I'm sorry that I couldn't have had one more chat with you than I did, but that was always going to be the case. However many I had, I'd have wanted just one more. We never ran out of things to talk about, did we?*

*I won't beat about the bush. I've nobody left in the world, so I want you to have my house. I've left Martin my money. They say it's hard for young folk to get a start these days, so I hope that this gives you one. Don't treat it like a shrine. Get rid of my stuff if you can't use it. Sell the house and buy one you really want.*

*Why am I doing this, you'll ask? You were always an inquisitive girl. Because when I needed support, you were there. You befriended an old man and made his last years much better than he thought they would be. You made a difference to me, young Sylvie, when I was too old to expect anything good to happen.*

*What I'm giving you has a value, but what you gave me was beyond value.*

*Wishing you every happiness in life,*
*Herbert.*

Sylvie passed the letter to her mother to read, received it again, and returned it to its envelope. She went out to the shed, found their old ball, and lovingly threw it over the fence one last time.

---

Graham Brack is primarily a crime and historical fiction writer. One of his series is based in Prague while the other is set in the Dutch Golden Age. His Dutch detective, Mercurius, is a cleric who likes to muse about morality and law, punishment and mercy; his Czech counterpart, Josef Slonský, is more interested in beer, sausages, coffee and pastries. Originally from Sunderland, Graham now lives in Northamptonshire with his wife. They have two adult children and three granddaughters. He worked as a pharmacist for many years. His hobbies include reading and telling professional sportsmen where they are going wrong from the comfort of his armchair.

# A PACKET OF KINDNESS

*By Hannah Lynn*

"Oliver Jenkins, get your backside downstairs—now!"

The words rattled through his skull, dragging him out of his dream and into the dull light of his bedroom. Groaning, he pulled the pillow out from under him and slammed it down over his head. There was no way it was morning already. It couldn't be time to get up yet. It felt like he'd only just fallen asleep.

"If you don't come down here this minute, I am coming up there and, believe me, you do not want that to happen."

Threats like this from his mother were ten-a-penny and there was usually only a fifty-fifty chance she would ever make good on one. From the tone of her voice, she definitely wanted him up, but she was normally juggling a hundred other things, like feeding the dog, phoning his gran to see if she'd had a good night and remembered her meds, dealing with the fallout of whatever had happened at work the night before. She had a hard time switching off from work, which had its advantages. However, that morning, when he heard footsteps thundering up the stairs, it was clear she was entirely focused on him.

"Oliver Sebastian Jenkins!"

The movements were simultaneous. As the handle twisted down, he threw off the duvet and leapt for the door. It was only a short jump and would have been easy for someone of his size, had he been fully awake. He wasn't even close to that and when his shin caught the end of the bed, he swallowed the pain and pushed himself against the door.

"Mum," he grinned, as he put his face to the narrow opening he'd allowed her, although the smile didn't stick. While *he* might have felt like he hadn't slept all night, it was fairly clear his mother actually hadn't. She was still wearing her uniform, but it was unbuttoned and untucked, not to mention stained with something he'd rather not investigate. Her hair, which had been immaculate when she'd left the previous evening, was now dishevelled and fell across her face and eyes, and her eyes were tired and smudged with mascara. He tried another grin, but her scowl refused to shift.

"Two days, Oliver. Two days. You do realise that, don't you? I did the shopping just two days ago."

*Damn,* he thought. He'd hoped he would manage to get away before she opened the cupboards and saw their depleted state. Trying to ignore the niggling guilt, he dug his toes into the carpet and avoided her gaze.

"You are going to eat us out of house and home at this rate."

"I was hungry," he mumbled.

"Obviously. That was a twelve-pack of crisps. It was meant to last you all the way to next week. If you were that famished, why didn't you make yourself a bowl of pasta, or a sandwich?"

His shoulders rose and dropped in a shrug.

"I suppose your bedroom is now full of wrappers too, isn't it?"

As his mum shifted to peer over his shoulder, Oliver narrowed the gap between the door and the frame still further.

"It's fine. I'll tidy it up now, before I go to school."

"It's that bad, is it?"

"Maybe." He grimaced.

The scowl hovered for a moment longer, before she shook her head and sighed.

"Honestly, it's no wonder you're so bloody tall. You eat enough for a weightlifter." She reached up and ruffled his hair. "I'm going to get washed up and head to bed. Remember, you need to pick up your cousin after school."

"I haven't forgotten him yet, have I?"

"Just checking. I promised your aunt I'd head over there this afternoon to give her a hand with Uncle Rob. You two will be okay to entertain yourselves for a couple of hours, won't you?"

"I guess."

"Okay. Well, you need to get ready pronto, or you're going to be late for school. Again."

As his mother retreated, the reminder about his cousin made him realise it was Friday, which in turn triggered another thought.

"Mum, can I grab a couple of quid from your purse?" he asked, just as she reached the bathroom door.

"Two pounds? Why?"

"It's non-uniform for World Book Day today."

"Again? I guess so." Her brow creased. "I thought non-uniform days were a pound?"

"They are, but there's a bake sale at lunchtime too. And as I'm not taking anything …"

She sighed again and an extra layer of guilt dropped onto his shoulders.

"I guess I've still got time to make myself a sandwich," he offered, but she waved his comment away.

"It's fine. All for a good cause, isn't it? All right, grab two quid on your way out. Although if that room of yours is a mess when I check later, you are going to be mowing our lawn *and* your grandmother's this weekend."

"I was going to do that anyway," he said, with a smile that finally forced its way through his mother's frown and caused a reciprocal twitch at the corners of her mouth.

"Well, if it's still in a state, then I'll hire you out to the guys at work too."

"As long as I get to keep the money that's fine."

"If you start earning money, you can start paying for all the food you eat."

"We could split it fifty-fifty," he suggested.

Another quick smile and his mum was in the bathroom. He turned back to survey the scene. As far as teenagers' rooms went—well, his friends' at least—his was in fairly good shape. There was the pile of unwashed clothes in the corner by the wardrobe that never seemed to make it as far as the washing basket. And there were a couple of dirty mugs which had probably been under the bed for at least three days and had something furry floating on the dregs. But you could see a good seventy percent of the carpet, and half an hour with the window open would make the place smell a little sweeter. Not that he had half an hour.

Hearing the shower running, he grabbed his school uniform and quickly threw it on. Then, seizing his bag, he headed downstairs, where he took two pounds from his mother's purse and a cereal bar from the cupboard, before springing out the front door. He'd give his teeth an extra good brush when he got in.

As he ambled down the road, his thoughts passed momentarily to what lessons he had that morning and how quickly he'd be able to get through the lawn mowing at the weekend. The new Batman film was out too, and he was desperate to see it. Maybe he'd ask Katie if she wanted to go to the cinema with him. She'd been hanging around with them every lunch break this week, and he was sure she'd wanted to pair up with him in science, before that bloody Lizzie had barged her way in. She probably liked decent films too. Katie that was. Ones with a bit of action, not just mind-numbingly boring romances. Then again, if she wanted to see a rom-com, that wouldn't be too bad either.

When he reached the main road he turned left, away from school, and took his phone out to scroll through his friends' latest Instagram stories while he waited.

Four minutes later, and now less than five minutes until they were meant to be at school, Jason appeared at his front door, dressed entirely in green, from his trainers to his T-shirt, not to mention the fluorescent tights that glowed beneath his shorts.

"Dude, it's dress-up day," he said as he flicked down a mask and surveyed Oliver with mock disgust.

"Yeah, I forgot," he replied, shoving his phone back into his pocket. "Anyway, I thought it was book day. What are you dressed up as?"

"Donatello," Jason replied, slamming his front door. "You know, from the Ninja Turtles."

"Isn't that a film?"

"Yeah, but all films are books first, ain't they?"

When they reached the main road, the two boys became three, as Tom joined them on his bike, staying close to the kerb and pedalling slowly, to join in the conversation about superhero film reboots and which Spiderman was the best.

Inside the school gates, the three headed their separate ways. They had come up through primary school together, even had the same teachers for seven years. Although they were in the same sets for most of their lessons, their form groups were different, so the first ten minutes of every day, they were apart. While Tom and Jason headed to the science block, Oliver walked into the main building and then on to the small, dimly-lit English classroom.

Dress-up days were a big deal here and a lot of people took it extremely seriously. Especially the staff. The previous year, his English teacher had come as the wardrobe from the Narnia books. Before that, the whole department had turned up as the different professors from Harry Potter. Loads of the kids were well into it, too. One time a group of sixth formers had got together and dressed up as different characters from the Mr Men books. That had been pretty cool, if he was honest, except for the kid dressed as Mr Tickle, who'd spent the entire day lurking around the corridors, attacking the younger kids with his extendable arms.

Yet not everyone was so dedicated. There were the people like Jason, who took it as a chance to go mad, but completely missed the theme; and the ones who used it as an excuse to just wear jeans and a T-shirt and offered up some lame excuse for their lack of imagination. Very few people came in uniform though. That day, in Oliver's class, there were only two of them. Him, and Alfie Caster.

"Oliver, Alfie, that's a shame," his tutor tutted from beneath a thick black-and-white Cruella de Vil wig. "I'm surprised at you Oliver," she added. "Your pirate outfit last year was great."

"Just forgot, Miss," he replied with a shrug, and the teacher nodded sadly, before turning to the rest of the class and speaking to each in turn about their attire and asking for their pound donation. Oliver and Alfie didn't have to pay as they were in uniform, although she didn't mention anything to Alfie about his lack of costume. She rarely mentioned anything to Alfie at all. No one did.

As far as the other students went, Alfie kept himself to himself. It wasn't that he had a small group of friends; from what Oliver had seen, he didn't have any. He would sit alone at lunchtime, eating his free school dinner, shoulders hunched as if trying to make himself invisible. When home time came, he would huddle beneath his rucksack, getting pushed and shoved back and forth as people tried to beat each other out of the gate. He never kicked up a fuss. He didn't do anything, other than try to make himself disappear.

But Oliver saw him. He saw him at the primary school, picking up his little sister, when he met his cousin on a Friday. He saw him in the park at weekends, sitting on a bench with his school books out, attempting to get his homework done while younger kids ran around, trying to get him to play with them. He saw the stains on his uniform and the way his trousers were patched and finished two inches above his ankles. And his grey jumper, that wasn't uniform at all, just a similar style to what they were meant to wear. He'd also seen Alfie at the food bank, before his mum had got her night shifts and the promotion that allowed them multipacks of crisps, chocolate bars and a takeaway treat once a week. Before a PlayStation and a new uniform each year were possible.

Worst of all, he'd seen him the day before, in the fish and chip shop. He'd overheard him talking to the girl at the counter, asking if there was anything going spare. That was the word he'd used. *Anything*. Was there *anything* she could give him to eat. He didn't care what. A bag of chips. An old piece of fish. It wasn't for him, he'd said, it was for his sister, and Oliver had believed him. That was when he'd raced home and taken the bag of crisps out of their kitchen cupboard and stuffed it into his school bag. The bag that sat bulging at his feet, although he had no idea what he was supposed to do now. Just go up to the guy and start talking about something random? Make up some reason as to why he had twelve packets of crisps that he needed to give away?

The second bell of the day rang out, breaking his train of thought. The rest of the class bolted for the door, their money donated and costumes admired. He hung back for a moment, casting his eyes towards Alfie.

"Come on the pair of you. I've got my Year Elevens in here now. You need to get to your own class."

"One minute Miss," Oliver replied over his shoulder.

He weaved his way through the chairs to the back of the room, to where Alfie was slowly packing his bag.

"Sorry, did you want to sit here?" he asked, noticing Oliver standing over him.

Oliver shook his head. "No, I just…I didn't know if—"

"Boys hurry up."

Oliver's pulse had kicked up a notch and his foot was bouncing nervously on the ground.

"You okay?" Alfie asked, standing up.

Taking a deep breath, he swung his bag off his shoulder, unzipped it and whipped out the carrier inside.

"My mum bought these, and I really don't like prawn cocktail flavour. I don't suppose you want them, do you?" His heart hammered as he held the bag out between them. He could hear the Year Elevens out in the corridor, waiting to come into the classroom.

Alfie's eyes narrowed, a mixture of scepticism and fear crossing his features.

*This was a stupid thing to do!* Oliver berated himself. He had got it wrong, and now he looked like an idiot. He was an idiot. Why would he think you could just go up to someone who hadn't even asked you for anything and offer them something? Swallowing repeatedly, he started to pull his hand back, when Alfie reached out and took the bag.

"Are you sure?" he asked. "My sister really likes those."

His default shrug was joined by a rapid nodding of the head.

"Like I said, we don't eat them. Just gonna go to waste."

The two boys' eyes met and, instantly, Oliver wanted to look away but at the same time knew he shouldn't. He realised at that moment that, however hard this felt for him, it wasn't really at all. Not like it was for the boy in front of him. And so, he let himself offer the smallest of smiles.

"Thank you," Alfie said.

Across the room, a gentle clearing of the throat brought their attention back to the moment, and their tutor still waiting to let her class in.

"Hurry up now, you two," she chided, but with a softness that hadn't been there before.

As the pair walked towards the door, Oliver turned to Alfie again.

"My mum gave me extra money for the bake sale today," he said. "If you want to get something with me at lunchtime?"

---

Hannah Lynn is an award-winning novelist. Publishing her first book, *Amendments*—a dark, dystopian speculative fiction novel, in 2015, she has since gone on to write *The Afterlife of Walter Augustus*—a contemporary fiction novel with a supernatural twist—which won the 2018 Kindle Storyteller Award and Gold Medal for Best Adult Fiction Ebook at the IPPY Awards, as well as the delightfully funny and poignant 'Peas and Carrots' series. Her latest works include retellings of classic Greek myths and saw her win her second IPPY Gold Medal for the first book in her Grecian Women Series, the heart-wrenching *Athena's Child*. Born in 1984, Hannah grew up in the Cotswolds, UK. After graduating from university, she spent ten years as a teacher of physics, first in the UK, then in Thailand, Malaysia, Austria and Jordan. It was during this time, inspired by the imaginations of the young people she taught, she began writing short stories for children, before moving on to adult fiction. Nowadays you will most likely find her busy writing at home with her husband and daughter, surrounded by a horde of cats.

# GOODBYE, WENDY

*By Heather Martin*

He was the main reason they went there. Not the only one, of course. It had a great vantage point on the crossroads, with a natural sun trap on the triangular concrete oasis outside, and a view down the facing street to patches of green and the church steeple beyond. The sandwiches were pretty good too. Choose-your-own fillings, wonky bread, Turkish or sourdough, never the same twice, all jammed together in the toaster but most likely falling apart on your plate, so you had to lick your fingers to get all the goodness from them. Red pesto or green, spicy or mild, all homemade and all just how you wanted it.

It was that kind of place.

But still, he was the main reason. There was just something about him. Didn't matter who you were. The bike shop guy from under the railway bridge. The music heads from the studio next door. The tattooist-to-the-stars from around the corner. The two French girls with pale skin and jet-black hair who sat side by side in the pull-down cinema seats at the front window. The old couple and their dog—a scruffy little scavenger who'd seen better days—who liked to tackle the crossword over tea and toast. Marv, who'd been coming in so long he had a sandwich named after him and whose preferred flavour of crisps had changed only once in two decades. Joe treated them all the same. Had a way of making you feel he had all the time in the world just for you, but whoever was behind you in the queue didn't get riled up about it, because well, he had all the time in the world for them too. No one knew how he did it, really. It was magic, but without the trickery. None of that hoo-ha with smoke and mirrors.

Nice smile, too. And generous with it. If time to time he made a mistake—let's face it, none of us is perfect—there was no blame and no bluster. He never tried to cover it up or brush it under the carpet. 'Sorry, man,' he'd say, and start over, so when whatever it was turned up it tasted better than if he'd got it right in the first place. Like a bonus ingredient, an added dash of humanity thrown in with the cheese and tomato. He was only a young lad, mid-twenties, at a guess. Friendly, but not flashy.

Wendy was a regular. Most people were, come to think of it. She'd pass most days, left to right across his field of vision on her way to the shops, then right to left on her way back again, hunched over a stick, pulling a powder-blue shopping trolley behind her patterned with a recurring Scottie-dog print. Always on her own. Didn't buy much, so far as he could see. Maybe a loaf of bread and a carton of milk to go with the extra-long cigarettes she picked up from the post office on the high street. Some Russian brand, he thought. She was always smartly turned out. Her dyed brown hair back-combed and set with rollers. Fire-engine red mock-croc shoes with a silver buckle over the instep and a bit of a point to them. Matching smear of red lipstick. A large-link gilt chain dangling across the front of her blouse. A proper overcoat whatever the season. All nice and laundered. Not that she had her own washing machine. Only faith that whoever she ran into at the laundrette would see her right: popping the coins in the slot, topping the machine up with detergent, and folding everything neatly into the trolley at the end.

Between shifts, or sometimes on his day off, Joe and Wendy liked to shoot the breeze outside over one of her bootleg cigarettes and, for her, a cup of milky tea with one sugar. Joe was still smoking in those days. They made an odd couple. Her all of four foot eleven and seamed with wrinkles like her shoes; him six foot and counting, swimmer's physique, smooth-skinned and close-cropped. Wendy was a sociable soul. Used to her own company, mind, what with her husband disappearing off the face of the earth fifteen years before. Hightailed it back to Burma, she reckoned. Hadn't seen hide nor hair of him since. Some fancy woman, most likely. She'd put good money on it—either that or a sentimental tour of the old POW camp. Wendy's laugh was loud, like her voice, just this side of abrasive, and always liable to crescendo into a fit of coughing. She had a son, holed up in some assisted living place, no one was quite sure why. Might as well be in Burma, for all the interest he had in his mother.

She told Joe how when she got home she would make toast and turn on the telly. He told her how when he wasn't making sandwiches he ran music nights at the local church—big, largely unused space like most churches, but different from most because the pews weren't fixed to the floor and could be moved into a circle, creating a stage in the round, which was magic. There was hot food too, made by a local Ethiopian family who ran a restaurant down the road. She should come along sometime. Ask for Joe at the door. Dinner on him. Wendy was up for that, a night out on the town in her pointy red dance shoes, and had it all lined up too, till her son stood her up.

One day, just like her truant husband, Wendy disappeared. No one noticed at first. The guy who'd been buying the same sandwich for twenty years was still showing up regular as clockwork, a Marv on the go as soon as he stepped foot through the door. The tattoo guy, the bike shop guy, the two French girls, the old couple with the scruffy dog: all present and correct. The crossword was still getting done, punters chipping in a speculative word here and there as they came and went. But there was something subtly off about the rhythm of his days. The beat was no longer steady. There was a flicker on the screen, a tiny blip on the monitor.

Then a woman passed in front of the window, left to right across his field of vision as he stood behind the counter ready to serve the next customer, smiling, but inwardly pensive. It wasn't Wendy, but it was someone Wendy knew, following Wendy's route. This woman never came in, but he'd seen the two of them stop and exchange greetings. 'You seen Wendy lately?' Joe asked, ducking outside. The guy waiting for his sandwich wasn't worried. He knew Joe would be back soon enough, with all the time in the world for him too.

But the woman hadn't seen Wendy, and nor had anyone else he asked as the days went by, the rhythm faltering more noticeably now, the vital signs dipping like the sun dropping behind the horizon.

One day, just like that, Joe went looking for Wendy. He'd finished his shift. It was about two in the afternoon. He didn't know where she lived, but he turned left out of the cafe down the slope under the railway bridge, and on a hunch, left again, into the nearest estate. She walked with a stick, right? How far was she going to go for a loaf of sliced bread and some fags? Eventually, someone buzzed him in to the first building and he started knocking on doors. A lot of doors, one after the other like he was canvassing for the Labour Party. Only a few surly brush-offs. Most people reacted like he was offering to make them the sandwich of their dreams.

'Hello,' he would say. 'Do you know Wendy? She's my mate, and I haven't seen her in a while, and I'm looking for her. I think she might live around here.'

The description was easy. Everyone knew Wendy. No one knew where she lived.

The second building had the same smell, mould and decay hanging heavy in the air. Same mix of hope, hunger and indifference. Then Joe stumbled across the woman from outside the cafe, the one who never came in, who didn't know where Wendy lived either but pointed vaguely to the next block along.

The first door he tried, a thick-set man opened up and said 'yeah, I think she's on the top floor', jabbing his thumb upwards in the direction of the nearest staircase. No lift that Joe could see. His head hurt. He could hear the slow tap of the stick on each concrete step, the irregular thump of the trolley as she dragged it up behind her, Scottie dogs bouncing merrily. The cough jangling like an out-of-tune guitar. The thick-set man hadn't seen Wendy. 'Been wondering if she died,' he said. 'Stinks in here.'

Joe took two steps at a time, heart thumping. He was there to find Wendy. Tried not to think about what might await him when he did. Tried not to breathe the foul air. He'd never seen a dead body. Didn't know what death smelled like. One thing he did know was he hated the thick-set man. He knew that for certain.

There weren't many people Joe hated.

He rapped his knuckles on the first door. A woman opened. Said nothing. Shook her head and shut the door on him like she didn't want to know. Joe swivelled. Knocked on the facing door. Waited. No answer. Knocked again. Nothing. Something stirred in his gut.

He bent down, pushed open the flap of the letter box and peered through the narrow horizontal gap. To his right a bathroom. Covered in grime. Put his own housekeeping skills in perspective. To his left, what looked like a bedroom. Straight ahead, a television, one of the old tube monsters, squat and bulbous, switched on but not showing a programme, filling the hallway with eerie blue light.

He called Wendy's name. Silence, apart from a faint electric hum. Called again. No rasping cough. No tapping stick, no dancing shoes.

He stood up. Bent down, took another look. Waited for his eyes to adjust to the glare. Then saw it. A jaunty repeat pattern. The powder-blue leached out by the virulence of the screen. The Scottie dogs, no longer bouncing, but watchful, patient. They'd wait forever if they had to. It's what dogs do. Wait till help comes.

Joe closed the flap softly. Stood up, took out his phone, and dialled the non-emergency number. The dogs weren't barking. Didn't look like an emergency to them, either. Someone picked up and Joe said: 'I work at the cafe on the crossroads. You know, the one on the corner. I was looking for my mate, Wendy. She's an old lady and I haven't seen her in a while. I think I've found where she lives. I think she might be dead.'

Someone would be right along, they said. His head was ringing. They gave him a rough ETA. Time to get out, breathe some air, buy a beer maybe. Sit on the wall and have a cigarette. Just a roll-up, no fancy Russian knock-offs for him. None for Wendy anymore either. Time for a mate to pass by, do a double-take and sit down on the wall beside him and ask what was up. Time to tell him. Time for the mate to go on about his business. For the sun to set. For Joe to pull out his phone and ring the non-emergency number again and ask if they were still coming. He got that it wasn't urgent, but all the same.

They were nice, when they turned up, the two officers. Two mid-thirties men in uniform, brisk and efficient. Concerned for his welfare. They buzzed a random number and said: 'Police. Open up, please.' Joe took them up the two flights of stairs to the third floor and they picked the lock, gently. Told him to stay outside. Went in, came straight back out again, and said: 'You were right. That's the smell of a dead body.'

Joe cried, then.

'We found her lying in bed,' one of the officers said. 'Like someone just switched off the light.'

He went home. He never did get a response from the son in the assisted living place. Never did hear about the funeral. The police were sympathetic. But there was nothing they could do, they said. Nothing more they could tell him, even if they knew. There were procedures and protocols. It was a family matter now.

'I don't know if there even was a funeral,' he told me back at the cafe. We were sitting outside in the sun in a lull between the lunch and evening crowds. Mine was a Marv. A new Marv, actually. No questions asked, but for some reason the guy had switched up from cheddar to goat's cheese. Everyone was OK with it. I was a fan.

Joe had a roll-up. Stretched out his long legs and turned his face up to the sky. We had all the time in the world.

---

Heather Martin is the author of *The Reacher Guy*, the first and only authorised biography of Lee Child (Little, Brown UK & Pegasus Books 2020). She was born in Geraldton, a few hundred miles north of Perth on the west coast of Australia. Aged sixteen she left home to spend three years as a music student in London, but never went back. She read Languages at Cambridge, staying on to do a PhD, then lectured in Spanish at the University of Hull and King's College London, where she was also admissions tutor.

More recently, after working as a freelance editor and translator and a stint as head of languages in an independent primary, she returned to academia as visiting fellow in the department of comparative literature at the Graduate Center, City University New York. Heather has always been a big reader, and though she never planned to become a biographer, once the idea of writing the Lee Child story took hold, it felt somehow meant to be.

# A FESTIVE TAIL

*By Holly Martin*

Cora stood on the doorstep of the little sandwich shop and peered out at the snow that had been steadily falling all day, showing no sign of stopping. The wind was rushing through the streets, piling the snow in great drifts in doorways and corners. For snow to fall on Christmas Eve in London was almost unheard of and completely magical. As a child growing up near the sea, Cora could count on one hand how many times she had seen snow like this; even when the rest of the country was blanketed in it, it never seemed to reach as far as the coast, or very rarely.

Maisie moved out next to her, locked the door behind them, and then turned to face the elements, pulling her snood tighter around her face.

"Are you really walking home in this?" asked Maisie, who would catch the tube for one stop rather than walk anywhere.

"It's not far," Cora said.

"You might die in the blizzard."

Cora smiled. "I think I'll be OK."

"Well, you have a wonderful Christmas, my dear. I'll see you in the new year."

The perks of owning her own sandwich shop, Maisie could open and close it as she saw fit. Maisie was taking her three kids to Disneyland in Paris the day after Boxing Day and though Cora had offered to run the shop in Maisie's absence, Maisie had insisted that Cora have a proper break for Christmas too. Little did Maisie know that Cora's plans for Christmas included a pizza and watching all the cheesy Christmas movies as she sat on her sofa in her pyjamas, alone.

"You too. Give big Christmas kisses to your little angels."

"Little devils more like. Pass on my love to your sister and her family as well."

Cora gave a vague nod. It had been a little lie. If Maisie knew that Cora was going to be alone for Christmas, she would have insisted on her coming to her big family celebration. It wasn't Cora's scene, and she didn't want to impose on anyone over Christmas.

Maisie gave her a wave and disappeared into the snow, a huddled figure trying to protect herself from the freezing onslaught.

Cora took a moment to watch the snow. The street was lit up with the most spectacular Christmas angels that seemed to be swooping over the street; she loved to see them and mostly she loved to see the tourists' reactions to them. And now they looked even more magical. There was an ethereal beauty as the Christmas lights sparkled off the snow that covered the cars, roofs and trees in a great duvet of tiny crystals.

She stepped out of the shelter of the doorway, glad she'd had the foresight to wear her snow boots that morning. The snow was not the gentle, romantic fluttering kind she saw in her favourite Christmas movies; this was harsh and whipped across her face so she could barely see. She took a little side road and then a small path that cut across St James's Park. There weren't many people in the park at this time of day. A few stragglers hurrying home, not paying any attention to the people they passed. There were sporadic lights that lit up the paths but tonight the snow made it so much easier to see.

She always took this route to her little flat, and she always took a slight detour through the park which made her journey a few minutes longer. She used to go that route primarily to see the pelicans that had made the lake their home but the last few months, as she had walked around the far corner of the lake, past the café, she had met a grey straggly dog she'd called Max. He always seemed to be hanging around that part of the park, probably in the hope of getting some leftovers from the café or its customers.

It had become a tradition for them both; Max was always waiting for her as she'd bring him any leftover meat from the sandwiches that day. As the shop was closed for the next week, her bag was filled with bits of ham, chicken and turkey; a perfect Christmas feast for her four-legged friend.

Little golden puddles of light cast their glow across the snowy paths as she hurried round the lake. There was no sign of the pelicans who were normally to be found near Duck Island Cottage. The park rangers sometimes took them to an indoor enclosure to look after them, and knowing the bad weather was imminent they might have taken them away for a few days.

There was also no sign of Max in his usual position. She looked around as the snow ripped around her in vicious gusts, but there was no sign of movement at all. No large dark straggly shadow sheltering in the trees. No excited waggy tail sticking out from behind a bush.

She called his name a few times and then felt foolish. Max probably didn't know his name. In her head she had called him that and she might have said it to him a few times, but he wouldn't know to come when that name was called. In fact, judging on past behaviour, he probably wasn't well trained at all.

She stood in the snow for a bit longer, hoping he would suddenly turn up but in this weather he was probably sheltering somewhere warm. She hoped so.

After a few more minutes, she turned and headed for home.

She had thought about trying to catch Max quite a few times since they'd met, but she could hardly look after a dog. She worked six days a week, most days from eight in the morning until six at night; it'd be unfair to leave a dog alone for that length of time. She had thought of taking him to an animal shelter in the hope of finding him a proper home, but he clearly loved lolloping around the park, tail in the air, smile on his face, and she didn't feel it was her place to put a stop to that and shove him in a cage until someone found it in their heart to give him a home. He was clearly well fed, probably giving the puppy dog eyes to anyone who was eating, including the hundreds of tourists that frequented the park every day. But she hated the idea of him being out in this weather; if she'd caught him and taken him to a shelter before now, he'd at least be inside on a cold night like this.

Cora walked up the stairs of the old Georgian townhouse that had been converted into six tiny one-bedroom flats, two on each floor. She unlocked the large black door and stepped inside the warmth of the foyer.

She checked her post box, which was depressingly empty, and then made her way up to the first floor and flat number three.

In a block of flats so small, Cora had hoped she'd make friends with her new neighbours when she'd moved to London from Cornwall, ten months before, but that hadn't happened. She remembered when her sister had moved to a different part of Cornwall and was welcomed with flowers, cakes and bottles of wine by the new neighbours. There had been no such welcoming party here at Sixpence Mews.

Cora had made some cupcakes with the intention of introducing herself to her new friends. But the doors of the flats had stayed resolutely closed when she'd knocked with her box of cakes, despite there being sounds of life behind at least three of the doors. She'd ended up leaving the cakes on the doorsteps. To her horror, when she'd come out later that day, she'd watched the cute guy, who she now knew as Angus, from flat number one, accidentally step on the cake and get icing all over his shoe. He hadn't been best pleased, and she hadn't been brave enough to confess that the cake was from her. No one else had knocked on her door to say thank you, in fact there had been no acknowledgement of the cakes at all.

Since then, she'd seen a few of the other residents in the foyer to say hello to and she knew all their names from the tags on the post boxes, but the long-lasting friendships she'd seen in TV programmes had never materialised. She'd never even met the couple who lived above her, though she heard them rowing often enough—and making up afterwards.

Living in London was a lot more lonely than she'd thought it would be.

* * *

Cora stared out the window at the snow that was quickly turning into a blizzard. It was gone eight o'clock and the weather was definitely getting worse. She was cosy and warm in her reindeer onesie but all she could think about was poor Max, freezing out there in the worst snowstorm that London had ever seen. It was entirely possible someone else had taken him in or the animal shelter had finally caught up with him, but she knew she couldn't go to bed that night knowing he was out there by himself. She had to look for him one more time.

She threw on some clothes and her snow boots and ran downstairs, pulling on her coat just as Angus came in through the front door, shaking the snow from his hair and stamping his feet from the cold. He had such a lovely face; nice eyes and a warm, friendly smile which always made her think talking to him would be easy. Unfortunately, the opportunity for that hadn't presented itself very often. She rarely saw him and when she had, he was always talking on the phone.

He stared at her in surprise. "Are you going out in this?"

"I have to. There's a stray dog I see regularly in the park and I always feed him on my way home from work, but he wasn't there tonight. I hate the thought of him being out in this. I have to find him."

"Ah, crap. Grey, straggly thing? Could be a Bearded Collie mix?"

"Yes, that's the one. I've called him Max, but I doubt he knows that name."

"Yeah, I normally buy him a sausage roll on my way home from work, but I didn't see him tonight either." Angus showed her the sausage roll still wrapped in its paper bag.

She was surprised at this. She had long since realised that people in London only seemed to care about themselves. There was a definite lack of the community spirit that she'd seen in Cornwall. To think that someone else had spotted Max and had been feeding him regularly warmed her heart a little.

"I'll come with you," Angus said. "It's too cold out there for anyone right now."

She hadn't expected that. She knew that Angus worked long hours and got back late most nights. She wouldn't blame him if he wanted to go straight into the warmth of his flat and have his dinner.

He escorted her out the foyer and down the steps. The icy wind whipped around them as they hurried down the road.

It was silent between them, and it occurred to her that their brief conversation inside the foyer was the most they'd talked in the ten months since she'd moved in.

"So, Cora, you moved here from Cornwall, right?"

She was surprised he knew that. They'd said hello on the odd occasions they saw each other, but their conversation rarely went beyond that.

"Yes, ten months ago," Cora said, wrapping her scarf tighter around her head.

"Most people move from London to Cornwall, not the other way round. What made you come here?"

Cora let out a heavy breath that was whipped away in the frozen air. "My husband was cheating on me."

"Crap."

"With my best friend."

"Oh wow, that has to hurt."

"Yeah, it did. I moved out, got a flat by myself, but we lived in such a tiny town that I'd be bumping into them nearly every day, all happy and loved up together. As soon as the divorce was finalised, they were engaged, then she was pregnant, and it was just too painful to see. Plus, all the looks of pity from all the other people who lived there. I needed to get away and thought it'd be nice to make a clean start where no one knew me."

"And how are you finding London?"

Cora paused before answering. There was a lot she liked about London, there was always something happening, always something to go and see at the weekends. She loved the shows and being single meant she could normally get a last-minute seat quite close to the front, but she couldn't say she was totally happy living here. "It's not what I thought it would be. With a population of over nine million, I thought it would be easy to make friends, but people are…very busy here."

"Yes, London can be quite…isolated in many ways."

"Have you always lived here?" Cora said.

He shook his head as they crossed over the main road heading towards St James's Park. "No, I grew up in a little village in the Cotswolds. It was quite the shock when I first moved to London, but I've lived here for around two years now, and you get used to it. People can be friendly and helpful once you get to know them."

"Do you know anyone in our flats?"

"Oh sure, Mrs Greene lives opposite me, she's nice. Retired. Used to be a headteacher. I think she left me a cake on my doorstep once, though I accidentally trod on it. I didn't tell her that though. And then there's Felix who lives opposite you, he's from Denmark originally, works in the theatre, I think he does the lights. And on the top floor we have Pauline and Daavid. She's from Wales, I think he's Finnish. Daavid has a dodgy taste in moustaches, but a brilliant taste in beer. I think Pauline is a veterinary nurse. And then there's Ganesh in flat number six, he works in computers, although rumour has it he might be a spy."

"But do you really know them, beyond where they are from and where they work?"

Angus was silent for a moment. "I suppose not. I went out with Daavid for a beer once but we mostly talked about football. Men don't really do personal conversations, not unless you're good friends. And I suppose being neighbours with someone doesn't really make you friends. It's hard to build up quality relationships with people you only see occasionally. Everyone at Sixpence Mews is in and out at such different times of the day, some days I don't see anyone."

She nodded. She understood that. She'd found the same thing.

"But you have other friends in London?" Cora asked.

"Well, work friends," Angus said. "And a few blokes I play tennis with once a week."

The wind started to drop a little bit as they walked into the park, but Cora assumed it was just a little lull before it started up again. The snow was still falling thick and fast.

"And do you have *personal* conversations with any of them?"

Angus thought for a moment. "Probably not. But I guess some things are too heavy for polite chat at work or over a tennis match. I wouldn't want to share those parts of my life with those friends. It makes things awkward and sometimes I prefer people not to know so I can have that normality for a change."

Cora hated the idea of Angus being alone with his problems, but it kind of proved her point about relationships in London being on the surface and nothing deeper. Where she'd grown up, everyone minded everyone else's business but largely it was because people genuinely cared.

"What could be too heavy for real friendship?"

Angus looked around the park that was now completely deserted and for a moment she didn't think he was going to tell her. But then they weren't friends, so why would he?

"My dad died six months ago."

"Shit, I'm so sorry."

She hadn't been expecting that and now she felt awful for almost dragging it out of him just to prove a point.

Angus nodded. "Sometimes it's easier just not talking about it, just carrying on with life as normal."

She put a hand on his arm. "And sometimes it doesn't do you any good to bottle up those feelings. I know we don't really know each other very well, but if you ever wanted to talk about it, I'm a good listener."

"Thank you," Angus said, as he looked around the park that was completely covered in snow. "Now is probably not the best time but maybe I'll take you up on that some time."

"You'd be very welcome."

He stared at her, warmth filling his pale green eyes before he turned away to look for Max.

They started walking towards the café but Cora couldn't shake the feeling of guilt. Angus lived directly underneath her and she'd had no idea what he was going through over the last six months. That would never have happened in the village she grew up in. If someone had lost a loved one, they would have had meals left on their doorstep every night at the very least. Cora brushed the snowflakes from her face. She had convinced herself that Londoners didn't care enough about other people to make friends when she had been as guilty of that too. Arriving in London with her heart and her dignity in tatters, she hadn't made any effort to make friends beyond making those cakes for her neighbours. She hadn't tried to make friends because losing her best friend to her husband had hurt a lot more than her husband's betrayal. She had been scared to put herself out there in case she was hurt all over again. She had closeted herself away, distracted herself with work and hadn't done anything more than that. She had told herself that Londoners weren't friendly when she had done nothing to be friendly either. At least Angus had taken the time to get to know where the people in the flat were from and where they worked, she hadn't even done that. If she wanted people to care and make the effort, then she had to do that too.

She turned her attention to the matter in hand because it was freezing and she could already feel her fingers going numb.

"I always see Max round here," Cora said. She looked around but there was no sign of the dog, no sign of life at all.

"I always see him in the top corner by the offices." Angus pointed. "On that section of path between the Artillery Memorial and the Guard's Memorial."

"Near the hotdog stand?"

Angus grinned. "Yes, I wonder why he likes that corner."

They made their way over to the Guard's Memorial and then took the path behind the offices. Periodically, Cora would call Max but there was no sign of him.

Angus paused at the entrance to the park offices car park. "Why don't we check around here? If he's still in the park, he's going to be sheltering somewhere and other than a few trees, there is nowhere else up this path that he'd be sheltering.

She nodded as they walked into the small car park. The buildings were in complete darkness so any hope that some kind-hearted security guard or park ranger had taken Max into one of the offices was quickly dashed.

And then she spotted something that made her heart lift.

"Look." She pointed at the paw print in the snow that definitely belonged to a dog.

"Yes, he must be here," Angus said. "Unless it's a fox."

"Bit big for a fox."

"Could be a bear."

Cora laughed. "I think we should take our chances."

They followed the tracks through the snow until they reached what looked like some kind of abandoned storage unit; the door was half hanging off and the wet footprints disappeared through the broken door.

Angus pulled his phone out of his pocket and switched on the flashlight, then cautiously bent down to peer through the hole.

"Well, that's a bit of a surprise," Angus said, gesturing for Cora to have a look too. She squatted down next to him and peered into the darkness. There was Max, lying amongst a pile of newspapers, wagging his tail at their arrival but then her eyes fell to the floor and her heart leapt. Cuddled into Max's side were two tiny balls of fur.

"It seems our Max is actually Maxine," Angus said.

"Oh my god."

Angus crawled into the storage unit and Cora followed him.

"Hey Max, look at you, you're a mum," Cora said, gently stroking Max's head.

"We need to get these guys somewhere warm," Angus said.

"They're so tiny," Cora said.

He nodded. "I'd guess they're just a few days old."

"Do you think she'll let us touch them?"

"Why don't I distract her with this sausage roll and you can see if she'll let you pick them up?"

They swapped places and Angus unwrapped the sausage roll. Max licked her lips hungrily as he broke the sausage roll into chunks and fed it to her.

Cora gently stroked the puppies who were fast asleep and to her surprise Max let her. Cora carefully scooped up one and popped it inside her coat and then placed the other in there too. Max watched her the whole time but she seemed to sense they weren't there to cause the dogs any harm.

Angus finished feeding Max and then took his belt off his trousers, looping it gently round Max's neck.

"Come on, let's get you and your puppies home," Angus said, softly.

To Cora's relief, Max stood up and whether it was the fact that Cora had her puppies or whether she hoped there'd be more sausage rolls, she seemed more than willing to go with them.

They crawled out of the storage unit, Cora keeping a careful arm around the two puppies. She looked around as Angus and Max made their way out of the storage unit too. Something wasn't quite right outside and for a moment she couldn't put her finger on what it was. The snow was still falling, giving a white glow to the park beyond the car park, allowing them to see much further than they normally would at this time of night, but something was different.

Angus moved to her side and then she realised what it was. “The lights have gone out.”

He stared at the street beyond; the electric lights in the park, the Christmas lights and street lights out on the main road, and even the traffic lights were in complete darkness.

“Oh crap,” Angus said.

“So much for warming up once we get back home.”

“I’m sure the power won’t be out for long and let’s face it, even our cold flats are going to be warmer than Max and her pups staying out in this.”

Cora nodded. “Let’s get home.”

They hurried out of the park with Max trotting along quite happily at their side, which made Cora think she’d definitely been walked on a lead before.

As they crossed the main street, which was also deserted, Cora skidded a bit on the snow and Angus immediately put his hand on her back to steady her.

“Thanks,” Cora said. “So much for my snow boots.”

“Ah, I think even the best boots would have trouble in this weather,” Angus said, but as they hurried along the street, he kept his hand on her back and she couldn’t help smiling to herself over that.

They quickly walked up the stairs to their flats, Cora holding her precious load tight against her. The foyer was in muted darkness although there was some limited light from the emergency lighting. There was a shadowy figure coming down the stairs, holding a torch.

“Hey Felix, you OK?” Angus said, ushering Cora and Max inside.

“Yes, I just wanted to check on Mrs Greene, I didn’t want her to be frightened in the dark,” Felix said and then his eyes fell on Max. “And who is this little fella?”

"Max," Cora said, unzipping her coat and producing the two balls of fur. "Or rather Maxine. She's been living in the park for the last few weeks."

Felix took one of the bundles and cradled it gently against his chest. "Hello," Felix crooned in the sweetest of voices. The puppy yawned and then snuggled in closer which made Cora smile. Felix was a huge, hulking man-mountain and to see him being so gentle with one of the puppies warmed her heart.

"Mrs Greene will love this, she's had dogs all her life but she says she'd getting too old now to walk one," Felix said, knocking on the door opposite Angus's.

"Mrs Greene, it's me, Felix," he called through the door. "I'm just checking you're OK."

There was the sound of the door being unlocked from the inside and then Mrs Greene poked her head out. "Oh Felix, you don't need to worry about me, I have my hot water bottle and…what's this?"

Her eyes lit up at seeing the tiny puppy in Felix's hand.

"Cora and Angus rescued a stray dog from the park and she's had two puppies."

Mrs Greene gasped. "They were all out in this weather?"

"Max had found a broken storage unit, so she was inside but it certainly wasn't warm," Cora said, as Max sniffed the puppy in Felix's hand.

"It's OK, Mama," Felix said gently, stroking Max's head. "You can have them back in a minute, let's get you somewhere comfy and then you can feed them."

Mrs Greene took the two puppies and started taking charge, clearly the headteacher habits never went away.

"Right, Felix, go and grab Pauline, she can check them all over and while you're up there get Ganesh to bring down that lovely gas heater he has in his flat. Angus, go and get some blankets and put them down in the corner over there. Cora, go and get some of those lovely candles you keep having delivered here. We need some light to see what we're doing."

Everyone sprang to action. By the time Cora had put all her candles in a box and found some matches and returned to the foyer, there were several other figures down there. Ganesh was lighting his gas fire and there were two other figures crouching down near the dogs.

Cora set about lighting the candles and placing them all round the foyer, golden pools of light flickering across the room. Then she turned her attention to the couple she'd never met before. Pauline was kneeling by Max and the puppies and so Cora brought a candle closer so Pauline could see what she was doing. It was then that Cora noticed Daavid's rather fabulous moustache that was thin and neatly manicured and ended in a splendid spiral on each side.

"These puppies are fine, nice and fat," Pauline said. "Mum has kept them well fed. We just need to keep mum well fed now."

"Is Max OK?" Cora asked as Angus came out of his flat with an armful of blankets.

"She seems to be, but it would be great if we can warm her up a bit."

Angus laid the blankets down in front of the gas fire and they placed the puppies on it. Max immediately lay down with them, licking the puppies and nuzzling them to make sure they were OK. After a while both puppies started feeding from her and they all stood around Max and watched.

"I'll get some food for Max," Mrs Greene said, shuffling back inside her flat.

Cora cleared her throat. "Hi, Pauline, we've never met but I'm Cora from number three."

Pauline grinned at her and stuck out a hand. "Hi, this is my husband Daavid. I've just been hearing about you and Angus and your heroic rescue."

"Oh, I don't know about heroic," Cora said.

"It sounded pretty heroic," Daavid said, his lovely Nordic accent quite clear to hear. "It's awful out there."

"I'm just glad we found them," Cora said.

Mrs Greene came bustling out with a plate of chicken and potatoes which she put down for Max, who snaffled it up.

"We were just having some mulled wine," Pauline said. "Would anyone like a glass?"

There were murmurs of appreciation around the foyer and Daavid was dispatched to fetch some glasses.

"I've got a load of party food I was going to use tomorrow," Felix said. "My friends aren't coming now because of the weather. It'd be a shame for it to go to waste."

Soon chairs were pulled out, and they all sat around the little fire as they passed around Scotch eggs and sticky ribs while drinking glasses of mulled wine and chatted between themselves. Max seemed content to be surrounded by so many people and the puppies were fast asleep after their meal, none the wiser that they had united seven people that had barely spoken before. Cora felt happier than she had in months.

"I can get a portable scanner from work next week, see if Max is microchipped," Pauline said. "But if not, we need to find a home for her, at least for the next eight weeks until the puppies are old enough to have homes of their own."

Everyone fell quiet for a moment and Cora wondered if anyone would have space in their lives for a dog and two puppies.

"I don't go to work until eleven," Angus said. "I could walk Max in the mornings."

"I could take her for a short walk in the afternoons," Mrs Greene said. "If the weather isn't too bad."

"I could come with you, or walk Max on days where the weather is bad," Felix said. "I normally work evenings so my days are free, though because of the very late nights, I tend to sleep in late in the mornings, but certainly afternoons are free."

"I could have her at weekends," Cora offered.

"I could take her for an evening walk," Daavid said. "I'm home from around four."

"I work from home some days a week," Ganesh said. "So I can look after her on those days."

"And I can make sure she has all her jabs and flea and worming tablets," Pauline said.

"And maybe, when the puppies are old enough, they could stay with their mum too," Mrs Greene said.

Cora liked this plan. It seemed they had themselves a dog share.

Suddenly the lights came back on and everyone gave a small cheer.

"Well on that note, I think we'll go to bed," Pauline said.

"This has been lovely," Cora said. "I've really enjoyed getting to know you all tonight. If no one has any plans tomorrow because of the snow, we could do all this again for Christmas Day."

There were nods of agreement and plans were made for lunch to be held in the foyer at one.

"Come on, let's get the dogs in my flat," Angus said.

There was a buzz of activity for a few minutes as people carried blankets and puppies inside Angus's flat. They settled the dogs down in front of one of the heaters which Angus had turned on and then everyone left, leaving Angus and Cora alone.

"I should probably go too," Cora said.

"You can stay for a little while if you want," Angus said. "Make sure the puppies are OK. Also, I have some mince pies and brandy cream if you're interested later."

"I could definitely be interested in that."

She sat down on the sofa and he sat down next to her as they watched the puppies sleeping soundly and Max looking at them fondly.

Just then they heard the church bells ring out midnight. It was Christmas Day.

Angus kissed her on the cheek. "Happy Christmas, Cora."

Cora smiled because she knew, despite all the odds, that it would be.

---

Holly lives in a little white cottage by the sea. She has been writing for 12 years, mainly romantic comedies but she has also dabbled in writing YA fantasy too. She won the Carina Valentine's competition at the Festival of Romance with her novel The Guestbook which led to a three-book publishing deal with Harlequin, now part of Harper Collins. She was shortlisted for the New Talent Award at the Festival of Romance and the following year was shortlisted for Best Romantic Read, Best eBook and Innovation in Romantic Fiction. She is the bestselling author of 28 books selling over 1.5 million books worldwide. Holly's books have been translated into French, German, Italian, Dutch, Bulgarian, Hungarian, Estonian, Turkish and Russian.

# AN UNGHOST STORY

*By Ian Sainsbury*

"What about you, Rachel? Any recurring dreams?"

The book group girls opened a bottle of port as the conversation moved from the usual themes to more esoteric matters.

"Well…"

Rachel took a sip. She'd already forgotten what this month's book was. Not that it mattered; not really. The four women's shared love of reading brought them together in the first place, but friendship keeps them meeting ten years after that first Sunday.

Winter had arrived. Biting cold; damp and dark. Boots dripped onto the stone flags in the hall, and the wind whistled in the chimney. The only light in the room came from the fire.

"Go on, Rachel. Tell us about it." Josie poured herself a second glass, having downed the first in an attempt to, as she put it, *reset her palate*. At the Christmas meeting, she reset it so thoroughly that she passed out during an unwise attempt at karaoke. Without accompaniment. Or being able to remember the lyrics and melody of her chosen song.

"It's not just a dream," said Rachel. "It's…well, it's sort of a ghost story."

Grace blanched. It was her rule for the book group. No horror or supernatural stories. She scared easily. She'd once called Rachel in a panic about a haunted room in a B&B, only to remember she'd left *The Archers* on when she had a bath.

"Don't panic," said Rachel, raising her hand to placate her friend. "I thought it was a ghost story at the time, but it wasn't. If anything, the opposite. An unghost story."

Chloe topped up Rachel's glass. Josie reached for the bottle. Chloe, the oldest, her children already through university, and the mother hen of the group, pulled it back.

"Rachel tells the best stories. I'm not having you falling asleep and snoring because you're half-cut."

Josie pouted. "How dare you. I never do anything half-arsed. I will be fully cut, or not at all."

Chloe put the bottle out of Josie's reach.

Robert put his head around the door.

"Ladies," he said. The corner of Rachel's mouth twitched. He called them 'ladies' to their faces. At all other times, he referred to the book group as the coven.

"I'm going up to watch a film. Don't talk about me when I'm gone. I know what you're like."

"Come on, Rach," said Josie, when he'd gone. "Tell us your unghost story. Just skip the bits with headless corpses rising from their graves, or Grace will have a fit."

"I promise."

Rachel closed her eyes. Thought back. Telling stories was her role in the group. They all expected her to write a book one day. Maybe she would. She had enough ideas simmering. She just needed to find the right jumping-off point. Start in the right place.

"I thought it was a warning," she began. "The dream, I mean. It was so real. Everything about it. And the way it ended, the moment I woke up, sweating, shaking…it scared me. But I had it all wrong."

*She's walking along a narrow track in the countryside. It's spring, and blossom crowds the hedgerows. Blackbirds hop across her path as if they've forgotten how to fly. Inquisitive robins perch on low branches and eye her as she passes. It's rained recently, and the track is dotted with puddles in deep tractor treads. About thirty yards ahead, a stile. Beyond it, to the right of the tidy rows of corn, a dense wood.*

*At this point, Rachel is not afraid. There's no sense of foreboding. She is a passenger in her own head. No thoughts, no past, no future. Just here. She smells wild garlic. A gust of wind lifts her hair, and she tucks it behind her ear.*

*She doesn't know she's dreaming. It's all so real. She walks faster. There's something ahead she wants to get to.*

*After climbing the stile, Rachel turns right. Faces the wood.*

*Sees the tree.*

*It's an ancient wood, and this tree might be the oldest. Behind the huge, gnarled trunk of the oak, rows of bluebells nod their heads. A silent choir.*

*Rachel notices how quiet it is. And, for the first time, she is afraid. The silence unnerves her. It's wrong. A strange fear, something nestled so deep she can't name it, gnaws at her.*

*She's looking for something, but what?*

*She looks left and right, her pace quickening as she approaches the massive tree.*

*Green leaves and new buds, blue sky between the branches.*

*Have the birds stopped singing?*

*She's nearly there when it happens. A high-pitched noise, a scream, rising in pitch and volume.*

*A trapped animal?*

*No, not trapped, because it's coming closer, fast, coming from behind the trunk, a blur of shrieks.*

*The thrill of anticipation. Is this fear or excitement?*

*She sees it. For a split second, she sees it. A flash of red. Now she's no longer a passenger. She can think again, and there's a word in her mind. One word.*

*The word is* monster.

Rachel woke up, breathing hard. Panicked. She sat up in bed, clicked on the bedside light. Let herself be reassured by her surroundings: Robert's jacket hanging from the cupboard handle. Two books on the table, more piled underneath. On top of the chest of drawers, Mr Clop, the faded yellow bear she'd had since she was three, the provenance of his name long forgotten. The sound of traffic outside. City noises, not countryside.

"You all right, love?"

Robert sat up beside her, put the back of his hand to her cheek.

"Yes. Yes. I'm fine."

"Same nightmare?"

She nodded. Exhaled through her mouth. Remembered the breathing exercises she'd been reading about that afternoon. In through the nose, out through the mouth. A book on giving birth. That particular volume was tucked under the bed. She didn't want Robert to think she was getting ahead of herself, getting her hopes up. This was their final round of IVF, after all. They couldn't afford to pay privately. Even if they saved every penny, Rachel would be in her mid-forties by the time they had enough to try again.

Don't allow yourself to get stressed. That had been the doctor's advice. Apparently, he'd been unaware of the irony. Third round of IVF, last chance to be a mother, which Rachel wanted more than anything in the world, no success in rounds one and two… but *don't allow yourself to get stressed.*

Out through the mouth.

Mr Clop stared at her from across the room, his expression inscrutable.

*It can't be scruted*, she thought, and laughed, the dream's lingering atmosphere finally evaporating.

"What's funny?" She pointed at the bear. But Robert's voice had been sleep-thick, and when she looked, he'd dozed off again. He always came home exhausted. Trying for a promotion with enough extra money for them to go private, but he'd lost weight, and he always looked tired. No. If this round failed, it was over. They'd have to learn to live with it, that was all.

Mr Clop stared on, always looking at something behind her. Something Rachel couldn't see.

She kept a diary back then. Had done since the first round of IVF. Monitored her diet, her bowel movements. Her mood. And, inevitably, her periods, which always came back, Rachel hunched over in the bathroom; alone, rejected.

She recorded the dreams in her diary. They began the night after the fragile fertilised egg was implanted, her body cradling the precious cells.

Rachel often pictured herself from outside in those early days; a careful, gentle, placid figure, thinking positive thoughts. Another piece of advice from the irony-free doctor. But Rachel did her best, treating negative thoughts like vampires, refusing to invite them over the threshold, denying them their power to wound.

She did everything she was asked to do. But—and this never made it into her diary—none of it made any difference. Because Rachel's biggest secret, the one she kept from her kind, insistent mother, the friends who had begun to filter out references to their own toddlers, and from Robert, especially Robert, was that she believed she was barren. Barren; an old word, a biblical word. A harsh, unforgiving word. But it echoed in her deepest place, and it named her, and she believed it. She didn't want to, but she did.

Still she went through the motions, followed the guidelines, did everything she could do to help nurture and nourish the speck of potential inside her.

*Maybe not everyone is supposed to be a mother.*

No one had said it to her face, but they must think it. And they were probably right.

Every night, the same nightmare. The lack of variation amazed her after the first week. Her subconscious didn't add a single bluebell, didn't change the fixed hymnal of birdsong. The puddles were a changeless map on the furrowed track. The smell of wild garlic, the moment at which the scent lifts to her nostrils. Always the same. Exactly the same.

The tree, the ascending scream. The flash of red.

After twenty days, Rachel started lying to Robert.

Three in the morning. Taxi idling down the street. Mr Clop staring. Robert half-awake.

"Same nightmare, Rach?"

"No. No. Indigestion. Go back to sleep."

And so it continued. Every night. Over and over and over. Days pretending the IVF might work. Drinking herbal tea while writing articles on the new cohort of female CEOs, a surge in human trafficking to the UK, or a puff piece about a fading pop star. She wrote the words, but it was more like automatic writing, Rachel's fingers finding the correct keys in the correct order, producing the kinds of sentences magazine readers would appreciate. Words that editors of those magazines would pay for.

She ate the right food, took light exercise daily. A walk around the park. None of the trees were like the oak in her dream. They were pruned, the grass cut, flowers in tidy beds. The dream wood was a wild place, as was the creature that rounded the trunk to confront her.

*The funny thing,* she wrote in the diary, *is that it's not scary. I wake up sweating, breathing hard, but I'm not scared. In the dream, too. I'm not scared. When I describe it, it sounds like a nightmare, but it's not. It's...something else. A warning? Yes. That's the closest I can get. It's a warning. Should I be afraid? It's not as if there's anything I can do about it.*

Rachel still had her eyes closed, but she had stopped talking. No one wanted to break the mood, but when Josie whispered, "Pass the port, Mother," to Chloe, Rachel smiled.

"Is that it?" said Grace. "Did the dreams stop?"

"Eventually, yes. After a hundred and forty-eight consecutive nights."

"Woah." Josie held her arms apart as if measuring the amount of dreamtime such a figure represented. The port sloshed dangerously close to the top of the glass and Grace stiffened beside her on the sofa. "Every night? And they stopped just like that?"

"Yes. And I never had the dream again. But that wasn't where it ended."

"No?" Grace shifted in her seat, looked at her watch. Of the four of them, Grace was the only one who finished every book, regardless of whether she was enjoying it. Even if she hated the characters and found the plot ludicrous. And now she was caught between her aversion to scary stories and her compulsion for completion.

"No," said Rachel, leaning forward to pat Grace's knee. "Part two happened here. In Suffolk, I mean."

Chloe put the cork back in the port bottle. It was gone ten. Usually, this would be the point she offered to make tea. More than two hours between cups and she got twitchy. Tonight, though, she sat on the edge of the armchair and said nothing. Waited for her friend to go on.

Rachel put another log on the fire. Sat back. Took a few moments to gather her thoughts. The flames crackled and spat, making Grace jump.

"We moved out of London three years later," she said. "Seven years ago, now. Robert got his job on the coast, and all of my work was freelance. We wanted out of the city. We settled in to the quieter lifestyle. Robert grew up in the countryside, so he adjusted quickly. It took me longer, but I got there. Then, one spring morning, a year after we moved, it happened."

Rachel and Robert sometimes played the *what if* game.

What if I hadn't gone to that party in Ealing?

What if I had stayed at uni, instead of dropping out to write for a music magazine?

What if Annie hadn't broken up with Robert that summer, and he'd gone to California after all?

What if he'd lost her number?

Robert, rational in so many other ways, inexplicably believed that some things happen for a reason. That not everything can be put down to chance, luck, coincidence.

Rachel disagreed.

When she looked back on what happened that morning, Rachel thought Robert might have been right all along.

Funnily enough, having her world view upended didn't upset her at all. Quite the opposite.

What if…

What if the central locking hadn't played up?

It took a few minutes for Rachel to lock the car, waving the key at various angles without success, then holding it to her head, as someone had once told her it improved the range. In the end, she put the key in the lock and turned it.

"Old school," she said, then hurried away from the lay-by.

It was one of Robert's workdays, and she wanted to explore. As it was their first spring in Suffolk, their next-door neighbour had recommended checking out one of the area's little secrets. Had even drawn her a map.

"What is it?" Rachel had asked. "What's there?" But Mrs Anniston, a tiny creature who looked like she'd borrowed a much larger woman's hair, had tapped a bony finger on her lips.

"You'll see."

She forgot all about Mrs Anniston when she reached the track.

It had rained over the weekend, and there were puddles to negotiate.

A blackbird hopped in front of her.

She followed the cornfield to her left. Looked ahead towards the stile.

It wasn't déjà vu. Rachel had written a piece about déjà vu for one of the Sundays. Although they didn't understand *why* it happened, scientists had dismissed any possibility of premonition. She'd interviewed a man who suffered from chronic déjà vu, some bouts lasting for minutes.

But nothing like this. Even the chronic sufferer had never anticipated his episodes, never predicted anything. There was no evidence to suggest it was more than a glitch in his brain functions.

This was different. Rachel's diary contained a detailed description of this exact scene. Everything matched the dream. Everything. The smell of wild garlic, the gust of wind that lifted her hair. The blackbird, the robins.

She reached the stile, mouth dry, no more able to stop herself than she had been able to when asleep. Her body followed the dream scenario as if the entire experience were playing back on film. She knew what was happening, registered the impossibility of what was happening, but had become an observer, a passenger in her head.

The screaming started.

Rachel stopped. Looked at the oak tree. Watched for the flash of red heralding the creature's approach.

And started laughing.

"You little *monster,*" she said, as Abbie shot out from her hiding place in a blur of shrieking chaos, her red mac streaming out behind her.

"Mummy! Mummy! I got you!"

And there she was, as loudly pleased with herself as only a four-year-old can be, allowing herself to be swept up by her mother and whirled around, stretching out her arms to transform from a monster to an aeroplane in an instant.

"C'mon, Mummy. You're slow. Come and see the flowers."

Grace looked away from the fire. "You're right. It wasn't a ghost story. So what was it? What did the dream mean?"

"I don't know. Maybe nothing. Robert disagrees, though."

Robert. Level-headed. Feet on the ground. Logical. Reliable. It was Robert who put it all together when Rachel told him what happened that day, showing him the description of the dream in her diary. The final dream came the night before Abbie kicked inside Rachel's womb for the first time. The night before Rachel accepted it was really happening: she was going to be a mother.

Josie's glass was empty, but she didn't ask for a refill. All three women leaned forward.

"Well?" said Chloe. "What did he say? What does it mean?"

Rachel glanced away from her friends for a moment, her eyes lingering on the photographs on the mantlepiece, the shelves, and the walls. Abbie as a baby, pudgy legs and a toothless smile. Abbie on Robert's shoulders at the beach. Abbie in her first proper bed, hugging Mr Clop. Abbie's first day at school. Rachel pictured her daughter asleep upstairs and smiled.

"In the diary, I'd written that the dream might be a warning. But Robert didn't think so. 'Not a warning, Rach. Don't you see? It's a promise' ".

---

Since *The World Walker* appeared on Amazon in 2016, Ian Sainsbury has—to his amazement—found he can do what he loves for a living without having to sell a kidney. In 2019, he won the Kindle Storyteller Award for his psychological thriller, *The Picture On The Fridge*. He lives in East Anglia, UK with Mrs S, two children, and a flatulent dog.

# COUNTING THE COST

*By Imogen Clark*

The tall glass jar with the slightly-chipped lid had been in her life for as long as Heather could remember. She had inherited it from her grandmother, who had kept it stocked with aniseed balls which Heather was given as a reward for good behaviour. Oxblood red and as hard as pebbles in her mouth, the sweets were a disappointing confection, but she'd sucked them anyway, always trying to get to the black pip at their heart.

Now the jar sat on her kitchen windowsill and was the repository of her family's loose change. Once a year, the children would tip the contents out onto the rug, collect the coins into neat piles and shovel them into plastic bags which Heather then took to the bank. The proceeds would be sent to the family's choice of charity for the year. It was a little thing but, as she often said to her children, the little things could quickly mount up into something bigger.

This morning her daughters were getting themselves into a steam about something. They stood huddled over Jessica's phone, peering at the screen. Heads as close as that always made Heather think of nits and she shuddered. You couldn't be too careful. There were children at school who always seemed to be humming with them.

Caitlin, eyes wide and indignant, looked up from the screen and mouthed a word.

'Bitch!'

'Caitlin!' came Heather's automatic response even though the word hadn't actually been uttered.

'Well, she is,' replied Caitlin. 'You should see what she's written, Mum.'

Jessica threw her sister a warning glance and closed her phone down, the glow of the screen fading from her eyes.

'That's no excuse for bad language,' replied Heather. 'Who are we talking about anyway?'

'Lily Connor. She's such a cow. And she was being vile to Sophie. You should message her back, Jess. Let her know that we're on to her.'

Caitlin's eyes shone at the prospect of a fight, but Jessica screwed her nose up, not convinced.

'You'll do no such thing,' Heather said sharply. 'That would make you just as bad as she is. You should treat people as you'd like to be treated yourself. And, anyway, someone might screenshot your reply and send it to a teacher, and then it'll be you that gets into trouble instead of Lily.'

'Who's getting into trouble?' said a small voice.

Max had wandered into the kitchen, hair tousled and fire-engine pyjamas riding up his little legs. Ten years younger than Caitlin, Heather worried that Max would grow up too quickly, tainted by the complicated world his sisters inhabited. When they had been his age, they had played with real toys. Max's world seemed to be worryingly two-dimensional.

'No one is getting into trouble,' replied Heather, sweeping him up off his feet and sitting him on her hip where, quite frankly, he was far too big to sit. 'Now—Cheerios or Weetabix?'

Later, with the children at school, Heather ran through a checklist in her head of the things she had to achieve in the narrow slither of time before they all came back. Today was the meeting of the fundraising PTA. They were a nice bunch with barely any of the backbiting you sometimes got on committees. They just got on with what needed to be done quietly and efficiently. Their reward was the job itself, of course, but Heather had asked everyone to write little pen-portraits about themselves to go on the school website. As Chair, her name and picture appeared at the top, not that she was interested in status at all.

A timer buzzed and Heather opened the oven door and pulled out the casserole. Her mouth began to water as she lifted off the lid to check that all was well inside. The rich brown gravy bubbled lazily, button onions and the odd cube of beef poking up through the surface. It was too hot to decant into plastic boxes just yet but there would be time to do it before she had to deliver them. Her cleaning lady had called her a veritable godsend for the old folk. Heather had remembered that, had even quoted it on occasion.

Her gaze settled on the glass jar of loose change. It was October and usually the jar would be nearly full by now, but the line of coins only sat around two thirds of the way up. The rise of contactless payments, Heather assumed. Everyone had less change in their pockets these days. In fact, if she didn't keep a little supply of pound coins in her bag, she often wouldn't have had enough to buy her copy of the *Big Issue*. She always bought it from the lady who stood outside Waitrose. There was another seller in town, a man, whose pitch was near the market in the rougher part of town, but Heather never seemed to be down there. Funnily enough, she had bumped into the chair of the Rotary Club the other day. Her *Big Issue* seller was down to her last copy and there had been some controversy over who should buy it. In the end, the Rotary man had gallantly stepped aside and let Heather take it. She had felt a bit guilty as she dropped it into the recycling bin in the car park unopened, but nobody really read it, did they? Everybody knew that it was just a ruse to make giving more palatable.

There would be less for them to give to this year's charitable cause, though, she thought as she glanced again at the jar. Perhaps she would have to top it up herself.

The PTA meeting ran smoothly. They had lots of creative ideas for fund-raising for the term ahead, and as she sat in the Head's office afterwards, she had that warm feeling that comes with a job well done. She enjoyed her private, post-meeting chats with the Head, especially when she was spotted by the other mothers through the window.

'We really can't thank you enough for the work that you and the PTA do,' said the Head, offering her the plate of rich tea biscuits. 'With funding as it is, we'd struggle to buy the extra equipment without it. Those replacement crash mats get used every day.'

Heather beamed. 'I'm so pleased,' she said. 'And I really hope that after the Christmas fair we'll have enough to buy that minibus. It's amazing what can be achieved when everyone pulls together. And with strong leadership,' she added. The Head nodded and smiled modestly at the covert compliment, although really there were two leaders in the room, Heather thought.

At teatime, Heather left Max with his sisters and nipped out to deliver her little boxes of casserole. She did Thursdays. She'd thought about offering to take on another day as well, but really there was a limit to how much one woman could do. She was already in danger of spreading herself too thinly and where would they all be if she was ill? She was the lynchpin for so many important things.

Mr Armitage was her last call. She rang the bell and then waited patiently for him to make his laborious way to open the door. Autumn was starting to take hold now and she shivered as the cold wind bit into her ankles. Come on! What on earth was keeping him? She had her own family to get back to. She didn't do this for the good of her health.

After an age had gone by, she saw the hunched shadow of Mr Armitage through the bevelled glass and then the door opened.

'Oh, it's you,' he said when he saw her.

Heather brightened her smile. 'Yes, it is. Just like every Thursday. I've brought you your meal.'

She offered the plastic carton to him. He looked at it suspiciously but didn't put out a hand to take it.

'What is it?'

'It's beef casserole,' Heather replied.

'Again? Can't you cook anything else?'

Heather pressed her lips together into a thin line. She was doing this out of the goodness of her own heart. No one paid her to produce these meals week in week out. The very least Mr Armitage could do was pretend to be grateful.

'I can,' she replied evenly. 'But the others all say how much they enjoy my casserole, particularly in the colder months.'

'Well, I'm sick to the back teeth of it. If you really want to be helpful, then why not make some food we actually want to eat.'

That stung. Heather had a good mind to take her casserole away and leave the old ingrate to go hungry. But he would no doubt report her if she did that. Instead, she said,

'I'm sorry that you find my food unsatisfactory, Mr Armitage, but I'm afraid there's nothing I can do about that. This is all there is. Now, would you like the casserole or should I take it away?'

Mr Armitage grunted a little and muttered something under his breath, but then he snatched the carton from

Heather's grasp and with one swift movement slammed the door in her face.

Anger raged in Heather. Who did he think he was? She would have a word with the coordinator, see if she couldn't knock him off her list. It took a lot of her precious time, not to mention money, to produce these casseroles week in week out. She wanted to be sure that they went to people who were truly grateful for her efforts.

It was three o'clock. Time to collect Max from school. Mothers gathered in small groups according to their status. Heather could have stood with the Alphas, but she chose to talk to the women on the edges, the ones who hadn't made it into any of the gangs. It was important that no one felt excluded, and Heather saw it as her responsibility, as a mother who knew and understood all the nuances of the playground, to make sure that no one was left behind.

Today, however, there were no stragglers and so Heather felt released from her obligations and went to stand with her own friends. Her options had been curtailed somewhat by some nastiness with Bernadette Fisher earlier in the term. Bernadette's son, Louis, had been mean to Max. Heather might go as far as to call it bullying, and indeed had done when she raised the matter with the Head at one of their post PTA tête-à-têtes. There had been no physical violence but rather what Heather saw as a conscious campaign of unkindness against Max orchestrated by Louis Fisher. She had listened night after night to Max's sorry tales until she could stand it no longer. A telephone call to the Fisher's house had ensued which had resulted in a feud of sorts growing up between the two mothers with no sign of the frost melting any time soon.

Heather's mother had had a view on the situation.

'You should never fall out with the other mums, Heather,' she'd said. 'The kids'll make it up, but adults find it harder. You never really get over a row with another mum. It always leaves a bad taste.'

And for once her mother had been right. The two women hadn't spoken since. Heather knew that she should be the bigger person and offer Bernadette an olive branch. After all, she was the more experienced parent and she prided herself on always doing the right thing, but this was her precious son they were talking about. Bernadette Fisher would need to meet her halfway. She eyed Bernadette now, taking in her shabby anorak and her boots with the heels worn down to the plastic and tried not to feel superior. It tested every one of her empathy responders.

Then the doors opened and out the children charged. She saw Max scan the women, hone in on her and then begin to trudge over. He dragged his book bag across the tarmac after him.

'Hi there, soldier,' Heather said as he approached. 'Pick your bag up, there's a good boy. Have you had a good day?'

Max thought about the question, face creased. 'It was okay,' he replied with a shrug.

'Only okay? Did something happen? Was someone mean to you?' Heather's eyes flicked to where Louis and Bernadette were standing.

'Louis said I was spoiled. I told Miss Venables about us going to Greece at half term and Louis said that anyone who had a holiday not in the summer was spoiled.'

Heather felt her hackles rise. 'Well, that's a lot of rubbish. Take no notice. He's probably just jealous that he's not as lucky as you.'

Heather firmly believed that it was important to be kind at all times. But some people just didn't deserve it.

There was trouble on the domestic front as well. The drama with Lily Connor appeared to have escalated and Jessica and Caitlin were teeming with righteous indignation.

'We'll just ghost her until she says she's sorry to Sophie,' she overheard them saying. Heather wasn't sure what 'ghosting' was, so she googled it surreptitiously and learned that it was when someone cut off all communication without explanation.

'Oh girls,' she said. 'You mustn't do that. It's unkind. And if she reports you then you'll be the ones that get in trouble.'

Caitlin, the fieriest of her children, turned on her.

'No Mum. It's not like that. You just don't get it.'

Heather was about to object when Jessica chipped in.

'And you're not bothered whether we're mean or not. You just don't want us to get caught doing it. It's all about being seen to do the right thing with you.'

Heather's jaw dropped.

'Well, I don't think that's fair,' she said. 'Of course, I care about you not being mean to people. It's important to be kind and treat others with respect.'

Still feeling stung, Heather reported their daughter's accusations to her husband when he got home from work.

'So basically,' she told him, 'what they're saying is the only reason I do all this charity work is because I want people to *see* me as a kind person, like it's all about appearances.'

Simon had adopted one of his infuriating diplomatic silences. When she pressed him, he had simply raised an eyebrow in reply.

But it wasn't true. She was kind. She was always helping other people. In fact, she was a pillar of the community. Everybody said so. And of course, she cared. It was ridiculous to suggest that she was only interested in how things looked. Wasn't it?

The following week the level of coins in the glass jar had dropped further still. There was only one conclusion to be reached. Someone was helping themselves.

'You haven't taken any money out of the jar, have you?' she asked Simon. 'For parking, or for the poppy appeal or something?'

Simon shook his head.

'I'm sure someone's taking it,' Heather said. 'And they've taken quite a lot.'

'Ask the girls,' said Simon. 'But tread carefully.'

He gave her a knowing look. Heather sighed internally. Of course, she'd tread carefully. Did he think she was completely stupid?

'You haven't borrowed money from the change jar, have you?' she asked Caitlin.

'No!' snapped Caitlin, going from nought to a hundred in a second. 'God Mum! As if I would!'

Jessica's response was similar and so Heather backed down, but someone was taking the money. Maybe it was the cleaning lady? Heather had always trusted her, leaving her jewellery out on the side when she came as proof of that fact, but perhaps a pile of actual cash was just too big a temptation. She would raise it with her the following week. She always tried to think the best of people, but in the face of evidence to the contrary what was she to do? She didn't want to have to sack her though. Good cleaners were so hard to find.

Max jangled as he walked, and the pockets of his school shorts rose up in lumpy bulges.

'Max?' said Heather. 'What have you got in your pockets?'

'Money,' he replied simply.

Max was too young for pocket money, so there was only one place he could have been getting such large sums. Suddenly all became clear, and Heather felt relieved that she hadn't yet accused the cleaning lady.

'Have you taken it out of the change jar?'

Max nodded but there wasn't a shred of contrition in his expression. Heather, feeling disturbed by his apparent lack of remorse, pressed on.

'Why?' she asked.

'It's for Louis,' Max said. 'I give it to him.'

Anger shot through Heather. This was it. Clear proof, if ever it were needed, that that Fisher boy was bullying Max. He must be demanding money with menaces and Max, afraid of the consequences of refusal, was complying in the only way he had available to him—by stealing.

She rushed over to her smallest child and threw her arms around him.

'Oh sweetheart. My poor little baby. What did he say he'd do if you didn't give him the money?'

Max wriggled out of her hug. His little forehead crinkled in confusion.

'Louis didn't ask for the money,' he said. 'I just gave it to him.'

Heather stared at him, not sure what he was saying.

'But you can't take things that don't belong to you, Max, even if you are going to give them to someone else. That's stealing.'

Surely, she had taught him right from wrong. He might be young, but he wasn't too young to understand the concept of theft.

'That jar is where we save up for charity,' she continued. 'If you take from the jar then you're stealing from the charity.'

Max paused, his eyes searching for answers on the ceiling. Heather could almost see the tiny cogs in his brain whirring round as he grappled with the idea.

'So, we put money into the jar to give to people who'—he paused as he tried to get the words just right—'people who aren't as lucky as us.'

Heather's disquietude slipped away. He did understand. 'Yes!' she replied enthusiastically. 'That's exactly it.'

Max grinned. 'That's what I thought,' he said. 'So, I gave it to Louis.'

Heather's shoulders dropped again, and she let out an infuriated sigh.

'No, Max. Louis doesn't count.'

'Why not?'

'Because, well, he's not less lucky than you. Not really.'

He was actually, thought Heather. He had that witch of a mother for a start.

'But he doesn't get any tea,' replied Max. 'That's not lucky.'

'What are you talking about, Max? Of course, he gets tea.'

Max shook his head. 'He told me. He only gets lunch, so he always eats loads at school. No breakfast either. So, I gave him money out of the jar for people who are less lucky than me.'

Heather stared at him, trying to work out which emotion to run with. Her son, it appeared, was smart, logical, honest and kind-hearted. She wasn't sure which of those warmed her heart the most. She swept him up in her arms again, ignoring his wriggling protestations.

'I'm so proud of you, Max,' she said. 'That was a very thoughtful thing to do. But perhaps don't give him any more money. Let me take it from here.'

Max slithered out of her grasp. He looked at her and shrugged. No biggie, he seemed to say.

It was Thursday—food delivery day. Heather was trying a new recipe. A wholesome shepherd's pie. In fact, she had come up with a few ideas that she was planning to cook on a rotation. As she stirred, she thought again about Max and Louis. She had had a quiet word with Max's class teacher and explained what had been going on. She'd done it discreetly without fanfare. Kindness it seemed really was about what you did, not what you were seen to be doing. But of course, she knew that already. She hadn't needed her seven-year-old to remind her, not really.

Heather knocked on Mr Armitage's door. It was chucking it down with rain and she could feel the cold drops trickling down the back of her neck. After what felt like forever, the door opened.

'What?' said Mr Armitage.

'I have your dinner,' said Heather, offering the plastic box.

'What is it?' growled Mr Armitage.

'Shepherd's pie,' Heather replied with a wide smile.

'I hate shepherd's pie,' said Mr Armitage, but he took the box and slammed the door.

Heather walked back to her car with a spring in her step. She'd try him on her chilli

con carne next week.

---

Internationally-bestselling author Imogen Clark writes contemporary fiction about families and secrets. Her books have topped Amazon storewide charts eight times and her third book was shortlisted in the UK for Contemporary Romantic Novel of the Year 2020. Imogen initially qualified as a lawyer but after leaving her legal career behind to care for her four children, she returned to her first love—books. She went back to university, studying English Literature part-time whilst the children were at school. It was a short step from there to writing novels. Imogen's great love is travel and she is always planning her next adventure. She lives in Yorkshire with her husband and children.

# THE LORD'S WORK

*By James Gilbert*

We were drinking again. The same place. We always started at the same place.

– I gave this up for a while.

– Eh?

– Drinking. Thought it'd be good to give it up for a few months. Made things worse in the end.

– How's that?

– Too much time. All those extra hours.

– …

– Mostly I read. But I got sick of it. So.

And I pointed a finger at the empty pint glass. Foamy and streaked.

Cousin Calvin nodded sagely before picking up the thread of the conversation I'd just tried to cut.

– It's not a good time. I'm telling you man. It's not fun to be alone again.

I nodded and tried to think of something to say. He leaned back in his chair and stared into space, eyes glazed. They were big and bright and blue and I didn't like to look into them for too long.

– But she wasn't mean about it, you said?

– Eh?

– I mean she wasn't mean about the whole thing.

– Ah no. He was shaking his head. Light gleamed off the hairless crown. – No it was – she was – it wasn't like that.

– Right. That's – well, that's good.

Cousin Calvin sighed and started massaging his eyes with a pale hand. He rubbed and rubbed.

*He isn't going to cry, is he?*

– Another one?

I gestured at the two empty pint glasses on the table. He nodded and I got up and stumbled over to the bar.

The bartender was young and good-looking. I knew it was wrong but I held it against him. Sometimes you can't help it. He put his phone down and pointed at one of the taps.

– Same again?

I tried to stand up straight, leaned a bit on the bar for support, pressing my hands onto its surface. Under my fingers, grease and dirt and nicks in the wood; indentations forming a map to indicate each casualty in the war between pint glasses slammed down by decades of excitable drunks and unmoving, solitary bar.

– Yeah. Please.

As he poured them I raised my eyes from the taps and looked around the place. The windows were black.

*In-out. In-out.*

– Darkness falls, eh?

I started, jerked my head back towards the taps. The bartender had been following my gaze.

– Right. Yeah.

And he handed me the two beers and I handed him the money.

– Cheers.

I carried them back to the table and collapsed in my chair. Cousin Calvin started on his right away and I watched as he tipped the glass heavenwards. His throat pulsed; beer descended down through oesophagus, into stomach. He let rip a loud belch.

– I'll be alone forever now.

– Ah, come on.

– It's true.

– Nah. Plenty of other people in the world.

– She was different.

I coughed, pushed my chair back a bit.

– You'll meet someone else. Someone better.

– You don't get it.

– I do. I get it.

He was rubbing his eyes again. I took a sip of the beer. It was awful.

– There are lots of people out there.

For a moment there was electricity, and suddenly he was alert, looking right at me, sitting up straight in his chair, excited. He pointed at his head.

– You see this?

– …

– You see the spot where there should be hair?

– Ah, come on.

– Women don't like it when the hair that's meant to be there isn't.

– That's not true.

– It's easy for you to say. And he pointed at my head. A long, bony finger. – You've never had to worry about it.

– Yet.

– Well. He took another gulp of beer. – I'm telling you. It makes things different. And this.

He looked down at his belly. It had swollen up like a balloon since she left him.

– You can lose that, I lied.

He was almost finished his beer. I took a long swig, tried to catch up. It was still bad, but it went down a bit easier this time.

*Just keep at it. Slow and steady.*

– We're getting old, Cousin Calvin murmured. – It's not like it used to be. It's harder to be alone.

I didn't know what to say to that; I had no idea what to say to that. Behind me I heard a glass fall to the floor and a woman laughing and suddenly there were four empty pint glasses on the table in front of us instead of two. They were multiplying aggressively.

– Like rabbits, I said quietly.

– Eh?

– Nothing.

– Next place?

It wasn't really a question. Cousin Calvin was already on his feet.

– Yeah. Yeah alright.

I pulled my coat tightly around me as we walked out into the darkness of the night. The cold, dry air tickled my throat and I breathed in and out, in and out. It was a trick my doctor had taught me. I was learning how to calm down.

*In-out. In-out.*

– The Lucky Strike? Or Sneaky Dees?

Cousin Calvin was huffing along beside me. For a moment I had been alone, away from him, from his problems, from my own, almost.

– Lucky Strike.

– Yeah.

We marched into the wind; on either side of us heaps of dirty snow shovelled clumsily up on the edges of the pavement.

The city buzzed and hummed and sang. Some of the shops had put up Christmas lights. I tried to remember what day it was and wondered how many there were between now and the holidays. Then I stopped and focused on walking in a straight line.

We crossed the street and turned up towards The Lucky Strike. Cousin Calvin slipped and I caught him.

– Alright?

– Yeah. Fine. Sorry.

*He is heavier. A lot heavier. Maybe he will be alone forever. Maybe I will be, too.*

A homeless man lay against the side of the closed-down electronics store next to The Lucky Strike. Old and grizzled. He moaned as we passed him and went into the bar.

A blast of heat, the smell of cheap beer and music playing loudly on an old sound system. My glasses fogged.

– It's a lot busier in here, eh?

– What you having?

– Whatever. I don't care.

I went up to the bar and realised I was buying two rounds in a row. It didn't matter, but I wished I had more money. It's easier when you do.

– It's true, a girl down the bar was chatting to her friend. – I'm telling you it's *really* true. He *really* said that. They both laughed.

*In-out. In-out.*

I got the bartender's attention. A Springsteen song was pumping loudly through the aging sound system. I tried to figure out which one, but I couldn't. And then the beers appeared before me as if out of thin air, and I carried them back to the table Cousin Calvin had seated himself at, spilling them clumsily as I went. I settled them on the table, looked at Cousin Calvin, a million miles away.

*Maybe more than that.*

I licked my lips and tried to think of something to say. I pointed upwards.

– Hey. Hey, you know which Springsteen song this is?

He closed an eye and cocked his head to one side. Listened for a moment.

– Can't tell.

– It's off *Born To Run* I think.

He paused, shifted in his chair.

– Nah. Nah this is from *Darkness On The Edge Of Town.*

And he clammed up on me again. I clutched my pint glass, slid it gently side to side on the table.

*One more try.*

– Hey you remember when we used to play that?

– ?

– The Springsteen. *Darkness*. When we used to play that at the local. With the other guys. In college.

Cousin Calvin picked up his beer and frowned.

– Yeah. Was ages ago.

– I thought we did a pretty good job of it.

– …

– I mean, with the set up we had and –

– I don't need this, he said flatly.

The speaker cracked and someone whooped loudly.

– Eh?

– I don't need this. It's not going to help me.

The pint glass hit the table hard. His lips tightened. Beer slopped over the sides of the glass, forming a little amber lake around the base.

– Well. Well don't have it if you don't want it.

I watched the little lake expand, imagined it was a flood, swallowing up all the dry land.

– No. I'm sorry man. This isn't – and it was my round. I'm sorry.

I coughed and put my beer down too. Gently, with no spilling.

– Don't worry about it.

– I just don't want to drink anymore tonight. I'm – I can't stop thinking about it.

The Springsteen song was ending.

– I can't stand being alone.

I put my hand out and gripped his shoulder. I don't like to touch people and I don't do it very often. It makes me feel strange.

– You're all right. I get it.

– Yeah. Yeah. He put his head in his hands. Then he let them drop to the pint glass in front of him. He shoved it gently across the table in my direction. – You have it.

I wanted it. I said:

– Nah. I don't need another either.

The song ended. Something else familiar came on. I started to say something – stopped – started again.

– Eagles?

– Nah. Yeah. Yeah, it's The Eagles.

– There's no 'The'.

– Eh?

– Everyone calls them 'The Eagles' but there's no 'The' in the band name. It's just 'Eagles'.

– ?

– It's true. I grinned and leaned back. – You surprise me. Musician of your calibre should know things like that.

– You serious?

– Course.

– Jesus. He was drumming his fingers on the table, trying to get the rhythm of the song. – I should know that. I've got *Hotel California* on vinyl and everything.

I shoved my chair back and stood up.

– Wanna head?

– Yeah. He sighed and smiled half-heartedly up at me. – Sorry about this man.

– Don't apologise. We'll try it another time.

It was snowing outside the bar. Across the street, outside one of the old, decaying nightclubs, a group of twenty-somethings were smoking cigarettes and laughing. A streetcar was groaning down the far end of the street, fighting its way reluctantly along the track.

– Cab?

– You got cash?

– Not enough.

– Hold on.

Cousin Calvin reached into his jeans pocket and fished around for a minute. He came up with a few dollars in coins.

– Here.

I thrust the bill and the coins I was holding in my own hand into his. He took them and counted, muttering quietly.

– Yeah. It's enough.

– Right. Good.

We turned to walk towards the road and look for a cab. Cousin Calvin stopped.

– Ah Jesus.

– ?

– Look at that, eh.

I jerked my head around. The homeless man was still there, slumped against the brick wall of the electronics store.

– That's rough eh, whispered Cousin Calvin.

I didn't say anything. We stood side by side in silence for a second and then he walked away from me and over towards the homeless man. He took the money and tried to hand it to him. The homeless man didn't say anything, just looked up, confused.

– Take it, said Cousin Calvin gently. – Here.

He held out the coins and bills. The man hesitated, reached out and took them and said something I couldn't hear. Cousin Calvin nodded at him and turned and walked back to where I was standing.

– We can walk, eh?

– Yeah. Sure. Yeah.

We turned and started off. Halfway down the block he stopped again.

Cousin Calvin coughed and cleared his throat.

– He said he was cold.

The streetcar was finally rumbling past.

– I bet he is.

He stopped. The snow was really coming down.

*If I shut my eyes and lay down it would bury me.*

– Hold on.

Cousin Calvin turned back again and walked over to the homeless man.

– What're you…

But he didn't hear me. I watched as he took his jacket off and handed it to the homeless man. I watched the homeless man try to refuse it, eventually take it. And then he was peeling his sweater off, his T-shirt underneath, undoing his belt, taking off his shoes and socks, stripping down to his boxer shorts.

*What the…*

Pot-belly, sporadic chest hair, albino-white, drainpipe legs. It was happening so fast it was in slow-motion.

He was back at my side now, a smile plastered across his face.

– We're the same size. What are the chances eh?

– …

– Come on, let's go.

He started off, naked except for his boxers.

– Calvin man…you're gonna freeze.

Ten steps ahead he turned and grinned and I stared at his body, glowing white under a streetlight. Bare feet in an inch of snow; the most realistic snowman in the universe. He spread his arms up and raised them and snowflakes gathered rapidly as everything else fell away.

– It's great, he smiled. – You should try it.

I laughed and he laughed and we started up the street.

– He'll be glad.

– Eh?

– The guy.

– Yeah. Well.

He rubbed his naked arms together, did a little twirl on the snow, faced me.

– You know what he said.

–?

– Said I was doing the Lord's work.

I laughed.

– My Grandfather used to say that.

– Yeah?

– Yeah. He did the Lord's work regularly.

– Good man.

– Paid off, too.

– How's that?

– He was never alone. Always surrounded by people. Maybe too many, sometimes.

I grinned and gave him a big, lazy wink.

– Hadn't had so much attention since the Nazis were shooting at him.

Cousin Calvin laughed and slapped me on the back and as we walked together flakes fell all around us and we were enveloped in a deep and welcome calm, pushing and shoving each other in the snow and the darkness.

– Least they missed, eh?

– Yeah. Pretty pleased about that.

– Me too.

And he slapped my back again and the city hummed and glowed and sang all around us as we walked and walked and walked, alive again.

*In-out. In-out. In…*

---

James Gilbert is a new writer from Toronto, and has lived and studied in the UK and Canada. An avid guitar player, he writes and produces music in his spare time. You can check out more of his short stories at: https://www.jamesgilbertwriter.com

# KIND IS IN THE MIND

*By Jane Corry*

*MAUDE*

She's a kind girl, is Annie. Always asking if there's anything I need. Nothing is too much trouble. This morning, when I ran out of my Earl Grey (we're allowed to order our own brands in here), she went out to the shops and bought me a packet.

There aren't many care staff who would do that nowadays. I know. I've been through a few.

Here's another thing. Annie brushes my hair. I didn't ask her. She just offered when she saw me struggling with my arthritic shoulder. That's right. It's got to the point where I can hardly move anything nowadays.

'Let me do that for you,' she said.

At first, I wasn't sure. I've never been one for letting people get close. But when you get to my age, you have to take what help you're offered.

In fact, I found it rather soothing. She doesn't do it briskly in a rushed fashion like my mother used to. '*Come on now, Maude. Sit still!*' It's more of a measured, respectful action.

Annie also hums when she's brushing. There would have been a time when I'd have found that extremely irritating. 'Maude has such a short fuse,' I once heard one of my staff complaining, back in my working days.

I got rid of that one pretty quick after that. You could dismiss people for all kinds of reasons back then. But the magazine world could be cutthroat. You needed people around you who were on your side.

That's the other thing about Annie. She doesn't mind listening to all my stories. 'You interviewed him?' she gaped when I mentioned a famous film star.

'I certainly did,' I said, a lovely warmth spreading through me at the memory. 'They flew me to Hollywood. After the interview, we swam in his pool.'

She raised her eyebrows.

'In fact,' I continued, 'I had a distinct feeling that the relationship might have become a bit more if I hadn't been married at the time.'

'Wow!'

Her admiration made me feel good. I didn't tell her that in fact we were disturbed by the actor's second (or was it third?) wife coming outside and asking when he was ready for the next interview.

Of course, he's dead now. Yet that old woman who looks back at me in the mirror with her double chin, wrinkled eyelids which have shrunk with age, and blue veins on her hands is still, in her heart, a young woman.

Mind you, I'm hanging on, thanks to the kindness of strangers like Annie. I look at her now as she tidies up around me and 'sorts out' my incontinence pad. I take care to hold my tongue when she's around because I've been asked to leave by too many homes before for being 'difficult'.

If she really knew the truth about me, I wonder if she'd be so nice?

Of course, if I could go back, I'd be different. But it's too late now.

* * *

*ANNIE*

I love my job at the care home. It's almost like a hotel. When I come in for my shifts, I breathe in the smell of fresh air spray and recently-vacuumed carpets. So much more comfortable than our cold flat with the boiler that doesn't work even though the landlord keeps promising to fix it. The canteen food is delicious! It's a real treat to have a meal put down in front of me. (Javed does his best although there's only so much you can buy on our budget. At least the girls get hot meals at school.)

But the best thing about working here is that you get a nice class of resident. Like Maude. To think I'm looking after someone who swam in a Hollywood pool with…No. I'd better not mention his name. I pride myself on being discreet!

Still, there's one thing that niggles me. Maude has got me all wrong.

'You're so kind, Annie,' she keeps telling me.

Actually, I'm not.

I try, but the truth is that when I finish my shifts, I'm exhausted. It makes me snappy sometimes. Last night, the manager asked me to do overtime and because I needed the money, I agreed.

It wasn't an easy evening. I had an emergency with old Mr Woodman's catheter which came out and then I had to help the new lady in room number three back into bed because she'd fallen out. Luckily, she hadn't hurt herself but it put my own back out a bit. (There was no one else available to help.)

Then I missed the last bus back—only by seconds but the driver wouldn't wait—and had to walk. A young lad stopped to ask if I wanted a lift but of course I said no. I'm not that stupid.

'Why are you so late?' asked my husband when I crawled into bed next to him.

But instead of explaining rationally like I should have done, I gave him what for. 'If you had to work my hours, you'd understand!'

I knew immediately that I shouldn't have said that. Javed's been trying to find work for months now but as everyone knows, it's not easy. Now I've offended his pride.

'I'm sorry, love,' I whispered.

'It's ok,' he said, turning over. But it wasn't. And I knew it.

Then, before I knew it, the girls were up and although Javed usually encourages me to lie in after a late shift, I want to see them before they go off to school. I like to hear their chat and find out what they're doing and check they've got their books together.

But today it all went wrong because Glenda and Posy both needed shoe boxes for a craft project. 'Couldn't you have thought of this last night?' I said.

Their faces fell. 'Sorry mum.'

'No,' I said. '*I'm* sorry. It's just that I'm tired.'

I managed to find two old boxes at the back of the cupboard (we haven't bought shoes for a while, although we're going to have to, before long) and gave them both a hug before Javed walked them to school.

'We've made up, haven't we?' I said to them as they went.

'Of course, mum.'

I went back to bed to try and catch up on my sleep before the next shift at the care home. But I couldn't stop reproaching myself. Why was it easier to be kind to patients like Maude instead of your own family?

And then I got an idea.

* * *

*SAM*

I keep thinking about that lady last night.

I've never done it before. Well, you can't, in this day and age, can you? It can be just as dangerous for the person who's trying to help. Someone could accuse you of taking advantage of them.

But I couldn't help noticing this woman running out of the care home, still in her uniform, waving at the bus.

Maybe the driver didn't see her or maybe it was too dangerous to pull in. I like to see both sides of things in life. My mum taught me that. She'd also done shifts, working late into the night.

Maybe that's why I found myself offering this lady a lift.

'No thanks,' she said, running on as if I was going to try and pull her into the car.

I get it of course. I could have been anyone. But even so, it made me think. My parents brought me up to think of others. 'Always be kind and courteous,' they used to say.

But kindness is often misinterpreted nowadays, isn't it?

'You know your trouble?' says Lucy when I tell her later. 'You're too nice for your own good!'

But she says this in a sweet way, giving me a big hug at the same time.

Lucy is the best thing that's happened to me since starting my Masters. (In fact, I'm on my way to morning lectures now.) We're both training to be psychologists. My mates tease me about this. 'You'll each know what the other is thinking,' they joke.

Actually, we kind of do. And it's nice. We both want to help others. The world stuff that's happened in the last couple of years has affected so many minds. It's going to take us time to get back on track. And one way to do that is to think of others.

Even though that's sometimes easier said than done.

Whoops! What's that?

The car has started to drive unevenly. That's all I need, especially as I'm meant to be giving a presentation today.

I get out to take a look. The front left tyre is as flat as a pancake.

'You OK, mate?' asks a voice.

It's a man with two little girls in school uniform.

'Not really,' I say. 'I'm meant to be somewhere and I've no idea how to sort this out.'

'Looks like a blow-out to me,' he says. 'If you can wait a bit, I'll just take my children to school and come back.'

'Thanks,' I say. But I can't help feeling worried. What if he doesn't come back? This presentation is really important. I'm not even insured with an emergency breakdown service. And I can't afford to join one on the spot with my bank balance at the moment.

Twenty minutes later, I'm just about to give up hope when I see the man running towards me. 'Sorry,' he gasps. 'I had to sort out something with the teacher about a school project. Now let's take a look at this, shall we? Got a spare in the boot, have you?'

'I've no idea, I'm afraid,' I say, feeling totally useless.

'No worries. Here it is.'

Within minutes, he's fitted it.

'Reckon you're good to go now,' he says.

'Thank you so much!' I put my hand in my pocket. Then I stop, remembering. Like many of us, I don't carry cash anymore because of hygiene.

'I don't want anything,' he says, noticing. 'I'm just glad I could help. Your thanks is payment enough. Have a nice day.'

Then he went.

I get to my presentation with minutes to spare. The topic is 'How to calm the mind in troubled times'. It's pretty important because it's going to count towards my post-grad. I don't want to sound boastful but I'm pretty word perfect. I've gone through it enough times. The only thing I'm rather worried about is my introduction, which feels a bit bland.

But as I'm standing here, in front of my class and professor, something different comes into my mind.

'Today,' I say, 'I'm going to talk about kindness and how it can change our lives. It might sound simple but if we are feeling down, the one guaranteed way of climbing back out of that black hole is to do something good for others.'

I see a few heads nodding.

'But it doesn't always go that way, does it?' I ask. 'Last night, I offered a lift to a stranger who had missed her bus. She declined and I felt rather silly. Of course she would! It's not always safe to accept a stranger's invitation.'

Everyone is listening. I'm beginning to feel nervous. Maybe I should have stuck with my opening script after all.

'Then today, I had a flat tyre on my way here and a total stranger offered to fix it. He refused to take any payment. He said that my thanks was payment enough.'

All eyes are on me. It's like I've struck a chord. It gives me the courage to go on more boldly.

'The thing is that his act made me feel really positive because it showed there are some good people out there after the awful time we've been through. And, even though this is only a guess, I reckon that he's feeling quite good now because he knows he's helped someone.'

Someone claps. This is the point where I can go into the rest of my presentation with all the diagrams and figures I've already prepared.

'Well done,' says my professor afterwards. 'You really got everyone's attention there.'

But I knew that it was my unknown rescuer who had really saved the day.

'Thank you,' I whisper silently.

* * *

*MAUDE*

'Maude,' says Annie. 'Are you napping?'

It's on the tip of my tongue to bark out that yes, of course I am. Can't she see that my eyes are closed?

But Annie is such a nice girl that I find myself trying extra hard to contain my sharp side left over from all those years in a tough working environment.

'I've got a visitor for you,' she says.

'A visitor?'

I straighten myself in my chair as a pretty young thing flounces in with bright red lipstick. She reminds me of myself, years ago.

'Hi, Great Aunty Maude,' she trills.

'Who are you?'

'Scarlet!'

I don't believe it. It's my niece's daughter.

'Goodness,' I say. 'The last time I saw you was at your christening.'

'I know,' she says. 'Mum said you weren't great at keeping up with family.'

I can't argue with that.

'You speak your mind, don't you, young lady?'

She beams. 'Mum says I take after you in that respect. I was doing a job round here, so I thought I'd pop in and say hello.'

'Hmph! What kind of job?'

Scarlet looks pleased with herself. 'Actually, I'm a journalist.'

'Are you now?' I sit up, my interest piqued.

She's taken one of the other chairs, making herself at home even though I haven't invited her to sit down. 'I always wanted to write for a magazine after the stories Mum and Gran told me about your life. It sounded so glamorous.'

'Hah! Not always.' I thought of the long hours slogging away to find case histories on the phone. Even those interviews with the famous weren't always easy. They could be real prima donnas. Not that I admitted this to anyone else.

'Who do you write for?' I ask.

She names a magazine I've never heard of.

'I interview celebrities,' she says.

'That's what I used to do.'

'I know. Mum kept scrapbooks of everything you had published. I brought one with me. Look!'

She hands it over. I'm amazed. I never thought my family was interested in my job but here it is. Feature after feature, including that one with the Hollywood actor in the swimming pool.

Scarlet's looking at me shyly now. 'Like I said, you inspired me, Great Aunt Maude. And I'm really grateful.'

I swallowed hard. I'm not used to getting praise in social situations. 'Really?'

'Yes.' She blushes.

I used to go red until I'd taught myself to be hard.

'In fact,' she continues, 'I was wondering if you could give me some advice. You see there's this woman I work for who's always telling me off even if I've got the slightest thing wrong. She growls good morning, snaps at me constantly, and gives me menial jobs when I know I could do more. She's also really rude about me to others. I don't know whether to stand up to her or change jobs. I don't want to move because it's such a great magazine.' Her face falls. 'But I'm not sure I can cope with her behaviour anymore.'

That woman sounds rather familiar. I did the same to some of my staff. Sometimes it was because I was worried the boss might replace me with someone younger.

'Actually,' I say, 'I've got a better idea. Why don't you take this boss of yours to one side and tell her that you're doing your best, but you'd appreciate her help in getting things right.'

Scarlet frowns. 'What if that doesn't work?

'Then be bold. Explain that you don't want to have to report her for bullying behaviour but that maybe you could both start again.'

My great niece's eyes widen. I realise that behind that confident exterior is a young girl, trying to get ahead in life.

'Sometimes,' I say, 'people think they can get away with being unkind until someone points it out and makes them feel ashamed.'

'Do you really think it will work?'

'It's worth a try,' I say firmly. 'Now let's have a glass of wine, shall we?'

'But it's only 10.30!'

'So what? You'll find the corkscrew in the drawer behind you, and my emergency bottle of red behind that copy of *Who's Who* on the bookshelf.'

Scarlet and I have a lovely time. It's nice to have a new audience to tell my stories to. I suspect that even Annie, who has the patience of a saint, is getting a bit sick of them.

'Shall I come back and visit?' she asks.

'Please do,' I say, kissing her soft cheek goodbye.

A fortnight later, I get a postcard from Vegas.

*Dear Great Aunty Maude,*

*Thanks for the advice! It worked! She liked some of my ideas too. I'm just about to interview this really famous actress!!! Are you free next month? I heard it was your birthday. Mum and Gran want to come too.'*

* * *

*ANNIE*

It was the girls' shoe box craft project that did it. The teacher needed them so the class could decorate the outside. Shen then wrote down 'inspirational tips' on the blackboard. They wrote them down, cut them out and put them in their boxes.

It's all part of a 'self-development' module. School has certainly changed a lot since my day!

'This is mine,' says Glenda, handing it to me at teatime. She's the eldest by five minutes.

*'It's ok to feel scratchy at times. Don't beat yourself up about it! Just try to think about what you're going to say before you say it!'*

'And this is mine,' says Posy, the 'little' one.

*'Think of someone you admire. Then pretend you are that person for a few minutes. It's amazing what a difference it can make!'*

They both made me think. So the next time I felt myself getting uptight, I pretended I was Maude. She's always nice to me! And what a life she's had! So when the girls mislaid a school shoe or their homework or hadn't washed up, I imagined I was lying by a pool in Hollywood, about to interview a famous actor.

Mind you, I'm feeling pretty happy anyway. Javed's got a job! He'd just finished fixing a stranger's car on the street—that's so like him—when a man walked past and said he owned a local garage and was looking for a mechanic. Amazing, isn't it? It's a lower grade than the job he had before, but like he says, it's a start. You can see from the spring in his step that he's getting his confidence back and it makes a big difference to our income. We can buy the girls new shoes now.

'We've got a lot to be grateful for,' he says.

He's right. In fact, I've started something new with Gloria and Posy. It was something my own mother had taught me which I'd forgotten. 'Think of one nice thing you've done for others today,' I tell them.

'What have you done, mum?' they ask.

I think of the phone call I made to Maude's 'next of kin' after I'd heard her weeping softly through the door the other month.

'I put someone in touch with someone else,' I said.

* * *

*SAM*

It was Lucy who gave me the idea.

We've all got to do a community project. It's part of our course. Some people are giving free advice sessions. But I'm collecting stories about kindness.

I've interviewed people in college and local shops and friends and even people in the local care home. The professor's partner works there and she introduced me to some amazing characters, including an old lady who was quite a journalist celebrity in her time.

A businessman (who owns a chain of garages round here) has offered to print it free of charge and we're going to sell it online and in local places. The proceeds are going to a school so it can buy some play equipment. It's going to be called KIND IS IN THE MIND. I hope it sells well. Wish us luck!

Meanwhile, I've signed up for a car repair course. I'll never forget that man who stopped to fix my tyre. He didn't just help me with my presentation (I got a distinction!) It also inspired the idea for my kindness anthology. I only wish I knew where he lived so I could tell him!

Still, that's the secret of kindness, I guess. It doesn't want fame. It just wants to help.

---

Jane Corry is a best-selling thriller writer who is published by Penguin. Her last six novels have all been in the top ten of the Sunday Times paperback chart. Jane's latest novel *The Lies We Tell* is about Sarah, a mother whose 15-year-old son Freddie comes home one night to say he's 'killed someone'. Sarah can't believe her boy would do such a thing. Her husband wants to go to the police, but Sarah takes Freddie on the run. It is a novel of forgiveness. Jane was inspired to write thrillers after working as a writer in residence of a high-security male prison. She has also taught creative writing at Oxford University and was a Royal Literary Fund Fellow at Exeter University. She's a regular contributor to The Daily Telegraph and swims every day in the sea.

# NOTHING MUCH TO LOOK AT

*by J.D. Kirk*

"She isn't much to look at, but she's got it where it counts."

Both women stood on the pavement, regarding the car that squatted on the road in front of them. Ellie, the younger of the two, swept a strand of hair behind her ear and shrugged.

"I mean…that's what he always used to say. Sounds pretty stupid when I say it."

It was a Honda Civic. Oh-seven plate. *A classic*, he'd always insisted, and about as close to a sports car as they were ever likely to own. The paintwork was a canvas for scuffs and scratches. Black. Mostly.

As long as you looked at it from the right angle.

Kate, the woman who'd come to see it, so far appeared largely unimpressed. She had given a tyre an experimental kick with the toe of a pointy black shoe. Ellie had a vague recollection that this was a bad thing, but she soldiered on regardless.

"It's got all the paperwork for the last MOT. Dad did the work himself." She saw the first flicker of doubt on Kate's face, and moved quickly to extinguish it. "But properly. He knew what he was doing. He worked in a garage for years before he took ill."

OK, technically it was a petrol station, but some people *did* refer to those as garages, so it wasn't technically a lie.

And he had known what he was doing. Better than most actual mechanics, in fact.

He used to joke that he'd been cursed with two opposing afflictions—a deep-rooted love of motor vehicles, and very shallow pockets. Money had always been tight, so when a mechanical problem arose—and they always did—he'd tackle it himself.

And it had worked. With help first from the Haynes manual, then more recently various YouTube tutorials, he'd kept the car running. Not running smoothly, necessarily, but running.

"He used to get me to help," Ellie recounted. "When I was little, I mean. He'd pretend he was a surgeon, and I was a nurse. He'd be like… 'Spanner,' and I'd pass it to him, and go, 'Spanner.'"

She smiled at the memory, then shook her head, remembering where she was and what she was supposed to be doing.

"Sorry. The point is, Bella's…" She fumbled for one of the phrases she'd memorised. "…mechanically sound."

Kate shot a glance at the watch on her wrist, gave an almost imperceptible sigh, then frowned. "Bella?"

Ellie's hands were sweating. She shoved them into the pockets of her jeans and blushed, just a little. "That's what we called her. It. The car." She nodded at the Honda, in case there was any confusion as to which car they were talking about. "He called it Bella. Stupid, really. It's just…it's a car. That's all." She angled her head away, like she couldn't bring herself to look at it. "Just a car."

"Oh." Kate took a sleek slab of a phone from her bag, rapid-fire typed out a message with two thumbs, then returned it to her bag. She smiled, but there was an impatience to it. "Sorry, busy day. How much did you want for it again?"

Ellie shifted uncomfortably. "Eh, I…We…My sister and me, we thought maybe…I mean, we did some looking up, and we thought something like…" She took a breath. Held it. "A thousand?"

"A thousand?"

The breath escaped as a squeak. "Or… Not necessarily a thousand. Something like that. Nearest offer."

She thought back over the research they'd done the previous evening. The sales techniques that Mia had drilled into her until Ellie had finally packed her off to bed.

"You need to get them to imagine themselves already owning it," Mia had told her. "Don't sell them a car, sell them a *lifestyle*."

Pretty wise words for an eight-year-old.

Ellie wished she'd brought Mia outside with her. She'd have handled this way better than Ellie currently was. She was a natural at this sort of thing. She was going to go places, that kid. Ellie was going to make sure of it.

"You'd, eh, you'd look good in it," she said. Then, to really try to sell the image, she moved her hands like she was turning a steering wheel.

Kate's brow furrowed briefly, then both sculpted eyebrows crept up towards her lightly greying hair. "What? Oh, no! The car's not for me!" she said, and she almost laughed at the very suggestion. "It's for my son. Well, stepson. It's his birthday next week. Seventeenth. We thought we'd get him a car, but nothing proper, just an old"—she stopped herself from saying 'banger' in the nick of time—"runaround."

"Oh. Right. Yeah," Ellie said. She gestured at it like a gameshow host presenting this week's star prize. Hand gestures, Mia had told her, were critical. "I'm sure he'll love it."

Kate looked doubtful. "It's more for my benefit than his. Get him out from under our feet every once in a while."

"Can he drive?" Ellie asked.

"He's not seventeen yet," Kate reminded her, and Ellie silently cursed herself for her stupidity.

"Oh, yeah. Of course. Sorry. You said that."

"He's going to start learning. Supposedly."

Ellie smiled. "Me, too. Don't want to rely on the bus forever. Not round here."

Kate glanced at the housing estate around them, so wary of *hooded youths* coming crawling from the shadowy alleyways that she almost missed the remark completely.

"What?" she asked, once it had filtered through. She looked down at the car, suddenly suspicious. "Then why are you selling it?"

"Lessons are expensive," Ellie explained. "Dad was going to teach me, after we found out about the…But, there was so much to sort out, and it all happened so fast, that…" She glanced down at her feet, squared her shoulders, then looked up again. "But yeah. They're not cheap. Thirty quid a time."

"Right. Yes. Well, they're cheaper if you buy them in blocks," Kate said, dropping her voice like she was sharing some big insider secret.

Ellie knew that, of course. She'd done the sums more than once. "Really? I'll look into that, thanks."

Kate's phone buzzed in her handbag. She ignored it, muttered a, "Thank God it's Friday," then turned her full attention to the Honda. "Right, let's have a look at it, then."

Ellie stood in silence, watching as Kate prowled around the car, squinting at the dings and dents, and rubbing her thumb on the scratches. Judging by the intakes of breath through her teeth, and her occasional *tuts*, she was not impressed.

Kate was around at the front of the car now. A few steps more, and she'd be on the opposite side to Ellie, rapidly approaching the angle at which the black paintwork was no longer anything of the sort.

Ellie hurriedly ran back over the list of potential responses that she and Mia had rehearsed the night before, preparing herself for the inevitable moment when—

"Oh!"

Kate looked at Ellie over the roof of the Honda, then let her eyes creep back down to the rear passenger door.

"This door's blue," she announced, in a tone that suggested she thought this might come as news to the younger woman.

"Um, yes. It is," Ellie confirmed.

"The rest of the car's black—well, it's a bit grey where it's peeling at the spoiler—but this door…" She stepped back and looked at it again, as if to double check. "…it's blue."

"There was an accident," Ellie explained.

Kate took a step back, like the car might be carrying some sort of contagious disease. "What, it's been in a crash?"

"No, nothing like that!" Ellie blurted. "A shopping trolley hit it. Blew across the car park at Aldi. Made a big dent. It looked terrible."

Kate pointed to the door. "And this looks better, does it?"

Ellie brought her shoulders up to about the level of her ears in a prolonged shrug. She smiled, but it was an anxious, unconvincing sort of thing.

Her eyes were drawn to an upstairs window of the terraced house behind her, where Mia watched from her bedroom. The glass fogged a little as the girl mouthed something, slowly and deliberately.

"Personality!" Ellie chirped.

"Sorry?"

"The door. Dad said it gave her personality. It. The car."

Kate tilted her head. Scrunched up her nose. "I suppose. But, is it the personality of someone you'd necessarily want to meet?"

She continued her appraisal, tracing her fingertips over scrapes, and bending to study the tread on all the tyres. "What's the mileage?" she asked.

Ellie momentarily closed her eyes, picturing the number Mia had made her go over and over. "Seventy-eight thousand, three hundred and twenty-six."

Kate flinched. "That's high, isn't it?"

"Not for the year. We looked it up. It's actually quite low compared to other cars of the same age." She could sense the older woman's doubt, and felt the sale slipping away. "Dad always said Hondas can run forever, if you look after them. And he did. It's been well cared for. Mechanically, I mean. She might not look like much, but—"

"She's got it where it counts," Kate concluded. "Yes, you mentioned that." She put her hands on her hips and clicked her tongue against the back of her teeth. "I'm just…it's a birthday present. I mean, the ungrateful little toad doesn't deserve anything, quite frankly, but still."

She stepped up onto the pavement, joining Ellie again.

"Is a seventeen-year-old really going to appreciate"—Kate gestured at the car with both hands, although with far less fondness than Ellie had—"*that*?"

"I mean…I would have loved Bella at seventeen," Ellie replied. And she had, too. "It's freedom, isn't it? A car. It lets you, I don't know, do stuff. Go places. That's why I'm going to get lessons. So my sister and I can…I don't know. See things." She put a hand on the roof, and let it linger there. "She's a good wee machine. I'd have loved to get her at that age."

Kate regarded the hand on the roof, and the look on the younger woman's face. "How long did he have the car? Your dad?"

"Ten years. Just over," Ellie said. She smiled. "I remember him bringing it home. It was the newest car he'd ever owned. Four years old at that point. He'd taken a loan, but he was so excited. He let me drive it. Well, he let me sit on his knee and hold the steering wheel."

"How old were you?"

"Nine," Ellie replied. She removed her hand, and watched as the sheen of an imprint faded.

Her hands really were *very* sweaty.

"So, you're only nineteen now?"

"Last week," Ellie confirmed.

"Jesus. You look older," Kate remarked, then she shook her head and widened her eyes. "Sorry, that just came out. I didn't mean…That's not…You look great. Just…mature, I meant."

Ellie smirked. "Like an old cheese, you mean?"

"No! Grown-up!"

Ellie tucked the persistently unkempt strand of hair back over her ear again, then returned her hands to her pockets. She glanced up at the girl in the window and smiled an apology. She had a sense that this was not going well.

"No choice, really," she said. "Someone has to be."

Kate followed the look up to the window in time to see a curtain fall back into place. Her phone buzzed in her bag. She ignored it again.

"Was it sudden? Your dad?" she asked. "Tell me if it's none of my business."

"It's fine," Ellie said, forcing a smile. "Yes, and no. We knew it was coming. Just…it came quicker than we'd been expecting. In the end."

"I'm so sorry," Kate said. She looked up at the window again. The top of a head ducked quickly out of sight. "Is your mum…? How's she taking it?"

Ellie looked off into the middle distance, nodding. "She's…I mean, I suppose she's…" She swallowed. "She's dead. Same. Cancer. Like…Dad. I mean, not the same kind, but…Yeah. Years ago. My sister was only a year old."

Kate's phone buzzed. She thrust a hand into the bag and pulled out the mobile.

Ellie caught a glimpse of a thick white envelope, and a suggestion of banknotes tucked inside. She tore her eyes away and watched as Kate pressed a button on the phone and held it until the screen went dark.

"Sorry," she said.

Ellie gestured to the phone. "It's fine. If you need to take it..."

Kate shook her head. "No, I mean about...everything. Your mum and dad."

"Oh." Ellie became fascinated by a spot in the middle distance. Her jaw clenched as she fought back tears that had been building for a while now. "Thanks. It is what it is."

Kate clicked her fingers. "Wait. Hold on. Sangster? That was your dad? Alan Sangster? Worked in the"—a smile tugged at her mouth, like she'd just got the joke—"garage?"

"Yes! That was him!" Ellie said, lighting up at the mention of his name. "You knew him?"

"Vaguely. Sort of. He was a year or two below me in school. I couldn't believe it when I heard." She looked up at the window, then back to Ellie. "So, you're on your own now? You and your sister?"

Ellie sniffed. Smiled. "She keeps me right," she said. "She quite practical. Very like Dad, actually."

"And she's happy with you selling the car?" Kate probed.

"Like I say, she's very practical. She knows we need the money," Ellie replied, dodging the question. She looked pointedly in Bella's direction. "So...?"

Kate smiled thinly, then took a step back so she could see the car in its entirety. "You were looking for a thousand, you say?"

"Or close to it," Ellie confirmed. "I mean, we can take some money off for the door."

Kate's eyebrows met in the middle. "What? The blue door?"

"Uh, yeah."

"The blue door gives it personality," the older woman reminded her. "The blue door's a plus. You can't take money off for the blue door. You should be charging extra, if anything."

Ellie frowned, confused. "What?"

"And what was that mileage? Under eighty-thousand? On a car of this age?" She puffed out her cheeks. "That's nothing. And they run forever, don't they? Hondas?"

"Um, if you look after them properly, yeah."

"Which you say he did."

"He did. He really did," Ellie confirmed.

Kate crossed her arms and slouched her weight onto one hip, like she was contemplating her next move. Ellie held her breath, trying not to get too hopeful. She could feel her sister's stare on the back of her head. The not knowing would be driving her crazy.

They needed this. God, they needed this. The insurance had covered only the most basic of funerals. No flowers. No wake. Nothing. Just a man in a box, two lost girls, and a handful of strangers on a wet, windy day.

"Given the low mileage, and the extra personality provided by the blue door, I'd be prepared to offer..." Kate tilted her head from side to side, doing some sums. "Twelve hundred."

Ellie blinked. "What? Pounds?"

"Yes. Twelve hundred pounds. Cash."

Ellie looked from Kate to Bella and back again. "But...I was only asking for—"

"You might want to rethink that sentence before you get to the end of it," Kate interjected. She thrust a hand out. "I'm assuming that's a satisfactory offer?"

"It's, eh, I mean... yes!" Ellie clutched the offered hand and shook it. "Yes. Thank you! This is...God, Mia's going to be made up."

"I'm sure," Kate replied. She reached into her bag and fished out the envelope, then handed it over. "I'll let you count it. Do you have the keys there?"

"What? Yes! Sorry!" Ellie fumbled around in her pockets until she found the keys.

An old plastic keyring *clacked* as the keys settled in her hand, a much younger Ellie and her dad smiling up from the photo pinned behind the scuffed acrylic. She stared down at it for a while, then gave a little jump of fright when the keys were plucked from her hand and the envelope was put there in its place.

"Count. Make sure it's all there," Kate instructed.

"I'm sure it is. I trust you," Ellie said.

Kate shook her head. "Best check. There are some dishonest people around."

She waited while Ellie took out the money and slowly counted it, sliding each note from one hand to the other, her lips moving silently as she tallied up the total.

"All there?"

"It is. Thank you," Ellie said, stuffing the money back into the envelope. "It's really generous of you."

"Nothing generous about it," Kate replied. "You under-priced it. I'm just paying what it's worth."

Ellie ran a thumb quickly across the underside of one eye, wiping away a tear before it could start to fall. "Well, I really appreciate it," she said, then she stole a glance back up at the bedroom window. "Weird request, I know, but…would you mind if I got my sister out? Just to, you know, say goodbye to Bella? To the car, I mean?"

Kate did not seem particularly enthused by this idea. "I don't think that's really necessary, do you?"

"What? No. I know. It's just…She knows we need to sell it, but I think if she doesn't, like, say goodbye or whatever, she might be upset later on."

Kate shook her head. "No. I mean, I don't think that's really necessary."

She held out the keys. From inside their Perspex prison, young Ellie and her dad both beamed happily.

Ellie frowned, her grip tightening on the envelope. "Sorry, I don't…Have you changed your mind about buying it?"

"*Her*," Kate corrected. "And no. I haven't. I'm buying the car for twelve hundred pounds, as agreed. But here." She jangled the keys. "These are yours."

"I don't…" Ellie looked from Kate to the keys and back again. "I thought it was a birthday present?"

"*She* is," Kate said. "She's your car, Ellie. You and your sister's. Not mine, and certainly not that ungrateful waste of space of a stepson's. He wants a Playstation, anyway. Bella? She belongs to you."

Ellie reached for the keys like they might be some sort of mirage, and appeared genuinely surprised when they turned out to be solid.

"I don't," she said again. "I'm not sure that I…"

"How does Monday sound? Have to be evening, though, I'm working until six. And I'll warn you, I'm an absolutely bloody nightmare."

Ellie blinked. "Monday? For…for what?"

"Your first lesson," Kate told her. "I mean, I'm not a qualified teacher, or anything, but I can give you some pointers. Cut down on the number of proper lessons you'll have to pay for." She patted the roof of the car, and this time it was her hand that lingered for a while. "We'll have you driving her in no time."

Ellie stared.

For a moment, she just stood there, staring, the muscles in her jaw straining.

And then, she lunged, throwing her arms around Kate and burying her head in against one of her shoulders. The older woman patted the girl's back as Ellie's shoulders heaved, and her breath came in faint, shaky sobs.

"You're OK," she whispered, tears tickling down her cheeks. "Shh. It's fine. You're OK."

She held Ellie close, and saw herself reflected in one of the windows of the car beside them. Her mascara was running, giving her a distinct Alice Cooper vibe, which wasn't a particularly attractive look for a women pushing fifty.

She didn't care. Truth be told, she'd never considered herself to be much to look at.

But sometimes—just sometimes—she had it where it counted.

---

Since publishing his first DCI Logan Scottish crime fiction novel back in 2019, J.D. Kirk has gone on to top the bestseller charts and win an army of international fans who can't get enough of his dark sense of humour, gripping plots, and vivid descriptions of different types of rain. He does write about Scotland, after all.

# THE BIG ISSUE

*By Jean Gill*

'Why doesn't he run away?' Alun pointed at the dog lying on a stripy blanket in the shoe-shop doorway. The brown mongrel and its owner looked back at him. Neither seemed too willing to waste energy on answering the question. Behind the man and his dog, Alun could see his own reflection shimmering like a ghost among the pairs of shoes, which were stacked in pyramids like a fairground game. If he had a stone with him and chucked it with a bit of spin at the black lace-ups bottom left, he could probably knock the red sandals smack into the bum of the shopper bending to pick up some trainers. Alun's image put its arm back down by his side and his thoughts returned to the question. If nobody answered him at home, he just kept on asking.

'Why doesn't he run away?' he asked again. The man's legs were stretched out in front of him, open, bent at the knees. His arms rested easily on them and he lifted his right hand now and then to take a slow drag. When he lifted his arm, Alun could see a hole in his trouser leg and the frayed ends of a woolly grey sleeve. Some kind of hat lay on the stripy blanket, with a few coins in it, but the man didn't seem to be making much effort to get attention from the passers-by. The dog was lying down, its head resting on crossed front legs. Its eyes guarded the hat and followed the passing shoppers, returning to Alun without much interest.

A second pair of deep brown eyes focused on Alun and the man spoke. 'He's a good dog.'

'Why don't you sell *The Big Issue*?' was Alun's next question.

'Why don't you?' asked the man, in that same slow drawl as if speaking were just another pointless effort. This answer was not nearly as satisfying as the first one and Alun had just opened his mouth to explain why the man should sell *The Big Issue* whereas Alun obviously had no need to, when the man spoke first.

'I gotta go somewhere. Will you look after the dog?'

Alun imagined sitting on the stripy blanket by the dog while the man went shopping. It would be just the same as waiting for his mother, who was taking so long that the man would probably be back before she came. He hoped none of his friends were in town but it would be worth it to talk to the dog. He could say it was a sponsored something. You could get away with anything if it was sponsored.

'All right.' Before Alun could sit down on the blanket, the man had stood, the dog following his movements with its head cocked, fully alert, and the blanket had been folded up. The man took a length of string out of a pocket, tied it round the dog's neck and gave the other end to Alun. The dog listened to the man, whispering something in the dog's ears, which drooped immediately.

'I'll be here again next Thursday,' he told Alun, and disappeared. The dog stood by Alun, waiting for something to happen and Alun stood by the dog, the string clutched tightly. The usual drift of couples, families and kids passed, chattering, but there was no trace of the man. Just as Alun thought his heart would burst from panicked beating, he saw a familiar face—not the man but his mother. This was as bad as it could be.

* * *

The argument was still going on in the kitchen and Alun could hear his mother's voice, shrill and angry, 'You just encourage him,' and then the lower, more dangerous tones of his father, 'He's only 11, Anne. If you want, we'll take the mutt straight to the vet and finish it off. It's half-starved anyway and there's no pain…just one injection and that's it'.

There was a silence as deep as a dog's brown eyes. Alun sat on the cold patio stone because he thought the dog would feel more at home with someone sitting beside him. The dog gave no sign of feeling anything. It lay beside him in the same pose it had kept on the blanket. If Alun had been braver he would have sneaked a blanket out of the airing cupboard, but one memory of his mother's face when he had tried to explain to her what had happened and he knew the dog would have to lie on the cold stone, at least for now. The silence lasted longer than he could hold his breath, which was a bad sign and very unlucky. He had told himself that if someone spoke before he breathed again then everything would be all right. The next words were spoken too quietly for him to hear but it was his mother's voice. Alun smoothed the dog's short fur, noticing how silky the forehead and ears were compared with the thickness of its back. He wondered how the dog's weatherproofing worked and considered how it would be to have a friend like this, who just sat beside you and thought doggy thoughts.

It was his mother who came out into the garden. Alun was reminded of those films where you saw two characters locked in mortal combat, then you couldn't see them anymore and it was only when the victor emerged that you knew who had won.

Except that with his parents there wasn't a goody and a baddy, and it depended what you wanted as to who you wanted to win. And it was always his mother who told him the verdict, whoever had won, so that meant nothing.

'I'm disappointed in you Alun.' This was nothing new. 'You're old enough to have a sense of responsibility. I can't believe you talked to a stranger at all, never mind bringing home a stray.'

'He's not a stray.' A glare from his mother shut him up.

'And we've said no to a dog often enough. But,' she sighed deeply, 'your Dad thinks it's a chance for you to show whether you can look after a pet. We'll try to take him back next week but if you ask me, this con-man just wanted rid of the poor thing, and you'll have had enough so we'll take it to the dog's home then and they'll do what's best.'

* * *

It was only three days since the dog had moved in but Alun could not imagine life without it. He didn't have to look down to know that the dog was at his side, following his every move, listening to his every word. The string had been abandoned straight away when it became clear that the dog was not going to run away. Quite the opposite: the dog wouldn't run on its own at all. It sat, lay, walked beside Alun, slept where it was told to, and it would even run—beside Alun, if he ran. It was not something he could say to his parents but Alun knew there was something wrong; the dog was just too good.

Day 4 was Sunday, one of those autumn days when the sun gave a last burst of heat and the garden flickered gold. Alun's dad stopped digging, groaned and stretched to ease his back. He idly threw a stick for the dog, shouting, 'Fetch,' and Alun watched as the dog's eyes followed the stick, while its body stayed rock-still, in its usual working pose.

Dad shook his head and frowned. 'We can't have that on a weekend. Anne?' he called Alun's mum and went off into the house, emerging minutes later. 'Come on, we're off to the beach. Bring the string, just in case.' Alun, his mother and the dog did as they were told, the back of the car being just another shop doorway as far as the dog was concerned. It didn't wince as Alun's dad sang along with the car radio, not even when his Mum joined in.

You could always smell the sea, before it appeared as a glint behind a field, hiding with the twists of the lanes and totally invisible from the carpark. Alun cricked his neck round to watch the dog. Perhaps this was its first time. Alun sniffed as if it was his first time; if you covered wet clothes in mud and salt, you still wouldn't come close to the freshness of the wet tang, with a hint of metal and machine from the small railway line which hugged the coast. Had he imagined it? Alun kept watching and sure enough, the dog's nostrils were flickering, twitching with interest, and the fine, straight hairs on the back of its neck were standing up, as if in a breeze which only the dog could feel.

The walk started sensibly, feet and paws moving as in a perfect fire drill, all straight lines and regular pace. Then Dad started zig-zagging and walking backwards, making Mum laugh until she skipped into pigeon steps and wrote his name in huge letters in the sand. Alun veered off his parents' course towards the low breakers, starting to run, his movements shadowed by the dog. They ran into the waves, Alun stopping as the waves lapped the calves of his wellies but the dog continuing to splash in deeper until it was forced to swim. 'You're out of your depth,' Alun told it. The dog carried on swimming. 'Dad!' Alun yelled, suddenly afraid, and his father, holding a stick, was suddenly at his side.

'Fetch!' The stick was thrown just in front of the dog's nose and retrieved without hesitation, the dog doubling its clumsy paddles to turn around and bring the stick back. When it reached the shallows, it dropped the stick in front of Alun, wagged its tail and gave a sharp bark. He was slow to understand and the dog nudged the stick with its nose, wagged its tail and barked again.

'Go on, throw it,' his dad told Alun, and the games began in earnest. In its excitement, the dog turned somersaults in the incoming waves. Even when the dog rushed out of the sea to shower Alun's mother with seawater as it shook itself right beside her, even then there was just shrieking and laughter, as his father encouraged the dog to chase his mother. It had been a long time since Alun had seen his parents playing.

"We'll call him Sandy," said his mother on the way home and Alun started to hope that they might keep the dog.

But the man was there the next Thursday, just as he had said.

'Where did you go?' asked Alun, despite his mother nudging him. The man just shrugged. 'Were you ill? Are you better now?'

The man looked at him steadily, ignoring his mother, who hovered anxiously beside Alun, not sure of the social rules. 'I wanted the dog to have a holiday. He's too young to understand this life.'

'You've got to give Sandy back, Alun.' His mother was impatient to get it over with but no longer because it was what she wanted.

Alun smoothed the dog's head and sent it back to the blanket with unspoken love. Man and dog greeted each other with a touch, a lick, a tail wag and a smile. 'If you sell *The Big Issue*, my mum would buy one, wouldn't you Mum?'

'Maybe,' she said.

'So you will sell it then,' Alun persevered.

'Maybe,' said the man, and he turned his attention to the dog, dismissing Alun and his mother even before they turned to go.

---

Jean Gill is an award-winning Welsh writer and photographer living in the south of France with two scruffy dogs, a beehive named 'Endeavour', a Nikon D750 and a man. For many years, she taught English and was the first woman to be a secondary headteacher in Dyfed, Wales. She is mother or stepmother to five children, so life was hectic. Visit www.jeangill.com to find out more about her work.

# GEORGIA GREEN

*By J.J. Marsh*

I almost didn't go to Charlotte. Reason being me and Ma had the biggest fight over that dumb dress. I put up all my best arguments for why I should wear my jeans but my mother ain't persuaded easy. Stubborn as a mule, just like me. Difference is, she got experience on her side.

She folded her arms and fixed me with one of her stony looks. "This discussion is over, Marybelle. You can wear the green dress I pressed for you and accompany your father to the city. Or you can wear your jeans and stay home with me. I could use an extra pair of hands."

It crossed my mind to call her bluff but I knew she woulda done it. She'd make me stay home and do chores while the boys got to drive across the state with Pa. So I put on the damn dress and sulked all through breakfast. Nobody noticed.

Scott and Glenn had both been to the city of Charlotte before and spent the whole week boring me and Frank silly with their advice on what to do and where to go and what to watch out for. Today was the day and their excited hollering gave me a pain in my head.

When time came to get in the truck, the boys scrambled into the flatbed. Scott had swept it clean of straw ready for the trip but what with the rust and oil and dirt, it was no place for a dress. Ma said I should sit up front with Pa. No arguments from me. Saved me three hours bumping around, listening to my brothers jabbering. Ma stood on the stoop to wave us off, smiling. I forgot about my sulk and waved and smiled right back.

Charlotte was the most beautiful place I ever saw in my entire life. Parks with golden trees and shimmering fountains, buildings so tall you had to lean back to see the top, people dressed up like as if it was Sunday, clean shiny cars driving down streets wider than Beaver Creek, billboards advertising everything from Cornflakes to eyelashes and a big ole courthouse so huge I swear you could fit the whole population of Oak Ridge inside.

My head was swivelling to and fro, telling Pa to 'lookit' every two minutes. He laughed and nodded even though he seen it all before. He parked outside a diner and bought us each a hamburger with fries and a Coca-Cola. He told us to be back at the truck by five o'clock or he'd leave us behind. And off he went for his meeting with the bank.

Me and Frank had a map each, drawn by Ma. Scott and Glenn said they didn't need one. Mine had a couple landmarks and stores and important sights to help me find my way, but there was only one place I wanted to go. I left the boys squabbling over ketchup and walked two blocks, checking my pocketbook one more time to make sure my dollar was still there.

Before I went in, I stood and gazed at it for a moment. Montgomery's Bookstore. First time in my life I saw a store which sold nothing but books. Closest thing Oak Ridge had to a bookstore was Ling's Provisions. Mr Ling kept a shelf at the back with paperbacks from all over the world. Every year, when Aunt Lilibeth sent me my birthday dollar, I'd pretty much decided which book I was going to buy weeks ahead of time. But this year, I was going to spend it in a real bookstore. My hand was a-trembling as I opened the door.

"Good afternoon to you," said a voice. Behind the counter, a short bald man with a freckled scalp looked over his glasses at me.

"Good afternoon, sir. I'd like to buy a book today."

"Would you now? Well, you've come to the right place. Do you know which book you want or should I leave you to browse?"

I turned to look at all the bookcases, shelves, recesses and tables all crammed to bursting with stories. "If it's all the same to you, sir, I'd like to take a look around before deciding."

He made a sweeping motion with his left hand, inviting me to explore. I wandered in and out of all those racks for hours, picking up everything that caught my eye and making a shortlist in my head. Tell the truth in the face of the Lord, it weren't all that short. Over the doorway ticked a huge clock with Roman numerals, like something out of a storybook itself. I vowed to choose by half four. Pa wouldn't leave without me, I knew that, but he'd be cranky as hell if I didn't get my butt back to the truck by five.

Good as his word, the ole guy left me in peace. Customers came and went, but nobody gave me a second glance. Who'd notice a fourteen-year-old girl sitting on a tea-chest in a dusty corner with her head bent over a book? Even if she was wearing a pretty green dress.

Panic started to flutter when I glanced at the clock and saw it was five minutes to four. I picked up the first on my list again.

"It's not easy, making a decision." The shop man leaned against the wall, hands in his pockets, his gaze ranging over the shelf behind me.

"Ain't that the truth? I been at it four hours but still no closer to choosing."

"Perhaps you'd like to sleep on it. Come back tomorrow?"

"No sir, I can't. Heading back Greensboro way tonight. I got a dollar to spend on a book and I want to be real careful what I pick. Worst of it is, I never saw so many books. Feels like this room has a thousand doorways and I only got one key."

He smiled. "Maybe I can help. What kind of stories do you like?"

I replaced *Goldfinger* on the shelf. "Adventures. Danger and excitement and foreign places. Brave heroes."

"We've got plenty of those. Anything else?"

I hesitated. "Well, sir, I'd like a hero..."

"Yes?"

"A hero who is not a boy."

He straightened up. "Not a boy? Hmm. You don't like boys?"

"I got three older brothers. I don't mean no disrespect, but there comes a time when you can have too much boy, if you catch my meaning."

He blinked over his eyeglasses. "What's your name, young lady?"

"Marybelle Calhoun."

"Pleased to make your acquaintance, Marybelle. My name is Mr Montgomery and I own this establishment. Let's see what we can find."

I tried, the Lord will testify, to make it last as long as possible. But come Thanksgiving, I'd already read *To Kill A Mocking Bird* twice. I wrote to Aunt Lilibeth and told her what I bought with her dollar and how much I liked it. She wrote back saying she'd read it too and I had 'superlative taste'. Would you look at that? Miss Marybelle Calhoun has superlative taste in literature, doncha know?

One afternoon in April, Frank and I trudged up the lane from the school bus, talking 'bout our favourite characters who ain't real. Mine was Scout. His was Linus from Charlie Brown.

Sometimes, I think Frank is smarter than he looks. Then Scott and Glenn ran ahead making fart sounds with their armpits and Frank joined in. I sighed. I might be the youngest, but I swear I am the most mature. Ma was shucking peas on the stoop in the sunshine.

"Marybelle, hurry now and change your clothes. Do your chores and come inside. There's a package for you."

I stopped dead.

Frank's half-lidded eyes sprang open. "A package? For Marybelle?"

"Who's it from?" I asked.

Ma shrugged. "I don't know but I'd sure like to find out. So change your clothes, feed the dogs and get the hens into the barn. Then we'll open it together."

Frank and I did our duties in record time and ran to the kitchen. There on the table was a brown paper package addressed to me, Marybelle Calhoun, in strong black penmanship. Ma pushed it across the scrubbed surface of the table.

"Open it."

I pulled the string, peeled back the scuffed brown paper and let out a little gasp. Inside, there was a big ole hardcover book, entitled *The Adventures of Miss Georgia Green.* The cover was all shades of sage and grass and emerald. The title and the author's name—D. Montgomery—were picked out in gold. I wiped my hands on my jeans and opened it. Inside, there was a sheet of paper, folded in two.

*Dear Miss Calhoun*

*Further to our discussion last fall, I find myself in agreement with your assertion. One can indeed have 'too much boy'. Therefore, I humbly submit this novel, of which I hope you will approve.*

*It has adventure, danger, bravery and foreign lands, and a very special hero, who is definitely not a boy.*

*Yours respectfully*
*Douglas Montgomery*

"The bookstore man in Charlotte! Look, Ma, he sent me a book!" I thrust the letter at my mother.

She was still leafing through the pages of my gift, shaking her head and smiling. "No, Marybelle. He *wrote* you a book."

She pointed to the dedication.

*To Marybelle, the girl who inspired Georgia Green*

---

As an English teacher, actor, director and cultural trainer, Jill has lived and worked all over Europe. Now she's a full-time author, publisher and audiobook narrator. Her crime novels in the 'Beatrice Stubbs' series have become international bestsellers. Psychological dramas *Odd Numbers* (shortlisted for the 2021 Bookbrunch Selfies Prize) and *Wolf Tones* dig deep into the world of emotional dependence. The 'Run and Hide' Thrillers chase a hunted woman around the world. She lives in Switzerland with her husband and dog, taking advantage of the landscape, languages, Prosecco and cheese.

# SNOW DAY

*By Judith O'Reilly*

Virginia Cafferty rapped so loudly on the window that the child she'd been watching dropped her chalk in fright. Maisie was a vandal in Virginia's opinion. Hopscotch on the public sidewalk was little better than a desecration of the neighbourhood. Virginia had her own chalk, of course, which she used on her walks to draw circles round the litter that was dropped and the foulings by dogs. But that was altogether different. That was a public service. One for which she should, by rights, be commended by the town mayor.

In the early dawn, when the mood came upon her, Virginia would zip up her sheepskin-lined ankle boots, button up her thickest tweed coat and patrol the streets. The chalk clutched in arthritic fingers, she'd stoop to write LITTER LOUT by the discarded food wrappers and tin cans. And FOUL!!!! by the poop, wrinkling her nose and careful that her sleeve didn't graze the stinking mess. It would have been quicker and simpler to pick up the offending garbage, but she was willing to admit that it would also have been a deal less satisfying. It was, after all, her duty to alert the lazy and the slack-jawed to the fact she was alive to their misdemeanours. Occasionally, she considered making her rounds in the daylight, but she wasn't convinced the rabble would understand her motivation, and to be frank, she loathed the idea of becoming a public spectacle if one of the miscreants challenged her or, worse yet, laughed at her. No, it was safer when there was no one about.

This morning, it was Maisie's turn to be taken to task and it was Maisie who stared back at her. Huge dark eyes and a look of indignation on her round face. The child was seven, and in Virginia's opinion, desperately noisy and a great deal too full of herself. Always in sneakers and the same denim dungarees, knocking and hollering for the other children to come play and shrieking with laughter when they did. The first out on the street after school and the last one to trail home at night. Not a nice child, in Virginia's opinion. She imagined herself drawing a chalk circle around the girl and writing the words TOO LOUD next to her. Her own mother would have made Maisie go without supper and learn by rote improving Bible verses from the Old Testament. EMPTY VESSELS. Yes, Mother would have soon knocked Maisie into shape, one way or another.

"Go on with you!" She gestured at the girl through the window, shoo-ing her off the sidewalk outside her house and across the road towards her own home. She knew why Maisie crossed the street. Maisie's house had no garden, only a small fenced-in yard at the back and the narrowest of sidewalks out front. It was a strange, sagging, excuse-of-a-house, which looked as if it had been thrown together by a builder who hated his job and resented whoever might go on to live there.

Having given Virginia's command due consideration, the girl poked a pink tongue out, picked up the white stick of chalk, and skipped away. OUTRAGEOUS thought Virginia. NO RESPECT. She considered phoning Maisie's mother to demand an apology from the child, not least because white splinters and powder now blotted the sidewalk where the chalk stick must have broken when it hit the ground. Just what she had been trying to avoid. SPOILATION. It really was too bad.

Her hand went to the phone where it sat on its crocheted doily next to her armchair. Hovered there. She lifted the handset. Put it down. Then again, it was past supper time and Maisie's mother would probably be drunk. Because that was the other thing about her dawn walks. Another civic service she contributed, free and gratis—organising her neighbours' recycling. People were so cavalier about mixing plastic and cardboard. It took only a few minutes to sort one from the other. And it was so informative as to who bought what. Not to mention the amount of junk food they gobbled up. Obviously, as she smoothed out and folded the cardboard, it was almost impossible to avoid noticing the empty bottles in the green plastic boxes that were put out for the refuse collectors every second Thursday of the month.

BOOZEHOUND. She chalked a ring round Maisie's mother as she watched her stumble out of her door, down the porch steps, and up the street. Virginia knew where she was going. The convenience store two blocks away. Virginia even knew what she would buy—two bottles of Californian rosé at $4.99 a piece. The woman got through seven bottles of the rosé a week. Out of curiosity, she'd bought one herself a couple of months ago. Although a pretty enough colour, it tasted like stale flower water and it was nothing she ever wanted to taste again.

Her gaze went to the downstairs window as the blue light from the TV came on in the gloom and she imagined Maisie sitting on the couch watching cartoon dogs and cats. Did children still find cartoons as entrancing as they used to? She had no idea. She did know this much though, children should not be left in the house alone—there really was no excuse for it.

Virginia's lips went to a narrow line. And Maisie was definitely alone, she knew that for a fact, because Maisie's father walked out on his family last year. Virginia had been woken by the screaming and the slam of the front door, then the splutter and roar of his beaten-up jalopy as it took off. Not been seen since. QUITTER, Virginia thought, drawing the chalk ring around her memory of Maisie's dad. ROTTER—to leave his little girl alone like that.

With her half-done crossword on her knee, she sat watching the flickering light of Maisie's TV. Should she call someone—the police perhaps? But then again, Maisie's mother would be back soon enough. Perhaps she should go over and check on the child? Her heart started to beat faster as she considered the idea. It wouldn't do for Maisie's mother to accuse her of interfering, and everyone knew drunks were quick to take offence. But she couldn't in all conscience do nothing. With a certain relish, she gave up on her original plan to watch her favourite TV programme—a particularly gory British detective series—and settled down to watch Maisie's house instead. She drew a chalk line between herself and where she imagined Maisy to be sitting and chalked the word VIGILANCE along it.

This way, if a bad man broke in or smoke and flames started to pour from under the eaves, she would rush to Maisie and drag the child from the villain or from the burning building. HERO, she wrote above her own head, sipping at a schooner of sweet sherry. *'Really, it was nothing,'* she imagined telling the local news reporter. *'Anyone would have done the same.'* Both of them knowing that to be a lie.

The clink of bottles alerted Virginia to the mother's return. Swaying, the young woman leaned against the porch as she attempted to fit her key in the door and Virginia noticed the lounge go dark, imagined the TV switching off, a pause long enough for a child to scamper upstairs, and then a first-floor light go on in what she guessed to be Maisie's bedroom. The key found the lock and Maisie's mother half fell into her hallway.

As she did, Virginia lifted her eyes. Maisie stood at her window staring directly down at Virginia, her round face a pale blur. Instinctively, Virginia lifted her hand. I'M HERE, she told her. NEVER FEAR. But Maisie drew her curtains together with what Virginia imagined to be a snap, and the chalk line blew apart into so much dust.

The night was a long one. In her second-best flannelette nightgown, stretched out in her feather bed, at first Virginia felt too warm under the quilt she had made herself, and then too cold. Laying first one way and then another, bringing out her arms and legs then curling up, but nothing felt right. Everything about her body creaked and hurt. Finally, she crossed her arms over her chest, closing her eyes as she would lay in her coffin—as she would lay in her grave. And as she listened to the tick tock of the grandfather clock in the hallway and finally surrendered herself to sleep, above all things, she wanted to be young again.

It snowed during the night, and as soon as she woke Virginia felt the itch in her blood to be out in it. As a girl she had loved snow. But the risk of a fall at her age was too frightening. A broken hip. A spell in hospital. A bout of pneumonia. And that would be the end of independent living. Growing old was no fun, she thought, entering the kitchen—itself lit up by the fallen snow outside, the branches of the old apple tree heavy with it. From somewhere the memory came of an old snowball fight and her brother's hand in hers. Dead now. Poor Teddy. All of them dead. Everyone she had ever loved and who had ever loved her. Really, what was the point of her? She shook her head as if to dislodge the past, filling the coffee maker with water and spooning in the fragrant, ground coffee from a battered tin. PULL YOURSELF TOGETHER, VIRGINIA CAFFERTY.

A bowl of oatmeal might be best, bearing in mind the weather—and perhaps she would treat herself to a drizzle of syrup in it?

Mother never allowed syrup or honey or brown sugar. *A waste,* she'd say and smack Virginia's hand away. *Not for the likes of you.*

As she did every day, Virginia took her breakfast in the dining room, although it was the coldest room in the house. The mahogany table was laid with a white linen cloth, the good silver and the best china. An African violet in the centre and a silver framed photograph of her mother across from her. For a moment, Virginia regarded her place setting then stood up and went back to the kitchen, opening the pantry door and reaching in to take hold of the unopened glass jug of maple syrup. *There's only me left, Mother. If not now, then when?* She closed the pantry door, headed back down the corridor, and sat back down at the breakfast table. Heady with recklessness, she unstoppered the jug.

In the hallway, the grandfather clock struck quarter of the hour. And in the dining room, Virginia waited for life to get sweeter.

At first, nothing happened, as if the syrup had decided to stay where it was. As if her mother was right, and it wasn't for the likes of her. Virginia waited it out. Tick tock. Tick tock.

And then in a slow amber river, the syrup dropped from the lip of the jug into the bowl of oatmeal. NOT ENOUGH, Virginia thought, putting down the jug to stare into the amber lagoon. Sucking a stray drop of syrup from the pad of her thumb, with her other hand she reached for the creamer, swirling the cream into the syrup, round and around. *Not nearly enough to make up for all those years without.*

Unusually, she didn't carry her empty bowl out to the kitchen. TROLLOP, she wrote, glancing back at the unwashed dish. Instead, she went through to the parlour, standing on slippered tiptoe, pressing her forehead against the cold glass as she leaned forwards to see what she could see of the new world.

The children hurly-burly-piled out of their houses, all but mummified in scarves and gloves and wearing heavy winter boots. SNOW DAY, Virginia thought settling herself in her usual seat by the window, drawing a rug over her knees. But for the first time in her forty years in the house, she felt self-conscious as she stared out. She had every right to sit in her own parlour, she reassured herself. No one had any right to think she was a NOSY OLD BAT. Not at all.

Her cheeks flushed as she made a show of shaking out and opening up the local paper she had scoured the day before. And out of the corner of her eye, she sensed as much as saw Maisie jump down the steps of her porch to join her playmates. At least she had galoshes on today. She waited for the child to acknowledge her, but Maisy appeared not to notice the old woman in the window. As ever, her voice was louder than the others and her laugh at a higher pitch. LET THEM KNOW YOU'RE THERE, MAISY, Virginia thought. QUITE RIGHT. After an hour or two, the rest of the children went in, called home by parents wanting them to get warm and eat their lunch, Virginia guessed. But Maisie stayed out.

Alone, the child played directly in front of Virginia's house, but for some reason Virginia found she didn't mind. The girl could hardly be expected to play out in the road, she thought to herself. As Maisie rolled the snow up and down the sidewalk, her feet slipping and sliding under her, Virginia found herself wondering if she mightn't happen upon Maisie's mother at the convenience store. If she mightn't ask her to carry home her shopping, and in return it would only be a neighbourly thing to do if she brought over a nourishing stew to thank her? Perhaps the woman was floundering, abandoned by her husband that way? Perhaps she was lonely and frightened and could be encouraged if someone reached out a hand? Seven bottles of wine weren't so many to give up. It was certainly something to think about.

For the first time, Maisie's eyes met hers, and Virginia nodded. CARRY ON, she thought. The child's focus was a THING OF WONDER as she patted and shaped the snow. At one point, Maisie had dashed back home and come back clutching a bundle. She settled the scarf and the baseball cap, the stick arms and bits of coal for the eyes. Finally, she took a step back, the snowman's smile complete. Maisie stood alongside, flushed and exhausted. She looked up at Virginia and beamed. TWO SMILES. The child's and the snowman's, Virginia thought, and both meant for her. Two more than on any other day in she couldn't think how long. Maisie pointed and called, and Virginia leaned closer to the glass again. "I made you a friend," Maisie shouted.

FRIEND. Virginia chalked the letters up in her mind. Drawing a circle around the snowman first, and then the girl.

Tears prickled her eyes, and Virginia reminded herself she was required to breathe again. She held up a finger as if to say WAIT THERE, then hurried out of the living room, the chalk crunching under her slipper on the parquet floor of the hallway. Her hand on the wall to support her, she flung open the door and the cold fresh air rushed into the house almost knocking her over. Blinking in the winter sunlight, her gaze found Maisie. And Virginia felt swept away by the most unfamiliar feeling of what she realised was gratitude.

---

Judith O'Reilly is a writer and journalist, whose books include, *Curse the Day*, *Killing State* (both thrillers) and the memoirs *Wife in the North* and *A Year of Doing Good* (which involved her doing a good deed a day for a year. It did not make her a better person!) She has two more crime books due out soon, and is a former journalist with the Sunday Times, Channel 4 News and Newsnight.

# ANOTHER WOMAN'S SHOES

*By Kelly Clayton*

"There! Take your damn ball, and if it lands in my garden again, you'll not be getting it back. I promise you that!" Fiona Barton punctuated her words with a satisfying slam of the front door, but not before registering the children's shocked faces and the small girl bursting into noisy, ugly sobs. Well, she couldn't help that.

Her tea was now lukewarm, and the TV programme finished. A quiet interlude in Monty Don's Garden ruined by those blasted children. The shouting and laughing made her head explode.

She got a little on edge before the weekly date, a butterflies-in-the-stomach, joyful anticipation kind of nervous.

Life wasn't easy, and that young woman at No 58 didn't help matters. The girl must be in her late thirties. Pretty enough, yet she always looked so tired. Goodness knows what she did most of the time. The youngsters were constantly outside, playing in the street. Why? These houses had sizeable gardens. Why couldn't she keep her kids in their own space? As for the music, well, that loud thump-bump was not on. She'd posted several notes through No 58's letterbox on that subject, and the builders and delivery vans coming and going all day long. This was a peaceful area, and one of the reasons Fiona moved here when she downsized.

Glancing at her watch, she realised it was past time to get ready. She was never late. That much she owed him.

* * *

Suzie Wilson would neither scream nor shout. She opened her mouth and yelled instead. "Katie, stop hitting your brother. That Barbie is for playing with; it's not a weapon."

Ross might be the victim, but he was looking sheepish. "And as for you, young man, did you start this. Did you?" She backed away from them, hands in the air. "No, don't tell me. Just behave. Any more nonsense, and you'll be back outside."

She figured that would keep them in order, as they'd be avoiding the battle-axe across the road. Thankfully, Katie had got over her tears quick enough.

Her first-born, Ben, was wearing those ridiculous earphones. Were they, and his gaming controller, attached to him, part of him? She yanked them off his head.

"Oi Mum, you caught my ear!"

"I'll catch more than that. Where's the baby?"

"Chill. Bella's over there."

Over there was the dog-cage they'd brought their brand-new puppy home in and curled up inside was her adorable 10-month-old daughter. She looked blissful, but that wasn't the point.

Suzie added two and two and got three. "Where's the dog?"

"Here, Mummy. Isn't he lovely?"

She followed Katie's pointing finger. Thor, a gorgeous golden Labrador, slept in the doll's pram, snoring away, a frilly bonnet on his head. He seemed content. Yet again, that wasn't the point.

"Ben, I asked you to keep an eye on them for five minutes whilst I dealt with the delivery men." She checked the time. "Dinner won't sort itself, I need to get the baby to bed, and the guy will be here to fix the broken paving stones soon. Plus, I've still got to clear the clutter from the front pathway. Why can't you put your outdoor toys in the shed? I've told you a million times."

She annoyed herself with her whining. Sighing, she ran a hand through her hair, pulling it away when she realised she couldn't remember when she'd last washed it. How had she become this woman? Not for the first time, she cursed her absent husband.

* * *

Fiona stared at her reflection in the mirror. There was something off about her looks, a part of her altered. Long gone were energetic walks, the occasional gym session and her morning yoga. She couldn't muster the energy or the inclination. Not that she'd been lazy. No, she'd kept her mind occupied with reading, downloading book after book. It was easy to know what subjects to avoid, preventing the accidental sear of a ragged nerve.

Her roots needed doing. Her long-term hairdresser was a talker, in touch with her own and everyone else's feelings. She'd ask questions that Fiona wouldn't, or couldn't, answer.

She slicked on some lipstick, a bright pink that was David's favourite. Grabbing her handbag, she headed outside—and halted. "What the…"

A flat-bed lorry blocked her in. With an angry huff of breath, she approached the young man directing the unloading of various crates. "Excuse me. I need to get my car out."

"Sorry, love. We'll be 30 minutes, and then we're out of your hair."

"No, you don't understand. I need to leave now." The sun dipped deeper toward the horizon. Her breathing quickened as her chest tightened and tears threatened. She was too late.

"You'll have to talk to our customer about any issues." He pointed across the street.

They had already placed several crates in the garden of No 58. Right, she was going over there.

* * *

The doorbell rang at the precise moment Suzie bent to unlatch the dog-cage to retrieve Bella. Blast. The path-guy was early. She whispered to her sleeping daughter. “Back in a minute, my poppet.” Straightening, she called out, “The door’s open. Come on in.”

The front door was in her direct sight-line, and she froze when she realised her caller wasn’t a welcome handy-man but her angry neighbour, dressed up in a flowery dress and flattering make-up. However, her tight-lipped grimace and glaring eyes said this wouldn’t be a pleasant social call. Suzie tensed, feet planted square on the floor, as she readied herself for what was coming her way. One wrong word against the children, and she would give her what for. “I’m Suzie Wilson. How can I help you?”

“My name is Fiona Barton. I live across the road at number 59.”

“I know who you are. To what do I owe this pleasure?” She knew the sarcasm was plain to hear, but she didn’t care. This woman was the stuff of nightmares. She could star in one of those horrible neighbour programmes on TV.

“I can’t get my car out, as there is a lorry blocking my driveway. I understand you are responsible.”

Oh, blast! Just her luck. She had rarely seen her leave her bungalow since they’d moved in. Maybe once a week? “Sorry, I’m getting some patio slabs delivered. The guys parked across the road to allow the mechanical arm enough distance to pick up the crates and swing them into my garden. They shouldn’t be too much longer.”

“It’s too late. You’ve ruined everything.” The woman spat the words out in a bitter staccato.

She could see now that Fiona wasn't just angry, but furious. "Look, I'm sorry you missed whatever you'd planned." Maybe she had a date? "I'll make sure no-one parks there again."

"The damage is done. This is a respectable neighbourhood. I came here for peace, and it has been my haven. Then you arrive with your horde of children, who are always playing outside my house—the noise is intolerable. Then there is your music, blaring away at night."

Suzie often played her old CDs at the weekend, and, lonely, and on her second bottle of rosé, she'd pump up the volume and dance, bopping in her living room. She'd felt a prickle of shame when the first complaining note arrived, then thought better of it. It wasn't as if the music carried on for ages, just half an hour max.

"I'm sorry if you don't like how we live, but my children only play out the front sometimes. They aren't there all the time. And the noise we make? That's called life. Maybe you need to get one yourself and stop sticking your nose into mine."

* * *

Affronted, Fiona drew in a deep breath to steady herself. Her stomach roiled and flipped, nausea catching in her throat, as she thought of the coming long, lonely week that would have to pass before next Friday. This girl wasn't worth wasting her time on. She turned to go when, horrified, she said, "Oh Lord, you keep your baby in a cage? What kind of woman are you?"

* * *

Damn. "You don't understand..." A now-awake Bella howled.

Fiona backed away from her. "You'll hear from Social Services about this. You just wait."

"No, please. You've got it all wrong. Let me explain." Panic fluttering in her chest, she reached out and touched the woman's arm, who acted as if boiling water had scalded her before she ran out the door.

Suzie called out, “Be careful of the toys and broken slabs. It’s not safe.” But she was too late.

* * *

The taxi driver carried Fiona’s handbag as she hobbled along the path, ungainly on crutches, her right knee bent as the injured foot dangled.

“Here, let me open up for you.” He unlocked the door, helped her up the steps and set her bag on the floor.

She hopped into the hall and said, “I need to go somewhere next Friday, early evening. Could you take me and then wait 45 minutes before bringing me back here? It would be a regular appointment until I can drive again.”

“Sorry, Friday’s my busy night. I could do a few quick jobs in that time, earning more than I’d feel honest in charging you.”

She briefly closed her eyes. Why was everything so complicated? “Oh, okay. Do you know of anyone else I could try?”

“Best you google a few companies, but it won’t be cheap.”

* * *

Suzie sipped at her drink as she sat by the window, the icy white wine numbing the shock. Good Lord, that woman had taken a nasty tumble. She couldn’t get the crack of snapping bones out of her head. She shivered, wishing she had someone to talk to about this.

Her husband was having one of his working weekends. She knew his job was important. It paid for the house, schools and all the other lovely things they had. But she didn’t have her husband, she didn’t have time with him, nor did their kids. He worked in Geneva during the week.

After the crushing despair of his redundancy, they'd not thought he'd get such a fabulous opportunity again. The plan they'd agreed was that Ed would be home by early evening each Friday, not leaving for Switzerland until late Monday afternoon. That seldom happened. He was always too busy with a pressing deadline or needed to socialise with an important client.

The frequent telephone calls weren't enough. Before each one, she promised she wouldn't moan or nag, yet that was all she did—pushing him from her as she longed to hold him tight.

Her eyes lingered on the lit front room across the road. She'd tried to talk to her, to soothe, while they waited for the paramedics, but Fiona shooed her away with flapping hands.

After the ambulance left, she fed the kids pizza and bundled them off to bed. She'd toyed with her meal, barely managing a few bites. Would Fiona call the authorities? Head pounding, she poured the wine back into the bottle. She needed the oblivion and safety of sleep, but not one fogged with alcohol.

* * *

Few visitors encroached on Fiona's space, which was how she liked it. Those closest to her knew she'd contact them when the time was right. How could she confide in them when she didn't know how to get past it or move on? She had no appetite for well-meaning advice. She always said she dealt with problems by taking to her bed. Today, she stretched out on a garden lounger, her broken foot resting on several plumped cushions, books and a flask of tea by her side.

"Coo-eeee!"

Oh no. The last thing she needed was Rachel from next door, yet here she was, hanging over the garden fence.

"How are you, Fiona? That looks nasty. You're lucky it wasn't worse. Imagine if you'd hit your head." Rachel was, as ever, the epitome of positivity.

"Yes, I suppose I got away lightly." If being bound in plaster, incapacitated and throbbing with pain was a blessing.

Rachel dropped a tartan plastic bag over the fence. "Here, I've prepped some microwave meals for you."

"Oh, thank you. That is kind." There was no need. Not in this age of grocery and takeaway deliveries.

"I couldn't help see what happened. You came out of Suzie Wilson's at some pace. No wonder you tripped on those paving stones. I saw her at the supermarket yesterday morning, and she said they were getting fixed that evening. You were just unlucky. I didn't know you and Suzie were friendly."

Aha—so this was an intelligence-gathering mission.

"We're not. I was complaining about the delivery people blocking me in."

"Didn't she take it well?"

Fiona had to be fair. "I guess she took it okay, but because of her, I missed an appointment."

"Oh, dear, of course—yesterday was Friday! What are you going to do until you can drive again?"

Fiona cursed her loose mouth. She'd told Rachel about herself when she first moved here. A foolish mistake. Rachel had subsequently shown her true colours by gossiping about everyone else on the street.

"Nothing. It's not an issue." And none of Rachel's business. "But I'll tell you what is. I'm appalled by that woman's behaviour. She keeps her baby in a cage."

To her surprise, Rachel laughed. "I saw Suzie this morning. She told me all about it. Her eldest was watching Bella when she crawled into the dog crate and fell asleep. Ben took advantage, as teenagers do, and got on his X-Box. She's a lovely girl, with a lot on her plate, but those kids are her world."

"The child was crying, sobbing."

"It's what they do. Over-tired, I expect. You know what they're like. Ah, that's right, you don't have children."

Fiona wasn't in the mood to pick that scab today. "Fine, but I'm keeping my eye on her. Where's the husband anyway, if there even is one?" She regretted the judgemental words almost immediately, pin-pricks of shame burning her cheeks. "That was uncalled for."

"He works in Switzerland. His last place closed down a year ago, and Suzie said they had a pretty rough time of it. I guess this new job is a lifeline."

"Not my concern. What bothers me is the racket those children make."

"It's just kids playing. I quite like the sound. There is something joyful in seeing them run around, not a care in the world. Look, I better be off. Give me a buzz if you need any help."

Left alone, Fiona considered Rachel's words. Memories of her own long-ago life crept out of her locked mind-box. She pushed them away, slamming the lid shut. It was done. She hadn't thought about Suzie's circumstances. Or her own. Did she not know what joy was any more? Was she merely existing and resentful of others?

* * *

Suzie arranged for Fiona to receive a fruit basket delivery. Her accompanying note gave her telephone number, just in case. She heard nothing, and it was now Friday again. Her husband said she'd done all she could. Yes, her actions were appropriate, but were they right?

Rachel's words played in her head on a loop. She realised Fiona had been distraught, not furious. You need to walk in another woman's shoes to understand her path. Suzie knew what she had to do.

* * *

Fiona got used to hopping about as she used the furniture for support. Her plastered foot throbbing as the bones knitted and reconnected.

She'd spent the week trying to organise transport, but the quotes from the cab companies were far too expensive. She couldn't afford the indulgence. Her Plan B was in place. She'd tidied herself up to look respectable, washed her hair and slapped on some make-up. She would sit in her garden and drink wine as the sun dipped lower. That would have to do.

The buzz of the doorbell intruded into the silence of the house. With a sigh, she hoisted herself to her feet and used the crutches to get to the front door, an automatic social smile plastered on her face. Then she saw who stood on her doorstep. Suzie Wilson. "What do you want?"

"Rachel told me where you go on Fridays. I'm beside myself that I've caused you such pain. I'd like to make amends."

Fiona had to give her credit for knowing when she was in the wrong and taking responsibility. "What do you mean?"

"I went to the hospital earlier and borrowed a wheelchair. Rachel is looking after the kids. She's at mine right now. I'm driving you to the cemetery and will wait to bring you home. I have my Kindle and will relish an hour on my own."

Fiona drew back. "Why would you do this?"

Suzie held her gaze. "Because I've been a misery. I know better. What you give out, you get back. Rachel told me your husband died before you moved here. That you said he'd worked away a lot, and your Friday night ritual was a glass of wine watching the sunset. And you visit his grave each week to do the same. Except for last Friday, when I made you miss it."

The weight of the words hung in the silence, as Fiona's defensive wall slowly crumbled. "You don't have to do this. I can't let you."

"Yes. You can. I won't take no for an answer."

* * *

Suzie engaged the brake on the wheelchair. David Barton's headstone was black with a golden etching of a setting sun at the top. Very fitting.

She reached into her carrier bag and drew out a small wicker tray, placing it across Fiona's knees, on top of the blanket she'd brought in case it turned cold.

Fiona's eyes widened at the contents. "You thought of everything."

Suzie smiled. She'd bought a couple of mini bottles of wine, a plastic glass, some olives and crisps. If you were going to do something, do it right. "Okay, so, shall we say 45 minutes? I'll read in the car. I can see you from over there. Wave if you need anything."

"Thank you."

Suzie walked away, but Fiona called her back. "My David worked in London during the week and came home each Friday afternoon. It wasn't always like that. We grew apart, different interests, no shared connection. He had his life, and I had mine. Not having children didn't help. I was lonely for a long time, even thought of divorce. We had a blazing argument. It could have been the end, but David made a promise. He said he would never miss a Friday evening with me. That we'd drink wine as the sun set, talking about our week, sharing and reconnecting. It saved our marriage. Just something to think on."

Fiona's words were raw, and Suzie could only imagine how much it had cost this private woman to speak them. Yes, she needed to think.

* * *

Fiona sipped her wine, surprised at how pleasant it was. She spoke to the breeze, the swaying trees, and her husband.

"David, we always said we'd be honest with each other. You'd not be proud of me and would surely be ashamed. I've not been kind to anybody, ignoring our family and friends, turning away from their offers of help. Grief and anger poisoned my every action. I promise to do better."

She let the tears fall, uncaring who might see or hear. She'd held it all in for too long.

* * *

*Eight weeks later.*

Suzie snuggled against her husband, careful not to spill her wine. Ed pulled her close, dropping a kiss on the top of her head.

"I'm glad you kicked off, Suze. You had every right. I'm doing well at this job. There's no need for me to work every weekend, just to prove myself. I belong here, at home."

"I thought you were avoiding your nagging wife, building-site of a house, and four screaming children."

"To be fair, the kids don't scream that much."

She swatted his arm, "You're hilarious."

"Here's to spending quality time together at the weekend." He raised his wine glass, clinking against hers in a toast. "I think I'm going to enjoy our Friday night wine-and-sunset dates. The kids are watching TV, and Bella is only a howl away." He waved at the baby-monitor beside them.

"Yes, a bit of reconnection for mummy and daddy. Oh, look, isn't it stunning?"

The setting sun trumpeted a last hurrah in a blaze of crimson, orange and deepest yellow, a welcoming salutation to the dusk and approaching night. Suzie thought of Fiona, sharing this exact moment with her and David's memories, an echo of their happy life together.

Time well spent and memories were the essences of life itself, together with compassion and understanding of the road another walked. Suzie would do her best not to forget that again.

---

Kelly Clayton lives on the Channel Island of Jersey with her husband and three cats. She writes contemporary crime and thrillers, including the DCI Jack Le Claire Mysteries. Kelly is also the author of historical romantic suspense as Julia Hardy. You can find out more at https://www.kellyclaytonbooks.com/.

# SOMEONE TO TALK TO, SOMEWHERE TO GO

*By Kim Nash*

She slowly raised her Dolce & Gabana sunglasses and glared at the rowdy crowd who had just run and jumped into what had previously been a peaceful and tranquil pool. "Bloody idiots!" she muttered, under her breath. She raised her glass of iced Bombay Sapphire and tonic to her lips and took a large sip before going back to reading the latest bonk-buster she had brought with her. This was supposed to be an exclusive luxury resort, not a hostel for uncouth plebs!

Saskia Duval was taking a week off from her high-powered, multi-million-pound lingerie empire which created beautiful, sexy and extremely expensive undergarments for the rich and famous. She was a complete control freak and had not taken a whole week off since her business started five years ago but was at risk of a total burnout if she didn't get away. And she was still in hourly contact with Alex, her operations director, much to Alex's disdain.

Surfing the internet one evening for somewhere to go, she had spotted the exclusive Sandy Beach Resort in Barbados. The soft white sand, clear turquoise water and tropical palm trees along with promises of peace and tranquillity and personal butler service had persuaded her to be spontaneous for once and book right there and then. And after all, it was only a week. Perhaps she'd finally find out if her business could cope without her. Perhaps that was what she was scared of.

Glancing across the pool, she saw the pretty blonde lady who arrived a few days ago and had smiled at her a couple of times but seemed to be surrounded in a cloud of mystery. She hadn't been anywhere far from around the pool either. She had a feeling that she knew her; she seemed very familiar. Saskia was normally great at people-watching and imagining their stories but couldn't quite get this lady right. Something was nagging at her that she had definitely seen her before.

Totally distracted by the noisy group around the pool, she slammed her book down on the padded rattan sun lounger with a huff and wandered over to the bar area, lowering herself onto one of the squashy armchairs. She ordered a skinny latte from the butler. The blonde lady was only seconds behind her, ordered the same and sat at the table next to Saskia.

"Well that's my peace shattered for the afternoon," she said disappointedly.

"Absolutely!" Saskia replied. "If I'd have wanted to go to The Solano in Benidorm, I would have. I thought this resort was supposed to be classy!"

The blonde lady grinned, stood up and came across to her table.

"Hi, I'm Melissa," she said. "Melissa Fox," as she reached out to shake Saskia's hand.

"Good to meet you, I'm Saskia. Saskia Duval. Fancy joining me?" Saskia indicated the vacant chair opposite, surprising herself immensely as she usually kept herself very much to herself.

"That would be lovely, thanks," replied Melissa, grabbing her coffee. "I feel a bit strange being away on my own. Never done it before."

"I haven't had a holiday in ages, so it's all a bit strange for me too! Normally working all hours but my doctor insisted on me taking a break before I make myself ill. It's been a busy year!"

"Yeah, I know what you mean. It's been quite a year for me too," said Melissa.

The two ladies chatted comfortably for the next half an hour about life in general and about how much they were enjoying the resort till the rowdy bunch moved in, both keeping away from personal topics but feeling like they'd known each other forever.

The butler appeared as if from nowhere, a bit like Mr Ben! "Your masseur is waiting for you Miss Duval. Would you like me to book a table in the restaurant again for you this evening?"

"Yes please, that would be lovely," she replied.

She hesitated slightly before inviting Melissa to join her for dinner.

"I'd love to. But only if you're sure you're happy to have some company," Melissa responded.

"It would be lovely to have some company for a change," she replied. "Why don't we meet for a cheeky rum punch at 7pm at the bar?"

"Perfect! I shall look forward to it."

* * *

At 6.45, Saskia was dressed to kill and beautifully made-up, ready to head to the bar and looking forward to having someone to talk to over dinner, instead of her normal meal for one.

For some reason she decided to pick up her iPad and typed the name Melissa Fox into Google. Her chin nearly hit the floor when she realised who the mysterious lady she was about to have dinner with was. She knew it. She knew she'd seen her before. What a dark horse!

* * *

At 6.45, Melissa had just finished getting ready in her room. After slicking on a pale pink lip-gloss to finish her natural make-up look, she looked in the mirror and felt grateful that her hair had grown back so lush and thick even though it was now curly which it had never been before. Wearing a wig out here would have made her feel so hot and sweaty, but there were lots of people who had no choice. With a few minutes to spare, she decided to do an internet search on Saskia Duval and read that she was a self-made businesswoman worth millions. "Bloody hell!" She put her hand to her chest. "Who knew?"

* * *

They met in the bar as arranged and after their first cocktail, had another and then decided that they should both eat as they were already feeling a little tipsy.

Over dinner, Melissa asked about Saskia's business and she told her all about how her company started after she was made redundant five years earlier—she decided to explore her creativity through sewing and she designed and made pretty lingerie for her friends and family. She explained that her darling mom was terminally ill with cancer at the time and one of the things that made her feel better was to wear beautiful underwear. Saskia was reminded once again, with a stab of pain to her heart, just how much she missed her mother and how she hoped she would be proud if she were looking down upon her.

Saskia was discovered by an American movie star who miraculously happened to cross her path one day, and who loved her creations so much, she insisted on giving her a loan to start the business. The business went from strength to strength, she repaid the loan quickly and was now more successful than she ever thought possible. She was eternally grateful to the helping hand she'd had along the way and felt that her mother had most definitely been looking down on her and was her guardian angel.

"So, what's your story then, Melissa?" she asked, already knowing the little that she'd discovered on the internet.

"Ah well, where do I start?" Melissa was normally very quiet about her experiences but felt that there was something about Saskia that made her want to tell her everything. So she did.

Melissa explained that as a working mom of seven children, just engaged and planning her wedding, she discovered a lump under her armpit. She had a mammogram, ultrasound test and core needle aspirations which all showed up negative. She noticed that the lump appeared to be bigger but the doctors still said that everything was fine, yet she knew instinctively that something was not right. Tired and constantly thirsty, she was told that she was being over-cautious. She felt that she had no one to talk to and nowhere to go.

By the following February, the lump was the size of an eyeball and hurt. Her left breast increased in size and again she went to the doctors who said that everything was fine. She still felt that she had no one to talk to and nowhere to go and felt desperately sad and lonely.

Next she discovered another lump next to her cleavage and went straight back to the doctor insisting on a blood test. It took two weeks for an appointment and she went through the same tests again. She was told that she was unlucky and was diagnosed with Grade Three breast cancer. She felt she had done something wrong and that it was all her fault. A course of chemotherapy followed by a double mastectomy was the agreed course of action.

Feeling desperately exhausted she looked for relaxation treatments which she knew she needed but couldn't afford. There was nothing for free. Still, she had no one to talk to and nowhere to go.

Then one day, her autopilot switched off and she decided that to get through this, she had to turn negative to positive and decided that she wanted to fundraise. In June 2011, the Melissa Fox Cancer Centre became a registered charity.

She set up support groups for women, men and families so that unlike her, they had someone to talk to and somewhere to go. She got experts in, offering weight loss classes. She researched food and set up a healthy eating bar. She set up art classes, and a beauty room for free pamper sessions. She distracted herself with fundraising and building a team of amazing volunteers.

"It's been five years now and I've just celebrated my cancerversary. I'm now five years cancer free!" she declared. Discreet tears rolled down her cheeks as she smiled.

"Wow!" Saskia was completely lost for words as she wiped away the tears that were now gushing from her eyes. "I really don't know what to say apart from what a remarkable lady you are!"

"I'm just doing what other people would do," she replied.

"I'm really not so sure about that my dear! So how did you end up on holiday alone at The Sandy Beach resort?" Saskia asked.

"My friends put me forward for the TV programme 'What a Surprise!' One of my many surprises was that I was given a luxury holiday here. No kids, no husband—just me, my thoughts and a whole lot of relaxation to rejuvenate me. I have so much to do when I get back. Not sure how, but maybe with the help of a miracle, I will get more centres. I have to for the sake of people with cancer everywhere."

"So, have you seen much of the island while you've been here?" Saskia asked.

"No, I didn't really fancy it on my own," Melissa replied.

"We should have a day sightseeing tomorrow, to celebrate our friendship," Saskia suggested.

"What a fabulous idea!" Melissa replied. "It's always much more fun with someone else."

"Leave it with me," said Saskia, excited about finally having a friend to play with. People thought that she was a hard-faced business-woman and didn't need friends. How wrong they were.

Melissa saw Saskia speak to the butler on her way to the ladies and she had a big grin on her face when she returned to the table. "All sorted!" she said with obvious delight.

They didn't realise how much time had passed while they were talking but there was no-one left in the restaurant. They had been sitting there for hours and the staff were closing up around them. After their very intimate conversation, they were both emotionally exhausted and decided to retire to their suites.

"Meet me in reception at 8am," Saskia said. "Remember your cozzie!"

"Now that sounds fun!" Melissa laughed.

"You are amazing Melissa!" Saskia burst out, completely in awe of her new friend. "Goodnight my lovely."

Saskia kissed Melissa tenderly on the cheek as they bid goodnight to each other, but then had the overwhelming urge to give this amazing woman a hug. While in their embrace, Melissa caught a waft of the most gorgeous smell.

"What's that perfume you're wearing?" she asked Saskia. "You smell incredible."

"Thank you. It's my own," Saskia replied bashfully. "I've just created it and am thinking of launching it as a product. It's a smell that's taken me ages to put together but I wanted something to remind me of my mom. Do you like it?"

"I love it," Melissa responded. "Beautiful."

"Why, thank you." Saskia was secretly delighted as an idea formed in her head.

* * *

The next day, the ladies were chauffeured to Bridgetown Port where a very handsome, uniformed young man with neatly-tied dreadlocks assisted them onto a catamaran. A bottle of Crystal stood proud in an ice bucket and two champagne flutes were handed to them by the captain. "Welcome ladies. We hope you will enjoy the next few hours with us!"

Saskia winked at Melissa. "I'm sure we will!" she replied, as she eyed up his perfectly-formed backside when he turned round.

"Please take some time to enjoy the beautiful sunshine until we reach our first snorkel stop."

Melissa snorted her champagne up her nose. "Snorkel! I've never snorkelled in my life!"

"Well, you need to sort that out then lady!" Saskia retorted, thoroughly enjoying herself as the boat sailed past a row of pastel-painted houses and the sun bounced off their windows. "Let's make some memories."

* * *

They left the boat around 5pm. What a day they'd had! The first snorkel stop had been hilarious with Melissa swallowing more water than she thought possible. However, once she'd mastered it, she was amazed at the multi-coloured vibrancy of the shoals of fishes and coral she could see. The second stop was to feed and swim with sea turtles and their babies, which they both found incredibly exhilarating. But the highlight of their day was when the captain shouted to the ladies, who were sunbathing on the deck, to look left. To their delight, two dolphins played alongside the boat in the sparkling azure sea and the scene completely took their breath away.

But their day wasn't over yet. They had been told that no-one can visit Barbados without visiting the famous Oistins Fish Fry where they danced to the loud calypso and reggae music with the locals, ate the most delicious Bajan fish and bought tons of traditional gifts from the sidewalk stalls.

They practically fell into the car that came to pick them up, laughing like two naughty schoolgirls. "I haven't had that much fun for years," Saskia declared, slurring her words ever so slightly.

"I'll never forget that day for the rest of my life," said Melissa as she shut her eyes and gently started to snore.

* * *

The two ladies spent the remaining day of their holiday lounging around the pool together, in between beauty treatments and massages. They were on different flights back to England, so said their goodbyes at the resort reception having immense respect and admiration for each other.

"Thank you for being a wonderful surprise holiday companion. I wasn't expecting to make a friend on holiday but I can honestly say I couldn't have met anyone nicer," said Saskia, with a tear in her eye. "I wish you love and luck for your future and I really do hope that you achieve what you want to."

"I feel like I've known you forever," said Melissa, sad that she was hugging goodbye to someone she'd known for such a short time but felt she could be great friends with. "I hope that one day we meet again."

"I'm sure we will," Saskia replied.

* * *

On her way into a planning meeting for the charity, Melissa bent down to pick up the post from the door mat. The first few envelopes were a mix of bills and letters but she spotted one purple envelope that smelled and felt different. It was then that a familiar smell came back to her. A perfume that she'd smelt before on recent holiday in Barbados.

"How bizarre!" she thought to herself. "I must be going bonkers!"

She ripped open the envelope, unfolded the letter and grabbed hold of a cheque before it fluttered to the floor.

She caught her breath as she read the words of the letter:

*My dear friend,*

*Thank you so much for being a fabulous holiday companion and for sharing your incredible story with me. I wish that your cancer centre had been around when my mother was dying from cancer. I know our family would have all benefited from the support of such an incredible place and group of people.*

*Last week, I met a thirteen-year-old young man who was painting rocks and selling them to friends and family to raise money for the homeless. When I asked him why he was doing this, he asked me, why not? He said if you could do something to help someone else, and you had the time and the resources to do it, why would you not? What a wise, kind and generous young man he is. I wish everyone could have a little of the spirit he has. Talking to him got my mind working overtime to see how I could help you and what you are trying to do to help others.*

*I would like you to take this cheque as a gift from me to show my admiration at what an inspirational, amazing and unselfish person you are. To take on the responsibility of making the world a better place for cancer sufferers and their families is an awesome task and you do it with grace, dignity and pride.*

*I would also like to be your first port of call if you ever need any business advice or if my team or I can help you in any small way. It would appear that while I was on holiday, my business ran smoothly and hadn't fallen apart. You made me realise that there is more to life than earning money so if you'll have me, I would like to dedicate one day each week to helping your charity achieve your goals. Time waits for no-one and you have to make each day count. You, lady, have made me see that.*

*You've also inspired me to go ahead with the perfume venture. It launches next month and I have decided to call it 'Foxy Lady' in your honour. 50% of the perfume sales will go to your charity.*

*When I was given a business loan all those years ago, it enabled me to start my business. Without that helping hand from my guardian angel, I wouldn't be where I am today. I hope that today, with a helping hand from your guardian angel, these gifts and my time will go some way to helping you to provide 'someone to talk to and somewhere to go' for cancer patients all across the country.*

*You are truly an angel!*

*Your friend*
*Saskia*
*Xxx*

Melissa looked at the cheque and read the amount, which said £250,000. She looked away and back again in disbelief. She breathed in the smell of the perfumed envelope and raised her eyes to heaven.

"Thank you for sending me a miracle."

---

Kim Nash, a finalist in the 2020 Amazon Kindle Storyteller Award, is an author of uplifting, funny, heartwarming, romantic feel-good fiction and lives in Staffordshire with son Ollie and

English Setter rescue dog Roni. Kim is Head of Publicity for publisher Bookouture (part of Hachette UK) and is a book blogger at www.kimthebookworm.co.uk. When she's not working or writing, Kim can be found walking her dog at Cannock Chase Forest, reading, writing and binge-watching box sets on the TV. She's also quite partial to a spa day and a gin and tonic (not at the same time!) Kim also runs a book club in Cannock, Staffs and organises reader/author events.

# LOVE IS LOVE

*By Leah Mercer*

The sun is bright in the sky and I can almost hear the greenery unfurling around me, coming out to play after a long winter huddled inside. Petals from the horse chestnut trees drift through the air like fragrant snow, and children race down the pathways as if they're wind-up toys. A few people frown at them, muttering that they shouldn't be here. 'A cemetery demands respect,' I've heard them grumble, grimacing as a toddler streaks across a grave. I don't care, though. I think the dead would like a little excitement. They have plenty of time to sleep.

Roya wouldn't mind, I know that much for sure. She loved kids—she must have done to have five of them. I pat the top of her gravestone, its surface reminding me of her cool, smooth skin. If I close my eyes now, I can picture the first time I touched her. It was at a barbeque; I can still smell the burning meat. Our husbands were jockeying for position at the grill and we were in the kitchen. The light caught her eyes, and I remember thinking I'd never seen anyone so beautiful. And then…

I catch my breath to stop the pain. People think that as you get older, your memories fade. But the closer I get to the end, the more vivid mine become. I'm not sure if that's a blessing or a curse.

'Excuse me.' I turn to see a little girl, maybe around eight, by my side. 'Can I fetch my ball?' Her bright red football has rolled on top of Roya and I didn't even notice.

'Of course,' I say. My voice is hoarse. I don't remember the last time I used it, actually. I've been alone for so long, with only my daily walk to Roya to keep me occupied. I shuffle back so the girl can move around me to pick up her ball.

'Who's that?' she asks, pointing at the grave. She leans forward. 'Roya. I like that name. Is she your sister?'

'Yes, yes, she is.' The lie emerges so smoothly, so practised, before I can even think about it. It's what we always said. It was easy: we looked so much alike that we could have been sisters; our husbands joked they might swap us one day. We'd catch each other's eye and laugh, a sickly cocktail of guilt and desire sweeping through us. I hated lying back then, and I hate it now. I hate that I can't even claim my love after death—after her husband's death, after my husband's death. I'm the only one left, and I still can't say she's mine.

Because she *was* mine, I think as I hobble home. Maybe not legally—back then, marriage wasn't an option for us—but in spirit. And she would have left her husband for me, just as I would have left mine. We talked about it for years: from the time we first met, when our skin was young and unlined, to when our hair became grey. But somehow the time was never right. The kids needed us, our partners needed us, there were moves to make and jobs to take. Attitudes may have changed, but in our world being together remained a dream.

And now her grave is all I have left—of her, of us. I try to keep it tidy, as if by clearing the weeds, I'm taking possession of her in a way I couldn't before. This tiny bit of her does belong to me. It's the only thing keeping me going. It's why I come here, time and again.

It's raining the next day when I open the door for my walk, but I don't mind. The cold water on my cheeks makes me feel alive again. I'm soaked through by the time I get to the cemetery. Despite the weather, it's surprisingly busy—everyone is desperate for space these days. I make my way down the usual path and over to Roya, murmuring my usual endearments. People here think I'm crazy, I'm sure, but I'm well past the point of caring.

But when I see her grave…my jaw slackens as I take in the wreckage. The stone that once jutted proudly upwards now lies on its side, sad and ashamed. The daisies I'd picked are trampled and torn, strewn like entrails. I stare and stare, unable to move, feeling like Roya has been ripped from me once more. The ground sways beneath me and I feel my legs give way. Blackness closes in and I start to fall. I don't even try to keep standing.

Maybe I'm finally going to be with her.

A soft hand pats my cheek and I smile. She's here. She's—

'Are you all right?' The hand pats my cheek again. 'Lady? Are you okay?'

'Matilda, what's happening?' A woman's sharp voice cuts into my reverie, and I open my eyes to see the little girl from yesterday and an older woman, with the same blue eyes, leaning over me. My heart drops and I draw in a breath. I haven't gone to Roya, after all.

'I'm okay.' I smile to convince them, then struggle to sit up. The woman takes my arm and as I thank her, I think how long it's been since anyone has touched me. 'It's just…' I gesture towards the toppled gravestone, my heart aching again.

The woman shakes her head. 'I'm so sorry. I really am. Apparently quite a few have been turned over—it happened last night. It's just awful.'

'It was her sister,' the girl pipes up, pointing at the stone, and I start to shake. A kind of rage, an anger, fills me, that someone could do this. That someone could take away the one thing I had in this life—not a sister, in fact, but my love. My *life*. I want to shout that out. But…I can't.

'Come, we'll help you get home. Do you live nearby?'

'Oh no, no. There's no need for that. Really. I'm fine now. It was just a shock.' I get to my feet, trying to ignore how dizzy I feel.

'We're taking you home. Lead the way.' The woman's voice is firm and I don't have the energy to argue, so I start to shuffle down the pathway towards my flat. Thankfully, it's not far and the little girl chatters as we make our way slowly there. I say my thanks and bid them goodbye, desperate to lie down and block the vision of Roya's ruined grave from my mind. Anger floods through me again when I realise that I'll never be able to afford a new tombstone. Roya will be lying there, unclaimed, forever. No one will know how much she was loved.

I can't say how many hours—days, even—pass while I lie here. Memories drift in and out of my head and when the doorbell sounds, I'm not sure if it's real. But it rings again and again, and then I hear shouts outside. I haul myself to my feet and gaze out the window, eyebrows rising when I spot the woman and the little girl who walked me home on the pavement outside. What on earth are they doing here?

'Can we come in?' the woman yells when she sees me. I shake my head, shame running through me. I haven't bathed since I saw them. I'm a mess and my flat is too. There's no way they can come inside. 'We haven't seen you at the cemetery,' the woman's saying. 'We wanted to make sure you're okay.'

I breathe in, their kindness bringing tears to my eyes. I'm not okay. Of course I'm not. But that they cared enough to check… well, that means something.

'I thought you might like to know that we tidied up your sister's grave,' the woman continues, and even though I appreciate the gesture, that same rage swamps me when I remember I can't afford to mark Roya's life like she deserves.

'She wasn't my sister.' The words fly from my mouth before I can stop them. I don't *want* to stop them. I don't have the gravestone any more to claim her in the present, but I can claim the past. I have to.

'She was the love of my life.' The phrase is so clichéd, but it couldn't express more clearly how I feel. I loved my husband, of course, but not like Roya. Nothing close to Roya. 'She was…she was everything.' And something inside me lifts. A sadness, a grief. I can picture Roya smiling now, her eyes shining down at me, bathing me in her love.

I wait for the mother to narrow her eyes and gaze up at me with disapproval and disgust, the same way Roya's husband did when he caught us together that one time before never speaking of it again.

But the woman's face softens and she takes her daughter's hand. 'How lucky you are to have found someone like that,' she says, and her daughter nods solemnly. Silence falls and I can hear the birds chirping as if they agree, too.

'Right, well, we'll let you get on with your day,' she says, when it's clear I'm not going to let them in. 'We hope to see you at the cemetery soon.'

I smile, but I know I won't go back there. I may have claimed Roya in other ways now, but I still can't bear to see her resting place destroyed. Just the thought of it makes me want to be ill, and so I crawl under the covers once more.

The days pass. I don't leave my little flat. I have no interest in the outside world—there's no one to be interested in, anyway. But one afternoon, the doorbell rings with that insistent peal. Footsteps echo on the stairs and there's a knock at my door. How did they get in?

'Hello? It's Matilda, from the cemetery.' The little girl's voice floats towards me, and I freeze. 'Please open the door. We need you to come. We need you to see Roya's grave.'

My eyebrows lift and I push a wisp of hair from my face. Roya's grave? Has something else happened?

'We have a car outside,' I hear Matilda's mum say. 'We'll give you a minute or two to get ready. Come down when you are—we're parked right out front.' She pauses. 'And we're not leaving until we have you!' She's laughing but I can hear the stubbornness in her voice. It reminds me of Roya, and I can't help smiling.

'Okay, okay. Give me five minutes.' I trudge to the mirror and make a face at my reflection, then go to the closet and pull on a red jumper and navy trousers. Roya loved red, and while I've no idea why there's such a push to get me to her grave, somehow it seems fitting. I pray it's nothing bad. I'm not sure I can take the sight of it.

I run a brush through my hair, grab my handbag and keys, then head down the stairs and out the door. It's the first time I've been outside in weeks. The air is a warm caress, and I can hear birds singing as I lower myself carefully into the front seat of the car.

A few minutes later, Matilda and her mother are helping me down the pathway towards Roya. There's a group of people gathered around her plot, and I pray once more that everything is okay. They see us coming and their faces break into smiles, applause and cheers floating through the air as we approach.

What on earth?

And then they part, and I see it. Roya's grave, covered in roses, with a brand-new headstone. It's smooth and shiny like before, and her name is engraved in sloping letters. And at the top, just three words.

*Love is love.*

I stare and stare until the tears in my eyes mean I can't see any longer. I take a few steps forward and touch the stone; trace the letters. In the past, now and forever, Roya will know exactly how I feel. That I'm not ashamed. I'm not afraid. Love is love, no matter what form it takes.

I turn to Matilda and her mother. 'How…how have you done this?'

She smiles and touches the top of Matilda's head. 'It was her. She was so sad that you couldn't replace Roya's gravestone. She wanted to do something.'

'I asked everyone in the cemetery for money! I told them Roya was the love of your life and we *had* to do something. It took ages, but we finally had enough.' Matilda's face shines. 'Do you like it?'

I meet her eyes, this little girl who's only a tenth of my age and already wiser. 'Love is love,' I say, smiling. 'I couldn't have put it better myself.'

---

Leah Mercer was born in Halifax, Nova Scotia, on the east coast of Canada. Her first ambition was to be a journalist, but after completing a master's in journalism, she soon realised she preferred anything other than reporting the news. After trying her hand at public relations, teaching and recruitment in various countries around the world, she finally settled in London and returned to writing… fiction, this time. Her first two novels, *Who We Were Before* and *The Man I Thought You Were*, were shortlisted at the UK's Romantic Novelists' Association Awards. Leah loves books, running and visiting historic houses with her husband and their son.

# THE BOY IN THE GREEN JACKET

*By Liz Fenwick*

'You're depressed.' Donna cast me a sideways glance before she refocused on the road.

'That's a surprise?' I raised an eyebrow. Two years ago, on a bitter January day, the love of my life exited this world. Unlike today, the earth had been bare and frozen brown. A week later, the gravedigger had told me the first shovel had broken. The earth was not ready for him, and I wasn't ready to let him go. I'd stood in front of the grave, broken too.

Now the wipers raced across the glass, contrasting with the leisurely pace of the falling snow. Four o'clock, the light had gone, and streetlights acted as beacons in the swirling white flakes. I hadn't been in this area in years. Coated in white, it appeared unaltered.

'Where are we going?' I asked, but I knew. In front of us the ice rink appeared.

Parking the car, she turned to me. 'Some things don't change.'

I forced a smile. 'Really?' My world had. I let the snowflakes fall on my face. They melted like tears from the warmth of my cheeks, still pink from the car's heater. Tears from without and tears from within.

She tucked her hand through my arm and moved towards the building. 'How many times a week did your mother bring us here?'

'At least three.' I huffed, thinking of my fourteen-year-old self. 'Why are we here?' I asked, knowing I couldn't do this.

'Because we had fun.'

I couldn't deny that. I was never any good a skating, but I loved the freedom, the speed and joy of it.

She handed me a thick pair of socks and white figure skates. Sinking onto the metal bench, I felt the cold through my jeans as I put the socks and the skates on, trying to find that balance of tight enough to support my wobbly fifty-year-old ankles but not so tight as to cut off all circulation to my feet.

She held out her hand and I took it. I knew what she was doing. I'd come to stay with her because I couldn't do anything else and didn't know where to begin. She knew me like no one else did or had—except Pete.

My legs swayed at the ankles, then the knees. I could barely hold myself upright and I wasn't even on the ice. I would be a disaster when it was slippery.

'When was the last time you skated?' She had gone through the gate and was waiting for me on the ice.

'Last week.'

She grinned. 'Hmmm.'

One foot reached the ice while I held tight to the battered wood that circled the rink. That one foot slipped sideways as I was placing the other one on the ice.

Donna grabbed my arm. 'Do you remember…that boy?'

I clung to the top of the wall. My mouth lifted. 'The boy in the green jacket.'

'Yes, him. Did you ever discover his name?'

I closed my eyes and moved fast through the past to a time when I'd never been kissed and the surface beneath me held no fear. This was a place of promise. Night after night, the boy in the green jacket and I skated around the rink and around each other. We never missed a free skate, he and I.

'It's good to see you smile,' she said.

I turned to her.

'I knew skating would help.' She placed my hand on the wooden rail.

'I wouldn't exactly call this skating.'

She laughed and skated backwards, encouraging me forward. My feet had other plans and headed in opposite directions. I clung to the wall again.

'Try. Let go of the wall.' Her look and her words pleaded with me.

I swallowed and watched the other skaters move in various states of grace about the rink. In the middle were the most accomplished. A young couple jumped and twirled, their movement in unison. I was never that skilled, but the freedom of speeding around the ice, it felt so good. Surely even after all these years I could still skate. I pushed both feet forward and left one hand on the wall. Remembering to breathe, I looked up and smiled at her. 'I'm going to try but at my own pace.'

She squinted at me and I waved her away. Shuffle by shuffle, I moved about the edge, giving encouraging smiles to other beginners. For I felt like a beginner again. I may have known how to whizz across the ice once, but now I was starting from scratch. This time with fear I'd never had before. In the past if I'd fallen, I'd be back on my feet in moments. Now, moving like a ninety-year-old around the fringes, all I could think about was the pain of the fall, the hardness of the ice, and the indignity of it all.

The sharp swish of people skating past competed with the soundtrack. Whoever was in charge liked the eighties. In fact, it could be the same soundtrack. All the old longings and the old possibilities settled over my heart. The boy in the green jacket. I never discovered his name. At the end of that season, he'd said goodbye. His family were moving. His hand had reached out and touched mine. Goodbye. His first and last word to me. His eyes had been the same colour as his dark green jacket. Funny how I could remember that, thirty-six years later.

A hand touched my shoulder. I turned, ready to say thanks to Donna, but the words died on my lips.

'Can I give you a hand? I've only just come back to skating after many years and you look…' His words trailed away. He wasn't in a green jacket, but his eyes were just as I remembered.

'You?' we said at the same time. He grinned. The dimples in his cheeks had become more pronounced. I nodded. He laughed, and so did I.

'I take it you haven't skated since?' He held out an arm, and I clutched it as he moved me away from the wall.

'No.'

'We'll take it slowly. It will come back to you. It did with me.' His eyes smiled, showing wrinkles that weren't there before.

'You stopped skating?' I tilted my head to look up at him.

'Life.'

I nodded.

'I took up skating again when my wife died three years ago,' he said.

'I'm so sorry.' My heart knew that pain only too well.

'Thank you. And what about you?' he asked.

'Skating today, and I lost my husband two years ago.'

He clasped my hand more tightly for just a moment. 'Now, slide one foot in front of the other.'

I did and wobbled.

'I won't let go.'

He was true to his promise and each slide became easier. Before I knew it, I'd made it round the rink. Donna skated past me backwards and said, 'Good to see you here again, Joe.'

I opened my eyes wide at her and she grinned.

'Shall we go round again?' He looked down at my hand on his arm.

'I'm holding you back,' I said.

'I have a feeling you'll catch up to me in no time.'

We set off, one shuffle at a time.

---

Writer, ex-pat expert, wife, mother of three, sale to two cats and dreamer turned doer…Liz Fenwick is an award-winning author of eight Cornwall based novels, dubbed 'the queen of the contemporary Cornish novel' by The Guardian. Her latest book is *The River Between Us.*

# THE LIAR

*By LJ Ross*

"How was the wedding?"

Mandy looked up from where she'd been filling a plastic kettle, her face blank.

"The—?"

"Your son's wedding? It was at the weekend, wasn't it?"

Bev's eyes were sharp behind the tortoiseshell glasses she wore and, suddenly, it all came rushing back.

"Oh!" Mandy let out a loud, tinkling laugh and hoped it didn't sound too forced. "Of course…the wedding. It was—"

*Fictional.*

*Non-existent.*

"Beautiful," she gushed, leaning against the Formica counter in the break room. "Mark was a little bit nervous, as you can imagine, but I was there to help. He looked so handsome, in his navy suit and tie. As for Ellie, she was radiant in her dress…"

"Aww," Bev said, reaching for one of the biscuits Mandy routinely kept stocked in the office tin. "Go on, let's see a picture—"

Mandy busied herself making the tea, while she thought of what to say.

"Well, you're not going to believe what happened," she said, casting an embarrassed look back over her shoulder. "I must have had one too many glasses of bubbly because I…well, I dropped my phone down the toilet at the end of the night. What a *wally*!"

Bev's pencilled eyebrows shot into her hairline. Whether it was surprise at the thought of Mandy ever being so clumsy, or being so drunk, she couldn't tell.

Neither seemed particularly plausible.

"Well, that's a shame," she said slowly.

"When the professional photographer sends through his snaps, I'll be sure to let you know," Mandy added, hastily.

They both knew Bev's interest would have waned long before then.

"Must be getting back to the grindstone," she said, with a pointed glance at the clock on the wall. "I've got a bunch of filing to get through before the end of the day."

With that, she hurried off, tea clutched in her hands like a lifeline.

*It has to stop,* Mandy told herself.

*The lies have to stop.*

* * *

"I can't seem to help myself, Mum. I've told so many lies, now, that I can barely remember the truth."

*You know the truth,* her mind whispered.

And she did, really.

She was a fifty-five-year-old woman with curly grey hair and brown eyes, and a body that had never lain naked beside another living soul, let alone grown a child or given one away in marriage at the weekend. She lived alone in a little two-up, two-down ex-miner's cottage that used to belong to her parents, with a cat named Freddy and a houseful of ghosts and memories.

There were no real visitors.

Oh, the postman came to deliver bills and flyers, and there was the occasional person canvassing for some political party or another, and she always invited them in for tea. Indeed, by the time she'd plied them with biscuits, cake and conversation, it seemed they were no longer too bothered about signing her up as a member or securing her vote in the local council elections.

*Must dash,* they'd say. *Lots of people to see.*

And that would be the end of that.

Over the years, she'd watched her schoolmates grow up and move on with their lives, kissing boys and marrying some of them, while she'd looked on with fascination, telling herself that, one day, that would be her. The perfect person would come along, and he'd look just like Mr Darcy, with dark hair and big brown eyes. He'd be a gentleman who'd take her hand and see beyond the painful acne, beyond the superficial skin she wore, to the burgeoning woman who wanted to blossom, beneath.

That had been a long time ago.

When Mr Darcy hadn't come along and her father had died, leaving her to care for Mum, there hadn't been much time or opportunity to look for him—or any other 'Mister', for that matter. She watched the same girls she'd known at school turn into women in smart navy suits, or mothers who pushed buggies along the high street, chattering amongst themselves while she looked on, always from a distance, with her nose pushed up against the glass.

Until, one day, those babies and toddlers had become teenagers she saw riding bikes to school, and then men and women who brushed past her in the street; unseeing and uncaring.

For she was invisible and unrecognisable.

"I didn't mean to do it," Mandy whispered, brushing a tear from her cheek. "I just wanted…I wanted to be one of them. I wanted to have the same things."

She couldn't remember when the lies started. Probably when she'd been chatting to a stranger on the bus.

*On your way somewhere nice, dear?* some old lady might have asked.

*Oh, just on my way to visit my son. He's got a new girlfriend, you know.*

*How lovely…and what does your son do?*

It was as easy as that, until the fantasy grew bigger and bigger—so big, she had created a whole world of friends and family to keep her company. Sometimes, she even made enough dinner for two or three, forgetting that there was only ever one mouth to feed.

Then, she'd be forced to eat it all.

*Waste not, want not,* her mother used to say.

"I think Bev knows something's wrong," she whispered, as she watched a leaf fall from one of the overhanging branches in the graveyard. It caught on the breeze and held on the air for a moment, suspended, before falling gently at the foot of her mother's headstone. "One of these days, she's going to stop all the polite small talk, because she knows I've been lying to her."

*Why not try telling the truth, then?*

"It isn't that easy," Mandy muttered. "I'd be so embarrassed to admit the truth. So ashamed. Besides, Bev has a family…two girls and a boy, all grown up now. She goes to the hairdresser every other week, and out for drinks with some of the other women from work once a month. She has a husband, and a sister. I don't have any of those things. We have nothing in common."

*You don't know that, unless you try…*

"Did you say something?"

With a start, Mandy swung around on the bench where she'd been sitting, to find a young man of around nineteen or twenty sitting on the grassy turf a short way away, beside another headstone which looked newly polished.

"Um, no. Sorry."

She reached for her bag, preparing to leave.

"I thought I was the only one," he said, with a twisted smile. "Who talks to their mum, I mean."

Mandy's eyes slid over to the headstone, which read:

SHARON PETTIFER
1970—2021
BELOVED WIFE AND MOTHER
GONE BUT NEVER FORGOTTEN

"I'm sorry," she mumbled, lifting a finger towards the stone. "How long since…since?"

"Six months," he said softly. "What about you?"

Mandy swallowed, and tried to work out what somebody might say when they had nothing but the truth to fall back on.

"My—er—my mum was a lot older than yours. She died a couple of years ago, after a lifetime of disability."

"That sucks," he said, with youthful compassion. "I bet you miss her."

Mandy blinked away sudden tears, thinking of all the times she'd said 'no' to cinema trips and outings, to the occasional and unexpected offer of a drink from a kind-hearted man. All the bed baths and pill boxes, the doctor's trips and nebulizers. But then, there'd been the laughter and the knitting, the games of bridge and Friday night telly marathons. She didn't regret having spent the best part of her life caring for her mother, because she'd loved her deeply and the choice had been hers to make. But now, her death had left a gaping void in her life, and loneliness had rushed in, taking root and making a home there.

"Yes," she said, eventually. "I miss her very much."

A couple of minutes of companionable silence went by, while they both watched the falling leaves and held private conversations with those they had lost, until the man rose to his feet and brushed the grass from his jeans.

Mandy prepared herself to bid farewell to another fleeting moment of human contact, and already had a cheerful smile in place, when he took her by surprise.

"I was thinking of getting a cuppa from the café," he said. "D'you fancy one?"

She stared at him, then at the headstone.

"A—all right."

* * *

They ran into one another every week, after that.

Mandy learned that his name was Jack, and that he worked as a mechanic in the local car dealership. He had a girlfriend called Isobel, a father called Steven, and an older brother called Daniel, who was married and lived in London. Jack learned that she had a tabby cat by the name of Frederick, who answered to "Freddy" and preferred salmon to chicken, who slept at the end of her bed most nights, and could open doors with his paw. Jack told her he was worried about his father, who had barely left the house since his mother's death, and had begun drinking a lot, especially in the evenings.

Mandy told him the truth.

"I don't drink much, but I tell a lot of lies."

And he'd listened while she untangled the web, tugging each thread until it had loosened, along with her tongue.

"It isn't too late," he'd said, at the end of it all. "It's never too late. That's what my mum used to say."

"I don't know how to speak to people. I've forgotten how."

"You're speaking to me, aren't you?"

It was as easy as that.

* * *

"Have the wedding photos come through, yet?"

Mandy drained the tea bag from her mug, and took a deep breath before turning to face Bev, who held out the milk for her.

"No," she said, taking the milk and setting it down on the counter. "There won't be any photos, because there wasn't any wedding. I don't have any children, or other family. I'm sorry, I lied to you."

Bev searched the other woman's face, and saw sincerity for the first time.

Compassion followed, on swift wings.

"Why, love? Why'd you say all that stuff?"

"I envied you," Mandy said, with brutal honesty. "I've never had a relationship like yours—or children. I wish I had."

Bev thought of all the times she'd waxed lyrical about her brilliant children or her romantic husband who whisked her away for anniversaries and birthdays, or 'just because'. She thought of Mandy, who always smiled and asked politely, who always baked biscuits and complimented her hair, her clothing, her make-up, while she hadn't cared enough to look and really *see.*

Well, it was never too late to change all that.

"What are you doing this Friday?" she asked, suddenly.

Mandy thought of the telly marathon she'd planned with Freddy. "Nothing special," she admitted.

"Good. You're coming out with me, and we're going to drink cocktails."

"Cocktails?"

"Haven't you ever had a 'Screaming Orgasm' before?"

*As a matter of fact…*

"Er, no, I can't say that I have."

"Well, it's about bloody time," Bev said, matter-of-factly. "In fact, I'd recommend multiple rounds."

Mandy grinned, but then her smile faded.

"I've never…I mean to say, I'll stick out like a sore thumb. I'm too old for wine bars and cocktails."

Bev stepped forward and put her hand on the woman's arm, giving it a gentle squeeze.

"This is only the beginning," she said softly.

---

LJ Ross is an internationally bestselling author, whose books have sold over seven million copies worldwide. Her debut, *Holy Island*, was released in 2015 and became an instant, international bestseller. Since then, a further twenty of her novels have gone on to take the coveted #1 spot, some even before general release and whilst only available to 'pre-order'. *The Bookseller* magazine has reported on Louise having topped the 'Most Read' and 'Most Sold' fiction charts, and she has garnered an army of loyal fans who love her atmospheric and addictive storytelling. Her eleventh novel, *The Infirmary*, is a prequel story to the chart-topping DCI Ryan series and is available as a major Audible Originals audio-drama. The first novel in her Alexander Gregory Thrillers series, *Impostor*, was shortlisted in the British Book Awards 2020: Crime & Thriller Book of the Year 2020. The audiobook of *Impostor*, narrated by Hugh Dancy, was also selected as a finalist in the New York Festivals Radio Awards, Best Fiction Audiobook of the Year Category. In May 2021, Louise was shortlisted for the prestigious Crime Writers' Association 'Dagger in the Library' award. Louise studied undergraduate and postgraduate Law at King's College, University of London and then abroad in Paris and Florence. She spent much of her working life in London, where she was a lawyer for a number of years until taking the decision to change career and pursue her dream to write. Now, she writes full time and lives with her husband and son in Northumberland, where she was born and grew up. She enjoys reading all manner of books, painting, travelling and spending time with family and friends.

To find out more about the many philanthropic ventures Louise has founded and sponsored through her publishing imprint, Dark Skies Publishing, please visit www.ljrossauthor.com.

# THE LIGHT ROOM

*By Louise Beech*

The fifth mother I've seen with a flower corsage pinned upside-down on her lapel asks if her daughter's 'monstrous' nose can be 'chiselled or something' and I have to explain without insult that only shadow and shade are alterable, not size or shape.

'But she looks like a circus extra in these pictures!' This latest mother prods my computer screen like her finger is a wand that might undo the ugly, change her frog offspring into a princess. 'You must help her.'

My screen bears the mark of so many wands. I'm almost too tired to request that she not touch it, but fear I'll slap her if she does it again. 'Please, don't—'

'There simply must be a way we can erase this bump. And how about the black lines under her eyes—goodness, she looks like she should be in a Rolling Stones video, not getting married!'

'Lines we can erase,' I say softly.

'Can you? Oh, you're just wonderful, dear. There's hope after all.'

I endure so many mothers; they come in all guises, parade the shop floor like I'm to pick one over the other in some pageant. There are those who want to show off their daughters. Those who want to change them. Those who want them to be everything they never were but instead say, *well, she's so wilful.* And I'm the magician. I'm the air-brusher. I can enhance any image, improve any bride, smooth out creases, whiten teeth, correct flaws, hide blemishes.

'I went to One Click on the High Street and they were going to charge me three hundred pounds. I mean, her nose needs help, but *quite*.' The fifth corsage-wearing mother flushes red. 'And I want the weather changing—can you do that?'

I nod and look, not for the first time, at the photograph, at the rain that bloats clouds behind this imperfect bride and her new husband. Her mouth is the loveliest I've seen, kind of wonky, shy, closed. She hides her teeth, keeps her lips together, two hands joined, almost praying, like she knows she'll later be analysed and asks for acceptance. But her eyes, they smile; they light up as if they have a choice.

'We can add sunshine,' I tell her, always reluctant to mess with what is. 'Blue sky, an archway, full moon…snow. How would you like it to be?'

The fifth mother's phone rings and she rummages in her bag for it. She cries out her conversation as though from afar—*But they can improve you! Yes, really! You need not have held your breath or clamped your mouth shut like you were doing long division in your head! You're going to look divine, perfect!*

'I think I'll have to come back in a while,' she says then, to me. 'I need to discuss with my obstinate daughter what's to be done. She can't see the need to airbrush. She thinks I'll hang her wedding pictures on my wall like *that*.'

My screen is once more prodded before I can react. On her way out, the fifth mother picks up one of our leaflets (*At Fantasy Fauxtograph we can transform your Magical Day into something really Memorable!)* and the bell above the door, quaint compared with the minimalist decor, tinkles her departure like a wedding supper announcement.

Alone, I save her images, as yet untouched. I wish I could develop them as art, how they are. True. I wish I could be kind.

At Fantasy Fauxtograph we still have a dark room; we're the only place in town that does. Digital photography has rendered it frequently unused, but some dedicated artists still request we develop their images the 'true' way, and so it remains. I prefer the dark room, letting the images develop as they will, no intervention, only time. I love the smell of fixer, the tickle of chemicals on my skin, the soft slosh of liquid, the otherwise quiet.

With the fifth mother gone and Billy in for a few hours, I go to this place. There are some black and white prints that Mr Crooks, a regular, has requested be developed so I turn on the safelight. Its amber glow warms my mood. Black and white papers are ruined only by blue light, or green, while colour paper, being sensitive to all parts of the visible spectrum, must be kept in complete darkness until the prints are properly fixed. After doing a test strip to ascertain the exposure time, I immerse Mr Crooks' paper in the developer and watch it sink.

I wait.

The image emerges, centre first, its heart.

I wait.

Black spreads like spilt tea, darker in parts, lighter in others.

I wait.

Faces appear, smiles, laugh lines, wind-blown hair, freckles, reality.

I wait.

The pictures are of children, three, and they're clearly Mr Crooks' own; a photographer cannot hide a love of his subject. They jump and he captures them forever in the air, weightless, flying. A girl, whose abundance of freckles suggests that in spite of the monochrome she must be a redhead, dances around a tree. Another girl, younger, looks over her shoulder at the photographer, flirting with him. A third, the oldest, waits by the bark, unsure, her hands at her mouth, hiding any expression.

We were three, I remember.

And I remember waiting, waiting for our mother.

At our granny's window, we didn't know what car to look for, not even the colour, so each one that rounded the street corner was a possibility. Granny called from the kitchen—*Don't touch the glass! Don't mark the glass!* My little sister Jenny's fingers had already left their impression and Baby Paul would soon add his. Mine never touched, not anything. I stood away from the window, away from the scene, from them. I knew. I don't know how. I was only nine. No one told me. I hated knowing.

When it came, the car was yellow, like hope. Our mother was with a social worker—time has given her this title, then she was just a lady. A lady who brought our mother from the hospital. Time has also given this place a name—Castle Hill Mental Health Unit. Time airbrushes. The mind tries to resist, to hear the heart, but memories are coloured by all that has passed since.

My memory cannot find Granny—I don't know where she was when our mother stood in the hallway, shy, hiding her teeth, keeping her lips together, two hands joined, praying, like she knew she'd later be analysed and asks for acceptance. We hadn't seen her in eight months. Little Jenny wrapped chubby arms around her leg and Baby Paul raised his open, wiggly hands, asking to be picked up. She seemed not to know how to respond.

In the living room, she perched on the rocking chair and smiled at the flood of questions. Have you brought my Barbie doll? Why have you been gone so long? Do you still love us?

Can we go to Scarborough? How long are you staying? I didn't ask. I knew. The social worker disappeared into the part of my mind where Granny was and I never saw her again. Our mother's teacup never left the saucer. The gold clock on the mantelpiece next to Jesus accelerated, I'm sure, an hour, two, each time I looked at it.

And then we were in the hallway again, and Granny came out of the dark, to help me. Our mother was leaving. I had known. Little Jenny clung to her leg, desperate now, not elated, not hopeful, but knowing. Baby Paul's fingers opened and closed, like an imitation of ambulance lights. On the bronze table in the living room her tea grew cold. We played 'cookery' when she'd gone, pouring the cold liquid back and forth between cup and beaker. Granny called from the kitchen—*Don't mess the table! Don't mark the carpet!*

In the dark room I always find light. Mr Crooks' pictures are born now, pure, untouched. I should have told them. I should have told Little Jenny and Baby Paul that I knew our mother wasn't staying, that she hadn't come to get us.

Would it have been *kinder* to do so?

I'm their memory now. I tell them things I remember, give them their history, but I've to be careful not to shade these moments with my own guilt or decoration of it, and to let their flashes colour it also.

I peg Mr Crooks' children on the line to dry and return to the shop. William, my assistant, goes out for lunch and a moment after his departure the bell heralds the return of the fifth mother. Her upside-down corsage is squashed against a pile of boxes, two of which she puts carefully on the counter near my mug of coffee. I resist asking her not to knock over my drink.

'I brought you cake, dear,' she says, removing one of her white gloves. 'A piece for you and a piece for the other young man. Yours is the one with half of an iced shoe—I thought you'd like that.'

I shake my head but can't find any words.

'Now, dear.' She removes the other glove and places it atop the cake boxes. 'I read your leaflet while I waited for my hair appointment and it says that you can remove people. *People*! You can make them disappear. Like they never were.'

From the place in my mind where Granny hid, I find—*No, I can't.*

'You *can*. It says here—look!' The fifth mother opens our leaflet, waves her red-nailed wand at the words, the promise. 'Now, in seven of the wedding pictures there's my husband's mother, and I want her out. Really, she should never have been invited after what happened, but I won't go into that, not here, now's not the time. I want you to do whatever it is that you do and remove her.'

'I won't,' I say softly.

'But it's what you do, dear. You're a Fantasy Fauxtographer.'

I click open an image of her daughter, one where she's closing her eyes to the blast of rainbow confetti, her fingers trapped in the froth of veil. 'This picture is beautiful,' I say. 'In its lop-sidedness and in the slightly stained sash and in the grey light of rain, it is beautiful. I won't touch it. You're changing the memory before you've even had time to let the moment pass and become one.'

'I'm making it *perfect*, dear.' The fifth mother looks at me, I think in disbelief at my daughter-like wilfulness when I've no right, but maybe with some respect. I'm not her child, but I speak for her, for all of them.

'I'm not going to change the picture,' I say.

This is the kind thing to do.

Let her daughter be true; beautiful in her imperfection.

'I'll go to One Click, you know,' snaps the mother. '*They'll* take my bloody mother-in-law out of the day. They'll trim my husband's nasal hair.' She pauses, looks at the boxes, and then back at me. Taking her gloves and putting them on she says, 'Oh, keep the darned cake anyway.'

The bell tinkles her second departure. I think I'd known she'd come back; I have a sense of these things. But I know she'll not return now, that she'll find what she wants at another place, just as I know I have to.

The mothers came and they asked me to give them the daughters they always wanted, and they thought I could take away the times they'd argued over boyfriends and the times they'd called each other names and then didn't speak for months, and they said—with tears in their eyes—that I must clean all that had been sullied, bring back the seven-year-old girl who'd loved without condition. But I can't now, and anyway, I already have a mother, one, and that's enough, and she's imperfect, flawed, real, and I love her.

---

Louise Beech is the author of seven novels. She was shortlisted for the Romantic Novel Award, longlisted for the Polari Prize, and won Best magazine's Book of the Year. Her newest book, *This Is How We Are Human*, hit the Top 100 on Amazon and was selected by the Clare Mackintosh Book Club as an August Book of the Month. A theatre usher at Hull Truck for seven happy years, Louise finally gave her job up to become a full-time writer this year, and is delighted.

# HENRY'S HOPE

*By Louise Jensen / Amelia Henley*

Dear Henry,

New year, new start. Isn't that what they say? But, without you, it seems more like an ending. Of all the times to be alone, surely this has to be the worst?

Journaling is meant to be therapeutic but it feels more like talking to myself, so instead I thought I'd write you letters. Letters I'll never send.

The house feels cold without you. I wander from room to room, the kitchen where I'd bake your favourites, hoping sponges swirled together with buttercream and jam or drizzled with lemon said all the things I'd stopped saying. Oh, how I wish I had said them. Did you feel taken for granted? It's too late now but this morning I made a cake and iced 'I love you' over the top. Stupid really.

I pass through the bedroom. I no longer sleep in our bed because it's too big, too empty. Not that I get much rest. Each time I'm nodding off, memories of you whisper on the periphery of my consciousness and I am jerked awake, my cheeks wet with tears, my pillow too.

It's when I reach the room we'd earmarked as a nursery there's a savage tearing at my heart. And that's when I think of *her* with her bump, new life growing inside of her, and I hate her with a ferocity that scares me. She took you away from me, and more than anything I want you back.

Love Hannah

Dear Henry,

Today, I go through some of the things you left behind. The shirts at the back of the wardrobe that were replaced by smaller, slim-fitting styles once you'd trimmed down.

Remember when I asked if you were having a mid-life crisis when you refused a second slice of the black cherry gateaux, patting your stomach by way of explanation?

I slip your pale blue shirt on over my pyjamas. You used to love it when I wore one of your shirts *instead* of my pyjamas. Now, it swamps me. I'm losing weight. I think of *her* gaining weight, shopping for maternity clothes, and I wrench your shirt from my body, stuffing everything back into the wardrobe and slamming the door.

Everything is too hard. Everything hurts too much.

Love Hannah

Dear Henry,

The daffodils are poking their hopeful heads through the tangle of weeds in the garden. Spring is another time for fresh beginnings isn't it, and as I glared at those yellow flowers, I was overcome by the unfairness of it all.

I marched to *her* house, was halfway up the path, knuckles poised to rap on the front door when I noticed, through the window, a half-assembled cot and that was my undoing.

I cried all the way home. I'm still crying now.

Love Hannah

Dear Henry,

This morning there was a letter on my mat, *I'm sorry, please forgive me.* It got me thinking about all those inspirational quotes you loved so much: '*You, more than anyone, deserve your love and affection*'; '*Forgiveness is a gift you give to yourself*'; '*Be kind, always'*, were some of your favourites. Does she know about your obsession with them? I think she must. She must know things about you that I don't, the way I have memories that are mine and mine alone.

I don't love myself right now. I don't treat myself with kindness, let alone anyone else. That much is apparent from the way I skip meals, drink too much in the evenings.

I don't forgive.

Even though I know you'd hope that I would.

I screwed up the letter and threw it into the bin.

Love Hannah

Dear Henry,

Today I gave away some of your things. Clothes you haven't worn for years, CDs of bands you'd grown out of, DVDs of movies that were popular before streaming was a thing. Nothing recent. Nothing that could evoke too painful a memory. I bundled everything into black sacks and took them to the charity shop. On the way I passed a man huddled in a doorway, sleeping bag rolled up beside him. His box asking for donations only contained a few coppers. I crouched before him and asked if he wanted anything from the bags. He shrugged on your old coat—you know, the thick tweed one we bought from M&S that you barely wore—and he stuffed some jumpers into his rucksack. I left him with £20 to buy some lunch and he thanked me for my kindness but it didn't feel like a selfless act. It felt like…revenge for you leaving me? A convenience just because he was there?

But then, if the outcome is the same does it make a good deed less valuable than if I'd purposefully sought him out?

I don't know. What I do know is that when I was heading home, I passed that baby shop on the High Street, 'Kids Kingdom', and she was inside, hunched over a pram—trying to figure out how it works before she bought it, I suppose. I ducked out of sight before I was spotted.

My chest aches with missing you. The house feels emptier now than ever.

Love Hannah

Dear Henry,

Today the lights went out and I had to brave the cupboard under the stairs to find the fuse box. I felt quite proud of myself when the bare bulb hanging from the ceiling lit up again, although I'd only had to push a button. The cupboard was full of clutter, always a dumping ground, but it was an old shoebox that caught my eye. My hands had trembled as I'd gently prised off the lid knowing what I'd find. Pale yellow straw still strewn over the cardboard base. Do you remember that day? You'd come home cradling a tiny baby bird.

'She fell out of her nest.' You had tears in your eyes.

'Poor thing.' I'd felt a constriction in my throat. 'She'll never survive.'

'Where there's life, there's hope,' you had said. Over the following weeks you nursed her, setting your alarm for regular intervals during the night to feed her via a pipette.

I remember thinking what a wonderful father you'd make.

One day, remarkably, joyously, she'd been strong enough to fly.

That was real kindness.

I put the box back where I had found it, unable to bear throwing it away, and then I went for a walk, eyes trained on the sky watching the birds as they soared across fluffy white clouds, wondering if I could spot our bird.

It wasn't intentional, going to *her* house, but again I found myself there. This time I ventured closer to the front door. Through the window, on the wall above the log burner there was a photo of you both grinning into the camera.

I ran all the way home but it wasn't the exertion making my heart hurt.

Love Hannah

Dear Henry,

All night I'd thought about you, her, us. In the morning I'd pulled on one of your t-shirts—the Ed Sheeran tour one we'd bought after seeing him at the O2—as though wanting to prove that there had been a part of your life that was just ours. Then I headed towards her house before I'd even had a coffee, before I could change my mind.

Rain blew into my face, streamed down my neck, my hair damp but the grey skies matched my grey mood and I could have put my hood up and tried to keep dry, but I didn't, wanting to feel…something. My heart was beating out my chest as I forced my reluctant feet to stand on her step, ring the bell.

The door swung open.

'Lydia…' My voice cracked and I couldn't say anything else.

She stepped forward and hugged me so hard I could feel her bump press against me and I pulled back, worried I'd hurt the baby.

I looked into her eyes and I saw myself in them, a woman grieving, hurting, lost, and then she was crying, I was crying.

'Come in, Hannah.' She ushered me inside.

Before I knew it, I was in your sister's house, surrounded by memories of you, photos of you, and then she apologised for killing you.

'You didn't.' I dropped to my knees as she sank into a chair, covering her face with her hands. I took them gently in mine.

'But it's what you think?' She sniffed. 'It's all my fault. It's what you said.'

'I'm so sorry I said that. I'm sorry I blamed you, I was incredibly angry and I wanted to lash out and—'

'But it's true. If I hadn't called Henry and asked him to fetch me a kebab late at night then—'

'You can't help your cravings'—I glanced at her bump—'and you can't help that you're on your own and you—'

'I could have driven myself—'

'But Henry *wanted* to help you. Henry always wanted to help everyone. It was his kindness that made me fall in love with him. I…I'm so sorry Lydia. If he'd seen the way I've treated you the past few weeks then he'd have been ashamed.' My cheeks burned at the truth of this. 'I'm ashamed of myself.'

'You're here now.' She placed her palm against my cheek and I leaned against it.

'Do you forgive me?' My voice was a whisper.

'There's nothing to forgive.'

Later, I told her about the letter I'd received. From Jenny, the mother of Sean—the boy who had mugged you, stabbed you as you'd punched numbers into the cashpoint because the takeaway didn't accept card payments. 'She said she felt so terrible about what happened but she still visited her son in the Young Offenders Institution. She said he was distraught, had never meant to hurt anyone.'

'Did you reply?' Lydia asked.

I shook my head. 'I can't—what can I say? It's okay? It isn't. The world is a hateful place.'

'Not always. You know what Henry would say?'

'*Be the change you want to see* or something else that's hard to do.'

'I think he'd say, *We win by kindness, we conquer by forgiveness*.'

I've thought about that a lot since she said it. It feels impossible.

Love Hannah

Dear Henry,

My thoughts are all over the place. This afternoon I had a coffee with Jenny in her local café. I'd expected Sean's mum to be....I don't know what I'd expected really but I'd thought the woman who had raised Sean would be...lacking somehow but she was...sad. Sorry. Normal. The sort of woman you'd pass on the street without a second glance, and perhaps that was part of the problem.

'We're invisible,' she told me. 'I'm not making excuses but people like us...' She gestured around the estate she lives on. 'Kids like Sean, they're almost expected to join a gang. Written off before they've had a chance to make anything of themselves. I blame myself. If I hadn't been out working all hours, I'd have kept a better eye on him.'

I didn't know what to say so I'd shredded the cake my anxious stomach couldn't eat, scattering crumbs over the table.

'Sean's my baby, only fifteen and...I'm not making excuses for him. Nothing can justify taking a life, but he *is* sorry.'

He might be sorry, but I've googled 'reoffenders' and I know the statistics. He's remorseful now but what about when he gets out? It's hopeless. I felt as though the walls were closing in on me, the celling pressing down. I shouldn't have come.

'I have to go.' I knocked the table as I stood, tea spilling over the Formica.

Jenny rose too, pushing her arms into the sleeves of her faded pink coat.

'Sean would like to see you,' she said. 'When you're ready.'

I'll never be ready.

Love Hannah

Dear Henry,

Last week, after I'd met Jenny, I'd woken up to the tap-tap-tap of a beak against the window. A bird—our bird—looking in on me before flying away. Was it you? I know that sounds mad. Perhaps I am mad because I took it as a sign and today, I did something I never thought I'd find the strength to do. I went to the Young Offenders Institute to visit Sean.

And I forgave him.

It wasn't easy. I couldn't even look him in the eye at first and I felt all this…anger towards him. Honestly, I wanted to… hurt him, and you know me, I never even kill the spiders when they scurry into the house. My blood felt hot, adrenaline was whooshing through my veins, but then I thought about that baby bird. Where there's life, there's hope, and I wondered whether Sean would have turned to crime if someone had showed a little faith in him rather than expecting the worst. A little kindness.

Love Hannah

Dear Henry,

The best news, my darling. In the early hours of this morning Lydia called me—she was in labour! It's a good job I've stopped drinking in the evenings—I'm looking after myself a little bit better nowadays—because I could pick her up and drive her to the hospital. She gave birth to a baby boy at 7.15am. I was there, holding her hand, cheering her on. Inadequate, but some comfort

I hope. Afterward she'd wrapped him in a crochet shawl that apparently your nana had knitted for you when your mum was pregnant, and later passed down to Lydia.

We'd marvelled at his wispy blond hair, his tiny fingers and toes.

'I…I'm going to call him Henry,' Lydia said softly.

We'd both cried and I vowed to always be there for him. To be both an aunt and an uncle. To give him the opportunities we would have afforded our own child. It got me thinking about all those children who don't get the same opportunities, kids like Sean.

The edges of a plan are forming in my mind.

Love Hannah

Dear Henry,

Sorry I haven't written in ages—I'm not forgetting you, I promise—but I've been so busy. Today was the grand opening of a charity I founded to help kids from underprivileged backgrounds find some purpose, some direction. I used much of your life insurance money to get it off the ground, but I know you wouldn't mind.

You'd be proud.

I don't know if I can make a difference, but I want to—I want to at least try.

Lydia and Jenny have helped me, we've taken on the lease of an old office on the outskirts of town and have worked tirelessly to renovate it ourselves to save money. I've watched YouTube tutorials and learned to plaster and tile the kitchenette. We've painted the walls a fresh white before stencilling an inspirational quote in huge letters with a gold pen, surrounded by transfers of soaring birds.

*Kindness is contagious, be a carrier.*

You'd love it.

We fizzed open champagne when the sign with the charity's name was erected above the front door.

We've called it 'Henry's Hope.'

Love Hannah

---

Louise Jensen has been nominated for multiple awards and has sold over a million English language copies of her International No. 1 psychological thrillers. Her novels have also been translated into twenty-five languages and are for sale in over thirty territories. Louise's books have been featured on the USA Today and Wall Street Journal Bestseller's List and have been optioned for TV. Louise also writes high concept contemporary love stories under the pen name 'Amelia Henley'.

# SIX STEPS

*By Louise Mumford*

It was there again on Tuesday.

"It's back," Eric said to Colin, who did not reply because he was a taxidermy squirrel.

Eric had watched them move in. Big van, some pieces of oak furniture, a bed with a curved white headboard and some neatly-labelled boxes. Not enough, he'd thought at the time. Not enough at all. They needed more.

His previous neighbours had been a quiet couple around his age, whose telly he'd heard in the evenings, the odd creak on the stair, sometimes the thump of a window closing. He didn't know what happened to them, or where they had gone, hadn't even noticed they had moved out until the new "For Sale" sign appeared in the front yard.

Eric pushed Colin's eye back into place and lowered the net curtain. Lauren could deal with it when she came: it would make her feel useful. Eric knew today was her visit day because he had checked the calendar. He did that first thing every morning to fix the day and date in his mind. Tuesday: Lauren day.

Also organising day.

It was always organising day.

You could at least see the floor in this room now. That was important. He had worked hard on that, carving a path out of the boxes and magazines, the unopened duvet sets and books soft with age so he could get to the window. See outside. Maria had picked the nets. She'd picked the wallpaper and the carpets and the paintings on the walls: prints of women and children with very big, sad eyes, holding flower baskets, or teddies, or dolls with the exact same big-eyed sad expressions.

The front door opened.

"Hello!" a loud voice called from below, as if about to announce the day's fun activities on a cruise ship. "Uncle Eric? Hello! I'm coming in!"

Eric wasn't sure why she always had to announce it like that—as if he had to spring to attention. His days of springing anywhere were long gone. By the time he got down the stairs she would be packing up and ready to go.

He stood on the landing and watched Lauren squeeze herself into the hallway, manoeuvring her ample bosom past the eight planks of wood propped up against an old door, a set of fire irons, a vegetable steamer in its box and a child's rocking horse. He hadn't got around to organising those things yet.

"Careful," he muttered, gripping onto the hand rail of the stairs as tightly as his arthritic fingers would allow. No one explained that old age would be such an adrenaline rush, he thought, edging his foot onto the first step—just walking downstairs was a thrill ride of fear. Would he make it to the bottom in one piece?

"How about that stair lift, hmm?" Lauren watched him from below, arms crossed.

"No—"

"—bloody stair lifts, yes, yes I know..." She smiled and Eric smiled with her.

Lauren liked a slogan t-shirt. The problem was that they had all been washed too many times and the lettering was beginning to flake away. This one said: "Li…e, L…u g…Love' which was now not quite the uplifting message it had once been. She was wearing a frosted lipstick that gave her the look of someone in the throes of hypothermia and enough bead bracelets to make a large abacus. Healing stones, she called them. Eric was sceptical that any stone cared enough about the human race to bother with healing them.

Getting down the stairs was not helped by the way that many of his shoes were lined up on the steps as if trooping themselves to bed. He couldn't remember his reasoning for that, though he was sure there had been a damn good one. He added it to his mental list of things to organise and stepped around an errant lace that threatened to unbalance him.

"It's there again," he puffed when he got to the last step, steadying himself against a small table in the shape of a dolphin carrying a tray on its nose.

"Is it?" Lauren bustled past him with a bag of shopping and Eric spied a few of his favourite chocolate mousse pots through the thin plastic. "You could come out with me, y'know."

Eric knew. He wasn't senile.

"Some fresh air would be nice for you, yeah? Have a look at the plants."

There weren't any plants. The ones Maria had left had died of neglect over the years and he had let them because it didn't seem fair that they should be alive when she wasn't.

Lauren sighed. "Have it your own way."

Eric stood at the threshold of the back door and watched her do it, just to be sure. The ball was bright red with a googly-eyed face painted on it, a stupid looking thing, incongruous against the weed-choked patio. Lauren picked it up and threw it back over the fence.

It was only as she began to walk back inside that he heard it. He wasn't sure because Lauren had been berating him about the new addition of a work bench complete with tools in his kitchen—"It's blocking the bloody fridge!"—but he thought he heard a small voice say, "Fank you."

* * *

The ball was there again on Wednesday.

On Friday, it had a friend—spongy and yellow.

Eric watched the little boy from the window. A scrap of a child, about five years old maybe, but he wasn't sure, had never been good at guessing the ages of children. They were small and shouty for what seemed like forever and then suddenly they shot up, all bad skin and greasy hair and gangly limbs. That had been Lauren anyway. He and Maria had never had children. No regret in that—he'd had her, and that was all he had ever wanted.

The boy pottered about in his back garden. They hadn't been in long but had already set up some garden furniture, a table and a few loungers though it was far too cold for lounging. The boy was dressed in a puffy jacket that made him look like a walking marshmallow.

Sunday brought a tennis ball.

"He's not a very good shot, is he?" Eric grumbled to Colin, whose eye wandered to the far side of the room. Eric pushed it back in again.

By the time Tuesday came around, Lauren had quite a few balls to throw back over the fence. Wiping her hands on her jeans, she walked towards the kitchen. This time her t-shirt said: "Dan… in the rain" and Eric felt sorry for this Dan person stuck in a perpetual downpour. "All I'm saying is—"

"No."

Lauren sighed, "All I'm saying is, I think there's mice in the front room. You can smell 'em, y'know."

Eric didn't care if there were mice. They could nibble up the whole of that room if they wanted to—they'd be doing him a favour. He never wanted to see it again. When he closed his eyes he could see the patch of carpet where Maria had slumped, lifeless, but at least when his eyes were open he didn't have to look at it, covered as it now was by baskets and tool boxes, piles of clothes and bedding and mismatched crockery wrapped in newspaper. He could hardly even open the door anymore, there was so much stuff piled against it. It had been easy, enjoyable even, filling the room with things. Essential things. Things he'd never known he needed, things that, had he owned them years before, might have been just the *right* thing to save Maria's life.

"You don't touch that room."

On Wednesday he would have missed it had Colin's eye not fallen out at just the opportune moment, rolling under the window sill and forcing him to spend a few torturous minutes jabbing at it with his stick that was meant to help him pick up things, except what it mostly helped him do was chase those things around the room with its jabby jaw until he gave up and left the fallen thing where it was.

The little boy-shaped marshmallow appeared in the back garden, stomping around with a toy dinosaur in his hand, making it roar at the daisies and terrorise the washing on the line. He picked up the red googly-eyed ball and bounced it a few times, before glancing behind him towards his back door.

Another bounce.

Another glance.

Then he climbed up on the stone edge of a raised flowerbed and, quite deliberately, placed the ball over the fence into Eric's garden.

Eric frowned.

The little tyke was doing it on purpose, taunting him, making poor Lauren bend and huff and throw them back. He raised his hand to rap on the glass, but stopped when he caught a glimpse of the boy's face as he turned from the fence and gazed towards Eric's house.

It was a face that reminded him of those big-eyed, solemn children in the prints on his walls.

There was a hunger in his gaze.

Eric's hand stilled, curled into a fist, ready to knock on the window. Colin gave him a reproachful look—or it would have been if he'd had both eyes.

"Don't know what you're staring at," Eric muttered as his hand fell to his side.

Anyway, he had a lot of organising left to do so he made a cup of tea. Drank it. Moved one box of magazines, took them all out one-by-one and then, one-by-one, put them all in a different box.

He made another cup of tea.

It went cold as he stared at the dried flowers in a vase for a while, then at the china dog on top of the container of records for a while longer, then the brass doorknocker on the arm of his chair…

… and, finally, he stared at the photo of Maria on his mantelpiece the longest.

Maria. With her ready smile and kind eyes he knew had been the colour of sea-washed stone, though he couldn't picture them any longer without the help of a photo. Maria who had always stopped to pat friendly dogs as they walked by, who had made conversation with people in queues, getting them to laugh, who had always stocked an overflowing treat bowl on Hallowe'en for trick or treaters.

He knew what Maria would have expected him to do.

By the time he got to the back door, his hand shook so much he could barely grasp the handle. There had been no need for him to leave the house since Maria had died, except for her funeral and the odd doctor's visit. So he hadn't. Why would he? He had spent the years growing the house around him, ordering from catalogues and online from his battered old computer, shoring those things up against the walls and the doors and the windows. It was his padding against the world. It kept him safe.

But.

He turned the handle.

Six steps to the ball, he counted them, keeping his eyes on his feet because around him a massive sky yawned wide enough to swallow him whole. He'd forgotten how large the outside was with its uneven grass and wind that tugged and pulled. He had forgotten there was so much air and that the air was alive, creeping its fingers under the collar of his shirt and up inside his cuffs.

The googly eyes on the red ball stared at him as he bent to pick it up, his shoulder creaking like an old ship's wood in a storm.

And then he threw it back.

A small voice floated over to him, "Fank you." A pause, a scuffle and then half a furry hood appeared over the top of the fence. "Mister…you've gotta squirrel in your window…"

"I do."

Another pause and the furry hood asked, "D'you wanna play catch?"

And, to his surprise, he did. He really did.

---

Louise Mumford was born and lives in South Wales. She studied English Literature at university and graduated with first class honours. As a teacher she tried to pass on her love of reading to her students (and discovered that the secret to successful teaching is… stickers! She is aware that that is, essentially, bribery.)

In the summer of 2019 Louise experienced a once-in-a-lifetime moment: she was discovered as a new writer by her publisher at the Primadonna Festival. Everything has been a bit of a whirlwind since then. Louise lives in Cardiff with her husband and spends her time trying to get down on paper all the marvellous and frightening things that happen in her head. *Sleepless*, a thriller, is her debut novel.

# THE PIECE OF PAPER THAT CHANGED A LIFE

*By Malcolm Hollingdrake*

*Bradford, 1960*

The flames licked the coal in a lacklustre effort at self-preservation and slowly Don could feel the heat. He leaned over the container holding myriad-coloured spills, took the poker from the old, brass, shell case and inserted it expertly into the heart of the fire. The effect was immediate. Air was dragged reluctantly over the cold floor, drawn by the growing warmth of the hearth before feeding the voracious flames; for the first time since arriving home, he felt some comfort.

The front door banged and the flames responded with a leap. A morsel of glowing coal was ejected before striking the fireguard, its bid for freedom all too short, leaving only a small wisp of grey, ghost-like smoke as evidence.

"It's only me, love. Your mother's fine. Just wanted a bit of fussing and her fire lighting."

Em popped her face round the door and smiled. "Don't miss your pools. I'll put the kettle on and make us some tea."

Don heard the gas stove burst into life as he collected his pools coupon from the letter rack on the mantelpiece before turning on the television. A small, white dot appeared which morphed into a thin white line across the centre of the screen as the set began to warm up. It would be ten minutes before the classified football results were read. This was a regular Saturday afternoon ritual, a religion, sacrosanct. Nobody would speak out of pure reverence to the god of fortune, but in reality, it was so Don did not miss a result or make an error. The whistle on the kettle seemed to signal the start of the proceedings. The two girls played quietly by the settee.

Em placed a large mug of tea on the table next to Don's chair and watched the black and white picture emerge. She crossed the fingers on her right hand and smiled; this was one of their week's highlights.

"Aston Villa one, Manchester United three. Burnley versus Blackpool, score draw…"

Don licked the pencil point and marked each score. On completion, he checked and rechecked before screwing up the pools coupon and tossing it into a hungry fire.

"Working another week, love," Don announced in his usual acceptant tone. "Funny how a piece of paper could change your life."

"Never mind, egg 'n' chips for tea and you're fishing tomorrow. We do all right. We're happy and want for little. Drink your tea."

They did all right, too. They had a lovely council house on the new Fagley Estate. It was luxury compared to their old back-to-back, now demolished to make way for the modern style high-rise flats. This house was easier to clean, close to new schools, and it had a lovely garden. In some ways they felt as though they had won the pools when they were given the keys.

* * *

Early Sunday morning was misty. Don breathed the fresh air as he collected the two pints of milk from the front step. A white crack had appeared diagonally in the dark, eastern sky; even the sun seemed reluctant to rise this morning.

The canal at Apperley Bridge had majesty of its own when cloaked heavily in the grey, damp mist of morning. A rising fish and wisps of grey steam rose along its length, rings occasionally breaking the water's still, mirror-like surface. It excited Don. The industrial surroundings and accompanying noise seemed smudged, almost blotted out by some ethereal thumb.

The float, the only hint of colour, lay motionless on the soup-like surface; Don focused as he bit into a beef-dripping sandwich. Suddenly the float dipped sending ripples, an alarm, towards the bank. Don placed the sandwich next to the box of wriggling maggots and gently took the rod in hand. The float bobbed again and with the flick of a wrist he knew that he had his first fish of the morning. By lunchtime he would be ready for a pint and home. Em's Yorkshire puddings smothered in onion gravy had a bigger draw than either fish or beer.

* * *

For Don, Friday evening in the summer months meant bowls, a few pints and a chat, but as winter was fast approaching it would be television instead and Friday was the night for *Rawhide*. The girls were safely in bed. Em had a sherry and Don a bottle of beer as they waited for the programme to start. Noises of cars outside made Don move to the window and draw back the net curtains. His old Triumph Mayflower, covered in light dew, had an uncharacteristic shine. It was all he could see until his eyes were drawn to two police officers moving up the path. He answered the door.

"Mr. Hainsworth?"

Don nodded and looked at the first officer.

"Mr. Donald Hainsworth?"

"Is there a problem, officer? Is my car alright?"

The policemen entered and explained that he would have to accompany them to the station for questioning over a serious matter. He was cautioned and it was explained that a solicitor would be appointed for him. They explained to Em that he could be kept in custody for up to twenty-four hours. Considering the intrusion and the bizarre circumstances, she remained fairly calm.

"I'll get my coat and hat." Don's voice was shaky and he moved to kiss Em. "Don't know what's going on but it'll be fine." His smile, she knew, was purely for her.

The black Consul police car pulled up outside Bradford's main police station and Don was escorted to a small room. A mug of sweet tea was placed in front of him before another officer and a man dressed in a dark suit, obviously a solicitor, entered and introduced themselves.

Don now felt very uncomfortable and it showed clearly in his posture.

"What the bloody hell is going on?"

"Mr. Hainsworth, can you tell me your whereabouts on Sunday last?"

Don looked at the man next to him and he nodded. "Fishing. I was at Apperley Bridge on the canal from 8am till 11, then I called at the pub, 'Ring o' Bells' and then home. Stayed home the rest of the day. Played with the kids in the garden."

"Did anyone see you fishing or in the pub?"

"Fishing was quiet and foggy, grew worse as the morning went on. Spoke with the landlord in the pub. Only had a pint."

One of the officers opened a cupboard and brought out a sports jacket in black and grey houndstooth.

"Do you recognise this, Mr. Hainsworth?"

It was his jacket. Don felt his face flush. "Where did you get that?"

The officer opened the jacket and clearly, on the inner label was a name 'D. HAINSWORTH'.

"It's not mine," Don erupted. "I have an identical jacket but that's not mine, mine's at home."

"Where at home? You see, we had a warrant and two officers searched your house tonight and they found no jacket."

There was a long pause and Don flushed again. His mind was a mass of confusion. He looked at his solicitor. The clear panic in his eyes stirred the solicitor into action.

"May I have a minute with my client?"

The officers left the room, taking the jacket.

"This is a murder case, Mr. Hainsworth—you are aware of that, yes?"

Don's jaw dropped. The words seemed to bounce around his head, but they failed to make a cohesive sentence. Don shook his head.

"What? No! I didn't!"

"Young girl. Canal near Apperley Bridge last Sunday. The jacket was found next to the body. If you know anything, I would advise full co-operation. Is that your jacket?"

Don nodded. "I have one like it, just like it. That's not mine. Mine didn't have my name in it." His mind rewound his actions of the previous Sunday, playing it over and over again. "I just fished. Didn't see nor hear anyone until I left the canal."

The officers entered and Don noticed the solicitor's eyebrows lift.

"Let's begin again, sir. Talk us through Sunday."

It seemed to go on and on. Don felt even more confused and desperate. There was a knock. An officer popped his head round the door.

"A minute, sir," requested the new face.

One of the officers left the room briefly. The silence made matters worse and Don was sure that his thoughts could be heard. The officer re-entered.

"Your wife tells us that you might have put it in for cleaning. Is that so?"

Don suddenly realised that he had put it in for cleaning nearly a month before and had totally forgotten about it. He breathed a deep sigh and a tear appeared in one eye.

"I did. About a month ago or maybe longer. Forgot all about it as I'd no 'dos' planned or owt."

"Remember which cleaners?" The officer's voice clearly showed little enthusiasm for this story.

"Johnson's at Undercliffe."

"Do you have the receipt for deposit, Mr. Hainsworth?"

Again, his mind went blank. He placed his hands on the table and stared at the tea. He shook his head. "Em'll be looking for it now, I would think. She'll have taken it out of my wallet and put it safe."

"Let's hope so because at the moment that's the one thing that might prove your innocence. An officer will visit the cleaners tomorrow to check their paperwork and the jacket. Until that time, you will remain here, Mr. Hainsworth."

Don looked again at his solicitor, who put a hand on his arm. "I'm sure this is a misunderstanding. Let's see what tomorrow brings."

* * *

Em stripped the whole house but found nothing. She leaned on the windowsill and looked across the garden; her thoughts were only for Don. She knew the man too well; he would not harm a fly let alone murder a young girl. It was then she thought about the car. She flipped open the glove box and moved the tin of travel sweets and a torch and there it was. A blue ticket marked *Johnson's the Cleaners* showing the date and Don's name.

The police took Don to Johnson's and they handed over the ticket. The assistant went to the back of the shop. Time seemed to stand still. Both officers looked at him and one drummed the counter with his fingers. She reappeared holding a hanger. She laid the jacket on the counter. Don suddenly felt very weak—it was identical to the one he had seen at the Police Station. One officer opened the jacket and checked for a name but just as Don had said, there was none.

* * *

A week later the "Bradford Telegraph and Argus" reported that a man had been charged with the murder of Christine Hetherington. Don read the article out loud.

"Police have arrested a Donald Hainsworth of Carrington Crescent, Yeadon for the murder of …" and then he stopped. "Bloody hell, love. Two men both bought the same Burton's jacket, shared the same name and lived not fifteen miles apart. And even worse, love, we were both on the same canal on the same day. Christ, it just goes to show that truth can be stranger than fiction."

Don could hear his two girls laughing in the garden as he contemplated the bizarre string of events of the previous weeks. Em brought him a mug of tea. He finished filling in his pools coupon, as it would be collected later in the day.

"You saved my life. I'd gone to pieces in there. Couldn't focus, nor think straight."

"They'd have found the jacket at the cleaners without the ticket, love, but it was such a relief. Funny how such a small piece of paper can change your life."

Don looked at the football pools coupon and then at Em.

She smiled and touched his hand. "Love is pure kindness. They go hand in hand. You know I'd fight with every last breath for you."

---

Malcolm is the author of ten novels in the Harrogate Crime Series and is now working on the third book in a new series set in Merseyside, published by Hobeck Books. Born in a library, it seems fitting that he should become an author. '*A Piece of Paper that Saved a Life a Life*' is set in his home town of Bradford. Malcolm organises two successful Noir events held annually, in Wigan and Harrogate.

# THE JAR OF IDEAS

*By Marcia Woolf*

I was still young, three or four years old, when I was first left in the care of my grandmother for the day. Lotte was my mother's mother: a towering, angular, pale woman with sleek grey hair and eyes the colour of water in sunlight. I was fascinated by her: she was strangely vague and distracted, and it seemed to me, even then, that Lotte was not really aware of my presence in the house. I followed her, asking questions, as small children do, always mindful that she might stumble over me, so far was I below her line of sight. From time to time, Grandmother would stop what she was doing, scan the horizon, eventually locate me in the room and then give a short, soft sigh: not a wistful exhalation, but a faint expression of impatience tinged with what I now recognise as disappointment. Her answer to my many questions seemed always to be "perhaps".

She didn't tell me not to do things, unlike those adults whose eyes would follow an unfamiliar child around anxiously, anticipating inconvenience, checking for damage and dirt. Lotte merely left me to my own devices. It was a miracle that I came to no harm in her charge: as an adult and a parent now myself I shudder at her haphazard approach, her unaccountable freedom from obligation, her overweening sense of self. I was seemingly insignificant to her. Meals came at irregular hours: foreign food, designed for adults wielding cutlery with expertise. She paid no attention if I used finger and thumb; made no attempt to teach either table manners or dexterity with eating irons. But I could watch her if I wanted, and I did. I learnt. I observed as she combed her lustrous silver mane; as she applied a veneer of lipstick, the colour of winter holly berries; as she rolled her long pale stockings onto her long white legs, snapping the suspenders shut. I looked on as she inspected her face in the mirror, turning this way and that, frowning. I could see when her neighbour came to call; watched as my grandmother slipped hastily behind the larder door, silent as a shadow lengthens in the dusk, ignoring his tap-tap for as long as it took for him to tire and leave, taking his flowers with him. I noticed when she climbed the uneven stairs to the attic room, clicking the ancient latch behind her, but it was a long time later, when I found the notebooks and discovered what she had been doing there, alone, that I really saw my grandmother. It was then that I opened her bureau drawer, cautiously, feeling the runner creak along its unaccustomed rail, and recognised with almost disbelief her name on the faded, fraying jacket of a book: and under it another, and another still, and some translated into other languages. And there were sheaves of paper, bound with rotting bands, strewn over with her fine, urgent, hypnotising script. But as a child, I watched as she wound the striking clock, and returned it to the dead centre of the mantelpiece, setting its ormolu feet precisely back into the footprints it had made in a powdery layer of dust, running her finger regretfully over the damaged corner of its case, remembering. I saw that she smoothed the bedlinen with her long veiny hand, and snipped at the dying flowerheads with vicious secateurs; handles worn, but blades still sharp as glass. Yet I came to no harm.

One day, in my first autumn holiday from school, I was listlessly trailing Grandmother Lotte around her faded old house when she suddenly turned to me.

"You must be bored. We shall find you something to do."

I looked up at her, wide-eyed, apprehensive at what she might have in mind.

"Come with me."

She beckoned. I followed her obediently, reluctantly, into the dining room, a dreary salon almost never used, filled with dark carved furniture and heavy Turkish rugs. Motes of dust glittered in the air as she strode ahead. There was a pungent, oppressive, atmosphere in that room; an odour of soot and sandalwood, at once familiar and exotic. Balanced precariously on the hideous ornate sideboard there was a porcelain figurine, a woman draped in flowing robes, fancy beyond all imagining, one leg extended, her arms outstretched in a balletic pose, a tiny gold crown perched on her aristocratic head. The ornament was too close to the edge: even as a child, I could see it was poised to fall, as if the dancer had it in her mind to jump. Lotte passed it by, her sleeve nearly sending the poor fragile thing to her death, but the dancer teetered on the brink and regained her composure, Lotte oblivious.

"Here," she said. "You see this pot?"

On a small mahogany table in a corner of the room stood the squat Oriental jar, octagonal, fitted with a neat lid. It was predominantly blue and white, with touches of red, green and orange highlighting its intricate surface pattern of scrolls. I approached it warily.

"Don't be afraid."

I studied her face for clues.

"This," she announced, with a flourish of her hand, "is the Jar of Ideas."

She laughed at my startled expression.

"How can a jar have ideas?"

Lotte gave me an enigmatic smile. Delicately, she removed the lid and set it aside. Then, holding back her sleeve with one hand, she extended the other delicately into the jar, as if trying to find something in there. I held my breath. After a few seconds, she carefully withdrew her hand, its fingers closed. Now I was curious.

"What is it?"

"What do you think?"

"Is it treasure?"

Lotte's eyes widened. She smiled. She winked.

"Tell me, Grandma. What is it?"

Still she kept her bony fingers tight around the mystery.

"Is it a chocolate? A krona? It must be something tiny…"

"No, it's something very big."

I giggled. "It can't be. What is it? Tell me!"

Slowly Grandma Lotte opened out her hand, and there, nestling in the palm, was nothing at all.

"That's silly. You've played a trick on me."

No doubt I pouted and made to turn away, but she stopped me.

"You can't see ideas, Ilse."

I looked more closely at the empty outstretched hand, as disillusion circled, scenting new blood.

"How do I know it's there?"

Grandma Lotte smiled again. "It's not there. It's here." She tapped her head. "It's flown into my mind. That's where ideas live. They can't exist freely, by themselves in the open air: they need to keep warm and be fed and grow big and strong, before they can do their work in the world."

I was staring at her now, wondering if she was one of the mad old ladies who populated my storybooks. Maybe she was going to sprout fangs and big hairy ears and eat me up. She pointed gleefully, mischievously, at the jar.

"Do you want to try?"

"No."

"It won't harm you. See: just put your hand inside, and when your hand comes out an idea will come with it and find a home in your head."

"I don't want an idea in my head."

Lotte laughed. I suppose the grown-up me would have laughed too. She took hold of my hand.

"So put your fingers into the jar, and find out what's inside."

"I don't want to!"

She was gripping me tighter now, determined that I should play her game, but, alarmed, I resisted and wriggled my hand free from hers.

"What's wrong? Ideas can't hurt you Ilse."

I hesitated.

"How do the ideas get *out* of your head?"

My grandmother was prepared for that question. She nodded, sagely, as if by answering this all possible objections might be overcome. As if she understood my trepidation; had once asked the very same thing herself. She bent towards me, and whispered.

"When they are big enough, and ready to come into the world, then you can write them down, that's how they escape. Or, you open your mouth—*and out they pop*!"

As she said this, she thrust her head and her wide parted lips towards me, sticking out her tongue and baring her teeth like the wicked old witches in my stories. I shrieked, stumbled away, and struck my head against the sideboard.

When my mother arrived at six o'clock, she was concerned to see Lotte at the kitchen table, carefully arranging pieces of broken porcelain.

"Mother? What happened? Oh, no. The dancer. Not the dancer."

Then she saw me, quiet by the hearth, reading my book of fairy stories.

"Ilse? Was this your fault?"

Before I could speak, Grandma Lotte scraped her chair back and rose, so that she stood head and shoulders over my mother, who was, inexplicably, a tiny woman sprung from the loins of a giantess. Grandma's hand waved airily over the broken ceramic limbs, dainty shards of gilded coronet and scarlet robe.

"Don't blame the girl, Grethe. We were playing. It was an accident."

I shot my grandmother an accusing look, which Mother detected immediately. She spoke to Lotte in a tone I'd never heard her use before; quiet, but hard and angry.

"Did you frighten her?"

Grandmother peered down at her daughter over half-moon glasses.

"Whatever makes you say that?"

Mother pursed her lips. I sensed it was time to go home, and slid down from my chair. I didn't know it then, but she would be lying in her coffin before I saw my grandmother again.

Mother and I went to the back door and she ushered me out into the chill evening air. It was dark, and the darkness smelt of fox. Underneath our feet the frost crackled and sparkled, platinum-white, like magical dust dropped from the moon. As we walked, Mother held my hand tightly and asked me what we had been doing all day. I was sure she was upset about the ornament. Because I felt she was annoyed with me, I talked to her instead about the Jar of Ideas. My mother listened in silence. I told her about Grandma Lotte sticking out her tongue and baring her teeth, and she laughed, but not as if she thought it was funny. I think she had heard the story before.

"So," she said, as we approached our own cosy little house, where the curtains were drawn and the lamps were lit. A thin skein of grey spiralled into the charcoal sky, and the sour odour of woodsmoke filled the air. Father was home at last. There would be a stew of venison and dumplings. Soon it would be Christmas, and I felt a child's tingle of excitement at the knowledge of it. A few transparent flakes of snow drifted tentatively earthwards, pioneers for the many that would follow before the night ended; the soft downy blanket that would suffocate every whispered endearment, muffle every footstep, stifle every snapping twig, all silenced, save for the mournful cries of wolves as they stalked the ridge, never finding solace, invisible under God's majestic canopy of stars. Mother paused as she turned her key in the lock.

"Did you put your hand into this Jar of Ideas?"

I thought I had done wrong; that Mother would be disappointed in me for betraying her in some way. I shook my head. Smiling, she stroked my hair.

"Good," she said. "We don't want Grandmother filling your mind with her nonsense."

The next day, and the days following, I stayed at our neighbour's house while Mother was at work. I sat at old Inge's scrubbed table in her whitewashed kitchen, drawing pictures of the wandering elk and spires of pine trees clad in pristine snow. And it was then that I began to write: stories about silver sprites who lived in the forest, and transformed themselves into icicles when the hunters came; and I knew, but told no-one, about the beautiful, wonderful, astonishing ideas growing in my head.

---

Marcia Woolf graduated in Art History from Leeds University. She is a member of the Crime Writers' Association (novels *Roadkill* and *Cut Out*) and is current Chair of Hastings Writers'

Group. She was a co-founder of the Hastings Literary Festival, and is Administrator of one of the UK's oldest charities, the Magdalen and Lasher, which has provided support to the local community since 1294.

# LOOKING TOWARDS THE FUTURE

*By Marcie Steele*

A cappuccino at The Coffee Stop was something Laura Smith looked forward to every Saturday. As soon as she woke up each weekend, she could almost feel her mouth salivating at the thought of what would accompany it. Would it be homemade carrot cake, with creamy butter icing? Or a double chocolate muffin? Maybe even a toasted teacake? No, it felt like a lemon drizzle sponge cake day. But not until she'd earned it. She and her friend Sue had a four-mile walk to do first.

Laura had met Sue when she'd moved into Hope Street, three years ago now. Sue lived next door and, over several conversations on the doorstep during that first week, they'd become firm friends. Sue was in her forties, slightly older than Laura, but you'd never tell. The two of them could pass for sisters, each sporting blonde bobs, trim figures and an easy nature. Sue was married with eighteen-year-old twin daughters, both of whom would be off to university later in the year.

As Sue had lived in the market town of Somerley most of her life, she'd shown Laura around and introduced her to people everywhere. In most of the shops on the high street, the indoor market, Ray's Café and The Somerley Stores. Then there was the community centre, the book shop and of course the local pub, The Hope & Anchor.

But her favourite place of all was The Coffee Stop, overlooking the square. There was a large oak tree in its middle and rumour had it that many of the locals sat underneath it when they were troubled and often came away with their problems solved. Sue said it gave them time to think, away from the busyness of life. Laura had liked the sound of that but was still unsure if Sue was winding her up.

The weather had been in their favour that morning, a clear blue sky and a sun that wasn't too hot to make walking a chore. A gentle breeze had wafted through her hair and she'd taken off her jacket halfway round. She and Sue had put the world to rights as they'd chatted. Now it was time for their treat.

Once inside, after they had given their orders, Laura followed Sue as she made her way through the tables to an empty one at the back of the room.

'I'm bushed after that session,' she told her once they were settled.

'Well, you'd better wipe that yawn off your face and replace it with a smile.' Sue nudged her arm. 'That guy I was telling you about is on his way over.'

'Which guy?'

'The one who's into running.'

Laura started to protest. 'But I told you I don't want to—'

'Hello, ladies.'

'Hi, Rob.' Sue patted the empty seat beside her. 'This is my friend, Laura.'

Laura held out her hand and Rob shook it.

'Wow, what a strong handshake! You can tell you've kept yourself fit over the years,' he said.

Laura didn't have to look at his face to see he was teasing her. But she was proud of the fact that she worked out on a regular basis. She could so easily have let herself go.

'Rob's a PE teacher at Somerley High School,' Sue told Laura. 'I believe he has muscles in his spit, he's so strong.'

'Behave,' Rob laughed. 'I run that department actually. Speaking of which, Sue says you used to be into running yourself, Laura. Ever thought about starting again?'

Laura shook her head. 'No, it's been too long now.'

'Give over.' Rob chuckled. 'Once a runner, always a runner. I know I'd miss it if I didn't do it. There's nothing like the wind in your hair, your lungs filling up with—'

'Car fumes,' Sue interrupted with a snigger.

'I suppose you're right. I do miss it.' Laura nodded sadly as she thought back to the times when she had hit the open road. It had always been the same route but in her head, she could imagine she was anywhere: across an empty beach one day, along cliff tops the next and through a park the week after. There was nothing like clocking up the miles, bettering your times and then running that little bit further.

It seemed ages since she'd competed in a race. Not so long ago, she'd entered at least one every few months but since Sam died last year, there had been no one to run with. Laura wouldn't train alone: it wasn't safe. Besides, without Sam the fun had gone.

'I could help, if you like?' Rob offered. 'I could run with you.'

'That would be brilliant,' Sue enthused, nudging Laura so sharply the cake she had on her fork almost fell to the floor.

Laura shook her head, appalled at the thought of running with a stranger. 'I'd slow you down,' she made up an excuse.

'I can take my time until you pick up pace.'

'I'm out of practice.'

'It'll be fine.'

'I don't want to put you out.'

But Rob wouldn't take no for an answer. 'A couple of sessions and you'll be wondering how you ever stopped,' he said.

'How about I call at ten-thirty tomorrow and we'll go from there?'

Once she and Sue were alone again, Laura pinched the bridge of her nose. 'You've set me up, haven't you?'

'Well, someone had to,' Sue cried. 'I know how much you miss it. And we can still do our weekly walk every Saturday.'

Sue nudged her again and Laura couldn't help but grin. Maybe she might enjoy it. It would certainly be worth a try to see how it worked out.

But the following morning, her nerves were getting the better of her and she almost rung Rob to cancel. If it weren't for Sue standing on her doorstep when Rob knocked, she would have stayed in the house too. Now there was no getting out of it.

'Be gentle with her,' Sue said as she waved them off.

They walked along Hope Street chatting about the weather. There was rain forecast but for now the sky was grey and it was warm for April. Then they started a steady jog as they got to the high street. The traffic was light at the best of times so it was a pleasant way to get to the park where they could run around the lake and up to the pavilion.

It was tough at first but she needn't have worried as she ran with Rob by her side. She lost count of how many times she had to stop to catch her breath, but he waited for her and then encouraged her to continue.

'Just one more corner,' he cheered, guiding her through the middle of a gang of teenagers on their way to play football.

'Wait,' Laura puffed minutes later as she felt him surging ahead. 'I can't go much further.'

Rob slowed down. 'You're doing fine. We're almost back to the high street.'

At last she was home. Despite herself, Laura felt exhilarated.

Rob patted her on the shoulder as she bent over to catch her breath. 'You did really well,' he said.

She grinned. 'I did, didn't I?'

'Care to do it again later in the week?'

'Yes, I think I would.'

'I told you,' Sue said when she popped round to see her. 'I can tell you enjoyed it. You have a glow to you that I haven't seen in a while.'

'It's still hard without Sam,' Laura replied with an ache in her heart.

'I can imagine, but didn't it make you feel good?'

'I was way too slow! It's embarrassing lagging behind. I need to get my speed up.'

'Does that mean you're going out with Rob again?'

Laura nodded and Sue hugged her fiercely. 'That's so good to hear. Because I've entered you for the 10k race this summer.'

This time last week Laura might have told Sue to stick her suggestion where the sun didn't shine. Now she laughed at her.

'You know I have a competitive streak. What date it is?'

'June seventh. It gives you plenty of time to get ready. And it gives you something to aim for. Hey, we could sponsor you, raise some money for a local charity.'

'Oh, I don't know about that.' Laura wasn't convinced. 'What happens if I don't make it?'

'Of course you will.' Sue nodded and picked up a notepad. 'Leave that to me. And Rob's great company, isn't he?'

Louise had to admit she liked the man's teaching style. He'd been gentle with her, pushing her when he felt she needed it, reassuring her when she thought she couldn't go on. All of a sudden, she felt spurred on to have a goal.

'Do you know what, Sue? Perhaps I can run in Sam's memory. I'll talk to Rob about it.'

When they met for their next run, Laura mentioned it to him.

'I think that's a great idea,' he said. 'Of course, it would mean more training, and I certainly don't mind spending time with you.' He squeezed her hand for a moment. 'Let the preparation begin.'

After that second meeting, their friendship grew as quickly as the distance they covered. Laura began to enjoy Rob's company and it wasn't long before she began to feel they might become more than running partners. Rob had given her confidence as well as a sense of achievement. She hadn't felt this happy for a long time.

On the morning of the race, she woke with a feeling of excitement mixed with trepidation. She hoped she wouldn't let herself down by being too ambitious, or trip at the finishing line and embarrass them both. But no sooner than she'd tried to talk herself out of her nerves, they were at the event.

The race was starting and finishing in Somerley Square, by the oak tree. The high street and some of the side roads had been cordoned off for a few hours and there were barriers along the pavements filling up with spectators.

As the crowds swarmed around her, Laura could feel the tension, the anticipation, building up. In the far distance she heard the squeals of the children on the small fair they'd erected overnight behind the shops. A strong whiff of onions floated by from one of the many burger bars.

The day was turning out to be bright and breezy and the atmosphere was electric. Laura felt anxious, yet proud that she had got this far again. Until now, she hadn't realised just how much she'd missed it all. If it weren't for Sue pushing her, and Rob helping her, she might never have started running again.

She gave Sue an impromptu hug. 'Thank you,' she said.

'What for?'

'For being so kind to me. I don't know what I'd do without you.'

'Ach, away with you.' Sue hugged her back. 'That's what friends are for.'

Laura secured her hair into a ponytail and began to march on the spot to get her legs warmed up. Then she fastened her laces with a double knot, making sure the ends were tucked into her trainers. She didn't need any trip hazards today.

'All set, Laura?' Rob asked as she stood up to his level. He rested a comforting hand on her arm.

'I think so,' she replied, her stomach flipping over at the thought.

'The race will be starting in fifteen minutes,' the commentator informed them through the loudspeaker. 'Can all participants start making their way forwards?'

'Come on then, partner. It's time to run.'

Rob helped Laura on with her luminous vest and carefully strapped her wrist to his, making sure that it wasn't fastened too tightly. Then they made their way over to the start line where all the other partially-sighted runners were gathering.

Laura looked up to the sky as they began to move forward. 'This is for you, Sam,' she spoke through her tears.

It didn't matter that the person behind might not be able to see she was running in aid of Guide Dogs for the Blind. Laura just felt great to be doing something in Sam's memory, and raising money too. After all, the golden Labrador had been more than her eyes over the past seven years.

And she didn't have long to wait until her new puppy, Ben, was properly trained. Then he'd be able to go running with them too.

The race was over in a flash. Laura laughed with glee as she ran across the finishing line and flew into Rob's arms.

'We did it!' She grinned.

Sue was through the crowds in seconds.

'I knew all you needed was a bit of encouragement.' Sue was hugging her too. 'How about another race soon?'

'I think that's a dead cert.' Rob took Laura's hand in his own. 'And even though I'm about to be replaced by a guide dog, I'm not letting this one go.'

As he kissed her gently on her nose, Laura smiled. Her future was certainly looking a lot brighter.

---

Marcie Steele writes down-to-earth stories about day-to-day people. She likes to explore relationships, families and friends and the things that life in general throws at us. She has written five novels and is busy writing her sixth. 'Marcie' is the pen name of crime author Mel Sherratt. In both genres, Mel likes to explore the emotional sides of life, whether it's good or bad. She is a firm believer that there is always someone there to help you up when you're at rock bottom. You will find her at wwww.marciesteele.co.uk, @marcie_steele and MarcieSteeleAuthor.

# TWO CHICKENS FOR LAURA LONG ARMS

*By Mark Stay*

*July, 1940—Just after the events of The Crow Folk*

1.

Tuesday night was coven night.

The Green Man pub's last patrons had gone home, and Faye Bright's shift was done. She had a date with two witches.

"I'm off, Dad," Faye called as she cleaned her specs with the hem of her shirt and crossed the saloon bar to the door. "Back late as usual, but I've got my key, so don't wait..."

She found Terrence Bright sitting silently by the fireplace, his wrinkled face propped up on his arm as he stared into a dark corner of the pub. The only sound came from the ticking of the grandfather clock in the hall.

Faye had made some kind of peace with her mother's passing, but there were moments like these when she found her father in the kind of silence that she knew she really oughtn't break.

There were no photos of her mother, Kathryn Wynter. Only memories. Sometimes, Faye or her dad would start off with,

"Do you remember that time when Mum…" and they would soon be laughing again.

But recently it felt like they had run out of memories, and more and more these days they sat in silence. And in Faye's dreams, her mother's face was ghostly.

Faye put her specs back on. "You all right, Pa?"

Terrence blinked and the lines on his face were pulled up into a hurried smile. "Sorry, Faye, drifted off there. You off, then? Witchy stuff?"

"Witchy stuff. You sure you're all tickety-boo?"

"All splendid, girl." He slapped his thighs and got to his feet. "All is right as rain. All is glorious and wonderful."

Terrence's natural enthusiasm came from years of pub landlord experience where a cheery disposition sold more pints. But this was a little too cheery, even for him.

"Is this one of them times when you're pretending to be happy, even though you're not?" she asked him. Faye had learned in her seventeen-and-a-half years that it was always better to be as forthright as possible with her father. "You don't have to put it on for me, Dad. I miss her, too."

Terrence's smile remained in place. "Just one of those moments," he said with a shrug. "They pop along and then bugger off. Go on, girl. You'll be late."

Faye gave her dad a tight squeeze, then hurried off to Mrs Teach's terraced house down the road for tea, scones, and tuition in the magical arts.

## 2.

Bright and early, Faye cycled down the Wode Road to the butcher's to collect the ration. She was surprised to see Doris Finch out on her milk round. The woman moved from door to door with her bottles, but there was none of her usual cheer. Her face was blank, as if she had forgotten how to smile.

Only yesterday afternoon, Doris got a telegram.

The one all mothers and fathers fear.

"Herbert Finch's battleship was torpedoed by a U-Boat somewhere in the North Atlantic," Mrs Teach had told Faye at the end of last night's coven. "Went down in minutes, they say. All souls lost at sea."

The last time Faye had seen Herbert Finch, he greeted her with a cheery, "Faye Bright, as I live and breathe." And her last words to him were, "Stay safe." He waved her goodbye, grinning his gap-toothed smile, as he went back to sea.

Faye shed a tear for the boy who had comforted her when her mother passed. The lad who was a handy midfielder in the school football team. The young man who was one of the first to volunteer. Herbert Finch was as invincible as anyone Faye knew.

So when Faye saw Doris, she pulled over on her bicycle and made a point of stopping to chat.

"The milk won't deliver itself," Doris said as she heaved a crate onto the back of the cart. She attempted a smile, but it didn't get far. "And it's a reason to get up in the morning."

Faye didn't know what to say to that, and so she stroked the mane of Doris's white horse. "Let me know if there's anything you need." Faye knew it was a trite thing to say, but she meant it.

A squadron of Hurricanes flew low over the village, rattling the very air and making the horse whinny. Doris calmed her down. Faye watched them bank over the rooftops in a battle formation, then out of sight.

"Hope," Doris said.

"Eh?"

"You asked me if I need anything." Doris's gaze remained fixed on the empty sky where the Hurricanes had been. "I'd like to know that he didn't die for nothing. But I s'pose we can't do anything about that, can we? Except wait it out and do our bit. So I'll get up every morning and deliver the milk." She got back on the cart. "Have a good day, Faye. Thanks for stopping, pet."

3.

That night at the pub, Terrence had to excuse himself more than once from the bar. Faye found him in the living room, sniffing and wiping a tear away. She sat with him and took his hand, and for a long time there was nothing to say.

"I can't see her any more, Faye," Terrence said, not looking up. "I close me eyes, and she ain't there no more. I blame meself. We could have had a fella take a few snaps on our wedding day, but he wanted ten shillings and I have didn't have it at the time. Who needs a photee-graph when you've got memories, I told him. What I wouldn't give for those ten shillings now."

Faye hugged her father tight and wondered what she could do. Mrs Teach had caused all kinds of trouble when she recently tried to speak to her late Ernie, and any kind of communication with the underworld was strictly prohibited by the Council of Witches. She needed magic, but the right kind.

4.

All the children in the village had heard the stories about Laura Long Arms. She lived in a bottomless pond in the wood and enticed you with wishes, but if you got too close she would grab you and drown you. Faye had always thought Laura Long Arms was just a silly story to scare children, but part of the legend said she could show you visions of the future, the past, and long-lost loved ones. Faye knew all there was to know about Laura Long Arms. Except if she was real.

“Oh, she’s real,” Miss Charlotte told her. The pair of them sat by the witch’s usual spot in the bar by the fireplace. Miss Charlotte lit her pipe and spoke between puffs. “She’s a naiad, old as the forest and as cunning as they come,” she said.

“And how would you know that?” Faye squinted at Miss Charlotte through her specs.

“I had an occasion to use her.” Miss Charlotte smiled enigmatically. “But she only gives you one favour. No repeats. She’s like a wet genie. And she always demands an offering.”

“What sort of offering?”

“It used to be small children, but I convinced her that was a bad idea. These days, she’s quite partial to chicken.”

“So…” Faye began, choosing her words carefully. “These visions—”

“No, it is forbidden.” Miss Charlotte, shrouded in blue pipe smoke, glowered at her. “Besides, you’ll never find her and I doubt she’s still alive. She’s even older than me.”

5.

How, Faye wondered, would she locate a hidden pond that didn’t want to be found? Her dad suggested a dowsing rod. He said old Larry Dell used one to find water for his brassicas all the time. You just held the y-shaped stick lightly in your hand and waited for it to twitch. Then you simply followed the pointy end until it took you to the source of water.

Faye left her Pashley Model A bicycle by the Old Roman Bridge, found a stick that was y-shaped enough for a dowsing rod, and strolled into the heart of the wood.

The forest that nestled up against Woodville Village could never make claim to being the biggest, but Faye had wandered through it enough times to know that it had an odd flexibility to it that other woods did not possess.

Tracks turned back on themselves, and trees shifted like children playing a game.

Mrs Teach said the woodland paths had the same flexibility as knicker elastic, and they would somehow fold and twist like a bra strap, or stockings that might never again resolve into a recognisable shape. She had told this to Faye while sorting through the underwear at the church jumble sale, which may have had some influence on her choice of metaphor.

After two hours of going around in circles, Faye decided that the only practical use for the dowsing road would be to teach her father a lesson and whack his backside with it when she got back home.

Faye found the Wode River, of course, and various brooks, weirs and a marsh, but there was no bottomless pond to be seen.

"I'm trying to help someone," she told the wood. It fell silent, save for the faint tambourine rattle of leaves high up in the canopy. She got the feeling it was listening. "So no more of this nonsense, thank you very much. I have business with Laura Long Arms."

Saying it out loud made Faye feel silly. What was she expecting? A beam of light showing the way?

Somewhere a raven cawed and was joined by the buzzing of insects and the flutter of birds. The wood was bored with her now and stopped playing.

Faye huffed and tossed the dowsing rod away.

It landed with a splash.

Faye turned to where the dowsing rod had spun through the air and dashed through high ferns. The air became humid, the sweet aroma of lilies mingled with the stagnant pong of still water.

Faye almost tumbled into the pond before she saw it.

Perfectly round, covered in duckweed, and surrounded by reeds, the pond water was a milky emerald, falling away to a darkness that might never end.

"Thank you," she said to the wood, remembering her manners.

"Hello?" Faye called to the still water, thinking that she should have asked Miss Charlotte and Mrs Teach how to summon a water naiad, but knowing that the witches would have thoroughly disapproved. "Laura Long Arms. You there?"

Somewhere, a frog went *ribbit.*

Faye made her fists into little balls and ground her teeth. Rituals like this were passed down from mother to daughter. But what use was that when your mother died when you were just four years—

A bony hand gripped Faye's ankle and pulled her into the pond.

Water shot up her nostrils, and Faye's dungarees clung to her skin, wet and heavy, weighing her down. The hand tugged and tugged, dragging her further beneath the surface. All sunlight was gone and she thrashed about in the dark as a second hand, clammy and skeletal, took a deathly grip on her other ankle.

It was all so fast. No time to take a breath. Water filling her mouth. Pricks of light filled her eyes and Faye's heart thudded in her ears.

Faye kicked out, the heel of her boot connecting with something hard. Both hands lost their grip, and Faye's arms and legs flayed about. She hadn't had a proper swim since they put barbed wire and mines on the beaches, and for a moment she wondered if she had forgotten how. Her fingers found a cluster of reeds and she heaved herself to the surface.

She croaked for air as she scrambled from the pond to the shore, pulling herself up through the reeds and rolling onto the woodland floor.

As she wiped the pond water from her specs and caught her breath, Faye saw a pair of bright green eyes watching her from just below the surface. Lank hair drifted about the pale creature's face. Her arms were like knotted rope with slender, spindly fingers parting the reeds.

Faye crouched, catching her breath, ready to flee, keeping her distance.

Faye coughed to clear her throat, and when she spoke, her voice was hoarse. "Laura Long Arms?"

The naiad retreated into the reeds, only then daring to raise her chin above the water.

"Who's doing the asking?" Her voice was a thin gargle.

"My name is Faye Bright. Miss Charlotte Southill told me you might be able to help me."

"Did she now indeed? Well, you can tell young Miss Charlotte Southill she owes me a chicken."

"I'll be sure to pass that on."

"Be sure that you does. What is it you're wanting, girly?"

"I was told you do…visions."

"Oh, yes." Laura Long Arms' big eyes glimmered and she shifted forward in the reeds. Her skin was soft and waxy, her scraggy fingers drummed impatiently. "I can show you what you desires. Only once. Don't be a greedy guts. A single vision of whatever you wants."

"It's not for me, it's for my dad. I want him to see Mum one last time."

Laura made a disapproving noise like a cat coughing up furballs. "Yer, I suppose so. But it'll cost you."

"How much?"

"Two chickens."

"Two?" Faye winced. Chickens had become something of a rarity since the start of the war. Farmers kept fewer of them because of a shortage of grain to feed them, and those left were guarded jealously. Eggs were hard currency in a village like Woodville. "Why two?"

"You smell all needy-like. Desperate and helpless. You reek of it. And I'm hungry."

"What about bacon? Or pork? I'll give you my ration for the week."

"Smelly pigs? No thank you stinky much."

"How about…a badger?" Faye ventured, thinking back to one she had seen dead by the side of the Wode Road a couple of days ago.

"No. No badgers. I'm sick of badgers. Two lovely chooks. Plucked and cooked." Laura closed her eyes and smacked her lips together in delighted anticipation.

"Cooked?"

"I might live in a pond, girly, but I likes my chicken roasted. Bring me what I asks for and you shall have your vision. Oh, yes."

6.

Harry Newton owned the biggest chicken farm in Woodville, along with the shortest temper and the biggest blunderbuss. He wouldn't be so easy to negotiate with. Ruby Tattersall, however, was a sweet girl. Terribly posh and one of the first Land Girls to arrive when the war started. After a few early mishaps—one bull still ran off at the sight of her after she tried to "milk" the poor thing on her first day—she had proven herself to be a natural farmer.

Faye set off to find her and soon came across a handful of Women's Land Army girls making hay in a field by the river. Ruby wasn't among them, but they pointed Faye to a tractor chugging down the road towards Larry Dell's farm. Ruby was at the wheel.

Faye leaned on the pedals of her bike and rode as fast as she could. It was mostly downhill and she had to gently squeeze the brakes as she drew up beside the tractor.

Ruby was one of the few women who could make the Land Girls' uniform of a green v-neck pullover, brown corduroy breeches and rubber boots look glamorous. Her hat sat back on her wavy hair, a little like a cowgirl's. She flashed Faye a grin when she spotted her.

"Faye, how delightful to see you! To what do I owe the pleasure?"

"Chooks, Ruby." Faye stood on her pedals as she coasted, raising her voice to be heard over the *chugga-chugga-chugga* of the tractor's engine. "Do you know if Harry's got any chickens that have stopped laying?"

"After a spot of Sunday roast, are we?"

"Something like that."

"I do believe he has a few that are due to meet their maker," Ruby told her, "but he sells them off to Mr Shackle for pies."

Mr Shackle was the village butcher and when word got round that he had a few chicken pies in, you could sure they would be gone by mid-morning.

"But I'll let you into a little secret," Ruby said. "He sometimes lets us girls get first dibs. I might be able to get you one."

"Do you think you could get us two?"

"Oh, crikey Faye. That's just greedy."

"I know, I know. I can't say why, but you'll be helping me make someone happy. And we all need a bit more of that these days, don't we?"

For a long and awkward moment, Ruby drove the tractor in silence, pursing her lips. Faye had blown it. Two chickens. Who on earth needed *two* chickens these days? Greedy water nymphs, that's who, but Faye could hardly bring herself to baffle Ruby with the whole story. She fell back onto her saddle and was ready to pedal away when Ruby spoke.

"Perhaps there is a way." Ruby slowed the tractor to a stop by the crossroads at the bottom of Gibbet Hill. As the engine idled, she leaned closer to Faye. "There's this chap."

## 7.

Ruby had a beau.

A Canadian officer at the Mansfield airbase. They had met at a village dance and fallen head-over-heels in…

"I wouldn't call it love, as such," she told Faye at the crossroads. "More a jolly keen infatuation. He has this very dashing moustache and cheeky glint in his eye and an accent that makes one tremble. And here's the rub: two days from now he leaves for a new assignment at Biggin Hill. I desperately want to spend some time with him before he goes, but…" She let the thought trail off.

"You're working," Faye said, catching on. "Though, if someone was to cover for you…"

"Oh, Faye, that would be darling. Could you?"

"Will it get me the chickens?"

"Wringing their necks is on my to-do list for tomorrow," Ruby said, a little too cheerfully. "Just leave enough for Mr Shackle. Otherwise, help yourself."

"That's a deal." Faye beamed. "What else is there to do?"

It began before sunup with the milking. Ruby loaned Faye her Land Army jumper, breeches, and necktie for the day, assuring her that Harry Newton had the uncanny ability to identify his own individual cows, pigs and horses, but completely failed to make a distinction between any of the Land Girls on his farm. Every one of them was addressed as "young lady" and treated with the same level of polite bafflement. Ruby brought the other girls up to speed on the deal, and Faye was able to blend in easily. After extracting more milk from the cows than she thought was possible, she had to check the rat traps dotted around the farm, after which she disposed of half a dozen poisoned rats in a burning brazier. Mucking out of the stables took all morning, after which Faye made her first mistake.

Stopping for a cuppa.

Moving around after that became considerably more painful as her body protested at being made to lift things, heave things, shove things and dig things. Even walking became onerous as her thighs, shins and soles argued with every step. Faye was never one to shy away from a bit of hard work, but this was proper graft. The other girls remained chipper, their bodies used to the daily slog, but Faye was reduced to a stagger by lunchtime. The girls took mercy on her, and after a couple of hours clearing a ditch and wrangling with the controls of an excavator, they gave her the almost sedentary task of harnessing a horse and riding it to Larry Dell's farm. There she was to collect the tractor Ruby had dropped off the day before and bring both it and the horse back.

The Land Girls made sure of Faye's reward. The birds were dead and plucked and in a sack when she collected them.

She roasted both chickens, fending off her dad who knew enough not to ask why she needed them, but still fancied them with spuds and gravy. She left them to cool overnight and flopped face down in bed, still wearing Ruby's clothes.

## 8.

The Local Defence Volunteers arrived at the scene before the Fire Brigade, but it was too late.

Doris Finch's home was consumed by flames.

She lived in a thatched cottage on Allhallows Lane. At Herbert's funeral she had been talking of moving, but the milk round had kept her busy and the idea faded.

The fire began with a spark in a light socket in the living room, and it spread while Doris slept. It was only when the clock in the hallway fell with an almighty clang of chimes that she realised anything was wrong. By the time she got her dressing gown on, the stairs were ablaze and the air thick with smoke.

Doris retreated to the bedroom, grabbed a box of belongings in a dresser drawer, clambered out of the window and shimmied down the drainpipe to safety.

Faye and Terrence took her in, offering bed and board and a sympathetic ear for as long as Doris needed it.

All Doris had left was the box of keepsakes, but Faye soon realised something was wrong.

"It's not…it's not here." Doris rummaged frantically through the box of letters, postcards and photos.

"What's not?" Faye joined Doris on the sofa as she tipped the box over, its contents spilling onto the floor. She got to her knees, checking each photo.

"I had a portrait of my Herbert in his uniform. It was the only one I…" She stopped with a strangled gasp. "It's on the mantle. I put it on the mantle in the living room. Oh, it's gone, it's gone. The only thing I have left. It's gone." Doris stopped herself, trembling yet nodding silently in acceptance, straightening the pleats on her skirt. Then she let out a sob and melted into tears. Faye held her neighbour tight, wishing she could take the sadness away.

9.

The next morning, Terrence wiped the condensation from his bedroom window to see Faye and Doris strolling in the direction of the wood. Faye had a full sack over her shoulder.

They returned a few hours later. Terrence couldn't help but notice that Doris's hair was somewhat straggly, as if it had recently been wet. And Faye's sack was now empty. He thought about asking Faye what they had been up to, but decided that the answer would only give him conniptions and, besides, he had a pub to open.

"Where will you go?" Faye asked as she poured tea for two. Doris's bags were packed and were neatly lined up by the kitchen door at the back of the Green Man pub. The villagers had rallied round with clothes, rations, toiletries and make-up for their favourite milk woman, and she almost looked her old chipper self. Her smile was back, there was colour in her cheeks, and a new light in her eyes.

Faye had insisted on making a brew before Doris left.

"Mr Barr has found me lodgings in a room by the milk depot," Doris told Faye. "It'll be easier for work, and a little place of my own."

"Oh, that's lovely." Faye placed a cup and saucer before Doris and sat opposite her. They sipped in silence.

"You're dying to ask me, aren't you?" Doris smiled.

"Yes. Come on. What was it like? I saw you go under, and then what?"

"The water was freezing for a start." Doris held her tea cup a little tighter. "I was scared, Faye. We all joked about Laura Long Arms at school, but when that thing came out of the reeds…I couldn't believe my own eyes. Then it dragged me under. It weren't half a shock. I swear, I thought I was going to drown. I mean, that would cap it all off, wouldn't it? If the fire didn't get me, then water would. But then…I saw him."

The pupils in Doris's eyes bloomed and she looked into an empty space just beyond where Faye sat.

"My Herbert. Clear as day. In his uniform, just as I remembered him. He gave me a hug and told me he was happy. I told him I was proud of him and that I loved him, and he told me back. He said it would all be good in the end. Things might seem bad now, but it wouldn't always be this way. And you know what, Faye? I believe him.

"I couldn't hold my breath any longer. I had half a thought about staying there with him, but then I wondered 'Who would do the milk round?'"

Doris turned back to Faye, half a smile on her face. "So I came up for air," she said. "And here we are." Doris took a breath, her chest shuddering. "It sounds half barmy when I say it out loud. Did it even really happen?"

"From the smile on your face, Doris, I'd say it did."

"Here's something else," Doris said as she opened the handbag that some kind soul had given her and rummaged through its compartments. "There might not have been a snap of my Herbert in that box of keepsakes, but there was this."

She took a dog-eared photograph out and handed it to Faye.

"It's not much—silly really—but I thought you might like it."

Faye's head felt light as she took it.

## 10.

"Dad, come and look at this."

The pub was shut and Terrence was just about ready to turn in for the night when Faye called him into the living room. She was sitting by the fire. The place where they would share memories.

"Still up, Faye?"

She had that grin on her face. The one he could never be sure was a good or a bad sign. All teeth and dimples. She held something in her hand. It looked like a photograph.

"What you got there?"

"Doris gave it to me," Faye said, getting to her feet and hurrying over to him. She held the photo to her chest and started babbling. "And she got it from some fella who was taking snaps on the day, and I can't believe this has been sitting in her keepsakes box for all this time without us knowing. In't it funny, people go looking for treasure, but sometimes they've got stuff right under their own noses and—"

"Faye." Terrence smiled and gently took her hand. "What is it?"

Faye bit her lip and handed him the photograph, face down. Someone had written "Woodville, Summer Fair, 1922" on the back.

He turned it over. The photograph featured a gathering of young people at a lemonade stall, but front and centre was Doris and another young woman. They wore gingham frocks, were laughing uproariously, and did not have a care in the world.

Terrence didn't have to ask Faye who the other young woman was.

"Mum and Doris," Faye said. "Look how happy they are."

Terrence felt his nose tingle and his eyes sting. He didn't much approve of blubbing and certainly not in wartime, but he blinked a few tears away and sniffed. It took a few moments before he was sure he could speak.

"Oh, that's…that's smashing," was all he could manage.

"We've finally got a photo of Mum." Faye took his arm and gave it a squeeze.

"Yeah, true enough. But you see that lanky fella there." His finger pointed to one of the young folk crowded around the lemonade stand. He had a familiar smile and only had eyes for Kathryn Wynter.

"No!" Faye gasped, looking from the photograph to her father and back again. "That's you? You're not wrinkly or nothin.'"

"Five minutes after this, I asked your mother if she wanted to dance, and she said yes. This is one of the best days of my life." He looked to Faye, the same smile on his face, albeit with a few more wrinkles. "Thank you."

Faye put the kettle on and they sat by the fire, only this time there was no silence. They shared stories and laughter all night. It started with her father saying, "Do you remember that time your Mum…" and it did not stop until the sun rose the next morning.

---

Mark Stay got a part-time Christmas job at Waterstone's in the nineties (back when it still had an apostrophe) and somehow ended up working in publishing for over 25 years. He would write in his spare time and (he can admit this now) on company time, and sometimes those writings would get turned into books and films. Mark is also co-presenter of the Bestseller Experiment podcast, which has inspired writers all over the world to finish and publish their books. Born in London, he lives in Kent with Youtube gardener Claire Burgess and a declining assortment of retired chickens.

# WAITING FOR THE WEST WIND

*By Natasha Bache*

The bus lurched to a stop. The whine and screech of the brakes snatched Tamsyn out of her reverie. The air was thick with the smell of dusty seats and warm bodies squashed alongside each other. She looked at the tiny windows, pulled open as far as they would go with not a slither of air passing through them, and reflected upon how each summer felt hotter and more unrelenting than the last. Even in mid-September, the sun seemed unreasonable; surely it was time it made its way to the other side of the world?

August had been the hottest "since records began," everyone kept saying. Even sundown gave little relief to the stifling atmosphere. This penetrating heat had arrived in late May, killing crops and revealing ancient patterns from lost buildings in the dried grasses. That reminded her, she would have to make a trip to Oswestry as some interesting—and familiar—patterns had emerged there.

A young schoolgirl ran up the stairs to the top deck, her shoes tapping out a melody on each step. Tamsyn watched her red face, glistening in sweat, beaming as she rounded the top stair. Then she stopped. The enthusiasm fell from her face. Someone was sitting in her favourite seat.

The bus started up again, throwing everyone back into their seats before the driver started negotiating the winding roads of Much Wenlock village. But the young girl barely noticed. She balanced with ease and turned sullenly towards the few empty seats along the back row. Moments later, the girl was followed by her mother who clambered after her, one hand gripping onto the backs of seats and the other a school bag. She swayed from side to side, then swung her body and landed heavily next to her daughter.

The girl turned and faced the window, angling her body as far as she could, scowling at the world down below.

Tamsyn smiled fondly at the memory of sitting on the bus with her grandmother, back and forth from the very same school as the girl. Although it was many years ago, and the uniform was a little different; there was no longer a bonnet for starters, and thank goodness they had stopped using that mustard colour.

To Tamsyn's disappointment, her grandmother had never been able to climb the stairs. Instead, at her insistence, they sat as close to the front as possible, nearest the driver. The other children from her school would giggle as they made their way to the top deck. It always sounded like fun.

The girl, filled with the sudden enthusiasm only the young can muster when all energy is depleted, span around and beamed at her mother.

'Mum, *please* can I go to Faye's house tonight?'

Tamsyn didn't think the mother could look any more despondent. She was wrong.

'Not tonight, darling,' the mother said in one long sigh. 'After we get home and I've made dinner, I promised myself at least thirty minutes lying on the bed with the fan.'

'Look, my darling,' she continued, seeing the disappointment on her daughter's face. 'Perhaps we'll have a thunderstorm tonight. They keep forecasting one—though they never seem to get it right these days—and maybe that will clear the heat up a bit and you can meet her in the park tomorrow.'

'You said that last week. What's even the point of having friends anymore, anyway? I hate the summer.' The young girl pressed her head against the window, giving the scorched grass and trees below the evil eye.

'I'll set the laptop up, you can have a chat with her after dinner. Okay?'

After being kept inside all winter, everyone had eagerly anticipated the changing of the seasons. It was a chance to enjoy a walk, meet friends outside, or just escape the confines of the house. Unfortunately, the suffocating temperatures cut short spring and thwarted any hope of a carefree summer. Even the fair and the festivals were cancelled after a couple of older ladies were taken to hospital with heat stroke and dehydration.

Tamsyn looked at the girl and felt her heart ache. Everyone in the village had had to endure a lot, and it wasn't fair.

* * *

Tamsyn's cottage lay on the edge of the village, and after waiting more than an hour under the partial shade of an oak tree, she decided her second bus had likely melted in the heat and was forced to drag her pale body and bags of groceries the rest of the way.

She could barely grasp the key in her hand, let alone slip it into the ancient lock. After a single turn, she paused, a curse slipping from her dry lips. With a sharp intake of breath, she threw her weight against the thick door of the cottage, green paint crumbling and cracking as her shoulder pressed against it. A cool breeze caressed her face. Rosemount Cottage, passed down over generations, had an almost uncanny way of keeping cool. Her grandmother liked to tell her it was the thick stone walls and thatched roof that kept out any unwelcome heat or cold, but she had an idea there was something else helping out.

Tamsyn kicked off her shoes and leant the groceries against the kitchen door. She then freed herself of the now sweat-encumbered clothing and left them lying on the floor while she gulped down water straight from the tap. Winnie, her cat, who had been lying stretched out on the cool kitchen tiles, surveyed her and the clothes with lethargic contempt.

'We can't all lie around all bloody day, Win.' She wiped her mouth with the back of her hand, then grabbed a bowl and one of the bags of groceries. She fished out a tin of tuna and slopped the contents out; Winnie meandered over.

Tamsyn unloaded the rest of her groceries onto the old oak table, averting her eyes from the picture of her grandmother, Silvia. The walnut frame was perched high on a shelf above the Aga and she scowled down amidst the dried herbs and old glass bottles; each filled with an unidentifiable brown liquid that had long seen better days. Silvia had raised Tamsyn on her own. She was equally strict and generous, warm yet distant, opinionated yet completely enigmatic; traits that could be confusing when you're a child. You never knew where you stood for a start, and the shift from one personality to the other made day-to-day life difficult to traverse.

She was also a witch. A hedge witch, to be exact. More herbs, remedies, and routine-cleansing-of-the-home type witchery, than the roasting children and praising Satan nonsense—although she did bake a very tasty gingerbread house for Midwinter Solstice.

Silvia raised Tamsyn strictly in the field of hedge witchery, as all the women in their family had been. Theirs was to be a solitary life of learning from nature, understanding and perfecting the recipes passed down from mother to daughter, then teaching the next generation. Men were for heirs and nothing more, they were a distraction and caused nothing but bad luck.

Silvia had also made it abundantly clear to Tamsyn that any practice that fell outside of her teachings was unequivocally forbidden. There was always a story, usually the same but with a few elements added or embellished depending on the question and subsequent lesson being taught, where an ancestor or distant cousin had dabbled in 'Knowledge beyond their ken' and met a gruesome, bloody end.

To Tamsyn, if she was being perfectly honest with herself, that just made her want to dabble more. There was only so much tea-making and sage-burning a girl could do before wondering if she could conjure up her own demon or familiar.

She ran upstairs to grab the tattered book she had found months before in an old bookshop in Ironbridge. She felt compelled to keep it hidden along with her other contraband, even though her grandmother was unlikely to find them from beyond the grave. After setting the book down on the table along with the ingredients, there was a sudden snap of static. Winnie's ears rotated to locate the sound and eyed the things on the table suspiciously. With barely any effort, she was on the surface, pink nostrils flaring as she sniffed around, then pawed at the brown paper bag to get at the length of red cord inside.

Tamsyn quickly set to work, lighting as many candles as she could find. She gingerly opened the browned book; it was barely in one piece, and pages were precariously hanging onto the spine.

The book fell open at the page marked with yellowed papers, each covered in her terrible handwriting. She double-checked what she had written against the wording in the book. Tamsyn had tried her best to modify it a little by combining the rituals with some interesting notes she had found hidden in Silvia's belongings. She shrugged, it at least resembled what she was trying to achieve.

Outside, the trees stood black against the ink-blue dusk that was fast approaching. Tamsyn didn't know much about casting weather spells, but she knew she had to get the timing right.

She stood in her garden, surrounded by candles, and let down her hair, as per the instructions. It was then that she caught her candle-lit reflection in the window. Her gleaming eyes and mousey brown hair conjured a memory of a sepia-toned photograph of her mother.

'Maybe this isn't such a good idea' she said to Winnie.

* * *

Tamsyn had little to no clue who her mother was, and that was exactly how her grandmother wanted it. One winter's evening, when she was six years old, she had asked her grandmother where her mother was. Silvia barely looked up from her knitting to say, 'Gone for good.'

Silvia wasn't known for her tact.

Tamsyn didn't mind back then. She held no preconceived ideas and hadn't dared to create any myths around her mother. There were far too many *real* myths in her grandmother's hidden tomes to draw her attention. In fact, it wasn't until her early teens when things changed. Her hair at that time was long and unruly, so she had taken to keeping it in a ponytail or plait, but one morning when running late for school—or later than usual—she left her hair down. She sped through the kitchen, shouting goodbye to her grandmother as she whipped past her, then stopped momentarily at the door when she replied with: 'Bye Anna.'

After a day of those words ringing in her head, Tamsyn begged her grandmother to tell her more. Silvia simply informed her that her mother had abandoned Tamsyn shortly after she was born, and that should inform her of all she needed to know of her character. Before leaving for bed later that night, Silvia stopped at the doorway and said, 'You're the spit of her, my Tam.'

It was a whole twenty years later—two years after her grandmother's death and inheriting the cottage—before she would uncover a few more details surrounding her mother's disappearance.

After finally admitting city life wasn't for her, Tamsyn had moved into the cottage she had grown up in. Initially, it was under the pretence of sorting and filing her grandmother's belongings, but Rosemount had a pull like no other. Before she knew it, the once-immaculate cottage was filled with Tamsyn's chaotic mess: magazines, books, makeup, piles of laundry.

On clearing out Silvia's oak writing desk, Tamsyn discovered a hidden compartment at the back of the cupboard. Carefully prising open the mahogany drawer, she unearthed a mound of old papers and letters, all written in the same flourishing handwriting. Dusk had settled long before she finished reading, barely able to make out the last few pages until forcing herself to light a candle.

The majority of the notes were adapted recipes for charms, herbal brews for various ailments, they were just like her own notes she had made experimenting with her grandmother's teachings. However, there were a few that made little to no sense to her. Before she could learn more, she came upon a letter in completely different handwriting. It was from a man.

It appeared that Tamsyn's mother, Annalise Pride, at the tender age of seventeen had fallen in love with an older man who worked as a tanner in the neighbouring village. He had a wife and children, and upon learning of Annalise's *situation* as he called it, he instructed her to kindly never darken his doorstep again. That is as much as Tamsyn knew, until she plucked up the courage to visit her grandmother's friend, Bridie. No one in the village knew how old Bridie was, but it was rumoured she had lived through both world wars.

* * *

'Well, hello my darling,' Bridie cheered after opening the door. She led her through to the sitting room, shuffling, painfully hunched, and smaller than Tamsyn remembered. The heat of the roaring fire hit her long before she saw it. The faintly-mildewed air was nicely contained by thick, partially-closed green velvet curtains. Eerie Toby jugs adorned every nook and cranny, and dust swirled in the beams of light streaming through the curtains. The house was deathly silent, save for the labouring chug from the grandfather clock in the corner and the distant sound of cutlery on china coming from the small kitchen just off the living room. Tamsyn brushed away stray strands of hair from her forehead, along with the thought that this deafening stillness could be her future.

Banished from helping in the kitchen, Tamsyn sat in the furnace on a frayed floral armchair, whilst Bridie prepared the teapot and Rich Tea biscuits. She ran her hand along the crochet covering the arm of the chair, imagining the hours her grandmother would sit here gossiping with Bridie about the salacious goings-on in the village.

Bridie clattered into the room and sat the tray down onto the glass table between the two wingbacks.

'You're looking very thin, my dear.' Bridie's eagle eyes surveyed her waist with disappointment. 'Would you like to take some pork pies home with you?'

'Oh, yes, that would be lovely. Thank you.' Tamsyn hadn't eaten meat since her grandmother died, but she knew better than to refuse food from Bridie. Perhaps Winnie would eat them.

'I hope you don't mind me popping round, but I was wondering if you could tell me anything about these?' Tamsyn pulled out her mother's papers. Bridie's eyes widened, and for a brief moment she seemed afraid.

'Don't you be interfering with them now, you hear me? Your grandmother'll haunt us both once she finds out you've got those.'

'But what are they, Aunt Bridie? It's not like anything I've seen in any of the standard books grandmother had.'

'You give those to me,' she said, making an effort the stand after only just sitting down. But Tamsyn simply stood up and gave them to her. 'We can't have you looking at 'em.' Bridie snatched them out of her hand, clearly agitated.

'You can have them; I just want to know what happened to her,' Tamsyn pleaded.

Bridie heaved her body out of her chair, her stooped frame leaning over to the open fire, and tossed the papers in. Tamsyn watched, her eyes stinging as the paper instantly curled and went brown, the flames enveloping her mother's distinctive loops and diagrams.

'You're a good girl,' she said, shuffling back into the sagging chair, wheezing from the effort. Bridie slurped at her tea and nodded at Tamsyn to have a Rich Tea. She dutifully took one of the stale biscuits and nibbled at it, lost in the thought that she had reached a firm dead end.

Bridie tutted and shook her head. 'So god help me, I'll tell ye.'

'Silvia, you'll never forgive me,' she said, looking up to the heavens. 'But a girl has a right to know about her own mother. Pour me some more tea, will you love?'

Bridie finished what was left in her cup, smacked her lips, then held out the brown-stained pink and white china cup.

'Your mam, she was fiery. Got into bad practices and the like. Dabbled in the darker stuff, or so your nan used to tell me. But as I used to say, "Ah, it's a bit of harmless water divination, Sil". Well, it turns out Annalise had a real talent for combining her hedge knowledge with this other stuff, you know, conjuring her own spells. Of course, the more your nan would come down on her, the more Anna just did it in secret...'

Bridie turned to look at the smouldering papers in the fire.

'And when that man didn't want anythin' more to do with her or the bab...with you... I'm sorry I burnt her papers, love. But I couldn't risk you going down the same road as your mam.'

'I'm not my mother, Aunty Bridie.'

Bridie fixed her faded blue eyes onto Tamsyn.

'Perhaps not. What's for sure is you don't know who you are yet, love. You're still a baby.'

'*Please.* There's more to this story, surely you can tell me something.'

Bridie sighed and placed her cup and saucer on the ring-marked table.

'Okay love, I'll tell ye. Now, be mindful that your mam had been jilted in the worst kind of way. My Lord, she were angry. One night, in a fit of rage, she took herself down to the river and made a deal with ol' Hafren.'

*Hafren*...The name echoed in Tamsyn's mind and for the slightest of moments she felt as if she was being dragged down by a current.

'Who's Hafren?' she said, snapping out of it. 'Another witch?'

Bridie laughed mockingly. Tamsyn couldn't help but think it was a little rude.

'Our Silvia really did keep you in the dark. Hafren is the ol' name for the River Severn, the locals call her Sabrina, but Hafren was her name.'

This all sounded a little too make-believe, even for Tamsyn, who had lived and breathed the life of a hedge witch for at least two decades of her life.

'So...what was this "deal" she made?' She tried to keep the snark out of her voice.

'What do you think? *Him*.' Bridie pointed a crooked finger at the fire. 'He scorned her, didn't he? And she wanted to make him pay. His tannery was right by the banks. She wanted him drowned.'

Bridie relaxed her shoulders and sat back, her face lost its joyful plumpness and was instead drained and tired.

'Instead, she made us all pay,' she said bitterly.

'The flood?' The realisation struck Tamsyn in the gut. 'In '87. The year I was born.'

'I've said enough. Too much. Forgive me, Silvia,' Bridie said, looking up again at the ceiling. A smile rounded her face back up again.

'Now, could I interest you in some kippers in tomato?' She asked, as if the conversation had never happened.

'It's a bit warm for kippers—thank you, though.' Tamsyn continued staring at the fire, her brain alight.

'Pah! It's never too warm for kippers.'

* * *

Tamsyn stood in the garden, her hair hanging over her shoulders, and looked down at the book in her hands with her mother's original papers inside. She hated deceiving Bridie, but those papers were all she had left of her mother. Intuition had told her to copy them, taking great pains to dye and dry the paper, before using one of her grandmother's quills to copy out the distinctive handwriting. However, the words from Bridie's story continued to dance around her head.

'This is not the same,' she said aloud, half to herself and half addressing her grandmother's well-versed hissing admonishments: *You can't do this. Don't do this. You will not do this.*

She removed the red cord from her pocket, then took her place among the candles and the intricate symbols she had drawn onto the earth with rock salt, an expensive choice but the only option from the farmers market.

The heady air already felt charged and buzzed about her, but the oncoming night had fallen silent in anticipation. A few droplets of perspiration clung to Tamsyn's top lip, and to her dismay, no whisper of wind could be felt.

With the cord held high, Tamsyn closed her eyes and took a deep breath, inhaling the smell of the dried grass and cracked earth beneath her feet. The aroma from the tea roses and the decaying apples piled beneath the tree lingered as she felt the scorching heat beginning to leave them.

She clenched her eyes, telling herself she was doing this for her village, for the little girl and her friends. Even if it lasted for a day, it would be worth it. *As long as it didn't backfire,* the unwelcome voice chimed in her head.

It was time.

Tamsyn pictured the first symbol from her mother's notes and whistled into the night. Clumsily tying a knot, she blew gently on the cord. Her voice pierced the silence as she recited the incantation she had seen in the book.

*'I tie this knot,*
*to wake the wind,*
*Each knot untied,*
*Will fill the sky.'*

Distant thunder rumbled over the nearby hills and Winnie, who had been uncharacteristically interested in what was happening, darted for cover under a garden chair.

Tamsyn whistled again, long and shrill, and pictured the second symbol. Then blew on the cord, harder this time, and tied a second knot. A flash of lightning and instant clap of thunder made her jump. She looked up, watching as dark clouds filled the sky and released a heavy rain. She heard the earth beneath her sizzle and sigh with relief. With the rain running down her face and her hands outstretched, she whistled again and held the final symbol in her mind. This time she blew as gently as she could, tying a third and final knot into the cord.

* * *

The next morning, as the sun began to climb over the Shropshire hills, the threat of blazing heat was abated, for now at least. Tamsyn sat outside with Winnie, cradling her warm cup of coffee as the birds twittered busily in the hedgerows. The cat was taking the opportunity to laze on the cool grass before the possibility of an unforgiving sun would give her cause to retreat inside. Tamsyn absentmindedly ate her sun-dried tomatoes on toast, all the while pondering the red cord that lay on the blanket at her side.

What might she unleash if she untied the cord? Tamsyn had modified her mother's incantations in the hope that the spell could cover a much wider area. According to Bridie, tampering with the weather had historically only ended in devastation.

Tamsyn recalled learning of the flooding of '87 at school. The sudden and unexpected surge of the river had taken the village by surprise. Buildings were damaged, cars abandoned before being washed away, livestock were lost, and someone lost their life. Tamsyn scolded herself. It was so obvious to her now that the flood had roots in unnatural causes, but as a child she had accepted the theory that it had been caused by a landslide further up in the Welsh mountains. Magic enacted for vengeance always lost control. The revelation of her mother's actions only further compounded the need to set things right.

Tamsyn stood, brushing off the crumbs, and holding the knotted cord high in the air. She closed her eyes and untied the third knot she made the night before.

*'I untie this knot,*
*Oh, west wind, be freed,'*

A light wind picked up, flipping over the corners of the blanket and throwing her hair lightly around her face. If the spell was successful, Tamsyn should be able to untie all three knots without causing a full-blown storm. She focused her mind. Exhaled slowly and untied the second knot.

*'Blow thine gale,*
*Your comfort we need.'*

The wind picked up significantly, and Winnie bolted inside. The weathervane on top of the house swung wildly around before pointing to the east. Drawing the air deep inside her lungs, Tamsyn pulled the energy from the air and blew lightly onto the cord, untying the first knot she had made. A huge blast of wind hit her from behind, and drawing it in, she channelled it through the cord and into the sky. The string sizzled in her hand, burning from her fingers up to the end, until it disintegrated into black soot. Frothy white clouds scudded quickly across the blue sky.

* * *

As the village began to wake, children excitedly pulled their bikes out of sheds and garages, knocking on doors and asking bleary-eyed parents if their friends could come to play. Kites dived and soared in the air as benches and tables were dragged out and dusted off. Tamsyn took her blanket to the village green to read, secretly people-watching over the rim of her book, behind her dark sunglasses.

A young woman and her boyfriend were lounging on a blanket not far away. He was squinting at his phone. 'This weather is so weird. It says they don't even know where this wind's coming from, but it's set to cover the whole of the UK.'

The girl sighed. 'Let's not worry about where it's from. Who knew the wind could feel so good?'

Tamsyn smiled to herself as she looked across the green. In the distance, she could see a group of girls, laughing as they walked with arms linked. She suddenly recognised the smallest girl on the end of the chain as the girl from the bus, hair whipping across her smiling face as she beamed at her friends.

---

Natasha Bache is Managing Director at Books Covered, a design agency specialising in bespoke book covers for both traditional and self-published authors. After graduating from Keele University, where she studied English Literature and Philosophy, she was Editor at HarperCollins Publishers, where she worked with estates such as Agatha Christie and J.R.R. Tolkien. Natasha lives in Shropshire with her husband and two children.

# THE HAUNTED TROLLEY

*By Nick Jackson*

It happened around March last year, when there was that spell of good weather, but everyone was supposed to stay indoors. The first pandemic lockdown had just been announced in the UK, and for many, pubs and restaurants were a memory only as distant as the previous weekend. Nobody thought it would last long, so when the schools closed, parents hoped they might reopen after Easter—we really had *no* idea. And yet, although classes were cancelled, we all still learned a new word: *furlough*.

We learned a lot of things, back then. The most important lesson is what I'd like to tell you about today.

I work for a supermarket chain, Right-Price (you've seen the adverts, where employees sing "There's only one Right Price" whilst gyrating down the aisles like your dad dancing), and last year we were considered 'essential workers.' That made us laugh, because the company never made us feel essential—heck, they didn't even give us paid breaks—but we knew that thousands in our community depended on us. Then came shorter opening hours, a chance to get the shelves cleaned and restocked. Then came longer shifts, as those of us not self-isolating covered for those who were. Then came the haunting.

That first night, there were four of us working…

"Hey, Ems, how's tricks, lady?" I turn at the sound of my name, grateful to see the always-smiling face of Nisha Kumar. We were born within three days of each other (though half a world apart) in April 1996, so we have a connection, and honestly any shift is more bearable when she's in charge. "You ready for another fun night?"

I pull the kind of face only Mr Bean could love and Nisha laughs. As we stow our bags into lockers she says, "being here is preferable to being at home right now, I can tell you."

"Sanjay's *still* not sulking because the football's been suspended?"

Nisha straightens her name badge in the wall mirror next to the shop floor entrance. "He's not cried so much since *Toy Story 3*." She rolls her eyes and I laugh. "Speaking of Woody and Buzz, it's me, you, Paul and Greg tonight."

"Is that all?"

"At least we're closed for a few hours."

Fewer hands will mean more work, but she has a point: we can crack on with our jobs, without watching for stray shoppers whilst wrestling a four-wheeled cage full of baked beans. But seriously, *four* of us? It's a big store, and it will feel so much bigger with so few people in it. It'll feel lonely, most of the time.

As the night wore on though, the four of us would discover we weren't quite as alone as we thought.

When it comes to the modern shopping experience, Right-Price likes to boast it offers everything—home delivery, click and collect, scan and go, you name it, we have it—except for lots of checkout operators. Most were 'redeployed' down the job centre when those self-scan Daleks were installed, meaning we were already short on numbers before the lockdown. Nisha I've already introduced, so let's meet the boys. Paul is our computer games student. His uni friends call him Baggins on account of his hairy feet (at six foot five, it has *nothing* to do with his height), and half the time I think he's speaking one of those weird languages too. For a month, whenever I overheard him talking about killing the boss I assumed he meant our store manager, not some end-of-level thingy in his games! Finally, there's Greg, who doesn't have a nickname, but if he could choose one himself it would be *RoboCop*. Greg usually works security, but as there's not much call for that once the doors are locked, he's been roped into shelf-stacking. Four of us, then, to disinfect and restock the entire store.

It is Paul who encounters it first.

"Emma, d'you want bakery, or shall I?"

I weigh up the back-breaking bread trays (which aren't heavy, until you've lugged dozens of them around) against the mouth-watering, freshly-baked smell. The smell wins, every time.

He gives me a thumbs-up, grabs a high-viz vest, and disappears into the cavernous warehouse. He'll be starting near the front of the store, which is toiletries. I head towards the rear, to sort into best-by-date the loaves still on the shelves before bringing out fresh stock. One thing about lockdown that I'm still getting used to is our deliveries arriving earlier.

Another is the funereal silence of an empty store. And just how far sound carries within it.

Nisha is out back with the frozen produce delivery, and Greg is doing a recce of the car park, which leaves on the shop floor just me and Paul. When I saw him a moment ago he was for once a small figure in the distance, and yet I could still hear him whistling an old earworm of a tune as he pushed a cage with a dodgy wheel going *squeak-squeak-squeak*. And, as I squeeze my shoulder-blades together and feel the tension in my aching muscles, as I glance up at the bakery clock and realise it's just past midnight, a loud crash echoes through the aisles. A crash, and a scream.

"Paul?" Nothing. "*Paul!*"

Sod the rules about not running—I leg it past rows of cereal boxes, cans of pop, biscuits, perishables—I keep shouting his name, not getting a reply—at the toiletries section I slow down, scanning the lanes for my colleague, but finding them empty—

Until I reach aisle six.

I see bottles of hand sanitiser scattered like bowling pins, and two have burst. I see a handheld Telxon scanner gun and portable label printer on a shelf. I see an empty shopping trolley, a half-full cage. And Paul, on the floor, scrabbling backwards, his shoes squealing as they propel him across the smooth surface.

Hang on, back up: two bottles have burst!

"Of all the things we sell, you have to go and drop sanitiser?"

But Paul says nothing, his back to me, his attention fixed upon…what?

Only when I shake his shoulder is there a reaction: a shriek so loud it sends the pigeons on the steel rafters into a flutter. Paul yanks out two earbuds, lending to our conversation a tinny Black Sabbath soundtrack, in keeping with his manic expression. As he tells it, I'm the first person he's seen since leaving the warehouse—but the *second* person to touch his shoulder.

"I ain't lying, Emma, there's somebody else here!" Paul's drip-white, shaking, and his eyes are at full beam. Ozzy would be proud.

Before I can explain that we're alone, pounding footsteps declare otherwise. Greg almost overshoots the aisle. He drags in jagged breaths. "I heard someone scream…from right over… other side…car park."

By now, Paul's on his feet. "You see anyone leave?"

"No-one *can* leave, mate: shutters are down." Greg sees the spillage on the floor. "Bloody hell, did you have to waste sanitiser?"

"It weren't deliberate! Somebody *touched* me."

"In your dreams," Greg laughs, and Paul's just about to snap when a fourth figure makes us all jump.

Nisha lifts her eyebrows. "Everyone okay?"

Paul explains again what happened. Nisha asks Greg to scout around and make certain there isn't somebody playing a prank, then she looks at the floor. The contents of two bottles are forming a mini galaxy of glittering onyx and unicorn pink.

"It *had* to be sanitiser, didn't it?"

I snigger, and even Paul cracks a smile. "You carry on with the shelves, Paul, I'll clean that up. My fingers need a chance to defrost anyway." Nisha rubs her hands together, then pulls the cage away from the glutinous mess. That is my first inkling something's not right, but I can't place what that is. "And who taught you to scream?" Nisha teases. "Some Baggins you are. Besides, aren't you supposed to whistle while you work?"

"Frodo was a hobbit, not a dwarf," Paul says, petulantly. "Anyway, I can't whistle."

"Middle-earth, flat-earth, all the same to me. Ain't that right, Ems?"

But I barely hear her, because I'm staring at Paul and thinking to myself, if he cannot whistle…then who was I listening to earlier?

"Earth to Emma…" Nisha only uses my full name when she's worried. "You okay?"

"Sorry, miles away."

"Not during this lockdown, lady."

I nod, but say nothing. I don't want to share what's on my mind until I've had time to think. As I'm about to leave, Paul stops me. "Don't forget your trolley."

I look at him, confused, then glance at that empty trolley. "It's not mine."

Before either of us can say anything, Nisha grabs the trolley's handlebar. "I've gotta get the mop anyway; I'll take it back."

And that's when I realise what had seemed wrong earlier. I'd assumed it was Paul's toiletries-filled cage with the dodgy wheel—after all, I'd seen him pushing it when I heard that noise—and yet when Nisha moved the cage a moment ago there came no sound. But now I know why.

As she walks away, her soft footsteps are accompanied by the *squeak-squeak-squeak* of a dodgy wheel on a trolley that had, somehow, been moving around the store by itself when everybody was busy elsewhere.

Well, not entirely by itself. It had been accompanied by that whistling.

By the next evening, I have put the whole thing down to the supermarket equivalent of cabin fever. I've worked nine days straight, and it's got so bad that at home I'm rearranging my kitchen cupboards so every label faces front.

I let Paul have bakery tonight, where the scariest thing that can happen is falling prey to jam doughnuts. As I walk down the wasteland that is aisle nine, I imagine the next *Indiana Jones* film will see Indy searching for toilet rolls, and wish him good luck with that one.

Nisha appears, bearing two mugs of tea. "Just found a bulletin about new shelf-edge-labels that need displaying." She blows steam from her drink. "They're implementing more multi-buy restrictions tonight."

"Which means more abuse tomorrow. Or today now," I say, glancing at my watch to see it's just turned midnight.

"I miss the days when folk just griped about the two-pack limit on paracetamol." Nisha sighs. "Anyhow, I've got John, Joyce and Rob starting early to…Can you hear that?"

Suddenly, there comes a faint *squeak-squeak-squeak*. It *could* be Paul or Greg pushing something…Heart quickening, I put a finger to my lips. Nisha frowns, but remains quiet. And so, we wait. And wait. And—

Nisha's widening eyes confirm that she too hears the whistling.

It's coming from farther down the toiletries section, where Paul had his accident last night. If an accident it was.

We check aisle eight. Nothing. We creep forward, towards aisle seven.

Again, nothing. So we tiptoe to aisle six.

To the aisle where, earlier that night, dozens of hand sanitiser bottles were placed on the shelves by me. To the aisle where, the previous night, Paul had dropped two bottles and we found an abandoned trolley.

To the aisle where that trolley waits for us again.

I swear softly. "Is it the same one?"

"How many trolleys do you think have dicky wheels?" Nisha sees the look on my face. "Fair enough."

We edge forward, step by silent step.

"If there's a pound coin jammed in the slot, it's the same one." Nisha's voice drops as we approach the trolley. Yep, we're giving it ears now. Part of me wants to laugh at this absurdity, but another part keeps thinking of that Stephen King book about the possessed car, which really isn't helping any.

The gleam of a coin can be seen—so it *is* the same trolley. The short, galvanised steel chain that connects one trolley lock to the next, releasing the coin when at the customer return point, hangs like a tail. I wonder if it will wag if I touch the trolley, but have no desire to find out. A static shock from the wire mesh is the least of my worries.

Without taking her eyes off the trolley, Nisha says, "Ems, go get a printer."

I dash to aisle nine, grab my handheld printer and hurry back. Nisha pulls out the label roll, peels off a label. She edges towards the trolley—as though about to swat a wasp—and slaps the sticky label onto the handlebar.

"Now we'll definitely know which one it is."

"What are we gonna do with it?"

"We're going to leave it the hell alone. Come on, we've got a store to prep."

With ten minutes to go, all the surfaces are disinfected and all the shelves are replenished, with new labels and signage informing customers of quantity restrictions. How many will pay attention is another matter, but right now that's less important than what Greg has discovered.

Nisha, Paul and I crowd round him in the poky security office, our tired faces illuminated ghost-like by banks of monitors. Nisha had asked Greg to search through the CCTV tapes for aisle six, and from the look of glazed excitement in his eyes, he's found something.

"The time-stamp made it easy locating footage from the other cameras once I knew when to start," Greg explains. He presses play on a silent-movie montage of an unmanned shopping trolley, making its way from inside the main entrance where we've started storing them, past the fruit and veg, before turning into and stopping on aisle six.

"I'd appreciate it if we keep this to ourselves, until we know what's going on," Nisha says.

"Whoa," Paul says, "a bona fide spook is what's going on!"

"I checked footage for previous nights"—Greg rubs his face—"and the same thing happened just after midnight yesterday. When Paul dropped the sanitiser."

"But not before then?" Nisha looks at me with eyes that can only be described as haunted. "So, why now?"

"Until two nights ago, we were open 24 hours," Greg says. "The trolleys were chained up in shelters outside."

"We've always closed Sundays though," I point out. "We don't leave the trolleys out then."

"But the doors shut at four." Nisha sips her black coffee. "All the restocking and cleaning is done, and everyone's gone by eleven. If the first people in Monday morning found a trolley in aisle six, they'd assume one of the last shift left it there."

"And the tapes stop recording when the final person leaves," Greg folds his arms. "No point filming an empty store."

Paul chews his knuckles. "We gotta get rid of it."

"There's the beck," Greg suggests. "I'm usually fishing our trolleys out of there, but…"

"No," I say, surprising everyone, not least myself. "I can't explain it but I don't think it means us any harm."

Nisha stifles a yawn. "Unless anybody's got the number for Ghostbusters, I suggest we go home, get some kip. We've got another shift tonight."

"You're coming back?"

"We have a job to do, Paul." Her voice is quiet but no less determined. "I'll understand if you don't think you can come in, but people are relying on us."

As we leave the security office and go our separate ways, I have no idea if they, or I for that matter, will return.

But of course, I do return.

Nisha's there when I arrive, and gives me a grateful smile. So is Greg. No Paul though.

My disappointment cuts deep. Earlier that evening, my neighbours and I had gathered on our doorsteps for the first time, to applaud the NHS staff and other key workers risking their lives, and as we'd finished a few people made a point of acknowledging me. That's when I realised: *I* was one of those workers. I've moaned about my job a few times, but tonight, getting ready for work, I've never felt so proud to wear the uniform. So, to lose Paul, to learn he does not feel the same, it hurts.

In the foyer, where the trolley nests are parked, the one with a label on its handlebar stands at the end of a row. Whilst its chain will connect to the trolley lock in front, none behind can plug into it, because of that stuck coin. I shove a couple more behind anyway, to pen it in. As I'm walking back through the store, which by its emptiness seems to have doubled in size, I'm greeted by an unexpected but welcome site.

"Bus knocked," Paul says, out of breath. "Reduced timetables."

I manage a "good to see you" whilst resisting the urge to give him the biggest hug.

"Your turn to have bakery, if you want it." Paul grins.

"Nah, you have it. I'll just eat my own weight in humble pie."

We crack on with our tasks, and I only realise it's gone midnight when from the foyer comes the sound of clattering metal. It reverberates around the store, like the clanking chains weighing down Jacob Marley's ghost. The cacophony draws everyone out, and together we hurry towards the entrance.

The trolleys I'd shoved in behind our stickered one are now pushed back far enough for it to manoeuvre free. Its chain has unlocked itself from the one in front, and right there before our eyes, it bumps through the welcome barrier of its own accord.

On cue, the whistling begins.

A thought strikes me. "Paul, give me that phone you've not got in your pocket."

We aren't allowed personal items on the shop floor (and by force of habit I'd put mine in my locker) but Nisha turns a blind eye as long as we get the job done. Paul hands me his phone. I find the right app and activate it.

"Quiet, everyone."

For a few seconds there is only the *squeak-squeak-squeak* of the wheel and that tune, familiar yet unrecognisable, as invisible as the person making it.

But not anymore.

The smartphone buzzes, as its music-recognition app finds a match. Gotcha!

"Our ghost likes the Bee Gees, because that's *Stayin' Alive*." I return the phone to Paul. "I *knew* it was familiar."

That's one mystery solved. But how it helps, I do not know.

At 3am I take my break. The air out back is cool enough to soothe my bare arms without waking the goosebumps. The whole world seems to be asleep except me. I google "phantom trolleys" and "haunted supermarkets" on my phone. My searches reveal nothing (and *Creepypasta* is so *not* what I expected) and I'm about to quit when I try *Stayin' Alive* and my store name.

And then I see it.

I see *him*.

If his recognisable old face is a surprise, however, that's nothing compared to the name near the end of the news report my search unearthed: Nisha Kumar.

I find her in the warehouse, near the cereal racking. She looks distracted, but when she sees me that ever-ready smile returns.

"Hey, Ems, you look as though you've—"

"Bill Wrigley," I say, watching for her reaction. And Nisha bursts into tears.

Bill Wrigley had been a regular at our store, usually visiting in the small hours after his night-porter shift ended. He'd retired two years ago but old habits die hard. I knew the face if not the name, but we'd given him a nickname anyway.

"Mr Minto," Nisha says, her voice fraught as we huddle together in the otherwise-empty colleague canteen. "He went through packets of those mints like other people buy ciggies."

I laugh sadly. “I remember how he always went to a manned checkout, not the self-scans, because he said he was protecting jobs.” A wave of sadness crashes into me as I realise I’ll never see him again.

“That Bee Gees song was his favourite. He used to whistle it all the time.” Nisha’s eyes glisten again. “I should’ve recognised it, but didn’t until you said what it was…They played it at his funeral.”

I take her hand, squeeze it. That’s when I realise.

“*You* went to his funeral?”

“It was a few weeks back, whilst you were away. The family invited me, Ems, and I met his neighbour, the lady he was shopping for. She must be in her seventies, but her kids live the other end of the country, so even though he should’ve been isolating too, he insisted on doing a shop for her. And that’s when it happened…”

Bill Wrigley had visited our store just after midnight at the end of February, when he’d collapsed. The on-site first-aider knew it was a heart attack, and despite others panicking that he had ‘the virus’, she’d stayed calm and stayed with him until the ambulance arrived. That night, our first-aider was Nisha.

“He died the following day, in hospital. Peacefully.” She wipes a trembling hand across her face as fresh tears fall.

I’d been on holiday then, one of the final lucky ones to go abroad before the commercial flights were cancelled. By the time I’d returned, so much of our everyday lives was changing that Nisha never told me about this. And now I know, now the truth about the haunted trolley is revealed, I can do nothing—nothing, except hold my friend’s hand as she cries.

I return home, but despite my exhaustion I cannot go to bed. Each day this lockdown seems to take a little more from me, and now that includes the ability to sleep.

Just as I start on the dishes, having made a note to buy more washing-up liquid, an idea appears so suddenly that I’m lightheaded—and fully awake. I ring Nisha, then after rechecking that news report, I cross my fingers and bring up an online telephone directory…

That night I arrive early for work, hurry onto the shop floor and help with the last sales. After this shift I'm off for two whole days. After this shift, I plan to crawl beneath my duvet and hibernate for 48 hours straight. And if all goes well, if my idea is sound and my plan works, then by the time I finish the ghost will bother us no more—after this shift.

Then the last customer leaves. The trolleys are collected and left in the foyer. The shutters clank down into place. The store is closed.

Then it begins.

"You're all clear which aisles need doing?" I ask, leading our little team huddle of four.

"We're on it like Sonic," Paul grins.

"That's the hedgehog, right?" I take their laughter as a yes—but you see what I mean about weird languages?

"The trolley's stood by itself, mate." Greg winks. "So there shouldn't be any problems."

"When it starts, I'll come with you," Nisha says. I'm grateful; even though the threat-level from our spook has been zero, I'll be glad of her company.

We have 90 minutes until midnight. The team breaks apart, hurrying to restock certain items in the short time remaining. And when you're rushing to get stuff done, hoping deliveries have arrived and been unpacked, 90 minutes is a very short time indeed.

*Squeak-squeak-squeak…*

I look up from my replenished shelves, unnerved at how quickly it's come around. Is everything ready? I don't know, and there's no time to find out. Nisha appears. We try to give each other reassuring smiles as we wait for the whistling. And there it is.

I let out the breath I've been holding. "I'll name that tune in one."

We follow the sound, though we know already where it will lead. And when we turn into aisle six, the trolley stands waiting.

During my earlier phone call, I'd asked if Nisha remembered the name of Bill Wrigley's neighbour. She did—it was a Mrs Arlington—and though she had no address, that news report included Bill's street details anyway. My plan depended on Mrs Arlington being listed on a telephone directory, but fortunately she was, so all that remained was to call her and explain how we wanted to honour his memory…

And bless her, she knew exactly the shopping list she'd given him four weeks ago, having saved a version on her phone's note app.

A handwritten copy of which I hold in my hand now.

"First item, shea butter hand sanitiser. Okay, here we go…"

Taking a bottle from the shelf, I approach the trolley. I'm trembling, as though about to pet a snarling dog, so I think of Mr Minto and that calms me enough to put the sanitiser into the trolley. Now, this will either work or—

With a fresh burst of *Stayin' Alive*, the trolley heads off towards the next item on the list, and Nisha and I break all social distancing rules with a delirious high-five. In your *face*, Ghostbusters!

In this manner we follow it around, filling the trolley with Mrs Arlington's list, until we arrive at the milk department. I reach for four pints of green-capped semi-skimmed—the final item. Except…there isn't any.

The dairy delivery hasn't arrived yet.

Our trolley waits expectantly. My hand hovers over the blue-capped skimmed milk, but is that an acceptable substitute?

I've got palpitations—like a contestant stuck on the final question in *Who Wants to Be a Millionaire?*—but just then, with pounding footsteps preceding him, Paul hurtles round the corner, holding one four-pint bottle of *green*-capped semi-skimmed!

"Got it from the canteen." He hands the bottle over, as careful as if it were a baby. I place it in the full trolley…And it starts back on its merry way, satisfied with this solution. Nisha and I cheer as Paul shouts, "level completed!" Now the trolley should head towards the checkouts and—

The trolley does *not* head towards the checkouts.

Instead, it makes for the confectionary aisle. Mrs Arlington forgot to mention her sweet tooth!

Nisha's all for ringing her, until she realises the time. "Right, let's try putting one of everything in, and see if…Ems, why are you *smiling*?"

On the shelf beside the trolley sits a box containing tube-shaped packets. I reach in, pull one out, and can almost picture a kindly old face nodding eagerly as I add the mints to the shopping.

With the task complete, the trolley trundles towards the checkouts. Which is when I spot the flaw in my plan.

"None of the till drawers are in!"

"You only think of this *now?*" Nisha laughs. "Besides, it's not like he's able to pay."

Which, all things considered, is a good point.

We follow the trolley to the front of the store, where Paul and Greg are waiting. It bypasses the self-scan lanes, heading for the few remaining manned checkouts—even though right now none are open. But when it stops before a stationary conveyor belt, it is clear we will still have to replicate a transaction.

"You put the stuff on the belt, Ems, I'll deactivate the scanner. If just one item goes through, head office will have kittens."

Nisha disappears under the checkout housing, and as the belt begins to move, the red lights on the scanner-scale fade out. With nothing now to read barcodes, as the items reach the end of the belt Nisha packs them straight into bags.

I wave my debit card. "What about payment?"

Nisha turns to our resident security guy. "Greg?"

"Terrible really, but all the checkout cameras *just crashed*, five minutes ago." If Greg ever swaps Right-Price for Las Vegas, he'll clean up with a poker face like that.

"As shift leader, I deem it in the interests of the company that we give this customer a freebie," Nisha says, as the trolley rolls itself to the end of the lane. "Besides, if we're not even worth paid breaks"—she puts the groceries into the trolley—"they can whistle for it."

With perfect timing, *Stayin' Alive* starts up and the trolley heads for the exit.

Nisha steps out from behind the checkout, and together the four of us follow the trolley on its final journey.

There's a strange, melancholy sense of an ending, like it's somebody's last day at work. Greg is ready to unlock the door and raise the shutter, but that squeaky wheel halts at the trolley nests. I lift the bags out, and it parks itself at the end of one row. The chain key swings up, clicks into the next trolley's lock, and with a ping the pound coin that has been stuck for so long hits the floor. We stare at it, mesmerised, as it spins…slows…stops.

Then the whistling ends.

Then it is over.

And then it was over.

As my last duty before going home that day, I took the groceries to Mrs Arlington's. Though she'd managed to get a few things from the local shop, my arrival still felt like Christmas had come early for her. Mrs Arlington tried to pay but I said it was a gift: our way of granting a loyal customer his final wish. She had tears in her eyes then, and truth be told so did I, but as I said goodbye to her on that warm March morning long ago, whilst the rest of the world edged closer towards despair, I felt an overwhelming sense of hope.

The trolley never moved by itself again. We left that label on, and it's still there to this day. Whenever I pass by, I give it a pat. I know many of you won't believe me, and that's fine. Those were crazy days, and whilst the pandemic brought out the worst in some, it brought out the best in others. It made heroes of everyday people. It united neighbours in ways our grandparents used to talk about. It showed that we can still give a damn, in the face of damnation.

All it took was a small act of kindness. Mr Minto taught me that.

---

Nick Jackson's fiction has appeared in several anthologies, including the Amazon bestselling charity collection *Dark Minds* and *Coming of Age*. His stories are sometimes about hope, and sometimes about ghosts, and occasionally they feature together. Nick was born in Cumbria, but now lives in Leeds, West Yorkshire.

# WHAT WE SEE IN THE SHADOWS—A JOE GERAGHTY STORY

*By Nick Quantrill*

1.

It's a cliché that a femme-fatale walks into the office of a Private Investigator. My office was currently the bar in The Queens pub. I'd yet to make my mind up about my new client. She was probably disappointed in me. I had no fedora to wear, no bottle of whisky to casually open and drink from, no blinds to peak through at a black and white world. It's often the way. But some things don't change. Husbands cheat and husbands lie. It was my job to prove it.

Tommy brought our drinks over, placed them down on the table, a smile on his face. I couldn't help but like the kid. He was fresh out of university, a drama student, full of life and ambition. Pulling pints in The Queens in Hull wasn't his dream, but it was getting him through. He'd also proved himself to be useful to me on occasion too.

I picked up and sipped at the orange juice he'd placed in front of me, waited for Keira Matheson to do the same with her drink. She was on the gin, but it was five o'clock somewhere. I put her in her late thirties, her short blonde hair sharply cut, sunglasses pushed on to the top of her head. I was no expert, but the jewellery certainly looked to be expensive.

'You were going to tell me about your husband,' I said, wanting her to talk.

She focused back in on me after looking around the pub again. A handful of late-afternoon drinkers were in place at the bar, but no one would overhear us in the corner.

'You'll know my husband as Paulo,' she said. 'One half of *Duo* back in the 1980s.'

I had to dredge my memory, but the name was familiar to me. 'The band?'

'The very one.'

I watched as she drew back a mouthful of gin, saying nothing more. Her silence spoke volumes. The band had been big for a while, the city's answer to *Wham!*. It hadn't been my thing, but I remembered them being everywhere for a short period, proper stars.

'There might be a perfectly logical explanation for his behaviour,' I said, getting us back on course. 'There often is.' She wasn't buying it. 'I've worked a lot of these cases over the years.'

'Let's call it peace of mind, then. His behaviour has changed and I'm not imagining it, before you say that. He's become secretive, hiding things from me. Before, he'd leave his phone lying around and it was never locked. Now, it's always in his pocket. He doesn't tell me where he's going, or who he's with.'

'Have you confronted him about your suspicions?'

She paused for breath, but didn't answer the question. 'It's been a tough time of late,' she told me. 'I run a small charity and funding is an issue. It's causing some tension, if I'm being totally honest.' She levelled her gaze on me, making eye contact. 'But if he's having an affair, I want to know.'

'It won't be easy,' I told her. I wasn't lying about having worked plenty of such cases. It was far from my first rodeo. 'Getting proof won't be easy,' I added. 'And it won't be easy for you to deal with.' I laid it out as best I could, pulling no punches. It was my bread-and-butter work, and her motivation wasn't my problem to grapple with, but it was still delicate. She deflated in front of me, the toughness an act, no femme fatale, which suited me. This wasn't the movies and I was no Philip Marlowe.

She threw back the last of the gin and readied to leave. 'Please.'

## 2.

I took a table in the corner of the bar, but one with a good sightline to Paulo Matheson and the woman he was with. His wife had told me where he'd be tonight. She'd overheard him set it up on the phone. She expected me to get straight to work.

I was sitting as close to them as I dared, but it was too far away to hear their conversation. The hotel was attached to the train station, all shabby chic with its thick carpets underfoot and dark wood panelling. Catch it in the right light and it was a film set for an Agatha Christie television drama.

I had to admit Paulo Matheson looked disgustingly good for his sixty years. His grey hair, neatly cropped to his skull, looked distinguished on him. His smart clothes looked reassuringly expensive. It was a long way from the 1980s and his blond-streaked mullet and dodgy double-denim. I'd done my research before setting out for the evening. *Duo* had enjoyed a string of hits, but it had been increasingly slim pickings after their first big hit. They'd hung on grimly to fame for a few years, and as the song-writer, Matheson had fared the best. I'd read an interview online in which he talked about his post-pop music life. As he'd faded from the headlines, he'd invested the money he'd made into property, back in the day when you really could buy a row of terraced houses in the city for loose change. He was now one of the city's biggest landlords.

I closed my eyes, trying to tune out the background noise. Travellers were coming and going, one last drink as they headed for the station concourse. The low chatter of the people sitting around me, the noise leaking out of a nearby function room. It was no good. I opened my eyes, knowing I wasn't going to be privy to the conversation. Instead, I watched them, searching for clues. Matheson was certainly friendly with the woman, leaning in to talk to her, a constant smile on his face. She had her back to me, though, and I couldn't get a proper fix on her. Maybe his wife was right. I'd read articles in which he'd hinted none too subtly about enjoying the benefits of life on the road in the 1980s. Things like that never really changed. I'd read up on Keira Matheson, too, saddened by how her literacy charity wasn't being funded any longer by the local council. She clearly did good work with struggling families in the city, but it was another victim of budget squeezes and austerity.

I stood up and made my way over to the bar and ordered another coffee. It was a chance to get a proper look at the woman with Matheson as I waited for the bar staff to make it. Taking my mobile out, I flicked it to camera and managed to get a snap of her without making it look too obvious what I was doing.

I waited until I was back in my seat with my coffee before looking at the image I'd managed to grab. The woman was half Matheson's age, thirty or so, professionally dressed in a suit. She leaned in when Matheson spoke, responding to his attention. They were at ease with each other, comfortable and not bothered about being seen together in public. Rubbing my face, a job was a job. Delivering bad news was part of it. I needed to put a name to the face as a starting point. I wanted to know who she was. Maybe Keira Matheson was right that her husband was having an affair, but I wasn't wrong when I said proving it would be difficult.

Paulo Matheson and the woman stood up, their conversation finished for now. The woman pulled on a coat, Matheson gestured to the door when she was ready to leave. I gave them a moment before following. Dodging through the people coming and going via the station entrance, I moved towards the car park. The darkening evening sky meant I couldn't track them easily. I swore under my breath. Scanning, I caught sight of them. They were standing next to a sports car, the woman half in, half out of the driver's door. Matheson leaned in closer and kissed her on the cheek. I was definitely too far away to hear what was being said as the woman laughed. I was also too far away to see the registration plate clearly. If I had that, it was possible I could call a favour in and get a name. Instead, I had to watch as the car's headlights illuminated the wall it was parked in front of, the engine roaring as she drove away. Stepping back, I didn't want Paulo Matheson to see me as he walked over to his own car.

'You spying on them?'

I turned to look at the man huddled into the corner, smiling at me with a collection of blankets piled up around him, a cardboard cup for loose change at his feet. 'You recognise them?' I asked.

He put down the well-thumbed book he was reading. 'He used to be a singer, right?'

'Very observant of you.' I kneeled down and picked up the paperback. *Black and Blue* by Ian Rankin. I wasn't familiar with it, or particularly a reader.

'Reading passes the time for me.'

I handed it back. 'Any good?'

'He's the best.' He glanced at it. 'Not got much of it left.'

I went to my pocket and took out a ten-pound note. Keira Matheson had part-paid me upfront and in cash.

‘It’s too much.’ The man pointed to the cardboard cup. ‘It says loose change.’

I stood up and rummaged around for some coins. Finding what I had, I handed them over. ‘If you’re sure?’

‘That woman your man was with, she uses this place regularly for her meetings. I hear her on her mobile when she stands next to me.’ He gave me a name. ‘She doesn’t see me, though.’

3.

I switched the car engine off and stared up at the Mathesons’ house, unsure why I was even there. It was a large detached property on the boundary of the city, an affluent pocket of exclusive individual builds. The price tag would be substantial, but so would be the views over the fields and along to the Humber Bridge. Sitting at the top of the hill, a security gate meant no riff-raff would get close to them without permission. Beyond it, I could see a single light on at the top of the house.

I wondered if any conversation had been had, what was going on inside their walls. Keira Matheson had called, demanding an update. I’d played it with a straight bat, saying there was nothing to report yet, as was my right. There was a lot to think about, a responsibility that came with any job I accepted.

The light from my mobile screen illuminated the car. The homeless man I’d spoken with at the train station was weighing on my mind; the coldness of the night, the fact he seemed happy with his book for company. There but for the grace of God go I, as someone far smarter than myself had once said.

He’d given me a name for the woman, though, and a lead, telling me he thought she worked in PR. Like he’d said, he was invisible to her. It had made her indiscreet. It also made her easy enough to track down, the city more like a large village. Google did the trick and I found myself looking at her website.

Gina Bellman was a one-woman agency, her work encompassing publicity, media management, event planning, social media and much more. More importantly to me, the photograph on it matched with the woman I'd seen in the hotel.

I lowered my mobile as a car drove past slowly. Looking out, the light I'd seen in the window had been turned off. Starting the engine back up, I pulled away and headed back into the city, hoping to make last orders at my office.

Tommy still behind the bar. He smiled as I approached, held a pint glass up. I said it was fine and asked for a soft drink. 'Driving.'

'Fair enough.' He bent down and reappeared with a can of Coke. 'That woman you was speaking to earlier looked like a piece of work.'

I shook my head and explained. 'She's not as tough as she's making out. The truth makes people scared.'

Tommy accepted the point. 'Bit deep for you?'

'I'm full of surprises.'

'What's her problem?'

'It's complicated.' I laid out what I'd seen in the hotel for him, knowing I was trying to make sense of it myself, testing theories. It's what I missed about not having a team anymore, people I could bounce ideas off. But that was my own fault.

'How do you think she'll take the news?'

'I've no idea.'

Tommy weighed up what I was saying. 'It's your job, though. You've got to sort it out. It's what you've signed up for.'

'Thanks for that.'

He shrugged and moved off down the bar to serve a last-minute drinker. I took my mobile out and fiddled with it, looking up Gina Bellman on social media. I found an Instagram page which showed a series of images taken on short breaks and holidays, nights out in bars, and meals with friends. Her Facebook page was similar and I found myself looking at photographs of the sports car I'd seen outside the hotel, the occasional post promoting her business. Her relationship status was set to single. I told myself not to be judgmental. I was as single as they come. Swallowing the last of my drink, I glanced at Tommy as he made his way back over to me. He was right. The job was frequently unpleasant. It was what I'd signed up for.

4.

Sometimes you have to look people in the eye and listen to your gut. It was a policy that had served me well in the past, and as I'd left Tommy and The Queens last night, it felt like it was pretty much all I had. It was why I was standing in an empty bedsit with Paulo Matheson, feigning interest as I paced around it. I'd taken the liberty of giving a false name when setting up the viewing. The real irony was that I did need somewhere to live, my brother's wife increasingly tiring of me sleeping on their couch.

'Boiler was only fitted last year,' Matheson said, 'as was the kitchen. Refurbished places like this don't come up very often.'

He was smiling at me, trying to look every inch the honest salesman. Fair play, and despite the threadbare carpet and the flecked paint I could see around the window, I'd lived in worse. I was surprised he'd answered the call personally and made the arrangements. But I wasn't going to turn the opportunity down. 'You're familiar to me,' I said, watching as he fiddled with his wedding ring, absentmindedly playing with it. 'Have we met?'

'I was in a band in a previous life. Long time ago now.'

'What was the name?'

'*Duo.* We were around in the 1980s.'

I gushed with enthusiasm, wanting him to drop his guard. He'd had this conversation a million times before, I was sure. 'You were big stars.'

He held his hands up and smiled, looked at me with false modesty. 'We gave it a go.'

'But property's your game now?'

'Nothing lasts forever.'

'I thought the nostalgia circuit was big business?'

'It's not my scene.'

'Must beat grafting, though?'

'You'd be surprised.'

'You must miss the female attention?' I made a show of recalling the details. 'You must have some stories to tell?'

'I'm a gentleman.' Matheson laughed and shook his head. 'I left all that behind me back then. I'm a happily married man these days.'

'Must be tempting though when you're famous? You'll get far more female attention than a regular bloke like me?' He didn't answer, staring at me for a moment before walking over to the window, hands in his pocket. I'd maybe pushed too hard. I followed him over and offered an apology. 'I'm just jealous.'

Matheson smiled. 'I prefer a quiet life. I've got my wife and dog, my hobbies. What more does a man need?'

'Your wife having a local charity rings a bell?'

'She does a lot of good work for underprivileged children here, but there's so little funding for that kind of thing these days. It's tough.' Matheson changed the subject back to the bedsit, taking me through its selling points again, keen to close a deal and hinting the rent was potentially negotiable. 'What do you think?'

I stared out of the window, watching the buses running towards the city centre, people dodging the rain as they hurried to wherever they were headed. 'I guess I'm a warning,' I said looking at Matheson.

'How so?'

I thought again about the homeless man I'd spoken to at the train station, wondering what he'd make of the place, how that contrasted with Matheson's large house. Thought about how we weren't that different in the final analysis. 'My wife left me,' I said, spinning him a tale. 'Actions always have consequences.'

5.

I returned Gina Bellman's smile and made myself comfortable in the chair. I'd pushed Paulo Matheson as far as I'd dared to before leaving. In truth, he wasn't what I'd been expecting to encounter. I'd expected him to be loud and brash, but he'd largely been the opposite. I needed to find a different avenue if I was going to make some progress.

Bellman's office was in one of the new blocks that had sprung up on the edge of the city, all bold steel structures and large glass windows so those driving past would see into hives of activity. On the other side of the road, a Porsche dealership added to the aspirational feel of the area.

Bellman's office suite was small and uncluttered, a laptop and telephone the only items on her desk, a collection of arty prints on the wall showing the industrial heritage of the city in new and unexpected ways. 'Very kind of you to fit me in so quickly,' I said, focusing back on her.

'It's my pleasure.' She tapped her mobile and glanced at the screen before turning back to me. 'What's your line of business?'

'I'm a consultant; image and brand protection, that kind of thing.' It wasn't too far from the truth, but it made it sound more glamorous than the reality. They were words she would like to hear. 'A bespoke problem-solver.'

'Sounds fascinating.'

'Not always.' I smiled and started to give her the story I'd rehearsed on my journey. The best I had was a spiel about representing a group of former rugby league players in the city, how we were looking to establish a support group, raise some money for good causes along the way. I felt bad for lying, not entirely sure if she was taking me seriously or not. I nodded politely as she explained what services she offered and remained non-committal as she asked what kind of budget I had to spend. Instead, I stared at her laptop, wanting to get a look at what was on it. If I got really lucky, I wanted to look at her mobile.

'Don't suppose you know any celebrities who might be able to help us with their profile?' I asked, sitting back in the chair. 'Non-sporting people, I mean. Might be good PR for everyone?'

Bellman smiled, toyed with the pen in her hand. 'As it happens, I might be able to twist an arm on your behalf.'

I returned the smile. 'Can you give me a clue?'

'I shouldn't really.'

'It would make it easier to sell this to my colleagues if I had a name.' Bellman smiled and I knew she was dying to give me the name. It was how her world worked, all about contacts and impressing the client. 'It could swing things,' I suggested.

She stood up and walked over to the window. Maybe she was looking at the cars on the forecourt, or maybe she was just running the calculation, weighing up if I was worth the effort.

'I could speak to a well-known musician from this area,' she said, turning back to face me. 'He's still very popular.'

'Is he a personal friend?' She started to answer, but we were interrupted by the telephone ringing. She hesitated. 'Take it,' I said, pointing to it. 'Not a problem.'

Bellman listened to what the caller wanted, tried to say she was busy before relenting. 'I just need to go to reception to sort out a parcel delivery,' she said. 'I do apologise.'

I waved away the apology as I eyed up her devices. 'Take your time.' Once she was out of the door, I stood up and was straight to the other side of the desk. Turning to the laptop, I stared for a moment at the various folders and icons. I took out a memory stick and quickly copied as much as I could, glancing at the details and the names of her clients. It was deeply unethical if I stopped to think about my actions, and it maybe didn't reflect well on me, but I was in the zone. Things were becoming clearer.

I removed the memory stick and pocketed it, headed away from Bellman' desk and walked across the room to the door, glancing along the corridor. She was still arguing the toss with the delivery driver in reception. I had a little more time. Back to her desk, I was surprised to find her mobile was unlocked. Scrolling through the text messages, it tallied with what I suspected. I used my own mobile to take shots of them, the proof I needed to finish the job, before heading for the exit.

6.

I stared at my pint of lager as Keira Matheson buttoned up her coat and left. She had the truth now. The bar in the hotel was much as it had been when I'd watched her husband meet with Gina Bellmen. People in suits repeatedly checked mobiles and glanced at the clock on the wall, making sure they didn't miss their train back home. A dribble of guests arriving to stay overnight passed through the reception desk. It was anonymous and bland, the perfect safe space.

The job was done. Keira Matheson stepped out of the door without looking back and disappeared into the night. I picked up the envelope she'd placed down, the balance of payment owed to me. I'd shared what I'd found in Bellman's office with her, laying it out calmly and without emotion. I'd watched as she'd taken it in and formed her own judgment. It was all I could do. That was the job. Picking up my mobile, I deleted the images I'd taken in Bellman's office, and placing the memory stick on the floor,

I ground it downwards with the heel of my boot until it snapped. I picked up the pieces and smiled as Tommy walked over to me.

'Fancy a drink, Joe?' he asked, taking a seat opposite me.

'I'm done for the night.'

'It's still young.'

I smiled and said I was too old to be out partying. 'You've got plans?'

'Meeting friends at the theatre when their performance is done. Just a quiet drink or two afterwards, a chance to catch-up.'

'Nice.'

Tommy picked up his drink, swallowed back a mouthful. 'How did she take the news?'

'Good question.' I wasn't sure what she'd expected me to say, nor had she shown any emotion.

'You told her the truth?'

'I did.'

Tommy shrugged. 'You can't do any more than that.'

'True.' I passed him over the money I owed him. 'Good work.'

He pocketed it and stood up, ready to be on his way. 'Any time.'

I drank up too and headed out of the bar. Closing any investigation left me feeling melancholic. I wasn't sure if I'd believed Paulo Matheson when we'd spoken in the property he'd tried to rent me, but I'd been proved wrong about him. He wasn't having an affair with Gina Bellman. It was a professional relationship, the woman helping him with a rebrand for his wife's charity, a fresh start designed to help attract new funding streams. A surprise I'd now ruined. Beyond that, the state of their marriage was none of my business. It was an act of kindness in the final analysis.

Tommy had done as I'd asked, playing the part of the delivery driver at Bellman's office to perfection. It wasn't how he wanted to be using his acting skills, but it kept him sharp and put some money in his pocket. He'd delayed Bellman returning to her office, arguing the toss with her over a fictitious parcel, giving me the time to do what I needed to do.

Standing outside the train station, hands in my pockets, I drew in the cold night air. Maybe I'd let cynicism win the day and I shouldn't allow it to happen. I'd thought the worst of people, and although I could justify it in all kinds of ways, it was a lesson to learn and take forward.

The homeless guy was where I'd seen him the previous night, huddled into the corner and staring back at me. I walked over and kneeled down in front of him. 'How's it going?' It took him a moment to remember me, shuffled under the blankets he had pulled up around him.

'You were following that couple?'

'I was doing my job.'

'Funny job you've got, then.'

'You're not wrong there.' Gina Bellman maybe hadn't seen him, but I had. I stood back up and took out the book I'd bought for the man. A smaller act of kindness, maybe, but one that felt right. '*The Hanging Game,* the next in that Ian Rankin series you wanted to read,' I said, holding it out to him. 'I thought you might like it.'

---

Nick Quantrill was born and raised in Hull, an isolated industrial city in East Yorkshire. His Private Investigator novels featuring Joe Geraghty are published by Fahrenheit Press with the latest being 'Sound of the Sinners'. Nick is also the co-founder of the Hull Noir crime writing festival.

# TO INFINITY AND BEYOND

*By Nicky Black*

*Newcastle upon Tyne*

1.

1996

*"My wings are standard issue."*

My mam says I am a proper miracle, like the way they make Terry's Chocolate Orange. I am an itty-bitty angel with wings, she says, wings that can take me to the moon and space and everywhere, and that's canny lush coz I spend hours and hours watching the dust when the sun shines which Dad says is moon dust. It dances to the music in my head which is fuddled and beyond repair to humans, but not to angels or astronauts.

My head is normal to me, but the other people in my house have different-normal heads where the words come all out of the mouth instead of staying in the head like mine. My dad's head is the different-normal, even though my mam and Our Mo and Chloe look at him funny sometimes. His *gueee-taars* are bigger than me and there are three of them, and he sings brilliant—mostly about the lovey-dovey because he is soft as clarts.

Sometimes he sings about stairways to heaven and the boys being back in town and that, but I like the softly ones the best—like the *Isn't Shhheeee Looooooovvvvvvely?* which he sings after the black beer, and it makes my mam's face go all red, and she slaps his arm and tells him to give over the slop. She tells Our Mo she only married him coz he had the number one hit in the Eighties, and even though the bastards kept all the money, and they haven't seen a bloody penny of it, she still fancies him like mad.

He's not a pop star now. He's a binman which he says is boring and hurts his back, but it pays all right and keeps my mam in the life she was born to have, which is to drink wine with Our Mo and laugh loads and say bad words. Dad calls me "Big Man," but I'm only itsy, and I've been in the room when the doctor says, Alistair will never be a big man coz he won't make it to double figures, which is the number ten, and I'm already at the number six. The doctor gives Mam the crying, and Dad always does the cuddling which makes the crying worse. And then they take all the bags of medicines and wheel me out and put me in the car and give me a kiss and say not to listen to the doctor coz he doesn't know shite, which is a shame after all that learning of the body inside and out and everything. But they don't have to say all that. I believe them more than I believe the doctor who's got a hairy face like the Gruffalo and only talks to them and not to me.

When I was borned from my mam's lovely soft floppy belly, they could hold me in the palm of their hand. A baby bird, all googly eyes and baldy-coot. So, they put me in a glass box for ages and ages under a purple light that Our Mo said gave me a better tan than she got from Lanzarote. And they left me there until I was the size of a proper bairn, and they took me home to here, even though my brain would be beyond repair after it did bleed and make me a bit special. But they don't care about that coz it is just the way the cookie crumbles.

'Love and kindness served here all day.' This is what my mam says when we eat our tea.

They are good words.

"Kindness" means to be nice to people even if they're in a fettle, and "love" means lots of things—too many things to count—like the number of stars in the sky or dusts on the moon, or the number of wet towels Mam has to pick up off the floor. I know it's true because there are lots of things in the world I love—like my mam and dad and my sister, Chloe, who was borned early too, but not as early as me. She can do everything, especially the dancing to the Spice Girls coz her feet aren't stupid. The dancing goes around the kitchen, and it should make me sad, but it doesn't coz she holds my hands and I get to join in, and listening to her laughing and singing makes me smile the big goofy smile that makes her go, Eeeeh, Our Alistair's Sporty Spice!

I love that feeling.

I love sausages.

But more than anything in the whole world I love *Toy Story* on the telly.

And even more than that I love the most best thing in the intergalactic universe, which is the space ranger, Buzz Lightyear, coz he can fly and turn on the lights in his head to get it working whenever he wants. And he always has the goofy smile on his face, even when his lights are off and he's still as a statue, which is something I can hardly ever do coz of my Cerebral Palsy and that.

Buzz is *my* Big Man. When I got to the number six, my mam unwrapped a big present for me, and inside it was the actual Buzz Lightyear and I peed in my nappy with the excitement of seeing him in real life. He had come to live with me and my family coz he knew he would be looked after, just like me and Chloe and Rocky the cat and the spider plants are looked after. Mam showed me how to press the button on Buzz's arm, and when I did, I got the biggest and best fright, because he could speak!

*'I am Buzz Lightyear. I come in peace.'*

And I thought I might burst like a firework, all sparks and dazzle and twinkly stars.

## 2.

## The Millennium

*"You don't want to be in the way when my laser goes off."*

I have made it to the Double Figures!

It is all party party here in the kitchen, even though Doctor Gruffalo at the hospital dropped the bomb yesterday: that even though I can do the blinking and my head works a bit after all, I am still a broken biscuit and my head will probably always be stuck at the number ten, maybe eleven. This is fine by me coz I like being ten, what with the grown-ups always worried about stuff and that.

It's the biggest cake I've ever seen, and it is Buzz Lightyear with ten candles sticking out of him. One minute everybody's laughing and the next they're crying like big girls' blouses saying I'm a miracle and all that, and all I can do is hope they will all stop shrieking so I can watch my best present yet which is Toy Story 2 on the video.

Our Mo is here, and she is my mam's sister. She goes around people's houses cutting their hair and she is my aunty, but everyone calls her Our Mo. Our Mo hasn't got a husband anymore coz she got a Toy Boy which ended in tears, and Uncle Brian got a flat in town which ended in a girlfriend who Our Mo calls Pocahontas on account of the hair and the lips and the sunbeds. I've watched Pocahontas on the telly, and she's cush and she can sing, and when she sings, I sing along in my head which doesn't seem to be beyond repair in the musical department which is pretty belter coz I'd like to have a number one hit like my dad.

I was eight and three quarters when I started doing the music in my head. They'd had me at the doctors coz Mam kept thinking I was having a wobbler which is called the epileptic, but I was only doing the music and needed to concentrate. There's nothing I can do with it except keep it in my head and play it over and over, coz the only sound I can make is *Gahhh*. It's a good sound, though, so I do it loads, and sometimes I see Chloe put things in her ears and I see Dad close his eyes and count to ten, which is the number I am now, and it is mint, so I don't mind staying at ten, maybe eleven.

Chloe blows the candles out coz I can't make my mouth blow. Then they sing the Happy Birthday and I kick my legs and shout, "*Gahhh, gahhh, gahhh!*" and I keep shouting it coz I'm loving the singing from everyone and want to join in. It's quite a while before I notice they've all stopped. They are staring at me like I'm Mister Potato Head with his face on upside down. They stare and stare and my last few *Gahhh*s are a bit pathetic. Then my dad plonks his hand on Chloe's shoulder which makes her jump, and he says he'll go to the top of wor stairs because Alastair is singing!

And they all go mental like they did last week when I did the blinking: two for Yes and one for No—which made Doctor Gruffalo say maybe the biscuit isn't so broken—and we all start singing the Happy Birthday again, and even if I can't say the words, I can sing the tune and everybody's jumping about, even Mam who isn't so tired today.

And then all the tunes that were in my head since I was eight and three quarters start coming out, and I sing for two whole hours, even with Buzz Lightyear birthday cake in my mouth.

It's all quiet now. Dad's in the front room watching the football, and Mam and Our Mo are sitting at the kitchen table finishing the wine and whispering. I'm sleepy-tired—too tired even for Toy Story 2—and I'm hoping they'll put me in my bubbly bath and to bed soon so I can sleep, which is my third favourite thing to do next to pressing Buzz Lightyear's karate chop button and eating sausages. Then Chloe comes in in her nightie to get a glass of water, and she kisses me on the forehead and tells me goodnight even though it's only eight o'clock. Mam and Our Mo watch her leave, then they look at each other all serious and say how she's got little boobs and everything.

Then all I can hear is the fridge humming its own tune, and Mam puts her hands to her chest where her own boobs used to be.

I'm pleased to be under the duvet with Buzz next to me, but Mam won't get off my bed. She's sitting there, swaying a bit and grinning at me and asking if I had a nice day. I do the two blinks and she puts her hands on my cheeks and gives me big fat face-kisses which are a bit wet for my liking, but I let it go. She tells me I'm a smasher, and in my head, I tell her she's a smasher too, even though she's all baldy-coot like I was when I was in the glass box. I give her my best smile, and when she's wiped my dribble away, she gets all wet in the eyes and asks me to sing her a song. So, I belt out the tune to *Mambo Number 5*—instrumentals and everything—and she laughs so much she pees herself and she isn't even wearing a nappy.

## 3.

## 2004

*"There's a snake in my boot."*

My dad says the estate we live on is Baghdad where the war is, but Mam won't move because she says why should she? And most of the people are canny, and it's dead convenient for the town where the shops are for her work for Superdrugs which she does while I'm at proper school. Let *them* move, she says, and anyhow, the shop on the corner does better corned beef pasties than Greggs and she's not giving them up for no worky-ticket scumbags.

But sometimes the noise at night keeps me awake—the shouting, and the bikes and glass. And tonight, I'm a bit scared too, coz tomorrow they're going to try to fix my stupid feet and it's going to hurt. They say it'll mean I can walk a bit, but that it might not work at all, and it makes me wish I could fly like Buzz and not have to use the chair or my stupid feet and just sail in the air like the itty-bitty angel with wings.

My mam pushes me into the hospital. She's doing the striding thing and showing off her new boobs which Our Mo says are bigger and better than the old ones and that makes her a lucky cow. Mrs Chang is going to cut up my stupid feet and make them straighter. She looks at Mam and Dad and Chloe and Our Mo and says they all look scareder than me, but that they shouldn't worry at all; that I am in very safe hands, and they should be brave like me, right Alistair? She's talking to me and she winks, so I give her the yes blinks and I know now that my feet probably won't be stupid for very much longer which means I might get to be like Kelly Holmes even though she's a girl.

When they're putting me in the gown—even though Chloe told me to think good thoughts before I go to sleep—I can't help thinking about all the bad things I've seen on the telly instead: the war a million miles away, and the prime minister all covered in purple paint, plane crashes in Egypt and bombs in Spain. Manchester United winning the FA Cup.

I think about all those terrible things and I look at the nurses all fussing over me, and I look at Chloe and her black eyes and big boots and worried face; my mam trying not to cry and Our Mo jangling her bangles. My dad being all jolly and jokey and brave for everyone. I look at it all, and I feel like the dancing moon dust, glad not to be an Iraqi or the prime minister or Bobby Robson.

And I realise, it doesn't matter if my feet stay stupid and I have to use the chair for ever and ever and I'll never fly like Buzz or angels, because Mrs Chang is not the only one with safe hands.

I'm already a bit woozy when they put me on the trolley and wheel me to the operating theatre which they've already shown me so I won't be scared.

But not so woozy that I can't sing.

So, when my mam lets go of my hand and the doors swing open and she's standing there with her hand over her mouth, I give her some *True Colours* coz it's her favourite song, and she gives this big gulp and then she is gone.

## 4.

### Two months later

*"Approaching light speed."*

My mam and dad and Chloe are run ragged trying to stop me falling down the stairs and breaking my bloody neck and knocking things over and breaking them too. But I am *free,* and I am *tall,* and I am *Buzz Lightyear to the rescue!*

Our Mo's hair has turned blue, and I stopped walking and stared at it for ages when she came in the house. She stared back, all *what-you-looking-at,* and said that for someone who wasn't supposed to make it to ten, I was doing quite canny, and Mam said, aye, fair enough, but she was knackered because Alastair's gone all Speedy Gonzalez, and Our Mo said, Julie, you cannit begrudge the laddie his feet.

I'm standing at the living room window and a car whizzes past, then a police car with it's lights flashing and sirens going, and I'm doing knee jumping with the excitement and because

I can. Our Mo says, this place is full of radgies, and Mam is all, no it isn't, and that there are some here that are the best and salty like the earth. And she's right too, coz every day I walk with my walker down the path on my new feet to the bottom of the front garden, and people say, Howay, Big Al, or Keep A'haad, Lanky, or Mind out, here's Ali McFastPants!

Another cup of tea is made, and while I go and stand at the mirror with my sticky hands either side of if, looking at my face with the bum fluff which isn't on my bum and isn't fluff at all, the tea is slurped, and Our Mo asks what the doctor said. Mam doesn't answer, so Our Mo says Mam does her bliddy head in, and she gets the phone off the little table by the telly and presses the buttons all angry and says, Aye, yez can help. I want to make an appointment for my dollop of a sister.

5.

2008

*"I'm proud of you, Cowboy."*

She's been gone three years, now.

Buzz stopped talking and the guitars got put away and Rocky went to live with the smelly cat lady up the road. The council gave us new windows and doors and Our Mo fought with all the tooths and nails to get them to put a stair lift in now that I'm a bigger Big Man and my dad's back is stupid like my feet used to be.

I can't tell a lie; I didn't feel ten-maybe-eleven for a long time because of the worry and the pain in my heart and all the sadness everywhere. We were all there at the hospice where the angels worked, all in white, peaceful and floaty like clouds. They let me lie down next to her on the bed, and she was too floppy to give me a cuddle, but she said that she would always love us—me and

Chloe and Dad and Our Mo—and she told us all to be kind to each other and everyone else, and that she was never prouder of her Big Man and his singing. So, after they'd stuck the driver needle thing in for the pain, and she went to sleep, I sang the Whitney Houston, *Always Love You,* over and over again, dead soft and quiet until her tummy stopped moving up and down and I didn't want to sing anymore.

Our Mo and Chloe helped loads at first, but now there's a nurse here to do stuff for me, and she's called Poppy from Down South. Her and all the people on the estate did coffee mornings and raffles, and after two years of being a right old nag she got the money for me to have a screen on my chair so I can do machine words and tell people my name.

Poppy from Down South is a proper smasher, and she has a son, too, who is a Big Man like me, all grown up, and still lives in Chingford, and even though he's a bit radio rental and has to take tablets, she loves him a lot because that's what families do. Poppy from Down South is quite bonny, and last year, after she started coming to help, my dad started running around the estate in shorts and has lost half of me which is five and a half stone. It was Our Mo what did it; said she hoped her sister wasn't looking down from heaven at the sight of him with the belly and the long hair and the whiff coming off him, and that Mam would have wanted better for Bugger Lugs, who is me. Dad stared at me for ages when she said that, and when he'd slammed the door shut behind him, Our Mo looked at me and said, sometimes you've got to be cruel to be kind, hinny. But then Poppy from Down South turned up like Mary Poppins in Crocs, and he got the shorts and everything, and now Our Mo calls him *'Slimcea Boy,'* which makes Poppy from Down South laugh, and when Poppy from Down South laughs, my dad can't help but laugh too.

My eighteenth birthday was purely belter. Dad took me for my first pint which was lemonade for me and the black stuff for him, and everyone said how grown-up Alistair was with a bit of a beard and that, and when a drunk woman said, Aww, how handsome Alistair would have been if he hadn't been in the glass box and have the chair and the open mouth all the time, I used my eagle eyes and looked at the "fuck off" words on my screen. Then the voice came out with the Geordie accent, and everybody laughed at the bad words, even the drunk woman.

Now we're having battered sausage and chips with scraps and gravy from the chip shop and watching Newcastle United get beat on the telly. It's so bad that Dad doesn't even say, 'Buggery shite,' when he drips gravy down his Number Ten Michael Own shirt. Instead, he says that Poppy from Down South has found me a grown-up school since now I'm eighteen and have to leave the school I'm at. And then he goes all shifty like his bum hurts, and he asks me how I would feel if Poppy from Down South was to move in with us now that Chloe was finished the university and was teaching bairns and getting a flat and there was a spare room at ours.

My rendition of the *Hallelujah Chorus* goes down a storm and the next day he's up in the loft, and by teatime all three guitars have been tuned and are resting all shiny against the wall next to the fireplace. Dad strums and I sing the tune to *Father and Son* which we haven't done for donkeys, and afterwards when we feel a bit sad, he tells me there's music lessons at the new school. And the sadness *pops!* And my heart sings and goes full-on fuzzy, and *boom!* There are sparks and firework stars for the first time in three years, and when Poppy from Down South arrives, she's got a new Buzz Lightyear with her, and I think I can love her almost as much as my mam.

And when she smiles at my dad, I think she probably won't be sleeping in Chloe's room—ever.

## 6.

### One year later

*"Reach for the sky!"*

Dad says, why aye, course he knew I was proper talented even though my head was still only ten, maybe eleven.

My music teacher is called Mrs Markey and she is from Rwanda which is in Africa and she is a refugee, although she doesn't look like one with the happy smile and the pudgy cheeks. She came to England when she was just a bairn, all alone because her mam and dad and brothers and sisters were all dead—chopped to bits by radgies. She's married to Mr Markey, and he's the physiotherapist and is from Ireland where they all drink the black stuff which is manna from heaven.

Mrs Markey says, Ten, maybe eleven my butt-hole, and asks my dad and Poppy from Down South if they're ready. When they nod, she puts the CD into the stereo and out comes my music, and it is as lush now as it was when I first heard it all in one piece in my head. Mrs Markey doesn't play it all, just the first minute. Then she turns it off, and my dad and Poppy's faces are all scrunched up like they haven't got a scooby what's going on. So, my dad asks, when will they hear the pop music because he was pretty sure I was going to have a number one hit like he did in 1982, and Mrs Markey smiles with her lovely white teeth and says, It's not pop music anymore, Mr Peacock, Alastair's been composing classical pieces on the new computer software with his very own eyes.

They are all looking at me and the room is peculiar silent like a spook. Poppy is blinking, and Dad breathes in loads of air to try and stop the twitch in his chin. He asks if I did that, and I blink twice, and I wonder if he is disappointed coz I'm not likely to make even the top 10,000 with all that airy-fairy shite. But instead, he nods his head and says he wants to hear the rest, and when it's finished, they all applaud and call me 'Maestro.'

## 8.

## 2012

*"This isn't flying, it is falling with style!"*

London is busy and noisy and colourful and absolutely bloody brilliant!

They've put us in a hotel that Poppy from Down South says is like Buckingham Palace on speed. The room is massive, and the walls are pink and yellow, and the furniture is spikey and weird like something from another planet, and I decide to spend some of the money I'm making from concerts and the YouTube to make mine and Buzz's bedroom like this back at home. The rest is going to buy a house away from Baghdad for Dad and Poppy, and there'll be no arguments, coz I've put it in writing to a legal man just in case I'm not here anymore and they refuse to spend any of it, like they are now.

It's been six months since Mrs Markey told my dad that me, Alistair Peacock of Newcastle upon Tyne, Geordie Land, had been asked to write something for the opening ceremony of the biggest and best Olympic Games in the history of the world. There were lots of whoopings, and *well done, son*s, and *I cannit believe it*s, and after a few cans of the black stuff my dad had said that if my mam could see my now she'd be pissing herself with pride, and I made the screen say, she *was* looking at me now, and he bubbled like a bairn until Poppy from Down South told him that was enough of the black stuff and he should go to bed.

Tonight is the night, and we go to the park which is named after the Queen and it is buzzing with volunteers in purple jackets and people from all over the world. Poppy's son is here and he's no longer a pain in the jacksie now he has a bairn of his own which Poppy says is the making of him. She cuddles that baby girl like she is the mam and not Karina who is from Poland and can do the splits and dances in shows.

Me, Dad and Poppy are dressed all Bobby Dazzler, and we have special tickets around our necks, so we don't have to wait in the queue with the people dressed in jeans. We're inside now, right at the front and there are people in chairs like me all around—and some of them are children, and some are grown-ups, and some are proper old men with hunchbacks and everything who have been at war with Nazis and are still alive against all the odds, like me.

I close my eyes. A speck of moon dust, drifting amongst the thousands and thousands of people whose faces I cannot see but whose voices I can hear like the roar of a million lions. I flit between them, and they are like notes on staves, every single one playing their part in the concerto of the here and now.

My music comes on after two hours, and my face is on a screen that is bigger than our house, and the lions roar and roar! It lasts for three minutes and eighteen seconds, and it is the best three minutes and eighteen seconds of my twenty-two years, with Poppy holding my left hand, and Dad holding my right, and my mam holding my heart. I know Our Mo and Chloe are watching from home and will be holding hands too. They will probably be blubbing, and Our Mo will be looking up to the ceiling and saying, I told you, Our Julie. We said we'd look after him and look at him now.

I am three minutes and eighteen seconds of moon dust. I am flying like Buzz. I am here, I am now, and I am a smasher. I have had all the stuff done to me to keep me alive. All the medicines hidden in my yoghurts and chocolate puddings.

All the sucky things on my head measuring waves. I am the swaying stadium, and the huge, triangular lights, and all the folks dancing and singing, the music from all the geniuses and rock stars and people alive and dead. I am all the totally brilliant things that are Great Britain, and the world and the universe. I am the fireworks, bursting, blazing bright, then dying, but always remembered.

And my hands are safe in other hands, and I know in these three minutes and eighteen seconds that I am here, now, alive, not because of Mrs Chang or the other doctors, hairy or not. I am no miracle. I am here because of the love. I am here because of the big hearts, whether beating or silent.

And I am here because of the kindness.

I am infinity. And I am beyond.

---

Nicky Black's gritty, bestselling 'Valley Park' novels are a collaboration between two friends, Nicky Doherty and Julie Blackie, who have known each other for over 20 years. Both have had careers in urban regeneration, working at the heart of disadvantaged communities in the North East of England. During that time, they experienced the real grit and struggle of peoples' every-day lives, as well as their humour and determination to lead a happy existence, whatever that meant to them. *To Infinity and Beyond* is written by Nicky, a Northumberland lass who is currently living out her middle years in North Tyneside.

# BROKEN WING

*By Patricia Gibney*

The coffin was open.

She stood statuesque, staring at his alabaster face. It was a mask of combed hair, closed eyes and tight lips without expression. The broken wing had not healed and she wondered how his soul could ever fly up to the heavens.

Her tears fell softly and she was astounded that she had tears left after all she had been through. She'd believed he would survive. Had prayed, begged and bribed any power above to cancel the horror and allow him to live. But her pleas had fallen on ears glued shut. She felt she had lost one of her own wings now that he was gone and she might not be able to take another step, let alone fly solo through the rest of her life.

And then she saw her grandmother standing by his head, her eyes emerald green, her hair silver-grey at fifty-five. She looked the very same as the last time she'd seen her.

* * *

It was early in the summer of 1969, and ten-year-old Rosie was filled with excitement despite the car sickness on the drive to her grandmother's cottage. She was sure her daddy was annoyed with all the stops he had to make to let her throw up over the blackthorn bushes along the road.

"Sorry, Daddy," she said each time. He just nodded and pulled out the gear stick on their gold-coloured Renault 4 (her friends called it mustard and laughed) and continued on their journey.

Black rosary beads swung from the rear-view mirror and Rosie thought maybe it was Jesus swinging on the cross making her stomach swirl and lurch. She closed her eyes for the remainder of the drive.

Her first sight of Granny Kate was of the tall, strong woman standing in the open yard, the door open behind her, and the thatch on the roof secured against the summer wind.

"Good to have you with us for a few days, Rosie," she said and waved Dad away.

On unsteady feet and a roiling stomach, Rosie felt tears sprout at the corners of her eyes as the car disappeared from view down the narrow country lane. A whole five days away from her parents and sister had sounded like a little bit of heaven when it was put to her, but now, she wasn't so sure.

Her granny lit up and pulled hard on a Sweet Afton, (Rosie loved the yellow box, because yellow was her favourite colour, after gold), then hacked a cough loud enough to send the chickens fluttering, their feathers flying into the air. After Granny Kate ground out the butt with the sole of her black rubber boot (cut crookedly around her ankles), Rosie felt the pressure of a calloused hand on her shoulder and she was steered inside.

"Don't fret, pet, you'll be fine with us. Want to help me flour the table? I've got the dough in the bowl."

Rosie sniffed the air.

"Treacle cake?" she said, her mouth watering with the delicious aroma filling the stone kitchen.

"Sure is, Rosie. Want a slice now? Straight out of the skillet."

"Can I spread butter on it?"

"That's the only way to eat my treacle cake, pet."

Seated on her grandfather's chair by the fire, a plate on her knee and melted butter dripping down her chin, Rosie sighed with relief as her stomach settled with the sweet cake. Something skittered across the stone floor. She yelped and hastily pulled her legs up, folding them beneath her bum.

Granny Kate laughed. "Sure, it's only a mouse. Won't touch you."

"He might, so he might."

"Don't you think he's more afraid of you than you are of him?"

"I don't want to find out."

Laughing hoarsely, Granny Kate plopped the brown bread dough onto the table. Rosie had forgotten she was supposed to flour it, but her granny didn't seem to notice.

"Where's Grandad?"

"Down the fields. Cutting hay. You can help us stack it later."

"I'm not that strong. I'm only ten."

"A few days here and you'll be as strong as an ox."

"What's an ox?"

"A cow. We do the milking at six. Another job for you. Eat up and I'll bring you to the barn to have a look."

"I thought they were in the field."

"In and out, sure they are."

Rosie ate up and wiped the crumbs from her good Aran jumper her mammy had knitted. She wore it over her best dress (the yellow one with the daisies) and she didn't want to get either dirty. She hadn't brought much clothes because she only had a small red case, and anyhow, she didn't have many clothes. She wondered if her granny would have boots to fit her as she looked down at her brown Clarke's sandals. They were all she had with her.

"You know what, pet, I need to get cigarettes. We'll have to go to the shop before I show you the cows."

"But you don't have a car and daddy says the shop is two miles down the road." Her daddy had told her granny got her groceries from the pub, and she'd thought that was hilarious. A pub with groceries? Ha.

"God gave you two feet, pet. But it's your first day so I'll bring the bike and you can hop up on the back."

Rosie had no idea how this worked but she found out. With a shopping bag on the handlebars, her granny stood tall with her feet on the pedals, Rosie sitting on the saddle, her hands around her granny's waist. Granny Kate pushed off and down the road they went, wind sailing through Rosie's hair which was now loose, having lost her ribbon somewhere along the way. She felt the breeze giving her freedom.

"Wow!" she yelled. It was funniest thing she'd ever known, not counting the day Mrs Wright in first class had made Denis the Messer learn how to knit with pink needles and pink wool.

By the time they reached the pub, she was full of energy and her granny was wrecked. "That was great fun," Rosie said.

"You won't be saying that when we have to walk up the hill, pushing the bike between us."

Rosie waited outside the pub while her granny got cigarettes, a box of matches, a pound of tea and a bottle of stout for grandad. There was nothing else in the village besides the church, with its single steeple and luscious flower beds lining the avenue.

Granny hung the shopping bag on the handle bars and began to push the bike.

"Can I get back on the saddle?" Rosie said.

"Get away with ye! I'm not pushing you and the bike. Now hurry up or your granddad will be home, looking for his tea."

It was tough going. Rosie's sandals flapped against her bare feet and she felt a blister rise on her heel and another on her big toe. This was no fun. But she didn't say it. As they crowned the top of the hill, she saw something lying in the middle of the road.

"What is that, Granny?"

"Whisht a minute, child," Granny Kate said. "Will you look at the poor creature?"

"Ugh, it's a bird." Rosie wasn't fond of anything that could fly around her head. Bats and other things that might stick in her hair. Her sister had got chewing gum stuck in her hair once and Mammy had to cut a lump out of her fringe. Not that it had anything to do with birds or bats, but all the same.

"Hold the bike." Granny Kate pushed it towards her.

Rosie felt the weight of the black monstrosity and wondered how her granny had been able to push it up the hill. She supposed older people were stronger. Granny looked strong, but now she was gentle, bending down to the little bird in the middle of the road, her long fingers teasing the wings out to see what had happened.

"Ah, sure it's no use to anyone."

"What's no use?" The bike was too heavy, sure it was nearly bigger than herself, Rosie thought, and she didn't want to let it fall and break the bottle of stout. Grandad wouldn't be happy if that happened.

"The wing is broken. Must have been clipped by a car."

"What are you going to do?" Rosie asked.

"I'll have to bring it home and give it some water. Then we'll see."

"Bring it home?" Rosie said, horrified. "How?"

Her granny didn't answer. She lifted the mute bird in her big hand and placed it into the pocket of her grey gaberdine coat, took the bike from Rosie, and they headed home.

Back at the house, Granny Kate put the bird in a cardboard box that had a red tin of baking powder printed on the outside. She placed a saucer of water in there too.

"He's not drinking." Rosie sat cross-legged on the stone floor, a little distance between her and the box, for fear the bird hadn't a broken wing at all. She wrapped her hair around her fingers too, just in case.

"The poor thing is tired," Granny said. "God knows how long it was lying there waiting for me to come along and pick it up."

"Birds don't think like that, Granny."

"How do you know? I'd say they have brains like us. Well, maybe not big brains like ours, but little brains. Who's to say they can't think like us?"

Rosie mulled over this and couldn't come up with a sensible reply.

"Maybe," is all she said.

"It needs time to heal."

"Granny?"

"What, pet?"

Granny Kate had her back to her, washing dishes in a basin of water. She'd boiled the water in the kettle on the open fire, and shown Rosie the correct way to stack the turf beneath it.

"Why can't a bird fly with one wing?" Rosie said.

"Sure, how would it balance itself? How would it be able to flap to fly away? It needs two wings, pet."

"Is it a hopeless case?" Rosie had heard her mammy say someone was a hopeless case one time and she wondered if that person had tried to fly with one wing.

"Nothing is hopeless. It might heal itself. But if it can't we'll have to leave it out in the bushes and let nature take its course.

"Hmm," Rosie muttered, not at all convinced. She moved away from the baking powder box and went to the door. "Can I go outside?"

"Of course you can. Mind the road. You don't want to end up with one wing like our little birdy."

"Silly, Granny, I don't have any wings."

"We all have wings. You just can't see them."

Yeah, in fairy tales, Rosie thought.

Out in the yard, she ran around, flapping her arms up and down, just to make sure she wasn't daft. No, no wings.

She skirted around the pecking hens and walked towards the barn. She really needed to wee, but Granny told her she'd have to go into the back field behind the stack of hay. Suddenly Rosie missed home. She even missed her annoying little sister.

There were no cows in the barn. They were out in the field. She wondered if it was nearly six yet, so she could see how they were milked. Maybe that would be fun. Or maybe not.

"The little—" Granny Kate yelled.

Rosie ran back to the house. There she found her granny running around the kitchen, waving a tea-towel. Her bun had come undone and her hair flailed around her head sticking to her forehead with sweat. The bird was hopping from one picture to the next along the wall, and came to rest on top of the Sacred Heart lamp.

"Catch him, Rosie, pet."

"I can't touch it. I'm afraid."

"Let me tell you, I'm wrecked. That bird shit all over my good Sunday scarf and it there hanging behind the door minding its own business. I'll break his other wing if he doesn't get back in his box."

Rosie's heart filled with dread for the damaged bird. "Don't kill it, Granny. Please don't!"

"Will you whisht, child? I wouldn't do that. This bird is one of God's creatures and no one should hurt it but I think it can fly on one wing. Must be a miracle."

The bird flapped its good wing and moved from the holy lamp to a photograph of Granny's mother that was taken by a photographer. A treasured heirloom, she'd been told before. The bird pooed down the glass. Rosie clamped a hand over her mouth, to keep her giggles inside.

"That's it!"

Rosie watched as Granny Kate picked up the baking powder box—forgetting about the saucer of water which smashed on the ground—and she ran around the kitchen trying to trap the bird with the broken wing inside.

"Success!" she cried when at last she got it on Granddad's chair. "Hold that there, Rosie."

She did as she was told and watched as her granny fetched a thin baking tray and slid it under the box and on top of grandad's cushion.

"What are you going to do now?" Rosie asked, tired from all the excitement.

"We'll bring it out to the bushes and set it free. The other birds will help it."

"How do you know that, Granny?"

"I don't, but I know it'd rather be free with a broken wing than being captive in here with the two of us running around after it. Help me now, pet."

They lifted the tray, with the box on top, and carried it out to the yard between them. The box trembled and Rosie was afraid the bird would knock it over and fall to the ground and die. But they reached the buses with it still safe inside.

"What are we going to do now?" Rosie said.

"You're a right little parrot, aren't you?" A butterfly flew by Rosie's face, so close she could almost touch it. Granny Kate added, "That's another soul on its way to heaven."

"Will it come back for our bird with the broken wing?"

"When the time is right, I'm sure it will. Same for all of us. On the count of three you pull out the tray and I'll lift the box. Be careful now."

Rosie did as she was told but her little fingers shook. The bird just stood on the grass beside the bush and didn't move. Rosie held onto the tray and said, "Shoo, birdy. Off you go. The other birdies will help you fly again."

"Ah it won't fly too far, but it's wing might heal with time."

"And what will happen if it doesn't heal?" Rosie couldn't get her head around all the things her granny had said in the few hours since she'd arrived.

"Sure if I knew that, I might as well get myself a throne and become God. Inside now, and we'll make your grandad's tea. The poor man will be parched from the hay."

Rosie stood for ages looking at the little bird. She heard her grandad tug off his wellington boots at the door before she turned around.

"Rosie child, how are you?" he said, a Sweet Afton dangling from his lips.

"I'm grand," she said. "I'm minding the bird with the broken wing."

"That's a great job altogether," he said and went inside.

When she turned around again, the bird had disappeared.

* * *

Granny Kate died one week after Rosie arrived home with her daddy in the gold Renault 4. A massive stroke, Doctor Ganley said. Rosie went back for the wake. Her daddy had to stop only three times for her to be sick.

Fifty years later, Rosie stood beside her dead husband's coffin, and stared at her granny hovering above his head. A butterfly flew by, taking her dreams away on the crest of a breeze. Granny Kate picked up a little bird and placed him in the pocket of her grey gabardine coat and then she was gone.

When Rosie looked down at her husband in the coffin, she could swear there was a soft smile on his face.

"Thank you, Granny Kate. Thank you for helping him fly away with a broken wing."

---

Patricia Gibney is a crime author from Mullingar, Co. Westmeath, Ireland. Her debut novel, The Missing Ones, was published by London based digital publisher, Bookouture, in March 2017. To date nine Detective Lottie Parker books have been published in the series with over one and a half million sales. The series is also available in audio format, and paperback editions are published by Sphere UK and Hachette Ireland. Foreign translations have sold to Spain, Norway, Italy, France, Poland, Hungary, Bulgaria, Slovakia, Czech Republic, Estonia, Taiwan and China, and audio to Sweden. Patricia is represented by Literary Agent, Ger Nichol of The Book Bureau.

# ONE MORNING IN THE LIFE OF HASAN D

*By Rachel Sargeant*

Hasan's waking breath tastes of rust and engine oil. He shuffles on his side along the cardboard under the Volkswagen and emerges on stiff legs.

There's a twinge in his ribs when he puts his arm into his jacket sleeve. Old damage, done back home. It hurts to raise his hand to his face, but his eyes feel gritty and he wants to rub them. The day isn't bright yet so he thinks it's early and checks his phone, forgetting it got smashed on the boat. He strokes the fractured images of Rima and Karam.

Other people are getting up. Elderly couples cough sleep out of their lungs, men light cigarettes, babies cry. The big man, a college lecturer, leans against a palm tree, his head lolling. He's afraid of rats and spends every night walking the road. There'll be a thud when he falls. Hasan leads him to the Volkswagen. Too tired to speak, the man pats Hasan's shoulder and slides under the vehicle into Hasan's night space. Hasan hopes he'll catch some sleep before it gets too hot, and noisy with car horns.

Hasan decides to make for the waterhole. There's no point heading straight to the white van; they don't post up the names this early. And it's not worth bothering with the seafront yet. He has to walk in the middle of the road because make-shift shelters block the pavement. The undulating line of plastic and canvas sheets, strung between a metal fence and ornamental citrus trees, reminds him of market stalls at home. There's a sudden hard feeling in his throat, and he looks at the parked cars instead.

The Suzuki SUV hasn't moved for the three days he's been here. He'd intended to sleep under it because of its high chassis, but two brothers got there first. They whisper to each other now as Hasan passes and he senses urgency in the murmured words. He knows they told the authorities they're eighteen and won't find out if they've been believed until their names appear on the white van. He could speak to them later, offer to be their uncle. Their best chance, if they are willing to trust him—but he wouldn't blame them if they don't.

There's still a nip of cold and he turns up his collar, but it will be warm later and more sweat will seep into his stale clothes. At least when he reaches the toilet cubicle he will be able to have a wash, and he'll take off his underpants to swill them in the hotel waterhole. They haven't been rinsed since the night he waded ashore. They can dry in the sun at the top of the metal fence with everyone's washing while he walks to the van in his jeans.

Someone runs into the road, a slight figure not much older than the boys under the Suzuki. Two men shout from beneath a tartan blanket lashed between two cars. The youth must have sneaked under it after they went to sleep. He raises his hands palms-upward in apology and trails off left towards the seafront. Hasan should go after him to explain that the holiday makers will still be having breakfast on their terraces. They won't be handing out Fanta and lollipops yet. If the wheelchair with the missing side panels is still outside the postcard kiosk, they could work a plan: father and invalid son. But it won't be there. A wheelchair is currency. Besides, a plan would need both names to be on the van. Hasan sighs at his own powerlessness. He hopes by the time Karam reaches that boy's age, he will be a proper father again, there to help with whatever his son needs.

A car appears ahead, spewing diesel fumes and noise. Hasan steps between the parked cars. The two men who chased off the youth raise their fists as he nears their temporary home, but they retreat under their tartan roof when the car gets level. The driver spits out of his window before speeding on. His spittle hits one of the parked cars. The saliva clings to the warm paintwork and rolls into the shape of Hasan's homeland. He walks away.

His skin prickles. There's a dog. They're attracted by the rubbish. A girl was bitten on the first day. Because they have to leave this country within the deadline or be deported, her parents tried to hide the bite, but the local police found out and sent the child to hospital.

The dog sniffs the ground and licks at something sticky on the tarmac. Its back end quivers and one eye weeps green fluid. Hasan could duck under the blanket and take his chances with the men's fists, but another car beeps its horn. The dog trot-limps into a side street. The driver accelerates and flicks his middle finger at Hasan.

At the old hotel car park, women stand straight-backed in the long line outside the toilet cubicle. Small children curl their fingers around the fabric of their mothers' robes. When Hasan catches a whiff of the stench ahead of them, he crosses the waste ground to where a thick stone pillar has collapsed, creating a privacy screen. He takes a pee. The concrete is wet and stinking where other men have been. He's about to go back and wait for the cubicle, but more women with children are arriving. Their need is greater; he and his underclothes can last another day without a wash.

The queue for the standpipe is even longer. Two policemen in surgical masks pace the line. Their gaze is over everyone's head. No one speaks. As Hasan waits his turn, he watches the waterhole. Rainwater collects in the exposed foundations of the demolished hotel. Several men squat at the side, soak rags and wipe their bodies under their shirts. Perhaps he should, too—a partial wash would be better than none. A woman strips two small boys to their grubby vests and washes their thin arms and faces. She fills a tin can and takes the children behind the remaining wall of a storeroom where some of the women go to wash.

The standpipe queue doesn't seem to move, but grows long with families. A baby cries tiredly into her mother's neck. The woman shifts the bundle higher onto her shoulder and rocks from side to side. The child will get heavier the longer the mother has to stay in line. The same for all the mothers behind him. Hasan wonders if he could leave the line and fill his cola bottle in the waterhole despite the nappies floating in it. He decides to come back for water later when the families have got theirs. The line shuffles forward to fill the gap he leaves.

Proper tents are pitched at the back of the car park. The authorities provided them until too many people came and hygiene became difficult. Hasan kicks through sweetie wrappers, a toy lorry with its wheels missing, and plastic bags swollen with unknown rubbish. He picks up a woman's shoe. The heel is broken but he removes the insole. He'll need a patch soon, or at least something to soak up the rain. He bought his shoes for his IT job, not for walking.

He checks the compartments of an abandoned rucksack: nothing inside. One strap is broken but he hooks the other one over his arm. His ribs hurt again, the injury from back home when the rebels caught Rima driving.

A truck pulls up when he gets back on the road. The driver opens his door and Hasan prepares to dash back among the tents. But the man is the one they call Good Friend. His chin has scabbed since yesterday when another local man threw stones. Hasan thought he wouldn't come again, but he steps out of the truck and holds up a string bag of oranges. Hasan clasps the man's fingers as he takes the bag, and the man keeps his hand there, allowing Hasan to thank him. Then he steps back, mutters at the ground and climbs in the truck. Through the open window, he passes Hasan a plastic bag and drives away. Inside the bag: t-shirt, socks and underpants.

A car veers towards Hasan and sounds the horn. He clutches the bags of clothes and oranges but slips the rucksack off his shoulder. If the driver makes a grab, that's what he can snatch. But the car keeps moving and blasts the horn again. Making a noise is enough for this one; he doesn't bother to spit.

Many others are on the road now. Most are men, younger than him, but there are women too. And children. His chest tightens. Families everywhere.

More cars. Shouts. Raised fists and fingers. The crowd keeps to the roadside as best they can. A car hit a woman yesterday. Hasan didn't see it but he heard the brothers under the Suzuki talking. He doesn't know what happened to her but hopes she kept walking.

He reaches the town square too parched to join another queue. He should have waited at the standpipe. He could have let the mother with the crying baby go ahead of him, but still waited. He pushes his way to the white van, keeping his head down, ashamed of his rudeness. It's reckless, too; he mustn't start a scuffle. Police trucks patrol the outer avenue and three officers stand on the town hall steps, shifting their weight.

The lists are in the van's windows but Hasan can't tell whether they're new or still there from yesterday. He scans them, peering over women and around men with children on their shoulders. His name is there, fourth sheet, second column. His face must register triumph because a policeman gestures him across the square towards a bus on the link road.

A blond family stands in the road, pointing and peering through the bus's dark windows. The father carries a girl of about five in his arms. She wears big yellow sunglasses. The bare-legged mother rests her hands on the handles of a pushchair. The baby has fat, pink cheeks. Hasan thinks the policeman has made fun of him and directed him to a tourist coach. But when he goes round the side of the bus, he sees three more policemen, arms linked, funnelling a crowd towards the steps.

A woman, holding a baby, sticks out her elbow to stop the child being crushed against the man in front. Her other arm reaches for the toddler by her side. There's a surge when the police let more people up the steps. The toddler trips over and cries out. Acting on a father's instinct, Hasan scoops up the child, but feels the boy go rigid in his arms. The woman's gaze darts to the policemen, but she doesn't call out. Instead she steps aside to let Hasan climb the steps in front of her and keeps her ashen face towards the child.

Hasan takes a window seat and puts the toddler on his lap. The woman hesitates in the aisle, but people want to get past so she sits down beside him with her younger baby on her knee.

"Hasan," he mumbles.

She looks away.

The bus gets stuffier as more people climb on and his head throbs with thirst. He takes two oranges from the string bag and offers one to the woman, but she doesn't take it. The toddler's big eyes blink at the fruit. Hasan puts both oranges away, feeling it would be cruel to eat in front of the child after the mother has declined the offering.

The bus judders when the engine starts. Every seat is taken, and the people having to stand grip where they can to keep their balance. Hasan closes his eyes, trying to shut out the smell of under-washed bodies, the angry shouts of passing drivers and the curious waves of the blond sightseers. The toddler falls asleep and his warm weight slumps against Hasan's chest. Hasan imagines he's holding Karam. But his boy is waiting with Rima in the first country they arrived in, where that government won't let him go to school.

As the bus joins the dual carriageway, Hasan stares out of the window. Tears—the first since the boat—bulge on his lower eyelids until they graze his cheeks. They catch on his lips, and their warm, salty taste makes him thirstier. He swallows and more tears fall.

Something taps his arm.

The woman is holding up a bottle of water. She pushes it towards him.

He takes the drink and nods a thank you.

For a moment the woman holds his gaze, her eyes watering. She nods too, then looks away.

---

Rachel Sargeant is a bestselling author of psychological thrillers and crime fiction. She loves reading in a range of genres and writes reviews of the books she's enjoyed on her monthly blog. She says: "I'm honoured to be included in this collection and hope you like my story and my character, Hasan. Even in the darkest times, small acts of kindness shine a light."

# SHEP'S MATE

*By Rob Parker*

Fin's favourite car was a VW T2 Camper Van, with tangerine flanks and a white trim. It still had all four wheels, which was nothing short of a miracle when one considered the terrain it was constantly pushed through. Crisp packets folded into bows, cigarette filters sucked to the quick, gnarled knobs of pork scratching and ash. Lots and lots of ash, which dusted Fin's fingers grey as he pushed his beloved car through all the obstacles on the floor of The Dog Inn. The bar stool legs were chicanes, his dad's booted feet the mountains and hills, their laces grasping snakes.

If Fin was honest, he was never happier than when he was playing on the floor of The Dog Inn, because if he was in there, playing on the floor, he knew exactly where his dad was. He wasn't out on the river, or at sea. He was on dry land, where Fin could see him. And in that knowledge, he felt sure and safe.

There was one thing Fin didn't like about The Dog Inn, however. One thing that made him wish that his dad would rather drink that smelly ale down at The Heron's Reach instead. And, as he pulled the T2 into a tight jack-knife turn around the downed husk of a dropped Quaver, he risked a glance up at it.

You couldn't hold eye contact with it for too long. Not according to the older men in the pub, who all had a story about Shep's Mate. They said that men had tried, tried their hardest to hold its gaze, but something within would always make you look away. Your nerves would give, or worse than that, you'd see something. Something, deep in those eyes, that you could never unsee.

At least that's what the old men said. The younger men, on the other hand, never talked about Shep's Mate, never gave it the time of day. And now, a further generation along, Fin found Shep's Mate both intoxicating and terrifying—so much so that he didn't dare look up, for fear of what he'd see.

Except for today.

He carried on his imitation of screeching brakes, so that his father wouldn't think anything was amiss, and catch him looking where he knew he shouldn't. But he looked up nevertheless, his eyes gliding slowly upwards towards the spot above the bar.

He found that Shep's Mate was looking straight at him, waiting for his gaze. And as their eyes met, Fin felt that buzz of dark mystery, of bleak spirits at play, and foul forces swirling that he couldn't see.

But he couldn't look away.

The eyes were flamed rings of amber around dead, unseeing inkwells.

The long snout finished on a black nose, painted to look wet as if belonging to the living.

The fur was off-white, almost yellow in parts, and Fin knew that was what happened to clean colours around cigarette smoke. They lost their lustre and went some kind of off.

And the horns, on top of the head, were twisted to points yet run through with ridges. They didn't match, one horn pointing higher than the other, which in itself was fatter and more stunted.

Fin knew that it was supposed to be a sheep, but he'd seen plenty of those, and none of them had ever looked like this.

And then he realised he'd gone quiet and wasn't doing his tyre screeching sound anymore. His Camper Van sat still on the floor between his knees.

'He can see you,' said a voice crusted and constricted by years of smoke and ale. 'Wherever you stand in this room, he can see you.'

Fin's head snapped to the source of the voice, which was a toad-shaped man in a faded blue shirt, a flat-cap with brown criss-cross lines on it, and cheeks the colour of past-ripe cherries. Fin had heard his father call him Muntjack, which Fin had heard before as the name of a kind of deer, not a person.

Muntjack, the man, smiled knowingly. 'How many times do you think they've tried to get rid of it?' he said. His voice was like fingers on baking paper, which was a sound that reminded him of his mother. It was one of the few things he remembered about her. Weekend pies and the smell of pastry browning in the kitchen. Fin looked wide-eyed at Muntjack and shook his head.

'To my knowledge, we've gone past four now,' the older man said.

Fin wasn't sure he should be hearing this, and he glanced at his dad. His father's face was still angled at the TV in the corner, horses surging on its screen, with a rolled-up copy of the Racing Post in one hand and that warm brown beer in the other.

'He's miles away,' Muntjack said, and Fin couldn't help but look back at the man. His eyes were wider now, as if he was sharing information of great importance. 'Four times bad things have happened in here, to someone or something in the pub. Four times they've thrown it in the river outside. And four times it floated back. He wants to be here, does Shep's Mate.'

Fin could feel his foundations wobble. Those formative rocks he had placed in his mind, upon which his understanding of the world now stood, were swaying. He looked up at the stuffed sheep's head near the ceiling. Malevolence now seemed to ooze from it, bestowing a black aura around it like a spurt of squid ink. Again, Fin found he couldn't break eye contact with it.

'Bad things?' he asked, his voice creeping out higher than usual.

'Landlord used to have a dog. Dog ran off, terrified of it. And you know what dogs are like, great judge of character.' Fin was shocked into stillness, but Muntjack only continued. 'Landlord said, in the days before dog ran off, that dog was constantly barking up at Shep's Mate. Like that thing up there was sending bad vibes down, and the dog had picked up on it. Apparently, the dog had never liked it, and it seems Shep's Mate up there didn't like it back.'

'What happened?' the boy whispered.

'Middle of the night, landlord hears the dog had come down into the bar and was whining and barking, and he thought it was an intruder. All landlord found when he got down here was an empty pub and Shep's Mate, staring at him. So he tore Shep's Mate down, and threw it in the river. Right outside, straight off the quay heading. Went looking for the dog, but couldn't find it anywhere. And Watersmeet isn't a big village. That dog knew everyone, and everyone knew that dog. No, that dog had run away for good, as far away as it could. Never seen again.'

Fin was frozen with horror, and felt himself falling into the glassy murk of the stuffed sheep's eyes. Felt evil pull at him, hypnotic and seductive. 'How did it come back?'

'Nobody really knows. But the landlord said when he came back from looking for his dog, he stood on the edge of the river, heartbroken. And as he looked down, there floating in the dinghy port was Shep's Mate, staring at him. So he bought it back inside. Something about the way that thing looked at him made him know. He had to bring it inside and put it back. Or worse things would happen.'

'Did that really all happen?'

'Why do you think this pub is called The Dog Inn?'

Fin still couldn't look away from the sheep's head, and found himself believing every word. But not only that, he was horrified to his core. The dinghy port was a short inlet off the river that led right up to the front of the pub, alongside the battered picnic tables that sat full of drinkers on sunny days. He and his dad used the dinghy port every day, boating being the easiest and quickest way to travel down from their caravan park home up-river. Fin had stared into the water of that inlet, just able to see the bottom in a gradually-solidifying cloud of silt, and couldn't help his mind for racing as to what might be down there.

The idea of that aged sheep's head floating in there, having been thrown away only to return, consumed him.

'Look at me,' said Muntjack and finally Fin looked away from the stuffed animal. The man's eyes were wide with enjoyment, yet sheened with something softer. 'You don't want to be looking too hard at Shep's Mate, lad. Bad things will be coming, you'll see.'

'Blast it!' came a voice from above, an explosion which punctured the tension in an instant. 'Always final furlong, always falling in the final furlong.'

The boots shuffled and reset by where Fin was sat, and he pulled his car out of the way so it wouldn't get crushed. He looked up, this time to see his father looking down at him. Fin knew his look well. Sad that a chance had gone, but hope still remained as there was always another race. They waited days like this, his dad hoping for the big winner to pull them up by their bootstraps. It just wasn't coming, no matter how hard Fin's father tried.

'Don't listen to that pillock,' his dad said. 'Full of fairy stories and nowt much else.'

That made Fin feel a little better, and he looked at Muntjack again, who was guzzling the dregs of his beer the way a grebe swallowed a fish—head back with a straight line from beak to gullet. 'And he drinks too much of the fizzy stuff to think straight half the time,' his dad added quietly.

Fin was soothed somewhat. At six, he found he could be swayed quite easily between panic and calm, influenced easily by a wild imagination given flight by plenty of time like this. Sat in pubs at his dad's feet with nothing much else to think about. He almost felt like smiling, because a smile would really go a long way to show his worries how silly they were.

Muntjack stood up, and looked less than perfect on his feet. 'See you tomorrow folks,' he said, before heading to the door—which he pulled open too quick, catching himself on the kneecap. He huffed, rubbed the joint and was gone.

The pub was quiet again in that midday-way that pubs get. It wasn't lunchtime, it wasn't teatime, the dockyards on the river hadn't kicked out yet, but you could sit quiet. That was Fin's favourite time. Quiet time, just him and his dad. He drank his beer, Fin played with his cars. They both knew just where the other was, and for them both, that seemed to be enough.

An engine was brought to life outside, banging and hollering is if it would rather do no such thing. 'He's not, is he?' Fin's dad said, looking around the bar for other patrons to share his surprise with, but they were alone. His dad sighed unhappily and folded his arms. 'I swear, one of these days he's going to—'

A gearbox screeched in the car park—just behind where the television sat in the corner, on which a jockey in blue leapt from a horse's back in triumph—before the entire wall collapsed and toppled, as a car sailed through it into the pub. Behind the wheel sat Muntjack, stunned, before Fin lost sight of him in a hail of brick and wood. The car kept going, and ploughed into the bar, which buckled immediately, before coming to rest under the optics and their overturned labels.

'Look out!' shouted Fin's dad, grabbing the boy and pulling him away, dragging him back towards the windows which overlooked the river just yards away from the glass. Masonry and horse brasses banged, clunked and clattered, as the wall of the pub and the bar was destroyed, an age-old Morris Minor having been unceremoniously inserted into it.

Fin's arms felt leaden, heavy, and his eyes couldn't take in what they were seeing. And there was a new sound that had only started since the crash. A hissing.

Fin's dad sniffed. 'Oh my god. He must have hit a gas line.' He dived at the wreckage, clawing at the bricks, and chunks of wood, to free Muntjack, who looked in a state of immovable shock. 'Get out!' shouted Fin's dad. A woman appeared on the other side of the wreckage, from the kitchen door. It was the lady who had poured Fin's lemonade. She also had that flop-jawed blankness that Fin supposed they all felt. All except for his dad, who was pulling Muntjack out of the seat.

'Gas leak!' he shouted. 'Go out the back, Shirley!' The woman was gone, the door swinging in her wake. 'Fin, get out into the car park, quick!'

Fin was torn. He hadn't collected his cars, and in the suddenness of the big vehicle crashing into the building, he'd lost sight of them.

'Now lad!' his father bellowed. Fin ran, his dad dragging Muntjack behind them, until they were out under the grey skies and even greyer tarmac of the car park. 'Good God, Muntjack, you could have killed us all,' said Fin's dad. Muntjack still couldn't seem to speak. Shirley joined them, but only for a moment to say: 'I'll get into the village, raise the alarm.'

'Good idea,' said Fin's dad.

Then, with a whump and an impact Fin would later remember as being shoved hard in the stomach, the entire front of the pub exploded. Chunks of brick and wood were vaulted high into the air, and rained into the trees and into the river. The tinkle of glass and metal took a long time to die down, and a column of black smoke began leaching upwards to the heavens like a fat worm.

Fin grabbed his dad's hand, and felt his father squeeze back.

Hours later, as dusk hunkered down over the river, and the fire had been put out, Fin and his dad were still at what was left of the pub. It was destroyed, a mere shell of a building, barely a wall still standing. Nothing was left of the bar, nor where Fin had sat with his father.

While his father was interviewed by the police—who Fin had been initially fascinated with until he realised they were really just here to ask questions while the firefighters did the really good stuff—Fin watched and let the weight of what had happened hit him, and find a place to sit in his own personal history.

They had nearly died. If his dad hadn't been so quick, they surely would have. Muntjack too. His dad was getting slaps on the back from people in attendance, including the nosey souls who'd come down from the village for a look—and he deserved every one.

But Fin was sad, their survival of something so incredible tanged with the bittersweet. Because he liked sitting in this pub. And all his cars had been in the pub when it all went to pieces.

He wandered around the charred frame of the building, trying to get a look at what was left of the floor, wondering if his cars were somehow untouched on the carpet. But he couldn't see a thing. Everything was burnt and broken.

As he walked around the edge of the picnic tables, themselves upended now like four-legged animals that couldn't right themselves, he heard a soft ripple of water, a splash almost too quiet to hear. He looked into the river.

There was something bobbing on the surface in the dinghy port. Something dark and scraggly.

Finn was upset. He hated things happening to animals. He'd seen enough dead ducks and birds on the river, and each time it had turned his stomach to heavy sadness. He worried that this animal had been hurt in the explosion, and that not everybody had been saved after all.

He moved closer—and his heart turned to stone, his knees suddenly liquid.

The fur was scorched, singed and burnt, but the shape was unmistakable. One of the horns was bent at an even more absurd angle and one of the eyes was missing, but Fin couldn't look away from the one that remained. It had lost its wooden mount, but that didn't seem to matter.

It was unmistakeably Shep's Mate.

Fin wanted to scream. Wanted to shout until his lungs could offer no more.

But then he noticed that the sheep's mouth was open. And something was inside it, glinting beyond the bared teeth in the car park lights. He leaned forward, until the flow of the river shifted the obscene head and rolled it enough for Fin to see exactly what was in its jaws.

He fell backwards onto the ground.

Shep's Mate was gripping in its jaws his very favourite, tangerine-flanked VW T2 Camper Van—and all the while, that one remaining lifeless eye bored into him, deep as his soul would go.

---

Rob Parker is a married father of three, who lives in Warrington, UK. The author of the Ben Bracken thrillers, *Crook's Hollow* and the Audible bestseller *Far From The Tree*, he enjoys a rural life, writing horrible things between school runs. Rob writes full time, attends various author events across the UK, and boxes regularly for charity. He spends a lot of time in schools across the North, encouraging literacy, story-telling and creative-writing, and somehow squeezes in time to co-host the For Your Reconsideration film podcast, appear regularly on The Blood Brothers Crime Podcast, and is a member of the Northern Crime Syndicate.

# UNFORGETTABLE

*By Rob Scragg*

Nothing prepares you for losing a parent. They're one of life's constants from the moment we're born. Our earliest memories are anchored to them. Futures shaped by them. There comes a point for all of us though, where we're expected to carry on without them. Whenever it comes, however it happens, slow or fast, illness or accident, nobody is truly ready. Mum's decline was like watching the first rise and fall of a rollercoaster. A slow crawl towards the tipping point, inexorable, unavoidable. Then her Alzheimer's crested, started manifesting in a dozen tiny things. A forgotten phone number. A hob left lit. It picked up pace, dragging her down with the weight of it, stripping away the woman who raised me, a layer at a time, leaving a shell behind who struggled to recognise her own daughter, and eventually, not even that, her memories lost like tears in the rain.

I open up her wardrobe, see the outfits that she'll never wear again. Reach out, running my fingers through the furry collar of her favourite coat, blinking back tears that I know will have to be let out eventually. Not now though. Not yet. Dad needs me to be strong, now more than ever. I nearly lost it this morning when I saw him fill up at the thought of going through her things. Watching his face dissolve into a cobweb of creases as he swallowed his own tears was almost too much to bear. I'll force myself through this for him, no matter how much it hurts.

The shelf above is lined with shoes, toes square with the edge, neat pairs in colour order. A rainbow line-up of footwear from left to right, black to white, and most colours in between. No prizes for guessing where my OCD tidiness comes from. I pull them down, placing them carefully in the cardboard box by my feet, wondering who might be wearing them this time next week.

I go up on tip-toes, like a ballet dancer on pointe, craning my neck to check nothing has escaped the cull, when I see it, pushed right up against the back panel. A rectangular shape; a book? An album? I reach in, pulling it towards me, blinking away dust that swirls around it in the sunlight like a blizzard, as it scrapes over the edge. My fingers slip, just for a moment, and it falls, bouncing against my chest. Not a book. A box. The lid flies off as it hits the floor, contents spilling out. I mutter a few words Mum would definitely not approve of, crouch down to pick them up, but my hand stops before I touch the first item, shooting back up like it's strung with elastic, hand covering my mouth.

I lower myself gently into a cross-legged position, into the eye of a hurricane of memories. All around me are scattered old photos, scrawled notes that a five-year old me had written to Mum, covered in hearts and kisses. Faded photos from holidays I can barely remember. A trio of black Moleskine notebooks poke out from underneath, elastic band biting into the leather covers. As I pull them towards me, I feel like an intruder. What if they're her diaries? The idea of sifting through her clothes was bad enough but her innermost thoughts might be too much to bear.

My forehead tightens, creased with uncertainty like the spine of a book, as I pop off the band, opening the cover of the first one. Two seconds later and I'm smiling. Not a trove of secrets, but treasure of a different kind. Mum's spidery writing crawls across pages as I flick through. Not a diary, more of a brain dump. Poems I don't recognise; her own work, or just ones that had caught her eye? Scribbled anecdotes, fragments of family history. I turn the pages so carefully, holding them gently as you would butterfly wings.

I drink in her words, every page like a time capsule. The one that breaks me is at the front of the second book. A list of present ideas for their silver wedding anniversary. A quarter century of unconditional love, more if you count the three years dating before they married. The day itself was a month ago, exactly a week before she died. How long ago had she written this? Had she known then that she'd not even recognise Dad, let alone the occasion, when it came? He'd spent the full day by her hospital bed, talking softly to her about how they'd met, trips they'd taken, never giving up hope, looking for one more flicker of recognition in her eyes that never came.

I screw my eyes tight shut, feel the warm tears matting my eyelashes together, and jerk my head back as the first few race down my cheeks, missing the pages by millimetres. I sit like that for a time, staccato breathing between sobs gradually slowing. When I feel like there's no more to come, I drag my palms across wet cheeks. One loud snotty sniff like a kid coming out the other side of a tantrum.

The last book sits unopened, daring me to look inside. As much as that last one hurt, whatever is inside is still part of Mum, linked to a previous version of her, the person she was before Alzheimer's wiped her out like a wet rag across a blackboard, and I cling to that, to the real her.

Something flutters out as I open the cover, a scrap of paper falls like a leaf, torn edge and faded ink, older than the book itself. I scan the first few lines, and can't help but smile. It's the perfect antidote for how I'm feeling. A recipe, a handwritten list of ingredients to what she called her special beef stew. She used to joke about this being part of my inheritance, family secret passed from mother to daughter, but I've not even thought about it, let alone seen it in years. It was the first thing she ever cooked for Dad, back when they were dating; the dish he's had every anniversary since I can remember.

I tuck it back inside the notebook, gather up the rest of the spilled contents, and place them carefully back in the box. How will Dad react to these fragments of her life? He's never been one to talk about how he's feeling, but lately it's written all over his face. Fresh lines carved deep in his forehead, and a thousand-yard stare, looking back into the past, happier times.

Canned laughter from an afternoon sit-com drifts from the living room as I head downstairs, box held tightly in both hands. I watch him through the crack in the door, unaware he's being spied on. Seems as if he's looking through the TV rather than at it. What I'd give to see him smile again. Last one I remember was months back, the last time Mum called me by my name. There must be a combination of words somewhere that can get through to him, cut through his pain and make him remember he's still alive. I stand like that for a full minute before the idea hits me, and the smile creeps across my face, melting away the blues.

'Just popping to the shops Dad. You need anything?'

His head jerks towards the door, snapping out of his trance.

'Hmm? No, no thank you, sweetheart.'

My trip to Tesco is more of a trolley dash, notebook clutched in one hand, trolley steered with the other, and I'm back at Dad's in less than half an hour. He hasn't moved from his seat, and I pop my head around the door.

'Just going to put the tea on Dad.'

'Ah, you don't have to go to any trouble' he says, twisting round, making as if to get up.

'No trouble, honestly,' I tell him. 'You stay there. It's a surprise.'

He pauses, looks confused, lost even, but slumps back into his chair. It's like he's been cast adrift, ambling through each day, but I'm hoping what I have in mind might jump-start him. Make him see that remembering what's gone before doesn't have to be sad. Better to have had the good times to look back on, than nothing worth remembering.

I head into the kitchen, shopping bags rustling as I set them down. Piling everything next to the cooker reminds me of the neat stacks we used to take into school for Harvest Festival; tins stacked up like they're ready to be knocked down at a fairground. Splashes of colour in the fresh ingredients. Fiery red peppers, dirty orange sweet potatoes in stark contrast to the brightness of the carrots.

I've been vegetarian since I was eight years old, and I've never tasted, let alone made, a beef stew before, but how hard can it be with her to guide me? I slide the recipe sheet out, setting it to one side, and set about bringing her words to life.

There's something about the rhythm of cooking that's hypnotic, cathartic. Strips of skin peel from the potatoes like stripping wallpaper, and the knife beats out a metronomic sharp snick against the glass chopping board. Carrots and peppers follow suit. I line a casserole dish with a multi-coloured bed of diced chunks, saving the onions till last, but now I'm smiling through blurred eyes as I peel, chop and dice.

Next is the meat. I drizzle a pool of olive oil in the pan, watching bubbles start to form. Cubes of steak hiss in protest as they slap against the hot oil, and I realise that even though I've never tasted the dish before, it's not just a recipe. It's a time machine, scents and sounds taking me back to when Mum was still around, still herself.

The rich purplish-red of the beef fades to brown, and I tip it, juices and all onto the veg, then drown the lot with a jug of steaming hot beef stock and a glass of red wine. When I get to the seasoning, Mum's writing has faded in parts, and I almost use tablespoons, not teaspoons, narrowly avoiding adding enough salt to stop an elephant's heart. There's enough veg left over to do a smaller version for me, the two side by side on the oven shelf reminding me of the Three Bears porridge, except without the mummy bear.

By the time I close the door and set the timer, I notice that the window has fogged up. I know I shouldn't, but can't help myself, and press a finger to the glass, squeaking the curves of a heart, finishing it off with Mum's name in the centre. It'll have faded by the time dinner's ready. No harm done.

Dad is snoozing when I go through. No sense waking him yet, and for the first time when I look at him, I see an old man. The last six months have worn him down, like waves against a cliff. Something you don't notice day to day, but over time, the changes happen. I lose myself in mindless TV until the timer on the oven chirps. Even as a vegetarian I have to admit it smells pretty good as I slide the dish out. Once it's plated up, I give Dad's shoulder a gentle rock, and his eyes snap open.

'Just resting my eyes love,' he mumbles, getting up slowly to join me at the table.

He stops a few feet away, clocking what's for dinner, and looks over at me.

'Is that what I think it is?' he asks, voice thick with emotion, eyes glistening.

My throat feels tight, as if it's closing up, and I nod. We both stand for a few seconds before he breaks the spell, shuffling to the table.

'Why…I mean, how did you…'

I tell him about the box, and everything I found, promising we can look through it together after dinner if he wants, so he doesn't have to sift through it alone. He nods, picks up his fork, stares at the plate for what seems like an age, then stabs a chunk of beef and carrot, chewing slowly. I scoop up a forkful of my own, and when I look back at him, my heart breaks.

Tears run down his cheeks, a handful splashing into his stew as he swallows the mouthful. The fork shakes, rattling against the side of his plate as he sets it down.

'Dad? What is it?'

He shakes his head, sitting back in his chair with a loud sigh. 'Nothing love, I'm all right.'

'What's wrong?' I say, reaching across, placing my hand on his. 'It's the stew, isn't it? Sorry, I should have told you what I was doing. I know it's not as good as Mum's, but I just thought...'

I'm crying as well now. How could I be so stupid, upsetting him like this? He clamps his other hand on top, sandwiching mine in between.

'It's perfect love. Bit different from your Mum's, but perfect.'

'How can it be perfect if it's different?' He's buttering me up now. I've messed up his favourite meal, and he's trying to spare my feelings.

A slow smile creeps across his face, the first I've seen in a while, and he pats my hand. 'Your mother was a wonderful woman, god rest her soul, but she couldn't cook to save her life. Used to drown everything in salt. I'm amazed I've outlasted her to be honest.'

I stare at him, see the smile widening as one of my own starts to break through. Looks like Mum was more a fan of tablespoons than teaspoons after all.

'But, you loved her cooking,' I say, not sure what else to come back with.

'I loved her. First time she cooked that for me, I nearly spat it out, it was so salty, but you should have seen the look on her face. Beaming with pride she was,' he says, and I can see the shift in his expression, as he pictures that moment, nearly three decades ago. 'Would have broken her heart if I'd said anything other than I loved it. Couldn't do that to her now, could I?'

We both stand, and as he pulls me in close, laughing our way through the tears, I know that we'll be alright. Mum will live on in moments like this, and a hundred others to come. It's okay to feel sad. Missing her is just a side effect of having so many happy memories.

Growing up, I've always known my parents were in love, but it's only now that I truly understand the magnitude of what that means. It's not the grand gestures that define it. It's the little things, things that sometimes go unnoticed, that set it apart as unconditional. The little things make us human.

---

Robert Scragg had a random mix of jobs before taking the dive into crime writing; he's been a bookseller, pizza deliverer, Karate instructor and Football coach. He lives in Tyne & Wear, is a founding member of the Northern Crime Syndicate crime writers group and winner of the Lindisfarne Prize for Crime Fiction 2021. For a full list of upcoming events and more info about Robert and his books, visit www.robertscragg.com.

# CHRYSANTHEMUMS

*By S.E. Lynes*

Whenever I see chrysanthemums, I think of Jimena.

When I was a child, we lived in Rome for several years. My father was a diplomat and my mother was what people called then a housewife, what we now call a stay-at-home mum. In reality, she didn't stay at home much at all, taken up as she was with her charity work, her tennis ladder, the many social events with my father, and her lunch and afternoon tea clubs with the other embassy wives. Despite the fact we didn't see my mother and father often, they were keen to impress upon us the importance of good citizenship, charity and kindness.

We lived in a large apartment, provided by the embassy, in the most salubrious area of the city. Our neighbourhood lay immediately north of the Villa Borghese, a huge park which stretched all the way to the Piazza del Popolo in the historic centre. The most expensive apartments were on the higher floors because they got the most light; in the basement, where there was no light at all, lived the caretakers, who did things like call the lift company if the lift broke down or change blown lightbulbs in the stairwell.

Our apartment was on the fifth floor. It had high coved ceilings, dark shiny parquet floors, and walls the colour of vanilla cream. The living area was so vast that my twin brothers and I used to roller skate around it when my mother wasn't home. There were two balconies, one of which overlooked the Vatican. We would often eat dinner there and watch the sun set pink over the famous cupola. My father told us that when a pope died, the Vatican would send a smoke signal from the roof. I remember I was always looking, watching for smoke. There were three bedrooms in our apartment: one for my parents, one for me, and one for the twins. A further room, beside the screeching lift shaft in the central atrium, had a narrow bed, a small built-in wardrobe and its own shower cubicle. Inside the shower cubicle was a toilet, which at the time my siblings and I found hilarious. This room was for the maid.

Most people in our area had live-in maids. Maids who also looked after children were called 'tatas'. Our tata was called Jimena and she was from Venezuela. The 'J' was pronounced 'H'. Because neither of my parents were at home much due to their good and charitable works, we spent most of our time with Jimena. Jimena would pick us up from school and we would call at the bakery where she would buy fresh warm bread and tear off chunks for us to eat as we made our way up the hill to our home. Jimena took us to swimming and tennis lessons, and to the park or the zoo on sunny afternoons. I would have been ten or so at the time, my brothers about eight. She always laughed at our antics and told us we were clever and well-behaved. The children looked after by the other tatas were nowhere near as clever and well-behaved as us, she said. She was as proud of us as if she were our real mother, and I confess that sometimes I wished she were.

As well as listening to our stories from school as if they were the most scintillating anecdotes she'd ever heard, Jimena would tell us her own funny stories about her husband who slept on a camp bed in the garage where he worked as a mechanic, and about her children back home in South America, who lived with her mother. It was strange for me to think that her children lived with their grandma because my grandparents on my father's side were dead, and we had only met my mother's parents once when I was very small. Once, when I was sitting on a park bench with Jimena, she dug out a photograph of her children for me to see. Her children were standing by a rope swing in the sun and they looked just like her. Jimena kissed the photograph three times before putting it back in her purse, which she then patted softly against her wide hip.

When we went to the park, Jimena let us wear our older, comfy clothes and never shouted if we ripped the knees or got them dirty. She always brought snacks like rice biscuits or red pizza which she carried in a bright pink cloth knapsack with rainbow coloured embroidery. If we fell over, she cuddled us; she tickled us out of our bad tempers, made steam basins that smelled of eucalyptus when we were blocked up with a cold. Sometimes, late in the evening, if we couldn't settle, she would sit on the floor outside our bedrooms and sing to us in Spanish. I would lie awake determined to decipher the meaning of the words but would wake up the next day with no recollection of drifting off to sleep.

On Sundays, when we went out with my mother and father, we wore our smart clothes. They would take us to one of the many elegant cafés where we would eat apricot jam tart and drink hot chocolate while they sipped cappuccino and read the newspapers. This was our treat. We were allowed to read our books, but we would get told off for kicking each other under the table, for making chocolate foam moustaches and for giggling. Sometimes we would dine in fine restaurants with white tablecloths and my father would make us try new and strange foods like oysters or artichokes, which we knew better than to refuse. On these evenings, we always went out so late that often, I had gone past the point of eating and longed to go to bed, though I never said this to my parents—just as I never confessed to hating artichokes.

One day, my mother was at home attending to her correspondence at the far end of the apartment. Jimena was helping my brothers get changed out of their uniforms to go to the park. They were giggling, shoving each other, and messing about like boys do.

'Children,' my mother called from her desk, in English. 'Can you keep it down?'

But one of the twins had put both feet into one leg of his tracksuit bottoms. I think he had done it on purpose, for comedy, and by now, all of us were laughing, including Jimena. When Jimena laughed, her shoulders shook and her whole faced folded into itself; her eyes became no more than slits and tears would roll down her chubby cheeks. This in turn made us laugh even more.

'*Ay, ay, ay*,' she said, shaking her head. '*Ay, Señor* mio.'

A shadow fell across us. I looked up to see my mother glaring down. Jimena dropped to her knees, suddenly silent and serious, and began trying to help my brother out of his trousers so he could put them on properly.

'Jimena,' my mother said in the harsh tone she used on us when we misbehaved. She spoke too fast for me to understand everything—as a family, we communicated in basic Italian with Jimena—but I caught words like 'scandalous' and 'trying to work' and was able to pick up the broader meaning, which was that if Jimena couldn't control us she would be '*fuori per strada*'—out on the street.

A hot feeling filled me. My mother's face was red with rage, her features small and spiteful. I had seen her with the other embassy wives when they came to our apartment for book club or for afternoon teas and knew instinctively that she would never speak to them like this. With them, she was always polite and would laugh in a high, tinkly way. It occurred to me in that moment for the first time that, with Jimena, she had a different way of speaking altogether—unsmiling and formal, never laughing. But she had not shouted at her before.

Once my mother had walked away—heels click, click, clicking on the parquet—Jimena, the twins and I got ready in whispers. I could not look directly at Jimena, but out of the corner of my eye, I could see her cheeks were aflame, her eyes shining with tears, and even though she was being playfully bossy, her voice trembled. Without disturbing my mother a second time, we crept out of the apartment and went to the park as we usually did. Jimena still smiled and told us we were clever and well-behaved, the best children in the neighbourhood. She still laughed and clapped her hands at our gymnastics or heroic feats of climbing on the wooden castle, and still gave us snacks from her bright pink knapsack with the coloured embroidery.

Later, on our way back from the park, we bumped into my father. He was on his way home from work, dressed in a smart grey suit and he looked tall and important. When he saw us, he smiled and told Jimena that he was going to take us for a fruit juice at the bar and that she was free to go. It must have been a Wednesday because on Wednesdays, Jimena had the evening off, and she would go and see her husband.

Opposite the bar, there was a florist's stall on the corner. The man there always said hello to us and, as we passed, I saw he was packing up for the day.

'*Ciao belli*,' he called to us three children.

'*Ciao*,' we replied.

'*Buona sera, Signor*,' he said, nodding to my father, who returned his greeting and smiled.

The man picked up a beautiful bunch of bright red flowers and held them out to me.

'*Signorina*,' he said, bowing low. '*Per te*.'

'*Grazie*,' I said, taking the flowers from him and flushing to the roots of my hair.

My father thanked the man too and told him he was '*molto carino*'—very kind. I waved goodbye, my cheeks still hot with pleasure.

In the bar, my father told me the flowers would have been thrown away anyway as they were not fresh enough to sell tomorrow, but I still loved them and still thought it was kind of the florist to give them to me. My father asked the barista how he was and ordered a beer for himself and peach juice in little green bottles for us. While he shook hands and chatted with the other customers, always smiling and friendly, my brothers and I drank our juice through our straws, careful not to slurp the last drops from the bottom. Later, as we stepped out of the bar, my father took my hand.

'In life,' he said, his forefinger pointing up to the sky, 'it's important to be able to speak easily to prince and beggar alike.'

I nodded, though I didn't fully understand what he meant, only that it had given me an uneasy feeling in my belly.

A little way along the street, I saw Jimena heading towards us. She had changed into her lime green dress and was wearing her red flower clip in her shiny black hair. I ran ahead to greet her.

'*Ciao Jimena!*'

'*Ciao Principessa!*'—hello princess.

She gave me her beautiful broad smile and I remembered how upset she'd been because of my mother. I thought about how she always laughed, always had snacks, and always told us we were the best-behaved of all the children. I looked at the flowers in my hands and knew that Jimena would trim their stems and put sugar into the water and that she would not think they would no longer be good tomorrow.

Before I knew what I was doing, I had thrust the bunch towards her.

'*Per te*,' I said.

Her brow furrowed; her hand clapped flat across her chest. But when I insisted the flowers were for her, she accepted them, pulled me to her with her free arm and squeezed me tight.

'*Grazie, Tesoro*,' she said when she'd released me, clasping the bunch in both her hands.

Her eyes were wet like before but this time she was smiling. The red of the flowers matched the clip in her hair. She told me the flowers were called chrysanthemums and that they were her favourite.

I suppose my brothers and my father must have caught us up; I can't remember anything more about that day. But I never forgot that moment. It might seem like nothing, like I simply gave some out-of-date flowers to my tata—so, what?—but that's not the way it was at all. Even now, fifty years later, I find it difficult to explain. It wasn't an act of kindness—of that I am sure. The fact is, I didn't want to part with my beautiful flowers. It was more like a flash, a flash of something that came from outside of me. The nearest I can get is that I knew in that moment, without any doubt, that the flowers were never intended for me; it was simply my job to keep hold of them until their purpose became clear.

About five years ago, after my father died, I repaired my estranged relationship with my mother. At the time, I believed I had done this in the spirit of forgiveness and compassion in order to be with her at her life's fragile and lonely end. But as I watch these carefully chosen red blooms descend into the earth on the top of her Italian oak coffin, it occurs to me that my final tenderness towards her came from somewhere out of understanding's grasp, that it wasn't out of duty, or kindness, but that it had more to do with Jimena and that moment on the street with the chrysanthemums.

---

S.E. Lynes is the Amazon #1 bestselling author of dark psychological thrillers *The Housewarming, Valentina, Can You See Her?* Her latest novel, *Her Sister's Secret* is out now. A former BBC Producer, she has lived in France, Spain, Scotland and Italy and is now settled in Greater London. After completing her MA, S E Lynes taught creative writing at Richmond Adult Community College for ten years. She now combines writing, mentoring and lecturing in Richmond Borough. For an author who specialises in writing about the darker side of life, *Everyday Kindness* is a real change, and she is thrilled to be part of this anthology.

# SVARVERKJÆR

*By Shelley Day*

Long long ago, in the thick dark forest that covers the steep rocky slope on the edge of the village of Rørholt in Telemark, there stood a small wooden house by the name of *Svarverkjær*. The forest, with its trees of spruce and pine, larch and birch and rowan; its undergrowth of juniper, so sweetly scented; its summer edges of harebells, raspberries, heather and fine fine grasses, and ferns as bright and fresh and green as you have seen; its autumn clumps of *blåbær* and *tyttebær* and a hundred different kinds of mushroom, this forest was home to *Svarverkjær* and the forest kept the house safe and that's how things were and that's how they had always been.

The little wooden house had been made many years ago by an old old man, a man who had always been old and who would always be old, a man who had lived all his long long life in the forest. He worked with the trees and he made his living from the trees; and the trees, in their turn, were kind to him and allowed him to fashion out of them such lovely things, and one of the loveliest things was the little wooden house which was his home and which he painted white and which he named *Svarverkjær*.

When the time came for the old man to stop being old, he went away; he went away and he left the little white house standing alone on the rocky hill in the forest where it had always stood.

Very soon after the old man had gone, the forest trees realised that a new freedom was theirs and they determined to take advantage of it. They allowed their young to take root willy-nilly all over the place and get into tangles. The cherry trees delighted in dropping their fruit anywhere and everywhere across the once-proud grassy paddock. The ash trees grew far bigger than they ought and dared creep closer in, bending and stooping and tap-tap-tapping their thinnest branches at the cobwebbed glass of the little windows of the house and peering in.

The stream that once trickled so sedately down the sloping *kve* from the deep dark well began to gush noisily, this way and that, any way it pleased, and at times it decided to cease its gush altogether and to make the well dry. The pond allowed its water to rise and fall without reason or warning; it invited so many rushes to live round its edges, and ferns, and even some wild roses, and sometimes you couldn't see its water at all. Ditches clogged themselves up with mud and silt; stones fell in and couldn't get back out, causing floods every time the rains came. And the track that leads up from the *Tokevann* to *Svarverkjær* all but disappeared under determined wiry grasses and sedges in the damper places. This is what happened after the old man went away and all these things made *Svarverkjær* feel quite gloomy and neglected.

But as the years passed, *Svarverkjær* survived and he learned to live by himself, he learned a new contentment in the movement of the seasons, he came to understand how new things come along to take the place of the old. Each year he noticed something new going awry, but he also observed how new solutions appeared, as if by miracle, as if by magic. One year, for example, when his chimney stack crumbled with the weight of the snow and the ice sneaked into the finest of cracks and fractured them open, no sooner had the chimney stack fallen than a pair of hooded crows moved in and made the ruin their home. They piled their nest high with twigs and sticks and pieces of bracken and kept themselves safe in the old chimney to raise a family of four.

It has been a long hot summer. And still, so still, the air so still, as though time herself had stopped to ponder; everything so very still, through the months of long warm days that stretched into nights and nothing moved. Now it's autumn, and the sun crosses the sky lower down and more quickly, spreading her evening pink across the *Tokevann*, she watches the dew gather on the tips of the grass, she follows the shadows as they climb up the bumpy track and into the woods and up to the pond and beyond until there are shadows all around the little house of *Svarverkjær*. The autumn mornings are softened by an early mist that rises as the warmth of the earth and water meets cooler descending air. When the sun nudges the tops of the tallest pines over there in the distance, the mist will retreat and wait for its turn again in the morning.

It is late September. A bee buzzes about its business, anxious to get finished before the long cold spell arrives and makes everything sharp. A chaffinch chirrups in the cherry tree. Rivalrous blackbirds keek-keek-keek at each other under the apple trees, each trying to get at the best of the pickings. A pair of magpies struts along the ridge of the old red barn. In the woods, a jay watches; a woodpecker hammers, demanding insects. A buzzard circles on currents high above the wild rocks at the top on the mountain, and mews. *Svarverkjær* listens, hears the mice scratching among his rafters, scuttling busy inside his walls; they too are fetching and carrying their stores for the winter. Bats, lined up in the loft, hang upside down, waiting for dusk to bring out the moths.

Dusk, in the autumn: this is the time when the sun settles down behind the shadows, the time for the Elk to come. The Elk will come to the orchard to enjoy the apples that drop from the trees and which no-one picks, not anymore, not since the old man went away. As the sun edges down behind the tall birches that stand on the hill to the west, *Svarverkjær* watches and waits anxiously for the Elk. A great lumbering animal, the Elk will nevertheless manage to arrive in silence. He'll stop by the pond and lift his great head, he'll sniff the air before bending to take a long drink of the cool clear water.

*Svarverkjær*, waiting, must have dozed—he's getting old, more easily tired—and dusk is already closing in when he wakes to the sound of the cracking of twigs and the soft thud-thud of apples dropping to the grass. He knows at once that the Elk had arrived. *Svarverkjær* looks out over the orchard, sees the Elk reaching up into the branches of the furthest tree with his great head, watches how he takes one old bough after another in his soft mouth and moves it lazily this way and that until, one after another, the ripened apples fall to the ground. The house watches as the Elk nudges his nose among the fallen apples, selects a good one and eats, his jaw moving from side to side as he chews. *Svarverkjær* watches for more than an hour as the Elk eats the apples one by one.

The Elk was late coming this year, later than usual, and *Svarverkjær* had worried he would not come at all. Then, when he finally arrived, it seemed to *Svarverkjær* that the Elk moved more slowly, that his gait was a little more stooped, his steps less certain. An outsider would see an elk, a plain old elk, a large one to be sure, male, getting on in years, his seniority indicated by the ten-pointed antlers proudly displayed on a head held high. But to *Svarverkjær*, who had watched and who had waited and who knew how everything has been and how it should be, the change in the Elk stirred something inside him, gave rise to thoughts in his bowel that would not go away.

He's like me, *Svarverkjær* thought, we're one of a kind, we're getting old. The old Elk is slowing up, as sure as the autumn slows everything up, as sure as we all gather ourselves up for the long cold winter.

And yet it seemed to *Svarverkjær* to have been not so very long ago when the Elk had been in his prime: brave and proud and strong, he'd stood two meters to the shoulder, he'd moved through the forest with a power, with a certainty of his high head, he'd stepped out with the confidence of an undisputed ruler. And he'd bellowed, how that Elk had bellowed! *Svarverkjær* can almost hear it from across the years, that bellow, the depth of it, the resonance, the message it carried right across the forest: this Elk is the King around these parts, and he intends for things to stay that way. And *Svarverkjær* didn't mind admitting how he himself had swelled with pride to hear the Elk—*his* Elk—claiming rulership of the forest at the very peak of his greatness; yes, all that, not so very long ago.

But greatness, thinks *Svarverkjær*, greatness is a passing state that one day will lose its significance and, at that stage, will readily be handed on.

And indeed the Elk had fathered many wild keen youngsters who now roamed the forest and who, each year, grew more proud, more strong; and all were looking to take their places, ready to fight for the top position.

*Svarverkjær* is still watching the Elk in the orchard as darkness closes in.

Yes, he is thinking, time moves on, and time moves us on. We must move with it or be left behind.

*Svarverkjær*'s roof creaked agreement; his walls creaked too, and the mice shuffled under his floorboards. In the darkness, the trees in the forest swayed and whispered.

Everything changes, thought *Svarverkjær*, it all changes as surely as the clouds dash across the sky in the autumn winds, as surely as the sun hides herself behind them, as surely as the moon rises and swells in the winter darkness and stills the long nights into silence.

This year, the apple crop had not been so good. As can be the way with apples, one tree had not produced any fruit at all but had remained defiantly barren, a warning that the winter would be a harsh one. The Elk would need as much food as he could get to keep him strong for the time when the bleak winds blow in from the north and the big snows arrive and settle for months on end, covering all the trees and making their branches dip, coating the ground and freezing up the *Tokevann*. The days would soon be very short, the nights long and so very cold.

Yes, the Elk needed to build up all his strength for the winter which would come soon enough, *Svarverkjær* knew. The winter would come quickly on the tails of the first frost that would change the colours of the birches, rowan and ash completely and make their leaves rustle and fall. The light would change and the sky would change and the trees would sway and lash and their leaves come landing damp and brown to the earth till the branches were stripped bare enough to resist the winter.

It pleased *Svarverkjær* to watch the plants and the birds and the animals around him preparing for the winter. The leaves of the *blåbær* reddened, and those of the shy tiny *tyttebær* smiled up before they thinned and fell; the heather too, its purple flowers curled dry and brown, hugged itself closer to the earth for shelter. The mushrooms took their final chance and swelled quick and huge, ripening proudly for the last time before their underground retreat from the dark cold months. The woodland creatures, the voles and the mice and the weasel, the polecat and the little red squirrel worked night and day with the help of the *Nisser-people* to gather up stores to last them through the snow-time. Toads and frogs and newts and salamanders crawled out from their watery homes and made for sheltered places in soft moss, among stones, piles of warm leaves and under fallen logs on the forest's edge.

*Svarverkjær* watched all these creatures; they knew what they were doing, he knew they would cope with the winter. Big forest owls screeched when darkness came; they too knew how to look after themselves. Many of the smaller birds had gathered themselves into flocks a month ago and made off to warmer places where they would stay until the snows melted at *Svarverkjær* and spring came once again. All these plants and animals knew how to look after themselves. It was only the Elk that *Svarverkjær* was worried about.

Darkness had long closed in but *Svarverkjær* was unable to rest. High winds from the North were beginning to bring icy cold; he tensed as they blew angrily round his walls, as they battled round and round, seemingly determined to get in. *Svarverkjær*'s walls shuddered as they resisted, they groaned their warnings for the wind to come no closer. But *Svarverkjær* knew nothing could withstand the real onslaught of winter and the great blasts of frozen air that would chill him to the core. He could rattle and shake his windows and his walls all he liked in protest, but to no avail; the wind was relentless. Winter was almost on the doorstep. The mice scampered and scratched to hide themselves in warmer places.

Wide-awake that long cold night, *Svarverkjær* knew the Elk had not gone back to the forest to sleep after his feed as he should have done. He had not returned to his mossy bed among the sweet-smelling juniper; he was still out there, in the orchard, where he'd been since dusk. He'll be freezing, thought *Svarverkjær*, freezing out there, in the orchard, standing by himself, in this wind.

But *Svarverkjær* had no way of helping the Elk. All he could do was to wait anxiously for dawn to open the dark into lightness so he could see across to the orchard and observe the Elk and make sure everything was alright. But the winter nights in Rørholt are long and they don't easily give up their thick black cloaks. *Svarverkjær* waited anxiously for dawn to show her pale face.

As dawn drew closer, *Svarverkjær* could just make out the Elk still standing under the apple trees. But the Elk was not at rest, he kept twisting round, nudging at his flank with his nose, and he wasn't taking any of his weight on his back leg on that side. Observing this, *Svarverkjær* knew that the Elk had been injured; there'd been a fight and he'd suffered an injury. He's been replaced, *Svarverkjær* knew at once; this is what happens. There's been a fight and a younger contender has taken over the top position in the forest. There's no future for this Elk, thought *Svarverkjær* sadly. The only future for this Elk is at the end of the barrel of a hunter's gun, his head and his fine fine antlers will go for a hunter's trophy.

*Svarverkjær* could hardly bear the thought of it, the thought that his magnificent Elk would end his days as hunter's meat, tracked down and chased through the forest, the very thought of it made *Svarverkjær* quake with grief and anger.

*Svarverkjær* had known this Elk for many years, for as many years as the Elk had been coming to *Svarverkjær*. The Elk and the little house had known and watched each other since the Elk was just a calf, a little suckling calf with big floppy ears and a hopeful face. He'd come with his mother, wobbling along on his gangly legs, up the track to *Svarverkjær*, to visit the old man. True, the old man had allowed the hunters through his forest, but for a reason he'd always kept to himself, the old man had made an exception for this Elk; this Elk was different: this Elk was not to be harmed, he was never to be harmed.

So *Svarverkjær* had watched the Elk as he grew up, had seen him as he ambled beside his mother as a cheeky yearling, then as a youngster, already showing early signs of the magnificent beast he would become. His mother brought him to drink at the pool. It was his mother who'd taken him to the orchard and, with the old man's blessing, had shown him the apples, taught him how to shake the branches to topple the ripe ones which were the best to eat.

Yes, this Elk had been the old man's Elk, and now he was going to be hunter's meat and *Svarverkjær* couldn't stand it. October, and the forests of Bamble Kommune are alive with hunters and *Svarverkjær* knows his Elk is in danger. And he knows the Elk, with his injured flank, will never be able to escape the long sure sight of a keen hunter's gun.

Dawn breaks, misty and cold as the pale sun struggles to see through the cloud. The Elk is still resting under the apple trees, the bleeding wound on his flank now clearly visible. And in the distance, *Svarverkjær* hears the voices and the steps and the baying of the dogs of the hunters as they make their way up the forest track.

Surely, he thinks, surely, the Elk hears them too, surely he smells the smell of death from the deer they'll be carrying over their shoulders, surely he'll sense the presence of the elkhounds whose job it is to locate their quarry and to chase them into clearings where they're visible enough for the hunters to take aim and to shoot. Surely, he'll know he's in danger, he'll run away…

But no, as *Svarverkjær* watches, the Elk continues to stand in the orchard, his head hung low; perhaps, thinks *Svarverkjær*, perhaps the Elk doesn't realise the danger he is in; perhaps he's too old and too sick to move.

The hunters and their dogs advance up the hill. *Svarverkjær* hears them talking and laughing, hears the elkhounds panting as they scuffle and scurry about in the undergrowth.

*Svarverkjær* braces himself and he clenches himself and he twists himself; he wills his every last ounce of strength to twist himself so that his walls creak and they groan and they creak some more and they twist and they bulge and eventually they begin to shift.

The poor walls have no idea what *Svarverkjær* is doing, twisting them about like that. Terrified of falling down, the walls are determined to stand their ground. They demand to know what in the Great Forest's name *Svarverkjær* thinks he is doing, why is he twisting them like that; is he seriously attempting to put them all out of shape, so they will all collapse? So they could never again be mended? Does he not realize he's putting their very lives in danger?

But *Svarverkjær* knows, and he knows very well, that a house cannot stand without walls, or not for long.

Stop it now! Stop what you're doing! the walls all plead in their loudest creaking voices.

But *Svarverkjær* is looking only at the Elk, watching him still standing there in the orchard. The house braces himself ever more strongly, and twists, he heaves and twists himself until his north wall begins to crack, and he twists some more until it crumples and he twists some more until finally it gives way and falls to the ground, shattered in pieces.

His mission achieved, *Svarverkjær* stands still and waits. The Elk can come now and find shelter in *Svarverkjær*'s collapsed north wall. Surely he'll come, the Elk will come and find refuge there. But as *Svarverkjær* watches, still the Elk stands unmoving in the orchard as the hunters draw ever closer.

The hunters and their dogs are coming round the corner now by the big red barn, their breath before them in clouds in the early morning air. *Svarverkjær* knows his one last chance of saving the Elk has been lost.

But just as he is giving up his very last hope, *Svarverkjær* sees something strange, something very strange is happening in front of him. Is that the old man he sees, leading the Elk across the track, coming towards *Svarverkjær* and guiding the injured animal for shelter at the side of the house that has crumbled?

If you go now to Svarverkjær, you'll see the little wooden house still stands at the top of the forest track, as it always did. You'll see the north wall has been mended and new people are living there. Children play by the pond and have made swings in the orchard; they're growing up to know elks and to love them and to share with them the apples in the orchard. The children will tell you how, every year, as autumn turns to winter, an old man comes, a very old man, he comes to the orchard, and he brings with him an Elk, and he sits and he watches as the Elk eats his fill of the fallen apples. Then, the two of them, they go away again, they disappear into the forest, as darkness closes in and winter comes once more.

---

Shelley Day is a former lawyer, psychology lecturer and research professor who now writes fiction. She was selected as an Emerging Writer by Edinburgh UNESCO City of Literature in 2013 and read at the Edinburgh International Book Festival. Her debut novel *The Confession of Stella Moon* (Saraband, 2016) won the Andrea Badenoch Award, was shortlisted for the Dundee International Book Prize, and was one of New Writing North's Read Regional 2017 titles. Her collection of short stories -what are you like- (Red Squirrel Press, 2019) won a Northern Promise Award and went on to win the 2020 Edge Hill Prize. *Svarverkjær* is a story from that collection. Please visit www.shelleyday.com to find out more about her work.

# A POSTBOX ATTACHED TO THE GATE

*By Sophie Hannah*

This is a mystery story without a solution. I'm not kidding. If you read that and thought, 'Ah, you say that now, but I bet you're going to solve it as a nice surprise for us at the end'...no, I'm not. You'll be disappointed if you go in with that assumption. I can't solve it for you because I still haven't solved it for me.

The story starts in November last year. That's 2020—the year that so many people describe unquestioningly as 'a terrible year', 'the worst year ever'. Every time I hear that description, I feel sorry for 2020, which did nothing bad on purpose. It was a completely innocent and blameless unit of time. Blame the virus, not the year—that's my motto. In fact, don't even blame the virus. Could it have done any different or better than it did? I don't think so.

My point is: 2020 was no more and no less than a container for human experiences, as all years are. If it had been cancelled before running its course, how would we have made it as far as 2021? We can't breathe or live outside of time. I might be just an estate agent and not the famous time scientist Stephen Hawkins, but I'm pretty sure he'd agree with me on this.

I see it all the time in the course of my work: failure to appreciate life's bounty. Most of all, I see the stupidity of holding an absolutely neutral space responsible for its sub-standard contents. People tell me nearly every day that they're not going to make an offer on a house, even though it's a fantastic bargain in a great location with more square footage than they could have dreamed of—and why? Because they've been put off by the flowery sofas or the pelmeted curtains. Why don't they understand that any container into which you can put horrible stuff, you can also empty and refill with good stuff—or you can fill it with good stuff simultaneously, if it's a unit of time like a week or a year.

I had only one really bad experience in 2020, courtesy of Tessa Pearson. Actually, the bad part happened this year, but the day I met Tessa was when it started. This was last November when she came to view a property I was selling: a Grade II listed, seventeenth-century former grain store with an impressive clunch-walled garden, in a tiny hamlet about twelve miles from town. The house had been done up to the nines inside: all white marble worktops, brand-new York stone floors and Venetian jade glass chandeliers. Tessa was one of what I like to call my 'Special Collection' viewers. She'd told me over the phone that she would never dream of moving out to 'the sticks', and nor could she afford The Grain Store even if she were tempted. She wouldn't have bothered to book a viewing if it weren't for the special circumstances.

I need to go a bit further back than November 2020 to tell you what that means—so I will, and if you want to disapprove of me, that's up to you. Short version? I saw a chance to improve ordinary people's day-to-day lives and I took it. When the first lockdown started at the end of March last year, I wasn't too worried for my own sake, but my mum told me a story that broke my heart. A lady who lives on her street, also elderly but fit and active, had turned up on Mum's doorstep in tears. The hotel health club where she was a member was closing for lockdown and she didn't know when it would reopen. The club was ten minutes' drive from her house and her routine was to go there every day to swim in the outdoor heated pool and have coffee or lunch afterwards with friends. Her whole life revolved around those things. What particularly upset her was that she'd done some research and all the experts seemed to agree that outdoor swimming in chlorinated water was extremely low risk. She felt as if she was being needlessly deprived of her favourite thing.

My mum didn't have much sympathy. She said it was silly to make so much fuss about swimming and that she'd said as much to her neighbour, who had (and this was the part that really broke my heart) agreed with her and started to backtrack. This poor elderly lady, older than my mum, who worked hard for decades and now lives alone in a pebble-dash two-up two-down and just wants to be able to swim in her club's pool every day and see her friends, actually apologised to the self-righteous arsehole who was busy telling her that what mattered to her shouldn't matter. Who knows how long that old lady has left to live? She might never have had the chance to swim again. It's not right.

Anyway, my conversation with Mum got me thinking. I happened to have two properties on my list at that time that had heated pools in their gardens—both a good size, too, and both unoccupied. One was The Grain Store, which had been given the full interior makeover treatment by an investor-developer, and the owner of the other had already moved into his new home in Wiltshire. And I had the keys for both.

I'm sure you've already guessed what I did next: found out where my mum's neighbour lived, went round, made a suggestion. Her name was Penny Skellett and she was lovely.

She couldn't have been more grateful. Every day until her health club opened up again, she and two of her friends met me at The Grain Store or The Old Rectory. Even when it was raining, they were determined to swim. I'd bring the all-important keys to let us all in. The old ladies would power up and down, doing their front crawl, and then we'd all have a cold buffet lunch in the kitchen. I tell you, those were some of the best lunches I've ever had. The three of them took turns to be the picnic provider, and there was even a bit of hamper rivalry going on, though all very amicable.

Mum never knew a thing about it and still doesn't. Neither did anyone else at first. Luckily both properties are nicely secluded, so there was little danger of any neighbours seeing me and my three elderly chums arriving or leaving. Penny kept saying how lucky she felt—almost as if this secret treat was 'meant to be'. Her two friends, Laura and Julia, were a bit bolshier. 'I don't care if I'm arrested,' Laura said. 'If the government takes away a perfectly safe form of fun like outdoor swimming then it jolly well ought to expect people to think "Get knotted!" and ignore its silliest rules. I'm following all the ones that make sense, and that's as far as I'll go.'

Julia went further: 'If happen to catch COVID and die as a result of swimming illegally with you lot, I'll be proud of having sacrificed my life for the noblest cause of all—freedom.'

Those three old women were an inspiration to me, and, not to blow my own trumpet, but I think I was to them too. They must have talked about me to their friends, because word got around. Soon I was fielding calls to my mobile from complete strangers who'd 'heard from an acquaintance' about The Grain Store or The Old Rectory—that I was conducting viewings of those properties and allowing potential buyers to 'try out' the pools. I had mixed feelings at first about the old ladies' indiscretion, which could easily have lost me my job, but then I realised that all Penny, Laura and Julia were doing was wanting to share the treat they'd been enjoying with as many people as possible. It was a generous impulse and, to be fair, I never had that many in my Special Collection at any given time—a couple of one-offs a week, maybe, in addition to my three regulars.

My partner at the estate agency, Martin Swainson, cottoned on eventually and told me that if the truth ever got out, I had to promise never to tell anyone that he'd known about it and turned a blind eye. I promised. He nodded solemnly and said, 'I think it's amazing. It's like an underground resistance movement with you as leader. If I had any guts or gumption myself, or properties with pools on my books, I'd do the same. I hope other estate agents are doing it. We get such a rotten press in our profession. It warms my cockles, thinking of us all coming together in defiance of tyranny and idiocy to make the world a better place.' I've never seen Martin get all teary-eyed before. I actually found it scary. He's the senior partner, at least ten years older than me. I've never seen him shaken by anything before.

When the November 2020 lockdown happened, the rules were different from what they'd been in March and April. We were allowed to do viewings, and there was no rule anywhere in the government's guidelines specifically forbidding swimming in the outdoor pools of houses for sale in a situation where a potential buyer insisted that they could only know if they wanted the house once they'd tried out its pool. It was mid-November when Tessa Pearson rang up and asked to view The Grain Store, telling me that she would certainly want to swim for at least half an hour, and probably more like forty-five minutes. "Fine," I said. "No problem."

She'd chosen The Grain Store because the pool there had Roman Steps. 'The Old Rectory's pool is a nicer shape, but I loathe having to climb in down a metal ladder,' she said with a shudder. 'It's so hideously school-swimming-lessons.' Then she asked me a question that no one had asked before: 'Why are the pools heated in November if the houses are unoccupied?'

'Erm…well, the owners are happy to help…anyone in your situation,' I lied.

'What, both of them?' Tessa queried. 'Two quite separate country-mansion owners, both totally happy to heat their pools for poor swimming-baths-deprived city folk like me?'

'Absolutely,' I lied again. The truth was that I had found the controls and turned on the heating for both pools without either owner's permission. Incredibly, so far neither one had noticed or queried it. I know that part of my heroic resistance effort was theft and therefore wrong, but one look at the houses and their land told me that anyone who owned places like these could easily afford it. One day the properties' owners would notice the heating bills, no doubt, and even though I'd offer to work extra jobs until I'd reimbursed them for every penny, I would almost certainly lose my estate agency job at that point and my little scheme would come crashing down. I didn't care. Well, I did—but not enough to stop me.

I met Tessa Pearson outside the gates of The Grain Store for the first time on Thursday 12 November 2020. 'Wow,' she said, looking at what she could see of the house above the high wall and gates. 'It's beautiful. If I weren't a city person to my core, I'd be very tempted.'

I used the remote-control device to open the gates. Tessa wasted no time in proceeding with her swim: almost hilariously slow breaststroke, neck and head poking up above the water like a duck. Afterwards, she asked me to show her round The Grain Store. When we got to the mezzanine lounge on the first floor, she sighed and said, 'Oh, God. I actually love this house. Do you think it's possible to fall in love with a house at first sight, as you would with a person?'

'I know it is,' I said. 'I'm an estate agent, remember? Seen it happen countless times.'

It's actually impossible to fall in love at first sight with a person, though I didn't say that to Tessa because I knew what she meant. Bitter experience had taught me how easy it is to fall in love at first sight with a gorgeous face-body combination plus your imagined version of who you think the person is. You might or might not end up loving the real them once you meet them.

'Do you think—I can't even believe I'm asking this,' said Tessa. 'Do you think the owner would knock a hundred grand off the price?'

'Unlikely. Though lots of people are having cashflow problems right now with the pandemic, and this place has been on the market for over a year, so…I could try for you, if you'd like to pursue it?'

'I think I would,' she said. 'I really do. I feel at home here. Although…oh God! My kids would kill me. They're 18 and 16. They love being in the centre of the city.'

'Wouldn't they love a huge outdoor heated pool?'

'Yeah, but they'd also wreck it, probably.' She sighed. 'They'd wait till my husband and I had gone to sleep and then they'd have all their mates over to smoke weed and drink Cîroc vodka in the garden, and they'd wake us and all the neighbours up with drill rap music about "whackin' man's face with the longest blade".' She gave me a pointed look that seemed to assume I would know what she was talking about. I didn't.

'I'd come out to the garden in the morning to find my beautiful pool full of old Rizla packets and greasy wrappers from the latest Deliveroo. Oh, God, I bet Deliveroo doesn't even come out here to the sticks.' Tessa stopped and peered at me. 'I can tell you're not a mother of teenagers from the horrified look on your face.'

'I'm not a mother of anybody,' I told her, thinking that life must be so much harder for parents than non-parents, and not only in the obvious ways. I wouldn't have taken any of the chances I was taking with my Special Collection people if I'd had children. It was one thing to risk your job and reputation when you were the only person who would suffer, and quite another to inflict the unfortunate consequences of your brave choices on your offspring.

Then Tessa Pearson did something strange. She asked me if I was familiar with the work of a rapper called Jace E-B. I told her I wasn't. Next, she asked if I knew any drill at all. No, I told her. This was the first indication I had that she was a slightly strange person. I mean, what kind of questions are those to ask an estate agent?

She started to sing in a strange accent that was very different from her own. I didn't catch most of the lyrics—it was too fast—but it ended with '…catch me an opp, then stab up his head, then ten toes back to the Grove.'

'That's Digga D, not Jace E-B.' Tessa said. She laughed, then said, 'You know, when I first heard my son and his friends playing that song, I thought "Ten toes back to the Grove" was a reference to The Grove in Hertfordshire, the luxury hotel. Stunning place. But no, it's Ladbroke Grove in Notting Hill, apparently. I'd always assumed Notting Hill was quite sheeshy too, but apparently it's also where one goes to "ching up one's opps".' She laughed. 'An opp is the drill-rap word for an enemy.'

I nodded. I had no idea where she was going with all this.

'It fascinates me, the way the authorial voice, as it were, in these drill rap songs—the narrative perspective—is always utterly convinced that all enemies deserve stabbing and shooting,' she went on. 'As I said to my son the other day, you'd never hear someone like Jace E-B rapping about not being sure how much of the latest feud was his fault and how much was the opp's fault. He's actually become a kind of role model for me.'

'Your son?' Surely that's what she must have meant.

'No, Jace E-B. Imagine the peace of mind you'd have if you sincerely believed all your enemies deserved a good "chinging".' She giggled. I wondered if she had a diagnosed, or diagnosable, mental disorder. 'I mean, when I get attacked by an opp—which I was recently, by a bitch called Lily Jeffries—I drive myself insane for days wondering if it was all my fault, descending into complicated spirals of self-torture, questioning what I did to merit such shoddy treatment and if I'm a rubbish person who doesn't deserve anything good to happen to me. Jace E-B doesn't do any of that! An opp is an opp, simple as that. It's his or her fault, not yours. You catch you an opp? You stab up his head, and you don't waste any time on self-recrimination. I love that kind of nice, uncomplicated justice model as a way of seeing the world. It's very *Godfather*-esque. How freeing and comforting, to be able to condemn your enemies so unreservedly and then set out to f— them up, pardon my French! I mean, can you imagine if I were a drill rapper, what my lyrics would be like?'

I couldn't, because I hardly knew her. She'd said it as if I'd known her for years.

What happened next was excruciatingly embarrassing, and I'm afraid I can't bear to describe it properly. She started to sing in the same strange accent she'd used before—kind of deep-voiced and rough-sounding—except this time the lyrics were clearly her own and made up on the spur of the moment. There were references to how she couldn't 'grip a sword' and 'get chopping' because she wasn't sure that retaliation was justified, and what if she was the one to blame, and wouldn't one accrue bad karma if one went round 'chinging' even the most reprehensible opps? She used those words: 'one' instead of 'you' and 'reprehensible'.

She meant it to be funny: a piss-take, the kind of lyrics a rapper would never write.

I can't remember how long this embarrassing singing episode lasted. It was all I could do to stop my skin from crawling right out of The Grain Store and drowning itself in the pool. Eventually, it was over. Tessa looked out of a window as if nothing unusual had happened and said in her usual upper-middle-class English accent, 'Ooh, is that a knot garden over there? Does it belong to this house?'

I cleared my throat and confirmed that it was, and it did.

'It's so beautiful,' she said. 'I think I'm going to make an offer. Do you know what? I think I'd even pay the asking price.'

That put me in a bit of a dilemma. If Tessa bought the house, what would happen to all my Special Collection people? Still, as an estate agent, I wasn't about to block a house sale.

The next strange thing happened as we were about to say goodbye. Tessa had put her swimming things back in her car and we were standing at The Grain Store's gates, which I'd just used the remote control to close. I was trying to draw her attention to the security cameras on the building's roof, and I noticed that she wasn't looking where I was telling her to. Instead, she was staring straight ahead, at The Grain Store's gates. A tear ran down her face. She wiped it away. 'What's that?' she asked, pointing.

'What?'

'This postbox attached to the gate.'

Why had she asked if she knew what it was? It was metal, black, rectangular. Solid and official-looking.

'I *have* to get this house,' she said. 'I'll pay the asking price. More, if I need to. Shit, don't tell the vendor I said that.' She was getting worked up into a proper state and I had no clue why. 'Can you get it for me? Promise you won't show it to anyone else. This postbox on the gate…it means this house *has* to be mine.'

I told her I was sure the vendor would be delighted with a full-asking-price offer, and then I said, 'If you don't mind my asking…'

Not only did Tessa not mind, she was so eager to tell me that she didn't even let me finish my question. This was when I heard more about the 'aforementioned opp', Lily Jeffries. The telling of this story took her a full half hour as we stood by our cars. By the end of it, I could have gone on Mastermind and had Tessa Pearson's fall-out with Lily Jeffries as my specialist subject.

Don't worry, I won't inflict the same on you. Here's the short version, which is all you need: Tessa and Lily had been best friends for years and their children had always attended the same schools. Then Lily's son had been expelled—justifiably, in Tessa's opinion—and Lily had wanted Tessa to withdraw her children from the school as a gesture of support. Tessa had thought it was unreasonable of Lily to demand that she do this, and said so. She had, she told me, kindly and tactfully said nothing about the obvious fair-enough-ness of the expulsion. Still, this hadn't prevented Lily from posting three handwritten pages of spiteful and unfair character-trashing through her letterbox, accusing her of betrayal, cowardice and 'nefariousness'.

The point was this: Tessa had felt that her home had been dirtied—'tarnished' and 'sullied', she said—by having Lily Jeffries's written attack posted through its letterbox: 'She pushed her vile words *into my hall.* Her disgusting envelope landed *on my mat*. Don't you see, Sonia? If I lived here'—she stroked the postbox—'and Lily Jeffries wanted to send me more poisonous words, or if anyone else did for that matter, *they wouldn't even be able to get their attack onto my land.* This is the closest any horrible words could get: out here, on the street. Not even into the garden, let alone the house.'

I saw what she meant, but I didn't agree. The postbox was fixed to the gate and the gate belonged to the house. Why did she care about a tarnished doormat and not a sullied postbox? I didn't ask. I couldn't have got a word in even if I'd wanted to; Tessa was too busy asking me if I thought she'd been disloyal to Lily, and then answering her own question: 'I mean, it's bloody outrageous to ask someone to remove her kids from a school where they're happy out of loyalty to your kid who's *hacked into his form tutor's laptop and replaced his screensaver with pornography*! Anyone would agree. Of course, the other brilliant thing is: if we're no longer friends and I move house, I don't even have to tell her where I'm moving. She won't know where I live anymore—ha!'

Tessa and her family bought The Grain Store and moved in in early February. Penny, Laura and Julia were disappointed to lose one of their two pools, but they understood the situation. 'Don't dare sell The Old Rectory, though, or we'll have your guts for garters,' warned Julia. Then, on 10 March, Tessa phoned my mobile in a rage. She'd been receiving anonymous letters, she told me, in the postbox attached to the gate. 'Oh, no,' I said, and actually felt a twisting in my gut. 'Not Lily Jeffries?' I hadn't forgotten the name of Tessa's opp.

'No, not her. I don't know who. And they're not horrible letters. They're nice. That's what's so creepy.'

'What do you mean?'

'I've had three so far—all of them going into detail about how Lily sounds awful and deranged, and I mustn't on any account feel guilty. They're *kind* letters. So, I have to ask, Sonia... is it you?'

'Me?'

'Writing the letters?'

'No! Tessa, seriously...Do you think I'm a crazy person?'

'Then who? The only other person who knows about my Lily trauma is my husband and I promise you, it's not him. Did you tell anyone?'

I closed my eyes and swore under my breath. 'Oh, God. I'm afraid I did, yeah. I told three people. Only three, but…' I left the sentence hanging, half-finished, because I had no valid excuse. The three I'd told were Penny, Laura and Julia: all massive gossips. They might have told dozens of people. 'I thought…it was just such an interesting story. I had no idea that—'

'Great.' Fury radiated from Tessa's voice. 'That's just perfect. Well, I can't live here now. You'd better put the house back on the market.'

'What? Why? You said they were kind letters—'

'*Why*? Because Lily Jeffries' name has been in my letterbox. More than once! Someone keeps writing to me and *reminding* me of her. What if they don't stop? Can you find out who it is and make them stop?'

I promised to try. I failed. Penny, Laura and Julia all denied being responsible, and I believed them. The trouble was, they also denied telling anyone else—and this denial was somewhat less convincing. Tessa stuck by her insistence that she had told no one apart from me and her husband, who was 'out of the question' and 'completely incapable' (she didn't specify how) and there was no one else to suspect.

The anonymous communications continued. Tessa rang me several more times, in tears, and read me extracts. The letters were indeed kind to Tessa: sympathetic, warm-hearted, seemingly designed to make her feel encouraged and understood, as well as to list all the ways in which she should practice self-care after such a horrible and abusive gaslighting episode. Clearly, Tessa had acquired a loyal, if shy and mysterious, friend and supporter. I wondered if she might be sending the letters to herself…but in which case, why ring me, weeping, and rant about how they were ruining her life?

On 26 March, I was asked by Martin, my senior partner at the agency, to resign. He was sad and reluctant, but I could see he had no choice. Unlike Lily Jeffries, I'm not unrealistic about what loyalty is and isn't.

Tessa had put The Grain Store on the market. She'd demanded my resignation, having decided that either I was the one who was sending the letters or else it was someone I'd told—which made it my fault either way. If I didn't resign, she said, and if the agency didn't waive the commission on any sale of her property by way of apology, then she would go to the *Daily Mail* with the story of my illicit swimming racket. In the same week, Martin had received an irate complaint from the owner of The Old Rectory, who had finally noticed how much he was forking out for the heating of his pool—heating he was certain he'd switched off in February 2020 when he'd first put his house on the market.

I resigned. I thought long and hard, and then I wrote Tessa a short letter and drove to The Grain Store to put it in her postbox. 'Dear Tessa,' it said. 'I'm so sorry. Everything that's happened is my fault. I shouldn't have told anyone your Lily story. That was wrong. Who knows, maybe the secret swimming thing was wrong too, though I really felt I was doing good. Anyway, I hope that one day you can forgive me.'

As I turned to go back to my car, I nearly walked into a tanned, bearded man with an envelope in his hand. He was wearing jeans, black Nike trainers and a blue North Face hoodie with the hood up and covering the top half of his face. Our eyes met. He smiled at me as if we were long-lost friends, then turned and walked in the other direction, stuffing the envelope into his back pocket. If there was any writing on it, I couldn't read it as he moved.

Had that letter been for Tessa? Had the bearded man written it or was he simply the delivery guy? Might he have been her kind, sympathetic correspondent? Who on earth was he?

I had a powerful intuition as I watched him disappear off into the distance—which I'm aware proves nothing, but I'll mention it anyway because it felt so important and real, almost like a revelation. I felt as if I knew that it was over, thanks to me saying sorry and taking responsibility for my mistake. I felt as if I knew that Tessa wouldn't be getting any more letters—that she could now safely stay in her new home if she wanted to.

Two days later I wrote to her again. This time I sent the letter by normal snail mail. I decided to trust my intuition and told her that it was hard to explain how I knew, but that I was sure the letters would now stop. I never heard back from her. Last time I looked on the website, The Grain Store was still for sale.

As I said at the start: this is a mystery story without a solution.

---

Sophie Hannah is a Sunday Times and New York Times bestselling writer of crime fiction, published in forty-nine languages and fifty-one territories. Her books have sold millions of copies worldwide. In 2014, with the blessing of Agatha Christie's family and estate, Sophie published a new Poirot novel, *The Monogram Murders*, which was a bestseller in more than fifteen countries. She has since published three more Poirot novels, *Closed Casket*, *The Mystery of Three Quarters* and *The Killings at Kingfisher Hill*—all of which were instant Sunday Times Top Ten bestsellers.

In 2013, Sophie's novel *The Carrier* won the Crime Thriller of the Year Award at the Specsavers National Book Awards. She has also published two short story collections and five collections of poetry—the fifth of which, *Pessimism for Beginners*, was shortlisted for the T S Eliot Award. Her poetry is studied at GCSE, A Level and degree level across the UK. Most recently, she has published two self-help books: *How to Hold a Grudge: From Resentment to Contentment—The Power of Grudges to Transform Your Life* and *Happiness, a Mystery, and 66 Attempts to Solve It.*

Sophie has recently helped to create a Master's Degree in Crime and Thriller Writing at the University of Cambridge, for which she is the main teacher and Course Director. She is also the founder of the DREAM AUTHOR coaching programme for writers. She lives with her husband, children and dog in Cambridge, where she is an Honorary Fellow of Lucy Cavendish College.

# THE PERFECT PRESENT

*By Victoria Connelly*

The trouble was, there was just too much choice. I'd already spent the best part of two hours trailing around endless shops and I still hadn't found anything suitable. I'd tried enormous department stores and tiny boutiques but had yet to be inspired. I'd sniffed my way through a dozen perfumes until they all began to smell the same and I'd decided that the bottles were far lovelier than the scents they contained. My fingers had tickled silky scarves, cotton scarves, velvet scarves and wool but none were *quite* right.

Then there'd been the jewellery. I'd so wanted to buy that special piece of jewellery that would brighten up any outfit: subtle and sweet. But all I'd found were ropes of gaudy beads in Caribbean colours which I felt would make my complexion look even paler than it did already.

But don't misunderstand. This isn't a present for me, but my sister, Jess. We have the same colouring, and it makes shopping for her a whole lot easier. I can hold a dress up against myself and tell instantly if it will do her justice. So far today, the dresses I'd inspected had been too dark in tone or too uninspiring in design or fabric. Who, I wondered, would pay good money to put one's body inside such creations?

So, I was stuck. I tried to think back to birthdays past. Things had been so much easier when we'd been growing up. Young girls were easily pleased, weren't they? Generally, it didn't matter what you bought them as long as it was pink! Our teenage years had been a doddle too. Make-up! You couldn't go wrong with make-up when you'd just discovered boys. Back then, though, it had been coloured eyeliner and sparkly eye-shadows in silver and purple. Somehow, I didn't think I could get away with that now.

Recent birthdays had been fun, though. I'd once treated Jess to an aromatherapy massage which she'd said was utter bliss and wouldn't mind having every year if I was stuck for what to get her. Well, I could book that, couldn't I? She'd been complaining about how tense she'd been feeling recently, and I wasn't surprised as she spent most of her days sat in front of a computer.

I sighed. That would be the easy way out. Besides, this was Jess's thirtieth birthday. That was special. You couldn't get a repeat present for somebody's thirtieth, could you?

Walking by a newsagents, inspiration struck me. A subscription to a magazine! I dived in the door and pored over the stacks of glossy gossip on the shelves. Where did one begin? A weekly title or a monthly? No, Jess always frowned at the magazines that littered my coffee table.

'Don't you have anything better to read, Grace?' she'd tease, but she wasn't averse to hearing the snippets of celebrity news I read out to her.

Okay then, so nothing gossipy. What about one of the lifestyle magazines? Jess was always going on about wanting to thrust her house into the twenty-first century. I thumbed through a few, my mouth watering at the deluxe kitchens, the sumptuous living rooms and the sort of bathrooms I could only dream of.

'Excuse me. Are you going to buy that?' A man's voice suddenly shocked me out of my reverie. 'Are you going to pay for that before you finish reading it?'

I turned round and came face to face with a short man with beady eyes that were doing their best to turn me into stone.

'I—er—haven't decided,' I said, quite honestly.

'Because this isn't a library,' he said.

My mouth dropped open and I instantly replaced the magazine before leaving the shop. Well, I wasn't giving *him* my annual subscription. And, let's face it, those magazines were all very well but, if you couldn't actually afford to do your house up, they'd only make you feel disgruntled. And what kind of a birthday present would that make?

I walked on feeling very disheartened. Why was I finding it so hard? The world was full of beautiful things, but I couldn't find the single perfect item for Jess and I wanted it to be special because *she* was special.

As I walked on, I noticed there was a bookshop coming up and I wondered whether or not Jess's special present could be found there. But, unlike me, she wasn't really a book person. There was nothing I loved more than a glorious hardback full of exquisite photographs or delicious recipes, or the latest novel by a favourite author, but they didn't do anything for Jess, and a paperback wasn't much of a present. Once read, what did one do with it?

And then I remembered what one of my work colleagues had bought for a friend: a dolphin! Not an actual dolphin, you understand—more of a small share in a wild one. I did rather like the idea of sponsoring an animal, but I wondered what the reality would be: a photograph, a sticker and a quarterly newsletter, probably. Was that special enough for my Jess?

I walked past our favourite restaurant and wondered whether I should book a table and have done with it. But, again, that was a short-lived present—gone in the space of a single evening, when what I wanted was something that would last—something Jess could keep as a token of my love for her.

Almost without thinking, I stopped outside our favourite jewellers. Why hadn't I thought of it before? It was a tiny shop which specialised in unusual pieces, and I loved it. If I was ever feeling particularly self-indulgent, I would treat myself to a pair of bright silver earrings or a new pendant for an old necklace. It never failed to cheer me up and make the world seem a more beautiful place.

And then I saw it: the perfect present. It was a slim gold chain on which was hung a simple amethyst pendant. It was exquisitely understated, and it yelled the name Jess.

I opened the shop door, the familiar bells tinkling merrily.

'Hello,' the shop assistant said. 'Are you looking for anything special?'

I nodded. 'I certainly am, and I think I may have just found it.' I pointed to the necklace in the window and the assistant took it out, placing it on a velvet mat where I could admire it.

'It's lovely,' I said, smiling as the dark jewel winked at me.

The assistant held up a mirror as I placed it against my throat.

'And there are matching earrings,' the lady said.

'Really?'

'I'll get them for you.'

*Oh, dear*, I thought, as she placed them next to the necklace a moment later. *They were divine*. I let my fingers reach out to touch them and then dared to hold one up to my ear as I looked in the little mirror. I was a real earring-addict. But this wasn't a present for me. I had to keep reminding myself of that and so I put the earring down. Besides, I really didn't have the funds for both.

'I'll just take the necklace today,' I said, making a mental note to catch up with the earrings another time.

I left the shop with a spring in my step. I'd found it. At long last, I could stop worrying. Relief flooded through me and excitement too because I couldn't wait to see Jess's face when she opened up the tiny box. The assistant had even gift-wrapped it for me—placing it in its plum-coloured box and wrapping it in a bright scarlet paper with a matching ribbon. It was actually going to be quite hard to part with it because it was so pretty. But wasn't that the test of a good present? One that almost hurt to give away?

We were meeting the next evening at my place. I'd decorated the front room with stargazer lilies and magnificent purple balloons and, because Jess adored candles, I had them everywhere: little tea lights winking in every corner as well as my silver candelabra in the middle of the table in which I'd placed three bright purple candles. I'd never been terribly inventive when it came to these sorts of thing but, by the time I'd finished, the room did look rather magnificent, and I couldn't wait for Jess to see it.

'Oh, Grace! It's so pretty. You shouldn't have gone to so much trouble,' Jess said as she entered.

'Nothing's too much trouble for my sister's thirtieth,' I said.

'Nor *my* sister's,' she said, and took out a tiny, gift-wrapped box from her pocket. 'I can't believe we're thirty, can you?'

I shook my head. 'It doesn't seem a minute since we were celebrating twenty-one.'

'Or eighteen.'

'Or thirteen.' I smiled as she handed me my present. It was a tiny, scarlet-wrapped box with a bright red ribbon and my heart skipped a beat as I took it from her.

'I have yours too!' I said, presenting her with an identical box.

Jess laughed. '*No!*'

I nodded. 'Great minds think alike?'

'One of the hazards of being a twin,' she said with a smile.

'You open first,' I said. 'You did turn thirty before me.'

'By a whole six minutes,' she reminded me in case I'd dared to forget her seniority. 'Come on, let's unwrap them together.'

I grinned. 'Okay.'

'After three. One. Two. *Three!*'

We both undid the red ribbons with infinite care before tearing open the tiny packages. My heart was in my mouth. What if we'd bought the same present for each other? It would be impossible, wouldn't it?

'*Oh!*' Jess suddenly shouted as she opened the box ahead of me. 'I don't believe it!'

I panicked. Was that a good response or a very bad one?

'It's beautiful!' She laughed. 'Go on—open yours.'

My hands were shaking as I opened the box to reveal a pair of perfect amethyst earrings. 'Jess!' It was all I could manage to say.

'I know!' she said, her eyes wide in delight.

'I love them.'

'And I love this. We're a matching pair!' she said.

'Always have been and always will be,' I said, hugging her and kissing her cheek.

'At least we never buy each other terrible presents,' she said, motioning for me to help put her necklace on.

I laughed and then took the earrings out of their box, grinning broadly as I put them on. 'It could never happen,' I said, 'because we both have excellent taste!'

---

Victoria Connelly lives in a 500-year-old thatched cottage in rural Suffolk with her artist husband, a springer spaniel and a flock of ex-battery hens. She is the million-selling author of two bestselling series, The Austen Addicts and The Book Lovers, as well as many other novels and novellas. Her first published novel,

*Flights of Angels*, was made into a film in Germany. Victoria loves books, films, walking, historic buildings and animals. If she isn't at her keyboard writing, she can usually be found in her garden either with a trowel in her hand or a hen on her lap.

# THE COLLECTOR OF MEMORIES

*By Victoria Cooke*

His scruffy appearance was off-putting to say the least. The torn, dirty clothing, shielding his modesty, emitted a stench that would repel even the hardiest of sewer rats. The face of the man was hard to distinguish beneath the unification of grime and beard hair; where one ended and the other began was anyone's guess. It was apparent to all that the card dealers had been unkind to this man, yet most carried on about their business without a second thought.

After some time, his eyes landed on those of a passer-by. His fingers fumbled the ends of his worn, woollen gloves as he summoned the courage to speak.

'Please—' was all he could muster. It was barely audible, a gruff croak rather than a word. It seemed obvious that the man hadn't spoken to anybody for a long while, his vocal cords fused and rusty. As the passer-by marched on, so did his hope. His final task, everything he'd set out to achieve, hung on these final few hours. He'd never failed at anything before, but he supposed this was a trip of firsts.

The cold air seeped beneath his skin, and his stomach growled but there was something else, which felt more akin to a burrowing worm in his gut. He looked around in confusion at buildings he didn't recognise. The streets were quietening down after the morning rush. His hands started to tremble. Time was running out. His eyes fell to a piece of discarded chewing gum on the ground. Pink and benign on the surface but practically filled with the makings of a human; teeth impressions, DNA and perhaps even blood but none of the parts one could bond with on an emotional level. His eye was caught by someone approaching; a lady with bushy, amber hair and a fuller figure, wrapped up in a green mac. She was carrying two of those shopping bags that you don't throw away, both were filled to bursting point. When her kind, green eyes met his, he felt a zap of something. Hope? The hint of a smile played on her lips before she looked away. He sensed kindness. He couldn't let her go. Once again he tried to summon the right thing to say.

'Help me, please.' His head was sludgy. Finding the right words was like trying to find a diamond ring dropped in quicksand. He was proud to determine that 'help' should be his first word, not 'please', like a beggar, but all that effort left him incapable of expanding. She frowned, sending his heart clattering into the deepest depths of his stomach. He lowered his eyes to the very pavement he had awoken on as a heaviness pulled on everything inside his ribcage. Unexpectedly, a firm hand landed on his shoulder. Human touch was so unfamiliar, both in his past and present life, that he flinched. Daring to look up, he saw the woman smiling, a warm, toothy smile and realised it was a hand of kindness. He felt a huge release of pressure, as if he'd shrugged off a heavy backpack.

'What can I do for you?' she asked.

His heart rate quickened. He wasn't sure he'd thought this far ahead. His fingers found the black thing in his pocket that held the rectangular papers containing everything he needed to know but there was no time to pull it out—he'd lose her. He had to remember. The notes detailed everything on seeking assistance, but there was nothing set out on what to do if somebody actually offered it—or if they did, he'd forgotten. His story was complicated and he had no idea where to begin in such a short encounter. It all seemed so confused and muddled in his head. The panic must have spread across his face; the woman spoke softly, as though she were nurturing a child.

'You look cold. Let's get you a cup of tea.' Delight welled in his stomach, but he still couldn't speak, for his throat was lined with sandpaper. Besides, his story had no decipherable beginning, middle nor end, not yet anyway.

The lady ushered him towards a café, a real *people's* café that smelt of hot fat and griddled bacon. Warm and inviting—he could almost taste the tea, feel the hot liquid comfort him from within. His saliva glands responded appropriately. She led him to a chair and shouted across to the counter an order for two teas before sitting opposite him. A few diners looked at him with bitter mouths and flared nostrils and he shuffled uncomfortably, not sure why they regarded him with such distaste. Normally, people looked at him with admiration for he always wore the finest suits. The kind woman glared at a few of them, then turned to him with a warm smile. Fine creases covered her face, crinkling like paper fans in the corner of her eyes. The emerald green of them reminded him of something comforting that he couldn't place.

'There's nothing a cup of tea can't fix, my dear.'

It couldn't fix him. No science, money, medicine or indeed tea in the world could fix him, yet somehow her comment gave him a feeling of hope. The touching warmth of someone looking out for him that was like small balloons filling his chest. He knew it was his turn to speak, he owed her something in return for her goodwill, but an efficient server broke the silence and placed two teacups and a metal teapot on the table with a loud clatter. The lady got to work, pouring the hot liquid and adding milk without even asking if he took it, not that he cared. He quickly took a delicious sip. The scalding heat seared his throat, shocking him. He coughed and sputtered.

'Oh, careful,' the woman said, wincing before heading to the counter and returning with a glass of water, which he gulped gratefully.

'Thank you for your generosity.' The words flowed easier for an oiled voice box. Her eyebrows furrowed in obvious concern. Oh dear. He had done this all wrong. His croaking for help from the pavement had given her and her obviously kind heart the wrong idea about him. He wished he could have attracted her attention some other way—now she was helping him in all the wrong ways and there was so little time. He had made a desperate mistake.

'What happened to you?' She spoke gently and placed a slight emphasis on the word 'happened' as though she knew something more was going on. People often ran around doing things for him but nobody ever stopped to listen. He wasn't quite sure, but perhaps this was his chance to seek what he needed.

'I always lived alone, never met a girl or had a roommate. It's always been just me.' He scrabbled with the spoon.

The woman raised her eyebrows, but it seemed more to express interest rather than surprise or concern at the admission. 'I don't make acquaintances easily, I mean.' She smiled again. He felt reassured by how accepting this woman was. She didn't pry and her face was round and affable. He already felt an affinity with her that consumed him like no other feeling he'd experienced before, and it made him feel comfortable like he was wrapped in a chunky knit blanket. A person had never made him feel that way before. Talking soon came easily, and he filled her in on some of his terrible attempts at friendship over the years, such as the time he accidentally stole a friend's clients at a dinner party. Trying to impress the table, he'd told them he could get a better return on their investments, unaware they were his friend's clients. At the time, he thought he was oozing charm and intelligence, but his friend said later that he never wanted to see him again.

'I lost my husband five years ago, so I know how it is to be alone.' Her eyes dropped to her teacup.

'I'm sorry.' He couldn't relate to loss. Not in the way she'd experienced it, anyhow.

'It's something I'm slowly getting used to. I don't have children and the few friends I do have are busy with their own lives.'

Her tone was matter-of-fact but he detected pain in her eyes—some instincts don't leave you. He'd felt similar when his life started to change. Losing control is a hard thing to come to terms with.

'Anyway.' She swept her hair off her face and sipped her tea. 'How did you cope living all by yourself?'

'I actually thought I enjoyed my own company and never felt the need for a companion until…' That was the difficult part.

'What is it, love?' She rested her face in her hands and looked at him with such intent, he wasn't sure if he was supposed to announce this year's Nobel prize winners. Even as he paused, the big green eyes set in her ruddy face stayed focussed on his own weary ones. He shuffled in his seat like a schoolboy in the headmaster's office.

'Did you lose your home?' she prompted softly. 'There are people we can call to get you some help.'

The man shook his head and almost laughed. His house was quite something—why would she think he was without a home?

'Then what is it? You felt okay being alone until…?' She tilted her head as though she were stepping aside to give him the spotlight.

He remembered now. 'Until my diagnosis.' He paused again to absorb the overwhelmingly fizzy lightness. The feeling of relief that came with letting go the expanding gas of a secret that, until now, had remained sealed in the compartment of his own mind.

'You see, I have been diagnosed with early-onset dementia. I found out earlier than most, so I'm both blessed and cursed with knowing what awaits me.'

Her brows pressed together, slightly curling down towards her nose in the middle. 'That's awful, you poor, poor man—at such a young age for a terrible disease too.' She reached across the table and covered his soiled, bony hand with her meaty one. He noticed she was wearing a ring on her right hand. It was silver with an amethyst gem, and the skin of her finger bulged round the band. When he lifted his gaze to her face, a look of concern had spread across her features. She took a breath before she tiptoed on to the next question.

'Have you anyone I can call? A friend? A family member? A doctor?'

He shook his head. The motion ruffled his matted, jaw-length hair and it felt strange, unnatural even. He lifted his hand and touched the ends. It wasn't right. His chest tightened.

'I must ask, when we met you were seeking help—what exactly is it you need? I noticed a sleeping bag by your feet; do you need help finding your home? Are you lost?' Her eyes glimmered with a sheen of moisture, her compassion erasing any anxiety he'd felt moments ago.

'Actually, I left home, weeks ago.' He looked down at himself, surprised by the filth on his trousers. 'Perhaps longer. I've been on a journey, and then I lost something, so I've had to stop travelling, but there's so much I still need to see and do.' The rush of relief engulfed him again when he opened the gas valve once more.

'So, it's like a bucket list? Your trip, I mean.'

The muscles in his forehead crumpled like a piece of paper that had been balled up ready for the bin.

'A bucket list. It's things to see or do before you…die.' She spoke in tender, soothing tones.

'Not quite,' he said. Then the valve closed tight. He stared at the woman before him and then the table. They were having a conversation, she was looking at him with big eyes filled with expectation.

'What did you lose?'

He pursed his lips and let his eyes fall to the floor. A few moments passed as he dug around in his own frustrating head. He wanted to answer her but he had nothing but black emptiness to give.

'You said you needed something for your trip.'

That was it. 'My black box. Filled with picture memories. I wore it like a necklace.'

The woman pondered this. 'Do you mean a camera?'

As soon as she said the word, he recognised it. Heat flushed his cheeks as he nodded. He felt such a fool, even though she hadn't been poking fun at him.

'When I got my diagnosis, I looked back on my life and realised that in order to lose my memories to dementia I must have some to lose in the first place. I had nothing of any merit worth remembering. My life was dedicated to making money—a task I was rather good at, if I do say so myself.' He took another sip of tea. 'This disease wants to take my newest memories first and I'm terrified of being trapped in an endless, solitary purgatory of reliving late-night conference calls and early morning meetings. That can happen, you know—you can believe you're still living a life from decades before.'

The woman whispered a quiet 'yes' and followed with a weak smile. He knew there was nothing more for her to say since his situation was helpless.

'A nurse suggested putting together a memory box. So, I've been trying to create better memories before it's too late.'

The woman leaned in a little. Her eyes, wide and embracing, comforted him somehow and he struggled to remember a time when someone had paid him so much interest. 'So you want photographs to look back on when things get worse?'

He nodded. 'Exactly. Only I didn't have any.' He pulled a small leather notepad from his pocket and flicked through its pages. 'A few weeks ago, I walked out of my front door and over the Pennine moors, the beauty was astounding. I came into the city and stayed a night in a very fancy hotel—I ate caviar. Me, caviar! Never in my life have I bothered with the stuff.' He laughed drily. He could only recall bits of those things; like when you wake up from a vivid dream and the details are foggy or missing. He clenched and unclenched his fists as he always did to try and ease the tightness in his chest. 'I visited Edinburgh and London, I saw an opera show and I volunteered in the soup kitchen.'

The woman glanced at the notebook and the corners of her mouth turned down. He followed her gaze to the words 'caviar, me!!!'

'My money ran out, so I spent time just watching people. It's been fascinating and liberating in equal measure. I can't believe how much of life I'd missed whilst I was chained to my office. I took pictures—here, you can see.' Excitedly, he pulled a small camera from his pocket and started to scroll through all of the pictures of the exciting life he had led over the weeks before.

'Brilliant—you've found your camera!' She smiled, and her cheeks puffed like pigeon chests. 'These really are fabulous, what an amazing tale! But where do I fit in? You said you needed help.' There was confusion in her tone.

'Ah yes, of course.' The tips of his ears felt hot. 'It's a little bit embarrassing really.'

'Go ahead. I won't judge.' She said it in such an assertive way that gave him the confidence to believe her.

'Well, once my memory has deserted me, I will have all of these pictures to look back on of places I've seen and things I've done, but it dawned on me that I have all these *things* to try and remember but *nobody* to remember. My notebook has instructions for each day, and now it says I have to return home. So, today, my final 'task' if you will, is to seek companionship. A face of comfort and kindness to remember fondly.' He had become so involved in his speech, he had barely noticed that the lady had slipped around the table and was sitting beside him, resting a hefty arm across the back of his chair.

'What's your name, love?' she asked.

That was easy enough. 'It's…er…' He almost laughed. He knew that; the shape of the word was on the tip of his tongue. A moment too long passed and the word didn't come. A light sensation of moisture broke on his brow. He lifted his gaze to meet hers, and she smiled and gestured forwards; his eyes followed hers and he heard a click before a bright flash almost blinded him.

'I'm Wendy. Whatever your name is, now you have *somebody*.'

---

Victoria Cooke grew up in the city of Manchester before crossing the Pennines in pursuit of a career in education. She now lives in Huddersfield with her husband and two young daughters and when she's not at home writing by the fire with a cup of coffee in hand, she loves walking, yoga and travelling. Victoria was first published at the tender age of eight by her classroom teacher who saw potential in a six-page story about an invisible man. Since then, she's always had a passion for reading and writing, undertaking several writers' courses before completing her first novel, *The Secret to Falling in Love*, in 2016. Her third novel, *Who Needs Men Anyway?* became a digital bestseller in 2018 and her debut was optioned for on-screen adaptation in 2020.

# THE RESERVOIR

*By Will Dean*

'Mum, I'm home.'

The hole in the kitchen wall is right there in front of me. A puncture mark through floral wallpaper. An outline of Dad's fist.

'Come in here, Tom.'

'Going upstairs, Mum. Homework.'

She walks through as I approach the stairs.

'Tom, you're going out for a bit tonight.'

'I'm not.'

She gestures for me to come to her, so I do. She rubs my shoulder and says, 'Geoff's taking you down to the reservoir. He wanted to do it. Just you and him for some fishing. Good night for it, he said.'

'I'm not going out, Mum. I've got homework. Chemistry. I'm knackered from school. Why do you—'

'Look,' she says, cutting me off, 'he'll be here in five minutes and I know I should have told you about it but…' She glances over at the damaged wall. 'I should have said, Tommy. But it's on now. Perfect weather for it, Geoff said.' She tries to smile. 'Go get your new jumper on, eh? Chilly later.'

'But Mum—'

'It's gonna be alright, Tom. You know that, don't you?'

'What about my homework?'

'Jumper. Now.'

I go up to my room and change my clothes and pull on the jumper I received from Mum for my birthday. It's from her, not him. I touch my posters in order. Not sure why I do it. Maybe to keep everyone safe or maybe I'm losing my mind. The Metallica poster, the space shuttle poster, the Nirvana poster, the Back to the Future poster, the Ferrari F40 poster. And then I walk downstairs.

'He's outside in his truck,' says Mum. 'Bang on time. Be polite, won't you? Here, take this.'

She hands me two one-pound coins.

'Look handsome in that colour, you do. All grown up.'

'You alright?' I ask.

'Get off with you! Go on, now.' She makes a sweeping gesture, pushing me out the door.

The truck is a relic from the past held together with rust and rope. The rear flatbed holds tools and boxes and planks of wood.

'All right, Pauline,' says Geoff from the driver's seat, his dark elbow resting on the open window.

'Thanks for this, Geoff.'

'Free labour,' he says, smiling. 'Get in, Tom. The big fish are waiting.'

I see Mum in my mirror as we drive off, spluttering up the country lane. She shrinks, and my stomach is uneasy at the thought of her being left home alone.

'Fishing,' says Geoff, rubbing his grey unruly beard with the back of his hand. 'Fly fishing. You any good, then, Tom?'

'Never been.'

He almost stops the truck. The frown on his face is deep and he turns to me and he says, 'Well, then, lad, let's get to it. Much to learn.'

'Mum said we're going down the reservoir.'

'Best spot around.'

'On the bank? I've seen a few fishermen there.'

He smirks. 'Much better. We're renting a boat.'

I don't say anything to that. A boat? I've only ever been on the car ferry to the Isle of Wight that time with school.

'Caught a seven-pounder few weeks back with me mate, Rick. Good man is Rick, works up the potato factory. You'd think he was a soprano or something to look at him but when he sings with us at church on a Sunday, he's got lungs like a bloody polar bear. Bass, he is.'

I nod.

'You want music, or peace and quiet?'

'Music.'

'None of that headbangin' rubbish. Got two tapes. You choose.'

He points down to the central console. There's a length of blue rope, a claw hammer, an oil can, and two tape cassettes. One is Hill Country Blues. The other is Skiffle.

'What's skiffle?' I ask.

'What's skiffle? Well, stick it in and you'll find out, won't you?'

I push the tape in.

Some kind of energetic jazz music flows out of the speakers and Geoff rattles his knuckles in tune on the steering wheel.

'Eh?' he says.

'Very good,' I say.

He grins and the sun picks out the scar on his forehead. Mum told me he had a mole removed in the spring.

'What is that?' I ask, pointing to the metal object between my trainers.

'Bit off the combine,' he says. 'Needs some work before I can get harvesting. Gonna cost me a few bob, that thing is.'

Twenty minutes later we pull up at the quiet side of the reservoir, the area with no camping or windsurfing or toilet facilities. Geoff takes rods and boxes from the back of the truck and passes me a canvas bag and a large net.

'Landing net,' he says. 'Keep your fingers crossed, but it ain't so much about landing a fish as it is about the sitting out on the water. That's what my old man reckoned and I'd say he was about right.'

We walk down a narrow dirt path to a timber cabin. It says *Boat Hire* above the entrance. We leave our gear outside and walk in.

'Jenkins,' says Geoff.

'Geoff. Who's your bodyguard, then?'

'This is young Tom, son of my sister-in-law is Tom. Good lad most of the time, aren't you?'

I nod awkwardly. Why do adults ask these things?

'Reckon on getting out for two hours or so. Maybe three if the weather holds out.'

'Decent forecast,' says Jenkins.

'How's Mrs Jenkins managing?'

'Oh, fair,' he says. 'Keeping her meals down.'

Geoff approaches the counter. 'Give her my best, will you? And Laura sends her love, she told me to say that.'

Jenkins nods curtly and says, 'You much of a fisherman are you, Tim?'

'Tom. Never been before. This is my first time.'

'Well,' says Jenkins. 'Better later than never, ain't that right, Geoff? Come here, Tim. Come on.'

I walk over to him.

'First time, you say?'

'Yeah.'

'Close your eyes, lad. Don't worry, I'm not gonna kiss you.'

Geoff laughs.

I close my eyes.

The shop smells of wax jackets and oiled wood.

Jenkins places a hat on my head, and I open my eyes.

'Looks professional, that does, Jenkins.'

'Suits the lad.'

I face the mirror. I was expecting Indiana Jones to look back. I was wrong. More like an extra from Last of the Summer Wine.

'For your flies, and that,' says Jenkins. 'Your hooks.'

'Good hat, that is,' says Geoff.

'That's a gift,' says Jenkins.

'You sure?' asks Geoff.

'Today is the start of this young man's fishing life. From this point onwards he'll be an angler and maybe even a future customer. He's part of the community and this hat should do him until he's your age, Geoff.'

We rent the boat and take the gear down to the small pontoons floating on the water. There are flies and midges buzzing around the reeds and the golden light of the early evening sun bathes the reservoir in a gentle hue.

The boat rocks as I climb in. It's more unsteady than I anticipated.

'Get your sea legs quick, Tommy. Engine's got a kick to it. Jenkins always gives me his best vessel.'

The engine is a joke. Dad's lawnmower has more power than this thing. We put-put out into the still waters, leaving the world in our wake.

The breeze on my face is warm and the air smells like summer.

'You reckon you can handle her all on your own, then?'

'What?'

'Come on, swap places. Rear admiral Tom, we'll call you.'

He's grinning again, except I can't see his mouth because his beard is so long. He has the same sense of humour as my five-year-old cousin.

'Don't I need a licence?'

He laughs again and sits me at the rear of the boat and shows me how to use the rudder.

'Just point her at the middle and feel the power of it. Let her rip.'

I'm driving. Sailing. Boating. Whatever. I'm in control. Dad would never let me do this. He'd never let me try.

'All right, nice job,' Geoff says. 'You didn't sink it or crash it. Ten out of ten.'

We cut the engine and the air falls silent. A faint scent of diesel fumes.

'That's your rod, that is, for tonight. My old un. Caught a great deal of fish with it. Go on, hold it in your hand.'

I take it from him.

'Feels good, don't it?'

I nod.

'Look around you, Tommy. What bugs and critters do you spot?'

'All sorts.'

'Such as?'

I slap my cheek and show him the result on my palm, and he roars with laughter to the point where the boat feels unsteady.

'I spotted a fly back a way with bright blue wings. Middle-sized, I'd call it. Don't know the Latin names but I know what I saw.' He opens a small tackle box. 'Made 'em all myself in the small barn. What do you think?'

'Nice,' I say.

He pulls out two blueish flies and holds them up against the light to inspect.

'Should do it. They're bits of old twine and rubbish but you go at them with pliers and some wire for a time and there's no telling what you can make.'

'You don't buy them?'

'Too dear. And I like working on them in my barn in the wintertime. Thermos of tea and a good hat. Something on the wireless. Can lose hours making flies, I can.'

He hands me one and then when he sees my reaction he says, 'let's get 'em sorted out together, you follow me.'

His hands are rough and his fingers have been flattened by decades of farm work but he manages to fix the flies and the hooks and floats to the lines. We take our rods and sit facing the boat shop in the distance.

'Best time of day for it, best time of year an' all. Watch me cast off and you do the same after.'

He gathers some slack fishing line in his hand and pulls and jerks the rod back and forth and then releases it so the line shoots out over the water. The only thing I can see is the orange float bobbing on the surface, and the line leading back to Geoff.

'Go on. Don't matter if you mess it up a bit. Practise makes perfect.'

I try to cast but it's a disaster. The hook gets caught in my birthday jumper. Geoff says, 'Go on, Tom—I did that my first time. We all did. Go on.'

Eventually I get the line to fly. It's not a swift, fluid movement like Geoff's casting, more of a spasm. But we're both sitting with our lines in the water. We're fishing.

'This is all right,' I say.

He smiles and then a few moments later he nods gently as if to himself.

The water is almost mirror-flat and all I can hear are the distant murmurings of ducks and moorhens, and the gentle lapping of water against the side of the boat.

'Get the landing net, Tom.'

I grab it and step closer to Geoff but his float's still there. It doesn't look like he has a catch. I've seen it on TV, the battling with energetic sailfish and the like. Swordfish, even. But then he starts to pull and reel. Not fiercely, but steadily. The expression on his face is one of calm focus. And then, after a few moments, the fish is up in the air wriggling, and I am placing the landing net beneath it, and we have caught an actual fish.

'How was that?' he asks.

'Brilliant,' I say.

'Just a littlun,' he says. 'Nice young littlun. Have a good look at him and then we'll put him back.'

'Not keeping him?'

'Just a scamp, he is. We'll catch him again in a few years, maybe. What should we call him, Tom?'

'Call him?'

'I always call 'em something before I put 'em back. Daft, really.' He removes the hook from the fish's mouth. 'But it's tradition. Who does he look like?'

I frown. 'Looks like a fish. Okay, all right, what about Michael J Fox?'

'School mate, is it?'

'Actor. Small, like the fish.'

Geoff bends over the edge of the boat and says, 'Michael J Fox, good to meet you, littlun. Be lucky, young fish.'

The fish sits in the water for a moment before coming back to life and darting away.

We sit and cast again, and we don't talk for a long time.

My jumper is warm. It was an awkward thing, on my birthday morning. Dad had said for months how things are tight, how we have to make things last, no spending what we don't have. He said birthdays and Christmases would be different from now on. That Mum would have half the housekeeping she used to get. We were all okay with it, even my little brother, Sam. We just wanted Dad to be happier. I don't need a Sega Mega Drive, really—I can play at my friends' houses. What Sam and I want is for Mum and Dad to be like they used to be. No more arguing and fighting. No more Dad sleeping downstairs in his armchair night after night.

'You missed a bite there, I'd say, Tom. You feel it?'

'Yeah, it didn't catch on.'

'Ah, well, you have to work for it sometimes. Not much of a current here, you need to move your line from time to time. You want a cuppa yet? Sandwich?'

'Yes, please.'

He places down his rod and unscrews a thermos and hands me one plastic end. The tea is steaming hot and when I sip it, I feel the liquid heat me from inside. Sweet, strong tea.

'Cheese and tomato or cheese and ham?'

'What do you want?'

'Not bothered one way or the other. Pauline made them for us, she always makes good butties, she does.'

'Cheese and tomato then, please.'

He hands me the aluminium foil that contains the sandwiches. I open it up. White doorstop slices with lots of butter. Slices of tomato and dark yellow cheese.

'Not bad out here is it, Tommy?'

'I like it,' I say.

He chews and slurps his tea and I do the same.

When mum gave me the jumper on the morning of my birthday, I hugged her and thanked her. She'd taken weeks knitting it at night while watching Dallas on TV and waiting for Dad to come home from work. It was too big for me, but I liked the colour. I still do. As well as the jumper, I received seven cards, a book token from Nan, and a painting from my little cousin.

But then Dad stood up and left the front room. He went out to his car and brought back a plastic bag. *Here you are, son,* he said. *Just from me, that is.* I didn't know what he meant. Gifts were always from them both. Mum's eyes were wet as I opened the carrier bag, but she was still smiling. Inside the bag was a games console and two controllers, and a new parker pen from the shop and a toffee crisp bar. All unwrapped. I hated all of it. What it meant. I didn't know what to say. *Thanks, Dad,* I said. Then Mum left the room.

'You finished them butties?'

'Yeah,' I said. 'Really good, thanks.'

'You tell Pauline to her face next time you see her. She'd like to hear that. Here, have a tart.'

He presents an old plastic Tupperware box with two lemon curd tarts and two jam tarts.

'You get one of each for pudding. We know how to live, us fishermen.'

The tarts are delicious. Sharp lemon curd with crumbly pastry washed down by strong tea. And then Geoff catches another fish.

'Littlun,' he says. 'Bloody littlun again. You reckon that's Michael Fox again or—?'

I smile.

'Same fish, is it?'

'No, this one has a mark on its gills. And he's fatter.'

'Need my glasses on. What shall we call him?'

'Jenkins?'

'You cheeky little bugger, I won't tell him you said that.'

'Gizmo,' I say.

'Gizmo? That Greek or something?'

'Name of the gremlin.'

'Sometimes I feel very old,' he says. Then he places the fish down in the water and says, 'God speed, Gizmo.'

The air cools. We drain the last from the thermos.

'Ten more minutes, I reckon,' he says.

My feet are getting cold.

'Happy to go back whenever you are.'

'Soon,' he says.

I know why Mum set this all up. Last weekend, I spent hours writing down ideas for Mum and Dad to make friends again. Things I could do differently to ease the stress for Dad: mowing the grass, bringing in coal, giving him some more of my paper-round money. I drew up compromise lists. That's what I called them. Charts of things Mum does that annoys Dad and vice versa. I thought if we can all talk it through and put in place some changes, things could go back to the way they were before. I've studied peace treaties in history class with Mrs Harrison. If people can reach a truce after a world war, there must be a way for my parents to sort things out. The chat started well, partly because Mum had made Dad his favourite food: lemon meringue pie. But then it descended into a shouting match. My compromise chart was screwed up into a ball. Dad smashed his fist into the kitchen wall and then he drove off. Maybe it was my fault for pushing them too soon? And this fishing trip is Mum being nice. She's letting me get away from my real life for a few hours. She's letting me escape for a bit.

'Heron,' says Geoff.

'Where?'

'Look.'

The heron is flying behind us, close to the water, and its wings are magnificent. It glides and dominates the reservoir. You cannot help but stare at it; you can try but you will fail.

'He's better at fishing than I am,' says Geoff.

'And me.'

'That's for bloody sure.'

And just at that moment, I feel a strong tug on my line.

'You little beauty,' says Geoff. 'Keep it steady, let it run on a bit.'

My limbs are alive with electricity. I stand slowly and keep a grip on the line and the fish feels strong. It has power.

'Start reeling her in,' says Geoff. 'I'll land her. Keep it steady, go on.'

I reel.

The fish breaks the water's surface and I see it for the first time, and I smile and my heart lifts in my chest.

'Bring it in gentle, nice and easy.'

Geoff lands the fish.

'You pull the hook out, Tom. Don't hurt the fish.'

I remove the hook.

'That's eating size, that is. A keeper. Decent specimen.'

'Are you sure? Looks the same as the two you caught. Maybe a bit smaller, even.'

'Different species, see. That one's for the pot. Well done, Tom.'

He shows me how he guts it and then we set off back to the rental shop.

'How was it out there, gentlemen?' asks Jenkins.

'One in the bag,' says Geoff. 'Tom popped his cherry, so to say.'

'Decent fish that,' says Jenkins, winking at Geoff. 'Here you go, lad. For your cap, that is.'

He hands me a turquoise fly attached to a hook.

'Put it on your cap, then.'

I hook it onto my new fishing cap.

'Keep well, Jenkins. See you soon I expect.'

'Safe drive.'

Geoff puts the fish inside a cool box he keeps strapped down in the flatbed.

On the drive back home, the skies are twilight and the cab of the truck is warm. There is no music.

My chest feels less tight than it did on the drive down. It's as if my lungs have loosened up and I can breathe normally again.

When we pull up outside my house I say, 'You want to come in for a cup of tea, Geoff?'

'Need to be getting back to Laura,' he says.

I climb out and meet him at the back of the truck, the engine still running. He opens the cool box and there's a large salmon there staring back up at us. It's sitting on ice next to my fish.

'Decent fish, they are,' says Geoff.

I frown.

'Well done, Tom. Tell your mother I'll check in on her later in the week. And give her these two quick, before they warm up. Nothing ever so good tasting as a couple of fish you caught yourself.' He winks. 'Take care, my lad.'

---

Will Dean grew up in the East Midlands and lived in nine different villages before the age of eighteen. His latest book, *The Last Thing to Burn* was chosen as Observer Thriller of the Month. His debut novel, *Dark Pines*, was selected for Zoe Ball's Book Club on ITV, shortlisted for the Guardian Not the Booker prize and named a Daily Telegraph Book of the Year. The second Tuva Moodyson mystery, *Red Snow*, won Best Independent Voice at the Amazon Publishing Readers' Awards, 2019, and was longlisted for the Theakstons Old Peculiar Crime Novel of the Year 2020. His third novel, *Black River*, was described by the Financial Times as a 'peerless exercise in suspense'. Will Dean lives in an elk forest in Sweden.